I0606671

Storm of Shadows

The Firestone Academy
Book 1

Hannah Haze

Copyright © 2025 by Hannah Haze

All rights reserved.

No part of this book may be reproduced in any form or by any electronic or mechanical means, including information storage and retrieval systems, without written permission from the author, except for the use of brief quotations in a book review.

Front cover designed by Covers by Christian

Edited by Buckley's Books

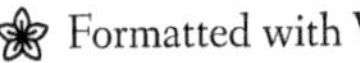 Formatted with Vellum

Foreword

This book is a 'why choose' paranormal romance with one female main character and more than one potential love interest. This story is based in a dystopian world where the powerful prey on the weak and where much inequality and unfairness exists. There is physical and verbal bullying of the female main character in this story (although not by the love interests) as well as steamy scenes. For more detailed content warnings, please visit my website.

If you spot any typos in this book, please drop me a line so I can make it right: hannahhazewrites@gmail.com (Or just drop me an email anyway. I love to chat!).

The Realm

Chapter One

B riony

Snowflakes swirl in the gray sky, catching in my hair and my eyelashes and the cold is biting. I blink them away and hug my bag more tightly to my chest, trying to ignore the stiffness in my fingers, the wetness creeping in through my boots and the ache in my chest.

I can't decide if I'm pleased to be leaving Slate Quarter for the academy or really pretty furious about it.

It doesn't matter either way. I'm going. I don't exactly have a choice in the matter.

I glance down the platform at the other kids my age, surrounded by family and friends – hugging each other close, wiping tears from their eyes, laughing and joking.

There's a sense of anticipation in the air, of excitement. I can practically taste it on the end of my tongue. These kids actually believe this is their ticket out of here. Their tickets to better things.

I snap my head away.

They're fucking deluded.

And, actually, not kids anymore either.

Young adults – that's what they call us when we hit twenty-one and that's why we're all lined up waiting for the train that's going to whisk us away to the Firestone Academy.

The old clock on the wall, its face cracked, ticks another minute.

Monday, January 3rd. 8:57am.

The train will be here in three.

My dad isn't coming to see me off.

Why am I even surprised?

He makes all sorts of promises in the evening, rarely keeps them in the morning. I know that, so why the hell did I think this time would be any different? Just because I'm leaving. Just because he swore on his life. The pull of the tavern has always been more alluring than the pull of his only daughter.

Only *remaining* daughter.

I swallow hard, trying not to think of that. Of the last time I stood on this platform waiting for this train. That day had been filled with glorious sunshine – rare out here in Slate Quarter – and my stomach had been full of that same excitement and anticipation that's buzzing around today.

I don't think it's full of anything today. Mostly because Muriel refused me breakfast. Partly because it's been years since I felt anything at all.

In front of me, the rail tracks vibrate, then rattle and then the station fills with the roar of the train. The people down the platform pick up bags, grab last-minute embraces, and kiss each other's cheeks.

I simply clutch my rucksack and wait as the train slides into the station, halting with a hiss like a giant silver snake, the blacked-out windows of the engine like soulless eyes. It's eerie and, as the doors part and an announcement instructs all young Slate Quarter adults to board, I can't help but feel like we're about to step inside the stomach of a monster.

I've no one to hug. No one to say my goodbyes to. Not even someone to wave to. So I climb on board, walking as far down the carriages as I can until I'm right at the front of the train and there's nowhere else to go. I pick a bench on the far side from the platform and slide along to the window.

I've no interest in watching any more of the spectacle out there on the platform – a reminder that others have people who actually give a damn about them. I'm more than aware of that.

It takes a few more minutes and another announcement over the loudspeaker, and then the others board the train – a trickle at first, just one or two. Then groups of friends, chatting away animatedly, talking over one another, so damn excited. The noise makes me wince.

No one picks the seat next to me on the bench, but I keep my bag on my lap anyway, clinging it tightly to my chest. I lean my head against the frigid pane of glass and close my eyes.

Soon, the train jolts and then slithers forward. I don't bother to open my eyes, to watch my home slip away from sight. It hasn't felt like home for a long time. I don't care if I'm leaving, even if I have no desire at all to go where we're headed.

Around me, the other kids keep right on chattering like monkeys locked in a cage. I wish I had a way to block out all the noise. I wish I was out in the forest, away from everything and everyone. I've never 'peopled' very well.

Or maybe I did once.

Then things changed.

Unfortunately, like everyone else on this train, I have no special powers, no remarkable abilities. I don't have a way to silence all the voices or block out all the sound. Just like them, I'll endure a year of hell at the academy – tested, assessed, probed to the extreme. Only for them to find out just how ordinary we all are and send us straight back to Slate Quarter.

An hour passes and another. Somewhere along the journey, I open my eyes and watch the passing landscapes outside the window. I can't help it. I've never left Slate Quarter before. This is the furthest I've ever been from home, and I am curious.

At first, it's all snow and ragged crops of mountains as far as the eyes can see, then gradually it thaws and trees and grass spring up from the ground – so much green it makes my head buzz. I want to press my nose against the glass and breathe it all in, pretend this is some magical adventure and not the start of a year of pain.

Unfortunately, any hope of escaping into a comforting daydream is interrupted by the slamming open of the carriage door. I should ignore whoever is swaggering through the doorway, but that damn curiosity of mine gets the better of me and I can't help peering over my shoulder.

Stanley Chandlers and his band of merry meatheads.

For a second, I catch his eyes and his top lip – one I've kissed – curls in disgust. Then I snatch my head back round and stare straight ahead.

I'm not interested in any of his bullshit.

"Hello, friends," he snarls, and I can almost hear the

others in the carriage shaking around me. Seriously, and they think they're actually going to make it through Firestone Academy? That they'll return home heroes to their families and not in a body bag?

I'd roll my eyes, but I know it'll only provoke a jerk like Stanley.

"You know the drill," he says, striding into the middle of the carriage, hands deep in his worn pant pockets. "Open your bags and hand over your lunches."

There's a menace in his voice, at odds to his laid-back demeanor, and no one argues. There's rustling as people unzip bags and root around for their lunches – lunches their moms probably packed with care.

From the corner of my eye, I watch Stanley's gang move around the carriage, snatching boxes and parcels of food, irritatingly smug grins plastered across their faces.

I turn my attention back to the window.

"And you too, Storm." I feel a hand slap down on my shoulder and then his hoarse voice by my ear. "We all know you think you're special or some such shit. You're not. Give me your lunch."

I'm trapped. My usual method of escape – running as fast as I freaking well can – is not an option. The only place to run to is right off the end of the carriage, onto the tracks, and most probably under the wheels of the train.

I snap my head around and glare at him. "Why? Did your mom forget to pack you one?"

It's a low blow. One I know will hit him hard. I doubt anyone else knows about his mom. Only me.

His brow furrows, his eyes turn cruel, and he shakes me so damn hard I feel my brain rattle against my skull.

It's hard to remember the sweet boy he used to be, the

one I spent that summer with three years ago. The one who was my friend. The one I kissed.

That was before he got tall and big and popular.

"Give me your fucking lunch, bitch," he snarls.

I keep my face blank. I learned from Muriel that if you show nothing, it makes them even madder. They want tears. They want anger. It's best if you don't give them anything at all.

"I don't have any," I say robotically.

He slams me back against the seat. The carriage is silent except for the rattle of the train on the tracks and the wind whistling past the windows. Everyone else is still, watching us.

"You're lying." He takes a fistful of the collar of my thin jacket. "You think you're special."

"I don't," I whisper.

"You think you're going to get to the academy and they're going to see how smart you are and you'll be assigned Granite Quarter. But you're wrong. You're fucking stupid. There's only a handful of us who are going to make it through the academy with enough points to be assigned some better quarter – who aren't going back to that shithole. And you won't be with us."

For once, he may actually be right. Although, I doubt it will be as many as a handful. One or two, possibly. Stanley, though, has a good chance. He's strong and athletic – he certainly won't make it to Granite Quarter with all the nerds and scholars, definitely won't be going to Onyx Quarter with the shadow weavers, but he has a good chance of Iron Quarter with all the other jocks and soldiers.

"Oh - kay," I say slowly, as if what he's saying is the most boring thing I've ever heard.

His expression hardens further. Since his glow up, he's

been used to people treating him with respect. I can sense the blood in his veins boiling.

"Last chance, you little slut."

I snort.

And he slams his fist right into my face. I hear my cheek crack and pain spirals right across my face and into the recesses of my skull. My mouth fills with the warm coppery taste of blood and my vision multiplies.

Despite the pain, I wrap my arms tightly around my bag and clutch it to my chest. He tugs on it, but I cling all the harder, refusing to let it go.

"You're going to regret this," he snarls, swinging his fist into my ribs and then against the side of my head.

I expect him to keep swinging, to beat me until I'm unconscious and he can take the bag from my limp arms. He doesn't. He stops and stalks away with his treasure, the carriage door slamming shut behind him.

He knows I'm not lying.

There may be something hidden in my bag, but it isn't lunch.

Chapter Two

B riony

I wait for everyone else to shuffle off the train, then stand and swing my rucksack up onto my shoulder. The action makes my bruised ribs ache and I wince against the pain, my head still pounding from the two punches I took to the skull.

It's fine. Sure, my reflection confirms my left eye's all puffed up and slowly turning blue, a cut striping across my cheek bone where Stanley caught me with his ring. But it will heal. It always does.

I lift my chin, walk to the train door and descend the metal steps out onto another platform.

This one's not covered in snow, but it's as cold and bleak as home, a frigid wind whipping around all the kids already lined up for some kind of inspection, the sun hanging low in the sky and shadows already descending.

I join the line, standing beside some girl who used to be in my woodwork class back at school. I lower my bag to the ground, positioning it between my feet, and wait.

There must be several hundred of us at least and we're the last ones to join. Not surprising. We had the furthest to travel because, of course, they'd build the academy closest to Onyx Quarter – can't have all those spoiled bastards traveling too far, can we? Plus, I suspect our train was the oldest and most decrepit. In fact, I bet most of the shadow weavers were driven in fancy cars by goddamn chauffeurs.

It's easy to spot who they are and an extreme sensation of disgust, hatred and fear spirals in my empty stomach.

They're furthest down the line from us and dressed in clothes that weren't handed down or retrieved from thrift stores. They're made from bright, expensive-looking materials and they actually fit them. Although, that isn't the only giveaway. There's something about the kids – an air of self confidence and arrogance that's discernible even over the distance.

Then there's the actual shadow magic – some of the kids tossing balls of it up into the air or at each other, making it clear to all of us losers just how special they are.

I run my gaze over the other soon-to-be students lined up along the platform – kids from the white-collar workers in Granite Quarter or the soldiers and athletes in Iron Quarter. They aren't as extravagantly dressed as the shadow weaver kids, but they still look a hell of a lot better than us.

It's why any one of the kids I traveled up with in the train would give their right arm to come out of the academy and all its trials and testing and be designated one of the other quarters, escaping a lifetime of hard labor in the factories, fields and mines of Slate Quarter. A better life for them and their family – if they choose to take them.

Not all do. Some want an entirely clean break. I can totally relate.

These Granite and Iron kids are ordinary, though, not a lot different from me and the others from Slate Quarter, and as a consequence, and to my utter shame, my gaze is pulled back to the shadow weavers.

To the magic. To the bright clothes. To the sense of power.

They are beautiful, all of them. And well fed and healthy.

It makes me hate them all the more.

They have so much — everything anyone could ever dream of — and yet they took the only thing I ever cared about.

Suddenly, my eyes meet the gaze of a boy peering along the line in our direction. For the briefest of seconds, we simply stare at each other – both stunned to be caught gaping.

Everything about him screams strength – from the way his shirt tugs across his muscular chest, to his square jaw and sharp cheekbones. He looks like he could crush me with his bare hands. Even his eyes are intimidating – an unusually pale color I can't make out over the distance, that contrast – startling so – with his dark brows and the dark hair that hangs to his shoulders.

For a moment, it's like everyone else around us melts away – all the noise, all the commotion – and it's just me and him staring at each other across the distance. A strange sensation shivers down my spine and I wonder if we know each other, if I recognize him from somewhere. Is that what this is? Or is it his magic? I've never met a shadow weaver in real life before – although I've heard a fuck-load about them.

But then the spell is broken.

He frowns like I've displeased him and turns his head away.

I shake my own head, annoyed that some guy could make me feel so disoriented, and concentrate instead on the set of guards marching towards us.

I wonder why they're needed. We're all here, aren't we? If we were going to run, we'd already have done it.

It seems no one's getting shot today, though, because the troop of guards halts in front of us, moves aside and the Empress herself steps forward.

She is a tall, willowy woman, with pale skin and pale eyes. A crimson gown drapes across her delicate shoulders, a pink thread woven through it that makes it glow in the dusk. It reaches the ground, her feet not visible and her arms, gloved in red leather, are clasped in front of her. On top of her head, woven into her golden locks, sits the steel crown of the realm.

All my life, I've seen pictures of her – on posters, in frames, in books. She is beautiful in an ethereal way. Delicate, fragile-looking, like the shell of an egg. Yet, this is the woman that controls the realm and all of us in it.

To see her in real life has me just as disoriented as a moment ago.

Or maybe that's just the two hits to the head. I'm not usually so awed. I don't intend to be. That isn't how my time at the academy is going to go. I know who these people are. I know how they treat people like me. I won't be bowing and scraping at their feet.

"Welcome, offspring of the realm." She smiles at us serenely, like we are her very own children. "One thousand years ago, this realm and its people were lost to the darkness and at the mercy of demons. It was only with the discovery of firestones, the taming of dragons and the emergence of those among us able to wield strong magic that we drove the danger away. From the ashes, our new realm was formed where each has their place, every one their role. However, I do not need to tell you that the threat still remains. The darkness encroaches us from all sides, the demons are an ever-present and deadly threat. It is only through the continued efforts and sacrifice of those able to wield shadow magic that we are protected from harm."

The soldiers stamp their feet and knock their fists against their chests.

"Today you become students of the Firestone Academy. Today you join the thousands of others before you in under-going the year-long learnings and trials that will determine your future." She casts her eyes over us, seeming to take each one of us in. "All of you have talents – whether it be your intellect, your brute strength, the ability of your hands – or the unique and powerful wielding of magic." She points to the shadow weavers, who smirk with self-satisfaction. "You all have something to offer the realm. You all have your place in ensuring the safety of its people and our collective prosperity. Whether that be by providing the food from Slate Quarter needed to feed our realm, or inventing new technology in Granite Technology to aid our fighters. Whether you will become a foot soldier from Iron Quarter supporting our more elite fighters or you are a shadow weaver protecting our realm with your magic." She lifts her hands into the air, sparks of magic exploding from her palms. "By trial and truth, your Quarter calls!"

The guards around her clap and, taking their cue, so do those lined up on the platform.

Not me though. I keep my hands by my side. This is all bullshit. My fate's already written – was from the moment I slithered from between my dying mother's legs and into Slate Quarter.

Stanley is right. I won't be going anywhere but home, where the 'ability of my hands' will be exploited, where there's nothing worth living for, where I'll be worked to the bone until I'm a broken wretch like my dad – unable to make it through the day without a bottle or two of spirits by my side.

Maybe once upon a time I trusted the system. I believed, like everyone else, if we gave our best, we'd be assigned a Quarter that would most suit our talents. Then I learned better.

My insolence goes unnoticed and finally the Empress lifts her hand for silence.

"I will not pretend that your year at the Firestone Academy will be an easy one. You will be pushed to your boundaries, stretched to your limits, driven to your breaking points. We intend to find the best among you – the most talented, the most powerful. And only the trials of the utmost rigor and hardship will reveal your true capabilities, your true selves." She pauses again, although this time there is no clapping. This time I'd say the realization has finally hit. There's a reason one or two students return home in a coffin each year. The Firestone Academy is a dangerous and forbidding place.

I know that better than anyone else.

"And so," the Empress continues, "there will be no delay. Your first trial begins this evening. In fact, it will start right now. You may leave your bags here – they will be transported up to the academy for you." She points off into the distance. Right there on the horizon, just visible above what looks like the dense tree line of a forest, tall castle turrets climb into the darkening sky. "You will make your own way to the academy. Points will be rewarded and, as you know, points will determine to which of the four Quarters you are assigned. Good luck." She smiles again and then, with a whisk of her cloak, she vanishes from sight, along with the guards that surrounded her, all of them melting into air.

What follows is confusion and chaos.

People swing their heads around in panic, others crowd around with their friends murmuring to one another, some call to each other.

Above the commotion, one of the shadow weavers jumps up onto a pile of bags – or did he fly up there?

"Yeah, good luck, you cock-sucking commoners. This is where you learn what real strength is. This is where you learn why we are the ones chosen to protect the realm. This is where you learn your place. None of you are getting any points. Because we're coming for you." He rubs his hands together with such glee it makes my blood run cold.

The powerful always prey on the weak. And tonight the powerful are going to show us just how weak we are.

The voices become more frantic. One girl is already crying. Another boy shaking.

Me, I'm not hanging about. I've heard what happens the night new students arrive at the academy. I've already taken one beating today. I'm not about to take another.

I swing my bag back up onto my shoulder, wincing again with the pain, and jump down from the platform.

"Hey, Slate scum, you're meant to leave your bag behind," some jerk calls out from above me.

I ignore him. There is no way I'm leaving my bag unattended. No way on earth I'm being parted from it.

Instead, I scan the landscape quickly as the sun dips behind the horizon and plunges us all into a black so thick it sucks away all the light. The temperature drops several degrees with it and cold caresses my body. Around us lie open fields and the distant forest. And perhaps the gurgle of a stream or a river. Already there are people running out across the fields – people, I bet, who aren't prepared to wait around and find out what's coming.

I peer up at the academy and then I start to run. Not towards it, away from it. I'm not following the crowd. I'm getting as far away from everyone else as I can. It's the tactic I've always used and nine times out of ten it's worked. Run and hide. Don't let them catch you.

Okay, it'll mean I'm one of the last to arrive at the academy. But so what? It's not like I'm going to ace any of these trials anyway. And if I'm punished? It's nothing I haven't handled before.

I run as hard as I can, although the pain in my ribs slows me down and makes every panted-breath agony.

At least I'm running in the wrong direction, though. At least no one is going to follow me this way. At least I'll escape the sadistic mayhem.

Yeah, so much for that plan.

Turns out, I'm wrong.

Behind me comes the pounding of feet on hard earth.

Loud, fast, determined.

Peering over my shoulder and through the darkness, I discover a figure racing towards me. Moving at a colossal speed.

I can't make them out, can't see their face, or determine their identity. But I'm pretty sure they're coming for me.

"Shit," I mutter, driving my arms and legs faster, even though it makes the pain spike in my body.

I scramble up a bank, then skid down the other side, losing my balance for a second, before I find my feet again.

A cloud of thick fog curls around me, drifts of silvery cobwebs swim past my face.

I keep running.

Maybe they'll get bored. Maybe I'll lose them in this mist. There must be easier prey than me out there. That crying girl for starters. I doubt she's going to last this first night at the academy. And they were all so freaking excited about coming here.

I tut, then berate myself for my smugness. I'm not exactly doing so great myself. The pain in my ribs is excruciating, and the shadow is gaining on me. I can hear them – their panted breath, their solid footfall. Shit, I can *feel* them.

I have no idea where I am. My head aches, my ribs sting and my legs are tiring.

I grit my teeth and keep driving forward through the swirling mist.

But it's no use.

My body lets me down, weakened by that goddamn beating.

Fucking Stanley!

I blink away tears of frustration. I try to keep moving.

My feet slow.

And a silvery shadow hooks around my middle, sliding around me, tightening its grip, and slamming me to the earth.

I land flat on my stomach and the air knocks straight from my lungs as my pursuer lands down on top of me, pinning me to the ground with their immense weight.

I close my eyes and try to breathe.

My lungs don't work, no matter how hard I suck at the air, no matter how much my aching ribs pull. Nothing. No air. No breath. Nothing.

The dark shadows of the world encroach across my vision.

Fuck it, Briony. I thought you were made of harder stuff than this.

I jolt myself back from the abyss.

I am made of harder stuff than this. I fucking am.

I suck more desperately at the air, screaming as my injured ribs expand, pain striking through my body.

Whoever has me pinned to the ground doesn't react. Their mouth hovers by my right ear, and their moist breath whistles over my skin.

They're much, much bigger than me, their scent woody and masculine, like the forest at night. Menacing, dark, enticing.

I attempt to shuffle from underneath them, but they hold me locked to the ground with their sizable frame.

"What's your name?"

A man. His voice is deep and polished, and if I hadn't guessed before, I know it now.

A shadow weaver.

"None of your fucking business," I spit, struggling against him. "Get the fuck off me."

"You think wriggling your ass against my cock is going to encourage me to get off you?" he says, with a hint of amusement.

I freeze.

Don't provoke the monsters. Don't give them what they want.

He curls a loose strand of hair around my ear. "Come on now, tell me your name."

I stare down at the hard earth, drops of moisture clinging to the brittle grass. I can feel the beat of his rapid heart pounding against me.

I say nothing.

He huffs a little, shifts his weight, and flips me right over so I'm lying on my back and staring right up at him, my hands pinned to the earth, his body caged over mine.

I jolt.

It's the boy from the platform.

Up close, his eyes are such a soft, pale blue they're almost translucent, almost silver, like the moon on a cool, clear evening. His skin is pale too and the lines of his face so sharp, so defined, they look as if they were carved from marble.

Around him the air crackles with electricity. His magic.

I wonder what power he possesses. I wonder what he can do.

I wonder what the hell he's going to do to me.

The thought has me struggling under him, attempting to break loose. But speed has always been my asset, not strength. I'm a tiny, pathetic weed compared to him. He pins my hands above my head and leans into me, his face mere millimeters from mine, his breath warm as it dances across my face.

He doesn't ask me my name again, instead he stares right into my eyes, like he did before, like he's trying to read my soul. It's so intense, my cheeks run warm, and I'm forced to turn my head away from him.

"How did you get that?" he asks, his voice less playful than before.

"Wh-wh-what?" I say, unable to help but peer back up at him.

"The black eye," he snarls, "the cut on your cheek."

I nearly add the bruised ribs to his list, but I hold my tongue. It's clear I disgust him. Weak, pathetic, easy prey. He probably saw that on the platform and that's why he chased me. Although, it seems dumb to me. It's a done-deal which quarter he'll be assigned. Only shadow weavers make it to Onyx Quarter. Yet, he's chosen to scupper his chance of securing easy points by following me in the wrong direction. Why?

"Who did this to you?" he asks.

Again, I don't reply. What's he going to do with the name? Congratulate the dude? Ask him to be his best friend? Yeah, Stanley's brute strength and large fists already give him enough advantages in this place. I'm not about to gift him a powerful new friend.

I stare over the dude's shoulder, letting my passive expression swamp my face.

He's going to do what the fuck he wants to me. But I won't give him the satisfaction of a reaction.

"Fine," he says. "I'm going to find out anyway. Your name and the name of the piece of shit that did this to you."

I blink. Confused by his words. Still waiting for the first blow.

Or worse ...

But then he's rolling off me and stumbling up to his feet.

His pale eyes glimmer in the darkness, flickering over my form, lingering on my face.

"Don't hang about, sweetheart. There are monsters out here," he whispers, and then he turns away and disappears into the swirling mist.

Chapter Three

B eaufort

I leave the girl lying on the cold hard ground and stride away.

My heart slams against my ribs and a million thoughts hurtle through my mind, but I walk away, the magic sparking in my fingertips.

Five minutes ago, adrenaline and excitement hurtled through my body, my magic hardly containable. Tonight is our night. Our opportunity to prove to the scum from the rest of the realm exactly what they truly are.

Pathetic.

Our opportunity to show them just how powerful, just how mighty, just how fucking awesome the shadow weavers are.

Just how grateful they should be.

I've dreamed about this moment for as long as I can

remember. For as long as I've known about the ritual of the first night at the Firestone Academy, when rules don't apply and actions have no consequences. A chance to establish the order of hierarchy for the next twelve months. To lay down our laws.

I should have rubbed that girl's face in the dirt. Forced her to eat the stinking mud. Made her lick it from my boots.

I should have given her a taste of my magic, made her writhe in agony, beg me for mercy.

This scum needs to understand how powerful we are. They need to understand why we are the ones who rule this realm. Why we are the only ones who can protect them.

And she is scum. Like the others.

Isn't she?

I shake my head. Trying to dislodge her from my head.

A thick soup of mist hovers above the ground. It dampens my hair and my skin and smothers the sound. But I know where I am. I can feel the academy waiting for me on the horizon. I can sense the others lost in the swirling mist. Shadow weavers and common scum among them. I can sense magic rocketing and shooting through the air. I can smell the fear.

It's not too late. The night has only just begun. There's still time – plenty of time.

Except I've lost my appetite for it now.

I have no desire for it at all.

Instead, I trudge over the land, under the trees, towards my new home.

And all the time, it continues in my head. Over and over again.

That vision. That flash of something.

Something when I looked into her eyes.

Chapter Four

B riony

I roll up onto my hands and knees and scrabble in the darkness for my bag. The mist is even thicker now, suffocatingly so, and along with the pain in my ribs, every breath is a struggle.

It takes five agonizingly long minutes to retrieve my bag, constantly peering over my shoulder – ears straining in the eerie silence – for another attacker. For that shadow weaver to come for me again.

Why did he leave me like that?

He could have beaten me to a pulp. Tortured me with his magic. Forced himself on me.

It's what the shadow weavers do.

To them, we are nothing but dirt on the soles of their boots.

I snort. A girl from Slate Quarter. We're even lower than dirt.

Why the hell did he let me go?

I push the thought from my mind.

What does it matter? I'm not safe yet.

Just because one self-entitled bastard chose to let me go, doesn't mean the next one will. The night is far from over.

With my heart in my throat, I rummage through my bag, checking nothing was lost or damaged in my tumble. Finding everything still there, I sling my rucksack back onto my shoulders, cursing because, after my fall, my ribs sting even more than they did, and then I start walking again. As I do, I listen acutely for any sounds, and glare through the mist for any flicker of movement.

I have no idea where I am anymore, nor which direction I'm heading in. For all I know, I could be strolling straight into the midst of all those shadow weavers, lying in wait for a powerless girl like me.

My feet catch on a small rock in the earth and I crouch down and dig it out with my hands, my already short nails cracking and snapping off as I do. Then I clutch it in my hand as if it is precious. A weapon I can strike with if anyone does attack. It makes me feel a little better, even if it is most probably worthless.

I walk for what feels like an hour. There has never been enough money for anything as luxurious as a watch. Usually I'd look up at the sky and the passing stars and traveling moon would tell me how much time had passed. However, the muggy mist makes it impossible to tell. Finally though, I hit a crop of trees. This could be the edge of the forest that lay before the academy. Then again, it could be somewhere different entirely.

Cautiously, I venture under the branches, walking a

little further until I find a tree I can climb. Its first branch hangs right above my head. With my bag still strapped to my back, I jump and grab the branch with both hands, kicking my feet upwards. It takes four attempts and then finally, I pincer the branch between my feet and swing myself up, climbing into the tree's boughs, as high as I dare go, the limbs of the tree becoming younger and weaker the further up I go. Then I settle into the crook of a branch, and, despite the cold, shrug off my jacket and use it to tie myself to the branch. Once I'm as secure as I'm going to be, I place my bag in my lap and hook my arms through the straps.

As carefully and silently as I can, I zip open my bag and peer inside, checking again that the contents have not been lost or broken. When I find it all safe and sound, I let out a sigh of relief and, zipping the bag closed, lean my head back against the tree.

I can't sleep. It's too risky up here in the tree. My precautions are probably not enough. If I drift off, I could drop my bag or fall to my death. Besides, I'm too wired.

I hope I'm safe up here, hidden and away from all the others. But I have no idea if I am.

Time passes and the mist drifts away. The sounds of the night are no longer muffled, they carry through the trees, bouncing off the trunks, amplified and echoing. Screams. So many goddamn screams. As well as sobbing and crying, yells and shouts, whoops of excitement, the crack of wood and the splintering of branches. Below me, I see magic flash through trees, sparking in the distance, shooting up into the sky.

I yank my rock from my pocket and grip it tightly in my fist.

If anyone comes for me, I will kill them. Better them than me.

More time passes. The noise fades. Replaced by the sounds of the forest. Creatures scurrying through the undergrowth, paws padding softly across the ground, the crack of wings.

I jerk awake. A pale light filters through the canopy of leafless branches and the birds that remain to weather the winter, call to each other weakly.

Morning.

My arms remain curled tightly around my bag. My fist is empty.

I peer through the branches below me and listen once again. Nothing, only the birds singing the arrival of the new day.

New day!

I groan and, stretching out my stiff body, hurry back down the tree.

I am going to be so fucking late for the academy. They'll think I bolted. They'll have soldiers out searching for me – or my body.

At the lowest branch, I glance down at the drop to the floor, then, taking a steadying breath in, jump. My legs buckle with the force of my landing and I roll across the hard earth, groaning at the pain in my ribs, until I right myself back on my feet.

"Chose a night up in the trees too, huh?"

I spin around. A tall, spindly boy walks towards me. His clothes are creased and grubby and a dead leaf rests in his mop of dark curly hair.

I freeze in indecision.

He isn't a shadow weaver. I can tell by his clothes. I don't recognize his face, which means he isn't from Slate Quarter either. Granite Quarter maybe?

Which means, while he may be smart, he probably isn't strong.

Should I be running anyway? He could still hurt me if he wanted to. Who says it's only the shadow weavers who get their kicks out of beating up weaker kids?

Look at Stanley.

However, before I've made up my mind, he's grinning at me and, maybe I'm naïve or stupid, or both, but it seems genuine. Kind even.

"Although, it looks like it didn't help you much." He points to my face.

"Nah," I say, "this I already had. No one caught me last night."

He applauds me.

"You know we're going to be so fucking late."

"Probably," I concur, waiting for him to catch up with me.

He chuckles. "No doubt about it, Cupcake. I'm just so glad I won't be the only one."

"Do you know where we are?" I ask him.

"I think ..." he says, pulling out a compass from his pocket – definitely Granite Quarter. "We're west of the academy which must mean we're in the Dankland Forest." I nod like I know what that means. I guess he sees right through me. "About an hour's walk from the academy."

"Shit," I mumble. "That far!"

Judging by the lightening sky it's already eight o'clock in the morning.

"Yeah. Afraid so." He smiles flatly. "Although, I have to say, turning up late and receiving whatever punishment we get given has to be a hell of a lot better than the beating we'd've gotten last night if any shadow weavers had caught us."

I nod, although I can't help thinking of the shadow weaver who let me go. "No points for us though."

The boy shrugs. "I think we made the better choice."

We walk on together, the dead leaves crunching under our feet. The cold air nipping at our faces.

He pulls something else from his pocket. A small parcel wrapped in a handkerchief. He unwraps it carefully, pulling out a lump of baked goods.

"Want some?" he asks, breaking a corner off and offering it to me.

"Is it poisoned?" I ask, side-eyeing him.

He takes a big bite. "Fuck, I hope not. Then again, I'm a massive disappointment to both my parents so maybe they decided to finish me off before I even got to the academy and could disappoint them even more." He chews. "Tastes okay."

"Not smart enough?" I say, taking a piece of the spongy concoction this time when he offers it again.

"Huh?" he says, watching me cram the piece into my mouth.

"Not smart enough for Granite Quarter? Is that why you're a disappointment?"

"No," he says gravely, "not – who knows the fuck what – for Iron Quarter."

"Oh," I say, my cheeks warming. Based on his appearance, I'd assumed he was from Granite Quarter. I don't like it when people make assumptions about me but I guess I'm guilty of doing just that.

I try not to, but I wolf that small piece of cake down quickly, licking the crumbs from my fingers when I'm done. I haven't eaten since the evening before yesterday and even my nerves aren't dampening my hunger.

"Here, have it all." He hands me the entire piece.

"I can't," I say.

"Slate Quarter, right?" he says, holding his hands way above his head when I try to pass the food back.

"How did you guess?" I ask just as flatly, taking another bite of the cake. I'm not sure I care if it is poisoned. It tastes so good and has my stomach rumbling in appreciation.

"Oh, you know," he says casually, "the general look of despair and malnutrition." He waves his hand in my direction.

I snort laugh, spraying crumbs real classily from my mouth and nose.

"I'm Fly, by the way," he says. "As in the act of, not the small annoying buzzing insect. Obviously."

I laugh again. It's a long time since anyone's made me laugh, since I found anyone remotely funny. It feels good, even if it hurts my ribs. Those nerves that have me tight-ening my shoulders and clenching my jaw, relax just a little.

"Briony," I say through gritted teeth, wincing against the pain.

He frowns. "Are you sure those fuckers didn't catch you last night?"

"Shush," I say, swinging my head around in mock horror. "You can't let anyone hear you call them that. They are our esteemed and respected betters."

"Still fuckers though," he says.

"Yeah," I say. "But, like I said, this wasn't them. This was from before."

"Before?"

"I wouldn't give my lunch up to one of the fuckers I traveled with from Slate Quarter. Not that I had any lunch to give him."

"Not got a lot of friends in Slate Quarter then?"

I hesitate, then shake my head. Maybe I'm opening myself up here, showing him my weaknesses – ones he could use against me. Then again, he'll learn soon enough that I have no friends. It'll be damn obvious.

"Yeah, same," he says.

I stare at him, finding it hard to believe. Okay, so he's not some muscle-man like Stanley or the shadow weaver from last night. He definitely could do with eating more of this cake. But he has a warm face – all smiles and bright eyes plus he's funny and friendly. How can he not be popular?

As if reading my thoughts, he adds: "Unless you're able to pump iron or run a sprint in less than a millisecond, nobody's interested."

"You can't do either of those things?"

"Nope. Can you?"

"Never tried."

I mine the handkerchief for any remaining crumbs, then fold it up neatly and pass it back to Fly.

"You must be pretty good at running if you made it to the trees to hide before any of those ..." I pause, "fuckers caught you."

"I'm not stupid. I knew what was coming. I wasn't going to hang about and let them catch me."

"Me neither." And for a moment we look at each other, understanding passing between us.

"Ahhh," he says, "looks like we've reached the perimeter of the academy." He points towards a fence woven from the branches of willow trees and blocking the way ahead. "Come on, Briony, we'd better go find out what punishment lies in wait for us."

We climb over the fence and step out onto mossy moorland. Immediately a murder of crows, feeding on the land, crack their wings and take off into the sky, skimming over our heads and cawing at us angrily.

"Great," I mutter, ducking my head. "I can't wait."

Chapter Five

B riony

The academy stands in front of us, my home for the next twelve months.

It sprawls across the landscape like a monster, many tall gothic towers twisting up into the gray sky like outstretched claws, and solid lower buildings, with long slitted windows and tiled roofs, crouching closer to the ground. It's a hodge-podge of constructions – some old, some newer, some spectacular and elegant, some decrepit and crumbling away.

It makes me shiver. It looks more like a prison than a school. A place to keep people locked away.

"Cheery, isn't it?" Fly says with a grimace. "I wonder if there will be doilies on the tables and frilly curtains by the windows."

"More likely chains and torture devices," I mumble.

"You're right. That would suit the overall aesthetic much better."

He grabs my hand and tugs me over the rough ground. "You're slowing up. Come on, the punishment will only be worse the later we leave it."

"Urgh," I groan but let him pull me, happy for once to have company.

I don't usually feel nervous. What's the point? But the place is so damn intimidating, about one hundred times bigger than anything back in Slate Quarter including the workshops and factories.

"Do you know where we should go?" I ask him, as we draw closer to the first of the towering buildings.

"There, I'm guessing," he says, pointing towards our left. We've been walking across rough moorland but this has given way to a manicured field, the grass green and even. Up against the stone building walls, a tent of pale canvas has been erected. There are a handful of people milling about, some slumped on the ground.

"Hey you, there!" a tall slender woman with a clipboard calls over to us, waving in our direction and calling to us in a clipped tone. "Stop dawdling and get over here at once."

We look at each other and then pick up our heels, sprinting that way. As we draw closer, I realize the people slumped on the ground aren't simply taking a rest, exhausted after the night's excursion. They're injured.

Blood pours from a wound on the head of one boy, an elderly woman crouching over him and attempting to bandage it up. A girl lies out cold on the floor. Another girl clutches an arm to her chest, tears rolling down her cheeks.

We halt before the woman who glares at us through jeweled spectacles, her hands on her hips, her raven hair twisted artistically onto the top of her head. Her lips are painted a deep red, her nails a matching color, and black liner rings her brown eyes.

"Fly Arison?" My new companion nods and she ticks his name off her list. "And Briony Storm?"

"Yes," I tell her, as she examines me with an up-turned nose. I didn't look great to begin with – especially with the black eye. But after rolling around on the earth, sleeping in a tree and trudging through the forest, I assume I look even worse. Plus I probably stink.

"Are you injured?" she asks us.

"No," we say together.

"Then what in all the realm do you think you've been doing? Eighteen hours? This is a new record for the slowest trek to the academy."

"We were trying to avoid that," Fly says, pointing to the unconscious girl.

"She's simply fainted from exhaustion." The woman scoffs. "Pathetic. It's a simple trek. No river to cross, no mountain to hike. If you hope to survive in Firestone Academy, you're both going to need to grow some balls."

"I don't think trekking did that to him," I spit out, gesturing to the boy who now, along with the girl with the broken arm, is being led inside the academy.

"He cracked his head on a branch. Total carelessness and an avoidable incident. So many of you low-lifers lack basic survival and practical skills. We see it every year. Too molly-coddled by your parents." She raps her knuckles on her clipboard. "Not here."

I glance towards Fly. He's staring straight ahead and I'm not sure he's even listening to this bullshit.

"It goes without saying neither of you earned any points in this trial." The woman snaps two pieces of paper off her clipboard and hands them to us. "Accommodation was allocated on the basis of arrival at the academy. This is where you will be staying. Your bags have already been sent to your rooms. I suggest you head there now, and freshen up. Arrival assembly starts in ..." She glances up to the tower behind her, where a large clock displays the time. "One hour. Do not be late! And you can collect your uniforms from the pile there."

"How about breakfast?" Fly asks.

"You missed it," she says, already striding away.

"Is that it?" I ask as we study our pieces of paper. "I was expecting something more ..."

"Don't get complacent," Fly says. "They've probably placed us down in the cellars with the rats and mice."

I shrug. If I was late back at home, the punishment was far more severe. Some less-than-desirable room seems pretty tame in comparison – especially given my room back in Slate Quarter was hardly worthy of a palace.

"And you know who that was?" Fly asks.

I shake my head.

"Madame Bardin."

"Is she a shadow weaver?"

"Cupcake, nearly all the faculty are. Can't have commoners teaching the elites. But Madame Bardin, she has a ... reputation."

"A reputation for baking her students cookies and handing out warm hugs?"

"Ahhh, no," Fly says with a smile, "imagine the opposite and then make it a hell of a lot worse. Much much worse. She's a bitch and we most definitely landed ourselves on her wrong side."

Chapter Six

B^{riony}

Our pieces of paper contain the names of our rooms, a map of the academy and some starkly written rules. I expected coming to a school like this the list would be endless – after all the rule book had been thick back home in Slate Quarter. But there are just three.

No Killing
No Maiming
No Stealing

I don't know if that's a good thing or a bad thing. I already know this place is going to be hellish – does it make a difference what the rules are? If there are hardly any rules at all?

We squint down at the map. The campus is so huge – more like a small town than a school – that the pictures and names are tiny. Eventually, though, we spy our rooms. Side by side.

For the first time, I feel a bubble of hope – yeah, I know that's stupid. But I seem to have made an acquaintance – I'm not sure if I can call Fly a friend yet – we've known each other less than a day, and it seems we're going to be neighbors. Maybe the next twelve months won't be all bad.

The campus is eerily quiet as we weave our way between the tall towers, so tall they bathe us in gloomy shadow, right to the east corner. Here the towers are oldest, made from thick gray stone, crumbling in places, the windows so small I can't imagine they emit any light.

"Cozy," Fly remarks with flared nostrils as he pushes his weight against the heavy wooden door and we step inside. The temperature drops immediately and the air is dank and smells of damp.

We climb a winding stone staircase, the steps worn in the center, passing other doorways as we go, and find our rooms right at the top underneath the thatched roof, a gale whistling through into the stairwell and making it colder still.

"See," Fly says, "this is our punishment. We're going to catch hypothermia or influenza or both and then we are going to die."

"It isn't a cellar," I point out, trying to be positive. "No rats or mice."

"There'll be both in that roof," he says, pointing above our heads before turning the iron ring on the door marked *Arison* and pushing his way inside.

I stare at my own door, marked *Storm*.

"How did they do that?" I ask, tracing my fingers over the embossed lettering.

"Magic," he calls from his room. I hear him flop down

on a mattress, the bed creaking under his weight. "I'm going to sleep. If I'm not out waiting for you in the stairwell in thirty, come wake me up. You owe me for that cake!"

I twist my own iron ring and push the door open. It's dark inside, the narrow window just as small as all the others in this tower and it's definitely no warmer than the stairwell. I find a switch on the wall by the door and press it. A dull bulb hanging from a cord in the exposed ceiling flickers on. Immediately, there's a scurrying in the roof. I'm guessing Fly's right about our furry roommates.

The bulb casts a dull light across the room and I stand and stare at it for several minutes. Back in Slate Quarter there's electricity in the factories and workhouses, places the like of me are sent to work. But in the homes, we rely on candles and gas lamps. I've spent a lifetime scrambling around for matches. Light has never been something that can be summoned at the flick of a switch.

Fuck the shadow weavers – this is magic. Invented by some clever nerd in Granite Quarter. And yet it's those damn shadow weavers who earn all the privilege, all the praise and all the riches. Just because they were lucky enough to be born with magic in their veins.

The room is bare, straw scattered over the cold stone floor, a wooden bed with a hard–looking mattress and rough blankets standing in the center, and an old wardrobe propped against the far wall, a cloudy mirror pinned to its door.

I half expect to find a bucket in the corner for me to do my business in, but as there is none, the bathroom must be elsewhere.

I stride directly towards the wardrobe, flinging back the doors. The left side has a rail, the right three shelves, and the door a hook. I hesitate. It's not exactly secure. I can lock the bedroom door, but if anyone gets inside …

I scoff. I'm being silly. Why the hell would anyone want to come into my room? Especially a room like this?

There's no need to worry.

Still, I unpack my bag, laying my few pieces of clothing and my meager possessions on the shelves – one photo frame, two books and a collection of broken pens and pencils. Then I lay my almost empty bag in the bottom of the wardrobe, beneath the rail and, pulling one of the blankets from the bed, bury it underneath.

I stand back and examine the effect. It's well hidden. Of course, someone might question why I'd leave a blanket in the cupboard when the room is so cold and if they were to go rummaging, they'd find it. I just have to hope that won't happen.

The final shelf I reserve for the pile of gray uniform clothes. The material is scratchy and repaired numerous times. It looks suspiciously like a potato sack.

With a sigh, I close the wardrobe, catching a glimpse of my reflection as I do. My hair has come loose, wisps floating around my head.

I remove the clip, unwind my hair, then brush in the loose strands with my fingers, wind it in a tight coil and secure it firmly to the base of my skull.

Then I follow Fly's lead and lie down on the bed. The one pillow is lumpy, the springs in the mattress clearly rusted solid, but it's more comfortable than the tree, better than the floor.

I close my eyes and the image of the shadow weaver comes hurtling back into my mind, his pale eyes boring into mine, the weight of his solid body pressing me into the earth.

I swallow, pushing the memory to the back of my mind.

There are hundreds of us at the academy and I'm betting they'll keep the shadow weavers separate from the rest of us. Wouldn't want us polluting their air.

I'll probably never see him again.

I wake to a pair of hands shaking me fiercely.

"You were meant to wake me up!" Fly says right in my face as I blink awake.

"Oh shit, are we l–?"

"Late? Not if you change into your uniform right now and we start sprinting." I glance at him. He's already changed into a pair of gray pants, a gray shirt and a tatty old gray blazer – the Firestone crest embroidered on one side.

"I'm giving you three minutes, Cupcake, and then you're going to have to fend for yourself."

"Shit," I mutter, as he dashes out the door and I strip off my grubby clothes and pull on the uniform. It scratches against my skin and smells of moth. At least I won't be the only one wearing this, though. It's the one benefit of this uniform. We're all going to look hideous together.

Once we're out on the cobbled pathways, we realize we're not as late as we feared. There are other new students out here too, all walking in the direction of the central campus building.

There are no shadow weavers among us. Everyone trudging along with us looks as exhausted and worn-out as we do. Most have gray shadows under their eyes, several have cuts and bruises to their faces. One or two are even hobbling.

I may have ended up with the worst bedroom in the

academy and no points awarded for the first trial, but it seems it may have been worth it after all. I think of the girl out by the tent. Madame Bardin said she'd fainted. Was that true?

However, it doesn't seem to matter that the shadow weavers spent the night torturing and abusing everyone else. The other students are still chattering excitedly about them as if they weren't responsible for the torture last night.

"What do you think they'll have us doing first?" Fly asks, chewing on his fingernails and ignoring the talk around us.

"I guess they're going to start testing us straight away. See what skills and talents we have."

"Do you have any? Talents, I mean?"

"Me?" I say laughing. "No. You?"

He shakes his head. "Except the ability to look good in anything including this shit." He peers down at the uniform, curling a lip in disgust. He's wrapped a belt around his lean waist. It gives the outfit some shape which is more than can be said for mine. It hangs off my frame exactly like a potato sack would.

We arrive at the Great Hall where we've been instructed to gather. It's not a gymnasium hall like I was expecting, or like the halls in the factories back in Slate Quarter. No, this hall is more like a cathedral. It's built from a yellow sandstone and around its high walls feature carved arches with no openings and long stained-glass windows.

Right outside the Hall's entrance stands a magnificent bronze statue – a giant egg and around it three swooping dragons their wings spread wide, their jaws filled with rows of sharp teeth, their talons long and deadly, and their eyes alert. Even in today's muggy light the statue glows, the egg itself seeming to brim with fire.

We all line up like we did on the platform, including, much to my surprise, the shadow weavers.

I see I was wrong. We're not all in this together.

Their academy uniforms are not hideous like ours. They're black not gray and the flames on the crest on their blazers flicker with life. The material is not the scratchy stiff kind our uniform is stitched from. It's soft, holding its shape and hugging the form of every single one of them.

They stare back at the rest of us with smirks on their arrogant faces, whispering to each other and laughing among themselves.

I hate them. I knew I would and everything I've seen so far only confirms it.

They are a bunch of self-satisfied jerks.

I don't care what I've been told. I've never believed it, and in this moment, I believe it even less so.

Because I see it clear as day – in their eyes, in their attitude, in the way they glare at us.

It was no accident. Whatever they did to her was deliberate. And I will discover the truth.

Chapter Seven

D^{ray}

"That's her," Beaufort says, leaning toward me and whispering into my ear as we line up outside the Great Hall.

"Her?" I say, following his gaze along the line of students, right past all the other shadow weavers, past the athletic kids who look like they might have some fight in them, past the ordinary kids to the freaks, losers and misfits right at the far end. My shoulders slump. "Fuck man, you can't be serious."

But one look at the frown on his face tells me he is. Beaufort rarely does anything but serious.

"But she's so ..." I groan. I'd had visions of our thrall being some curvy, pretty thing – an obedient and willing little pet. Fuck, I'd had wet dreams about it. Plenty and plenty of wet dreams.

The way that girl scowls at the air around her suggests she'd be anything but obedient or willing. I don't even think she'd be fun.

"I was hoping we'd choose someone more ... like her!" I say, staring straight at a stunning brunette who's making eyes at me, blushing when I wink at her. She's easily the most beautiful girl out here with a butt I want to slap and a chest I want to bury my face into.

"No, it has to be her," Beaufort says, eyes lingering on the scrawny girl. Her dirty hair is scraped tight around her skull, her clothes hang off her puny frame, and her expression is so bitter I can taste the sourness from here.

Definitely nothing fun about her.

I sniff the air, hoping to catch her scent, something that would explain why Beaufort has his sights set on her. But there are too many other scents swirling in the air out here on the field. Shadow weavers and the plain old commoners as well. Even if I strain my nostrils, I can't make out her scent. Not in my human form anyway.

I kick at the cobbled ground and adopt a sulk on my face.

Only the elite among the shadow weavers are awarded the privilege of picking a thrall to serve them during their time at the academy. And now it seems Beaufort wants to throw that gift away.

A handful of the other powerful shadow weavers are already making their way along the line, inspecting the other students, ready to make their picks. Kratos, Prentice, and Nathan stop right in front of the brunette. Kratos draws his hand down her arm, making her shiver as Prentice leans in, nose pressed to her throat and inhales her scent.

"Fuckers," I mutter.

That's the girl that should be ours. We outrank those

losers. We're more powerful than them. We come from better families. If we picked the brunette, they'd have to find some other student to be their thrall.

It doesn't look like that is going to happen.

Freaking Beaufort would have to have other ideas.

The Smyte sisters have their hands on a young-looking boy, his hair golden, his features beautiful. Elaine and Dahlia are talking to a boy from Iron Quarter, so big you'd think he was the offspring of giants.

"What do you think, Thorne?" I ask, appealing to my other friend.

He's glaring at Beaufort's girl, his square jaw hard as stone, his dark eyes black as night. He doesn't say a word.

I sigh.

"Can we at least give it some thought? I mean, it doesn't look like she'll last a week at the academy." I scoff. "It doesn't look like she'd last a night in my company."

Which gives me an idea. Maybe I'm best playing along. She'll be gone in a matter of days. Then we can choose someone better.

Or maybe I should trust my best friend. If he says it has to be her, then there is a reason for it. There always is.

"She'll outlast us all," he says cryptically in that way that really pisses me off.

"You want to go claim her now?" I mean, I doubt there's any hurry. No one else is going to pick the girl as their thrall.

Beaufort doesn't answer, he's already strolling down the line, oblivious to all the girls fluttering their eyelashes at him and all the boys flexing their pecs. They all want him to pick them. Even the brunette is no longer focused on her admirers, smiling Beaufort's way instead.

The only one not following his progress down the line, is the one girl he's heading towards. Her eyes are trained straight ahead at the morning's mist swirling across the stone walls. She seems oblivious to everything going on around her, lost in her own world. She doesn't even register Beaufort's presence when he stops right beside her, although she must feel him. His magic is powerful. It's impossible not to.

All the other students are watching, a silence falling over the crowd.

"Hey, Dray," Dallan calls my way, "what's your pal doing down there with all the Slate scum? You do know they carry infectious diseases, right?" He chuckles, probably expecting me to join right in.

"Shut the fuck up," I snarl, my eyes flashing at him. His gaze falls immediately to the floor. He's always been weaker than me.

I return my focus to my friend. He's stopped right by the girl, the distance between them mere inches – so close she must be able to feel the tingle of his powers against her skin. Skin that is bruised around her eye and scabbed along her cheek. Someone got to her last night which proves just how weak she is. I groan again and strain my ears to hear Beaufort's words as he speaks to her.

"Be at our rooms by seven o'clock tomorrow night."

She jolts as if she really has only just realized he's there, then swings her face up towards his. Recognition, alarm and something I can't read flickers over her face quickly, before she schools her features into something emotionless and void.

"Excuse me?" she replies. Her voice isn't how I thought it would be. I expected the voice to match the expression – sour, screechy – like fingernails dragging down a blackboard. It's not like that at all. Although she's trying to sound tough, her voice is soft. As pathetic as the rest of her.

"You heard me the first time," Beaufort says. "Do not be late."

Beaufort doesn't wait for a reply, he never does. He turns his back on her and strides right back up to his spot at the head of the line, ignoring all the other students staring open-mouthed at him.

"Seriously," Ashleigh Pickford whispers beside me, "you're picking *her* as your thrall? You could have anyone you want."

"Yeah," I say, peering back towards the girl whose name I don't even know. "But we've chosen *her*."

Chapter Eight

B riony

"Oh my stars!" Fly whisper-shrieks beside me, because Madame Bardin and two other teachers are now strolling our way and the line of students have dropped their voices.

"What?" I say, distracted as I watch the teachers. Apart from Madame Bardin, who is slim, elegant and wearing heeled boots despite the rough ground, the other two teachers are the size of small houses, stacked with muscle that seem determined to break free from their clothing. They are also identical in every way, from their shorn heads and beady brown eyes, to their solid shoulders and square jaws – jaws that could crack even the hardest of nuts.

"*What?!*" Fly scoffs in disbelief. "You just got picked as their thrall."

If I hoped to ask my new friend what the hell a thrall is or who *they* are, I'm not given the chance, because one of the bulldozer twins blows violently on a whistle clutched in his over-sized hand.

"Silence," his brother roars, "and stand the fuck to attention. This isn't some holiday camp, you suckers, this is Firestone Academy and there will be no talking, slouching or ill-discipline on our watch. Now keep your mouths shut and take your seats in the Hall."

Madame Bardin steps forward, wobbling slightly in her heels and drawing her black cape around her body. She walks towards the entrance of the Great Hall and the line of students snakes behind her inside – no one daring to utter a word under the beady gaze of the two male bulldozers.

Inside is even more magnificent than the outside. High stone-vaulted ceilings taller than trees, magnificently carved pillars, marble tiles on the floor and grand chandeliers hanging far above our heads.

"Wow," I mumble.

"They say the academy was built on the site of the first discovered firestones and that this Hall was built by the early shadow weavers back when the realm was created," Fly says, head tipped right back as he stares up at the colorful stained-glass window dominating the far wall of the Hall. "Built with magic."

His words make me shiver because it does seem far too beautiful to have been built by the hands of men.

It seems like it should belong inside a castle, not a school. Except instead of elegant thrones or great banqueting tables, rows of benches have been placed along its width facing a raised stage at the far end, the huge circular window framed behind, the colored panes forming an image of the Firestone crest – the academy motto written in the old language beneath: *Through trials to truth.*

On the center of the platform stands Madame Bardin.

She waits until the line of students has shuffled along the rows of benches and then she speaks.

"Welcome all of you to the Firestone Academy. We have already begun to test you and this testing will not end until you complete your twelve months at the academy. Your time here will determine your futures. Be mindful, we will be watching you." She glares at us as if to emphasize her point. "Even when you think you aren't being assessed, you are." She pauses, allowing that information to sink in. "However, as you will all be aware, what counts most at this academy is your performance at the trials we set you." I can't help but swallow. The academy trials are notorious. That one last night was mild compared to others I've heard about. Heck, I've seen what those trials can do to you. Every year, one or two return to Slate Quarter with their face scarred, their arm maimed, a leg missing. "Ultimately," Madame says, "it is your performance during the trials which will determine to which Quarter you are sent after your time at this academy ends. The first trial is now complete and points have been awarded accordingly. Remember, points will determine to which Quarter you are assigned and thereby your destiny. The next trial will take place in three weeks' time."

This statement causes much murmuring among the students, despite the death stares from the troll-like twins.

"It's so unfair," I mutter under my breath to Fly, "us kids from Slate don't stand a chance."

"Having said that," Madame continues, "we know some students have had a head start over others," I peer towards the front row where for once the shadow weavers are listening intently, "some among you may have untapped potential and skills. Potential and skills that have not been given the correct environment to blossom. The academy also provides the opportunity to learn, to be taught, to hone your skills. Use this opportunity wisely."

My heart sinks. Learning – that was the bit Amelia was most excited about. She'd whisper to me as we fell asleep at night-time about all the things she was going to be taught. She'd promised she'd make it out of Slate Quarter. She promised she'd take me with her.

Once upon a time, I was as optimistic as she was. Once upon a time, I believed in a different future. Now I know better.

"There will be no lessons or assessments today. You have the rest of your time to acquaint yourselves with your surroundings. Classes will begin tomorrow." A few students rise to their feet, clearly believing that's it. Madame Bardin glares at them. "If you'd be gracious enough to honor me with just one more moment of your time," she says with a sinister smile that has all those students dropping back to the benches as quickly as they can. "You all have a copy of the rules of the academy. Short and simple. However, there are a few more things you should be aware of. Those caught skipping classes will be punished. Those late for lessons will be punished. Those who forget the necessary equipment for lessons will be punished. And anyone caught cheating in any way will be severely punished." She smiles a second time, only this time it's a lot more genuine. I know her type and I suspect she likes the punishing a lot more than she does the teaching.

"And if you have any problems, any complaints, any difficulties," she smiles around the Hall, "do not bother me with them. Dismissed!"

Fly leans towards me. "I don't know about you, Cupcake, but I'm starving. I'm heading straight for the canteen. Unless you have some better idea?"

I laugh. "Can we please find some lunch? I may actually pass out if not and I don't want a bump on my head to add to the collection of injuries."

"Sure," he says, hooking his arm through mine and leading me in the direction of the canteen. It's in a squat, old-looking building towards the back of the campus. One that obviously hasn't been decorated or cleaned in half a century. Paint peels from the walls and grime is smeared across the windows.

"I warn you now," Fly says, "I've been told that the cuisine here is far from the best the realm has to offer." He crinkles his nose in obvious disgust. "Jeez, it smells like something died in here."

I have to disagree. The smells are many and tantalizing – sweet and savory, vegetable and meat, wet and dry – all sloshing together through the air and swimming towards my nose. In front of us, laid out across two tables, is more food than I've seen in my lifetime. Sure, it's basic – sausages, boiled root vegetables, hard looking rolls and some sort of sloppy stew – and has to stretch to feed several hundred of us, but it's still a feast.

I grab a plate and pile it high.

Fly follows along behind me, complaining that the vegetables are overcooked and the sausages are full of more gristle than actual meat. I don't care. I am in food heaven. What's more, someone else made this for me and someone else will be clearing it all away.

I thought the academy was meant to be a place of hardship. It seems like it might be anything but.

"Slow down there, Cupcake," Fly mutters. "You eat all that, you will definitely make yourself sick."

"I don't care," I say, as we carry our plates over to an

empty table. "I'm so hungry, you could serve me pig's eyes and lizard innards and I'd wolf them down."

"Well, you could do with eating," he says, poking at a limp-looking vegetable with his fork.

"What's that meant to mean?" I ask, stuffing half a sausage into my mouth.

"No offense, sweetie, but you're a little on the skinny side."

"You can talk," I say, jabbing my knife in his direction.

"I'm lean," he says. "There's a difference."

"There is?" I say chewing.

"Yeah." He jabs his own fork towards my clavicle. "No one wants to see that much bone."

"Jeez, thanks," I say, adjusting the collar of my shirt and darting my gaze around to see if anyone else is staring at my bones. It's then I realize several are in fact staring right at me, although they all dart their gazes away as soon as I catch them at it.

Bizarre. I shake my head and return my attention to my food.

When we're done, Fly smothers a yawn with his hand.

"Orienteering myself can wait. I'm heading straight back to my room and into bed. You coming?" My eyebrows shoot involuntarily up my forehead. Fly quirks one of his own. "Just to be clear, that wasn't an offer. I mean, back to our rooms."

"In a bit," I tell him. "I think I'm going to have a snoop around first."

"Suit yourself," he says as we shuffle out of the canteen and then out into the dim daylight. "Come call on me for breakfast tomorrow, okay?"

"You don't want me to wake you for dinner?"

He shakes his head and I wave him off, then pull my

map from my blazer pocket. Is it my imagination or are people out here staring at me too? I'm good at disappearing into the background and it is brutally unsettling. I pick up my feet and walk along the pathways until I find a quieter spot, then I study the map again.

Nyneve Tower.

I've never forgotten the name. It's been seared into my memory like every other detail.

I find it marked out on the opposite side of the campus from my own tower. Peering skywards at the surrounding towers, I catch my bearings and set off along the weaving pathways. I pass other students as I walk and am not immune to the funny looks they give me or the whispered comments. At one point I actually stop and examine my reflection in a low window, checking my skirt isn't tucked into my panties or I have dirt all over my face. The black eye does look pretty awful. Maybe that's the cause of all the sudden interest. Back in Slate Quarter, I'm ignored and I am one hundred percent happy with that situation.

Finally, I reach the base of the tower. I can already tell from its lack of crumbling walls and roof made from actual tiles that it's a hell of a lot nicer than the tower I've been assigned. Which must mean she made it to the academy ahead of a lot more students than I did.

A little pride has my mouth curling into a smile. I'm not surprised. Amelia was brave, determined and clever. She would have found a way.

The smile fades as I think of her, the sadness creeping in instead. I push against the door before the grief grounds me in one place altogether.

In the entrance way there is a group of girls, dressed in their gray uniforms, chatting together. Their eyes swivel my way and I am tempted to turn around and march right out.

"Can we help you?" a girl with thick brown hair arranged in waves about her shoulders asks me. She's no shadow weaver, but she still manages to make the uniform look a lot better than mine, plus, rather than cuts and bruises, she's wearing actual make-up on her face.

"I'm just heading to my room," I say, lowering my head and hoping to pass by without any trouble.

I just want a glimpse – just one little glance at her room. I'm sure it won't tell me anything. I know she is long gone. But nonetheless, I possess this insatiable urge to see it.

"Urgh," the brunette says, "I think you must be mistaken." I let that passive look overcome my face, one I hope disguises how keen I am to get up those stairs. "Slate, right?"

Even though I know I'd be better off with my eyes downcast and looking bored, even though I understand it would give me more chances of having this girl leave me alone, I can't help myself. I lift my chin with just a smidgen of defiance.

"I mean, you'd have to be, wouldn't you?" Her lip curls in disgust. "Look at your face. Did you walk into a wall or a shadow weaver's fist?" She titters and all the girls behind her do the same.

I notice there isn't a scratch on her – at least I don't think so. Maybe the layers of make-up are hiding her own injuries from last night.

"What's wrong? Did they rip out your tongue too, sweetie?"

"No," I say. "I have my tongue." I go to move past her. She clearly has the appetite to toy with me and I do not have the patience. I want to see that room.

I made a promise – to her, to myself. I intend to keep it and I intend to start right now.

"But obviously not a brain," she says, blocking my path. "You have the wrong tower. No Slate scum here."

"My room is just up–"

"I don't know what you think you're going to do, Slate scum. Steal our belongings, creep through our rooms? I don't think so," she says, taking a menacing step towards me, the girls behind her moving too. The brunette is about an inch taller than me and much curvier. I could probably outrun her, but in a fight, she'd probably win. "Beat it!"

I glower at her, knowing at this moment I'm beat. I'll have to come another time.

"Wait," one of the other girls says, just as I'm about to turn around and make my exit. "Isn't she the girl the Princes chose?"

"Her?" the brunette sneers. "I don't think so. Are you looking at her properly?"

"No, Odessa, I'm sure it's her."

Something flashes across the brunette's face. Something I don't like the look of, and though I don't know what the hell they are talking about, I decide I am better off leaving before I find out.

Back in my room, I tug the blanket out from the bottom of my wardrobe, pulling my bag onto my lap. I close my eyes. I will find answers. I owe it to her. I owe it to her to find the truth.

I reach inside my bag and check it's still there.

Chapter Nine

T horne

Shadow weavers are given their own private dining room for meal times – a room lined in dark wood paneling, large oil portraits of shadow weavers from the past pinned along the walls, dark candelabras hanging from the vaulted ceilings.

A long polished table dominates the room with high-backed chairs. Serving staff stand to the sides waiting to take our orders and soft music wafts through the room – although it's hard to hear it above all the excited chatter of all the other shadow weavers. They are already gathered around the table, talking excitedly about the last twenty-four hours' events.

Silently, I walk the length of the room and take the empty seat beside Beaufort right at the end of the table away from everyone else.

I expect this is a million times nicer than whatever rat's nest the commoners are given and I should be relieved we're not eating with them. I'm already tired of the way they stare at us, whisper about us, even follow us about.

However, I'm not pleased about it at all. Because it means the girl is not with us and the girl is someone I wish to study.

Though I would never admit it, I'm as intrigued as Dray is as to why Beaufort would pick a girl like her as our thrall. Dray is right. We could have anyone we wanted.

"I ordered you steak," Beaufort says.

I nod, straightening the cutlery on the table. Then tugging at my leather gloves, stretching my stiff fingers confined inside.

The dining room door opens and I expect the servers to enter with our dinner. Instead, the deputy headmistress strolls inside. She's an older woman – possibly in her later thirties or early forties – and she's dressed in a long tight dress, her hair piled on top of her head and her lips painted red.

The room falls silent as she walks to the head of the table and stops right beside me.

She smiles closed lips at Beaufort and me.

"Gentlemen," she says quietly before addressing the entire room. "I trust you enjoyed your first trial at the academy." Her smile widens and there are some chuckles and murmured 'yeses' from around the table. "I'm glad." She rests one hand lightly on the table, her long red nails splayed across the surface, and leans forward a little, providing a view right down the front of her dress. I lower my gaze to the tabletop, the wood so highly polished I can see my face in it. "I believe it's important that the other students understand where they stand. That they fully appreciate the extent of your powers and your abilities."

Beside me Beaufort nods his agreement.

"It is important that they understand this process of assigning our people to their quarters is sacrosanct and crucial to our continued survival. Our processes have existed for centuries. They have kept our realm safe and prosperous."

"Hear, hear," Beaufort says and several others around the table imitate him.

"And so, it is important we maintain our traditions even if over time we ... modify them. And so I move on to the tradition I'm sure you are all most eager to hear about." Around me I hear people lean forwards on their chairs. "As I am very sure you are all aware, the first shadow weavers had squires to aid them in battle and in their defense of the realm. The squire was bound to his master – not only ensuring he had the equipment necessary for battle, but cooking for him, washing his clothes, finding him shelter for the night and," she pauses and when she speaks again, there is a hint of excitement in her voice, "it is understood they provided other services to their masters too."

There is laughter.

"I bet they did," Dray calls out.

"In recognition of this highly valued relationship, one that served our realm well, this academy continues the tradition. The most distinguished and talented among you will be given the privilege of choosing a *thrall* from among the other students – someone who will serve and aid you during your time at the academy – just as the squire did his shadow weaver master. It is another way in which we, as shadow weavers, can demonstrate to the others how much more superior we are than them. How their role in our society is to serve and please us – while ours is to protect them from the darkness."

I lift my gaze and stare at the deputy headmistress. Her eyes are glowing and a twisted smile now rests on her face.

"Those given this privilege have already been informed. Choose your thrall wisely and ... do enjoy yourselves."

She stands up straight and strolls from the room, the incessant chattering starting up again immediately.

"Yeah, Beaufort," Kratos calls from down the table. "Choose wisely."

"Shut up, Kratos," Dray says in a bored tone. "We all know you have the worst taste in Onyx Quarter. Didn't you screw your own cousin?"

The room laughs – all except Kratos who stares daggers towards our end of the table.

Beaufort looks at me. "You understand why it has to be her." I nod. "You could look happier about it. Dray's been chewing off my ear."

I raise my gaze to meet his.

"Why would I be happy about it?"

My friend stares back at me. Then decides to change the subject. "What do you make of our competition here?"

I scoff, wondering why he's bothering to ask me. Most of the other shadow weavers we have known for years. We grew up together, went to school together, we were trained together. Okay, there are a handful we know less well, but that's because they come from the weaker, less powerful families. Of course, I've been watching them nonetheless, just in case.

"I see no threats."

"Kratos' acting like he's growing more powerful."

"It's an act," I tell him, sliding away from the server as he reaches around to lay my plate of steak and steaming vegetables on the table in front of me. I wait until the server is gone, then hesitate. Scratching the rough seam of my glove against my chin. "The girl could be a problem though."

"Girls always are," Dray says, turning away from Dallan on his other side and focusing his attention on us. He winks at me, his mouth full of food.

"I wouldn't know," I say coolly.

"How do you mean?" Beaufort asks, sawing through his steak, frowning. "How will she be a problem?"

"She'll be a vulnerability," I say.

"Exactly," Dray says, waving his knife around. "That's what I'm saying. She's so puny looking, a gust of wind would snap her in two."

Excitement sparks in my gut. I'd like to own something I could break.

"No one will touch her," Beaufort says lowly. "Not if she's ours."

Ours.

Why do I like the idea of that so much?

Because it is a problem. It's not good to want anything. It's even worse to desire it.

I push my plate to one side, stand up and walk the length of the table. And you can hear all that twinkling music now because the room falls silent like before, even the scrape of cutlery and the crunch of food ceases as they all watch me leave.

I don't know what I expected from the academy. It's an eventuality I knew was coming all my life.

For most it's an opportunity to thrive, to taste freedom, to indulge all their hidden desires. For me it already feels like a cage.

Too many people. Too little space. No room to breathe.

I descend the grand staircase, cross the elegant entrance hall and leave the building designated for shadow weavers only. At the front of the building is a wide courtyard, a fountain in its center, stone benches circling it, and cultivated trees at the edges. I cross this too and stride along the cobbled pathways, searching for an escape, swerving away when I hear voices or footsteps, choosing the less-frequented pathways, away from the curious glances of other people.

I'm at the edge of the campus, the oldest part, where the towers are solid but crumbling, the stonework basic but strong, when I hear the sound of more footsteps – hurried footsteps. I turn looking for a different way and then there she is.

The girl herself.

The girl whose name we don't even know but who Beaufort says should be ours.

Our thrall.

She spots me further along the pathway and freezes. Her eyes widen.

In horror? Fascination? Admiration? I don't know. The tall towers cast the pathways in shadows and it's hard to make out the expression on her face.

She is small. Her head barely reaches my chest. And like so many from the Slate Quarter, she is slim. Too slim. I bet she's all jutting hip bones and exposed ribs. Her hair is yanked back from her face so tightly it's impossible to discern its color and it stretches the skin of her face, making her look startled and cross.

I realize it disguises how pretty she is. Her features symmetrical. Her skin smooth. Her lashes thick and long. Her lips plump and soft.

This pretty little thing belongs to us.

I've never owned anything so pretty. So delicate. So fragile.

It makes me want to touch her. To destroy her. Nothing so beautiful deserves to exist in a world like ours.

I ball my gloved hands into tight fists, the leather stretching across my knuckles.

She spies the movement and flinches.

A sickness swims through my stomach and I take a hurried step away from her. Then another.

"I'm g-g-going to be late," she stutters, rocking on her toes as if she wants to be going. "For dinner."

Late?

She points up towards the clock tower – visible from any point on the campus.

"They stop serving soon."

She doesn't know who I am.

It's clear.

I take another step away from her.

And then another.

It doesn't matter.

She'll know soon enough.

Chapter Ten

Briony

Luckily, a bell rings out at seven o'clock in the morning the next day, rousing all the academy students from their beds, otherwise I think I would have slept right through breakfast and the morning's lessons. Although frustration about not finding that room last night kept me awake at first, the exhaustion of the last few days soon overtook me.

I haven't slept that well for as long as I can remember. I'm guessing it was on account of the full belly – that constant gnawing sensation in my stomach – the one that keeps me awake – sedated for once.

Even though I'd quite happily lie here for the rest of the day, I somehow find the strength to drag my tired body out of my bed and to the wardrobe, where I climb into a gray tracksuit that only needs a set of stripes to have it looking like a prison uniform, comb and tie my hair back and go to knock on Fly's door.

"Come in," he mutters and I find him still buried under the rotten blankets.

"Are you getting up?" I ask him.

"Do I have to?"

"I mean," I say with a shrug, "you could see what happens if you don't."

He throws back the covers and I squeal and avert my eyes – although, it's fine, he's wearing a striped pair of pajamas that look comfortable and warm – nothing like the ratty old t-shirt I wore to bed.

"We can both guess it wouldn't be pleasant." He yawns and stretches his arms over his bed. "How long do we have?"

"About forty-five minutes I think. But I'm not missing breakfast."

"Good," he says, rolling up onto his feet. "It's my mission to fatten you up. Now give a man some privacy." He ushers me towards the door. "I'll only be five minutes."

He actually takes fifteen and when he emerges, I can see why. Once again, he's somehow managed to make the horrible tracksuit look stylish.

"How do you do that?" I say, shaking my head in admiration as we descend the stairs.

"It's a talent I was born with." He grins. "It's not something you can teach. Although," he examines me with a rather hopeless look on his face, "I'm sure we could do something with you. Your hair for starters–" He reaches his hand towards my head.

I duck away. "No," I say.

"It doesn't suit you like that."

"I like it like this."

"Like a sixty-year-old nun."

"Yes," I say stubbornly.

"Oh-kay," he says, probably wondering why he bothered befriending me in the first place.

Luckily, Fly doesn't seem to hold a grudge and soon he's talking me through all the breakfast choices in the canteen – encouraging me to choose the ones that will fatten me up.

"Take some more sausages," he says, pointing to them, "and eggs. And lots of bread."

"The sausages look like they're the ones from last night," I say, picking one up with suspicion.

"Beggars can't be choosers."

"You're right," I say, dropping it onto my plate. "Besides, being unable to attend lessons because I have food poisoning probably wouldn't be such a bad thing."

"Although, not fun for those of us who have to share a bathroom with you!" he says. We take a seat and Fly stirs his spoon through his bowl of porridge. "So, are you telling me you aren't looking forward to lessons this morning, Cupcake?"

"I don't know," I say, braving a piece of the cold sausage and glancing around the full canteen. "I'm a little nervous they've got us wearing these tracksuits. It can only mean one thing–"

"Yeah," Fly agrees, "physical torture."

"Now, listen up," one of the gruesome twins says as we line up along the academy field, all of us shivering against the icy wind, "because Madame Bardin has your instructions."

He steps back and she, once again, hobbles forward in her perfectly impractical heeled boots.

I take my chance to glance down the line of students. Once again, the shadow weavers are at the far end. I should have known. No fucking potato sacks for the shadow weavers. Their academy tracksuits are made from a dark black material soft enough to stroke, with a deep crimson stitching and the academy crest.

"And so, let us start." She sweeps her arm to the left, her cape swooshing through the air. "You are all required to complete the assault course behind me. We are looking for speed, agility, strength and, most importantly, perseverance."

Fly groans quietly beside me.

The twin with the whistle steps forward again. "You heard Madame, get to it!"

And now I understand why the shadow weavers were so determined to beat the crap out of everyone else on the first night. If we're all barely able to stand, it gives them an advantage when it comes to our time at the academy. Not that they need it. They have their powers – several of the shadow weavers racing off across the field at speeds that are not human.

"Come on," Fly says, setting off at a jog. "The sooner we get this started, the sooner it'll be over."

"Yeah, but maybe we're better off–"

The blast of a whistle cuts through my next words.

"Get your butts moving!" one of the twins roars. I glance towards the retreating flanks of the shadow weavers and decide then and there the ogre twins are way more terrifying.

I chase after Fly, but despite his early declaration that he was trash at all physical activity, he proves to be a lot better at it than me.

I manage to keep up with him during the sprint across

the field, but as soon as we reach the first obstacle – crawling on our bellies under a tightly pinned net – he leaves me for dust. In fact, the shadow weavers are nowhere to be seen, and those from Iron Quarter are soon out of sight too. Leaving us weaklings from Slate and Granite Quarters to struggle through the course.

I crash through a moat of freezing cold water, swing over a ditch on a rope, scrabble through a tunnel and then meet my match. Monkey bars. At least, that's what the other kids around me are calling them. I've never seen any before. A ladder slung across another ditch of mud. The kids in front of me grip the rungs with their hands and swing from one rung to the next, moving along the ladder until they reach the bank at the other side of the ditch.

I roll my shoulders. I can do this. I pulled myself up into that tree the night before last. I'm not a complete weakling.

And maybe I could if my ribs weren't so damaged. I jump, grip the first rung, reach for the next with my right hand, and pain radiates through my side. I lose my grip and land straight in the mud below me. For a moment, I consider wading through the mud like I did the water and skipping the monkey bars all together, but then I spy a spike concealed in the mud, obviously placed there to stop any smart-asses from attempting that.

I climb up the bank and watch the next two kids make their way across. One succeeds, the other falls and I note the difference in their techniques.

Then it's my time again. This time I'm ready for the pain, and gritting my teeth, my eyes smarting, I swing across that ladder, every movement sending more agony through my ribs. I scream out, but I keep going. Being skewered by one of those spikes would be much much worse.

The other side, I step off the path and heave straight into a bush.

"Eww," two girls screech as they race past me. "That's so pathetic. The course isn't even that hard."

"She must be seriously unfit," the other girl replies.

"Isn't she the one ..."

I don't hear any more, their voices lost in the undergrowth.

I wipe my mouth with the back of my hand, spit twice onto the ground, wishing I had water to wash out my mouth. Then, wiping the tears and sweat from my eyes with my right hand, clutch my sore ribs with my left and keep on running.

I can't show any weakness. The weak will be picked apart like prey in the academy and I want to make it through the next twelve months with the least harm possible. It's the best chance I have of discovering the truth about my sister.

The best way to survive is to do the thing I've always done. Don't stand out – for good or bad reasons. Become invisible. Disappear.

If they can't see you, they can't hurt you.

Problem is, whatever the hell that was outside the Great Hall yesterday seems to have drawn attention my way. Attention I don't want and don't need.

Attention, I can't help but think, is going to bite my ass.

I keep running, although I'm much slower now, my aching ribs impeding every step, and reach the next obstacle. A cargo net reaching high into the sky. There are other students already climbing up this side and down the other.

I smile.

At least this is an obstacle I can do. Even if I know it's

much harder than it looks. You just need to know the right technique.

I find a clear spot on the net, and gripping one of the ropes that run vertically, use it to haul myself upwards as I use the horizontal ropes as stepping stones. It still hurts, but it's more effective this way and soon I'm nearing the top of the net.

It's here I find I was right. My cards have been marked already. There's a girl straddling the top of the net, dressed in her gray tracksuit. I jerk when I peer up and find her scowling at me.

It's the brunette from yesterday.

Despite the scowl, she's really damn beautiful: olive skin, big green eyes and thick glossy brown hair, braided down her back.

"You slut!" she says, and before I can respond, she spits at me, a large glob of her saliva landing right in my face. "You spread your legs already. When was it? In the forest on the first night? Is that why they chose you? Did you suck their cocks and let them fuck you in the ass?"

"What the hell?" I say, wiping spit from my eyes. How can all those vile words come flying out of such a pretty mouth? She looks like an actual angel.

"You're not going to have them! Do you hear me, Slate scum? You fucked them one time and one time only. Eat dirt, you slut!"

Before I can respond, before I know what the hell is going on, she drives her hands right towards my shoulders. Hard and violently. So hard, so violently, I lose my balance.

I scream. The netting slips from my grasp.

I fall, hurtling towards the distant ground.

Chapter Eleven

Briony

I screw my eyes shut.

I'm going to split my skull or snap my spine. Either way, I'm going to die. I only made it to the second day.

Except rather than hit the floor, my body stops flying through the air, and instead, it's yanked violently. And then I'm hanging upside down by the ankle, my left foot caught in the netting.

I hang there, swaying slightly, other students clinging to the net and staring right at me.

Realizing hanging around like this so that some other fucker can come at me and try to kill me, I grit my teeth and pull myself upward, free my foot and start climbing again. Only it's even harder than it was before, because now, as well as the pain in my ribs, my ankle is throbbing too. When

I try to bear weight on it, I have to chomp down hard on my lip to stop myself from crying out.

I climb the rest of the net on my knees, the measly tracksuit doing nothing to protect my skin from the harsh rope, my legs and hands sore with burns by the time I reach the top.

The brunette is long gone – obviously not bothered about watching me die.

I straddle the top of the net and catch my breath. From up here, I can see the end of the course, people crossing the line and collapsing in heaps, the gruesome twosome making a note of their times.

If I peer back in the other direction, the one I've come from, I realize I'm right at the back of the group now. Only a few stragglers behind me.

I swing my leg over the top of the net and start my slow descent. There isn't any point in hurrying and anyway it hurts too much. Then I limp the final four hundred meters, towards the finish line.

The two twins watch me come, making no effort to help me and grunting my time at me as I finally stumble over the line.

"If you're injured, get yourself to the infirmary," one of them yells at me as I collapse down on the cold ground. "You need to be ready for this afternoon's assignment."

I don't move. I can't, not yet anyway.

"Did you hear me?!"

"Yes, I heard you," I mumble. "I'm going."

"Sir!" he yells. "Yes, I heard you, *Sir!*"

I roll my head to the side and stare over at him. He's glowering at me, his two beady eyes bulging. "Yes, I heard you, Sir," I mumble, as I roll up onto my feet and hobble away.

I don't have that map with me so I have no idea where the infirmary would be. Instead, I limp in the direction of my room. I can bandage my ankle myself with one of my shirts and run my injured fingers under the tap; I don't need any help.

I'm halfway across a courtyard with an ancient oak towering in its center, its heavy boughs sprawling over the cobbled stones, when someone calls out my name.

"Briony!" Fly comes jogging towards me. He's already changed out of the tracksuit and into the actual academy uniform.

"What happened to you, Cupcake? I waited ages. They sent me away in the end. I was just coming to find you."

I point to my leg, pulling up my pants to show him a now purple and swollen ankle. We both wince.

"Ouch! Did you trip over?"

"Nope," I say, "some girl tried to push me to my death."

"Ahhh," he says, eyes flicking from side to side in their sockets. "Figures."

"It does?" I say. "I know this place is meant to be brutal. But ... I don't know ... I didn't figure ..."

"They'd come for you?" Fly wraps my arm around his shoulder, encouraging me to lean my weight against him before we start walking together. It's a little awkward. He's way taller than I am and is forced to crouch low to make this work, but I appreciate the help.

"Well, yeah."

"They come for everyone, Cupcake."

He's right. They came for Amelia, didn't they?

Maybe it's inevitable they'd come for me too. I just didn't expect it to happen quite so quickly. I need to be a hell of a lot smarter, especially about the people I trust.

"Plus," he adds, "you've given them more reasons than others."

"I have?" I say, racking my brains to understand what those reasons could be. Sure, there's Amelia but that girl couldn't know about that. I *was* last back to the academy yesterday morning. *And* I missed out on a beating by hiding out in a tree. Can that really be the reason?

"Beaufort Lincoln."

"Huh?"

"The hot shadow weaver who picked you to be his and his brothers' thrall yesterday."

I dig my good heel into the cobbles and lean all my weight on Fly, forcing him to stop.

"Could you speak English, please?"

"Seriously, Cupcake?" he says, examining my face. "You telling me you don't know about this stuff? You knew about the first night."

"I know some stuff," I say cryptically, "not all of it, obviously."

"Obviously," he says, rolling his eyes, then starts up the walking again. "The most powerful shadow weaver siblings are given the privilege of picking a thrall for their time at the academy."

"And what is a thrall exactly?" I ask, my stomach churning. I have a bad feeling about this. I already knew this place was trouble. Perhaps I had no idea just how much.

"A thrall is like a servant, I guess. Someone who serves and obeys those who have chosen them."

"What the hell?" I snap. "Then why did that girl nearly kill me?"

"Because in return for your ..." his eyes dart my way, "service, the siblings will offer you protection. If you're a thrall, no one else at the academy can touch you. You're safe."

"Siblings?" I ask. "That shadow weaver has brothers and sisters here?"

"Two brothers. But not regular brothers – not brothers by blood. Brothers by bond. Shadow weavers who are bound to each other by the forces of fate for the entirety of their lives."

"What?" I say. I thought I knew everything I needed to know about shadow weavers. Seems I was wrong.

"Please tell me you know about bonds." I hesitate, then shake my head. "I mean, I don't understand it exactly. I'm not a shadow weaver, myself." He draws his hand down his body. "Obviously. But from what I understand, it's when individuals find their other parts."

"Other parts?"

"Like a soul mate I guess. Although, it's not necessarily romantic," he muses, "or sexual. Although I'm gathering sometimes it can be that way."

"But what does it mean?"

"It means they're linked together for life. Their magic becomes bound together."

"And these other two boys are bound to Beaufort Lincoln? Are they happy about it?"

Fly laughs. "I have no idea, Cupcake. But considering they're three of the strongest shadow weavers the realm has seen, I doubt they care too much." He lowers his voice and adopts a mysterious tone. "They call them the Princes."

"Not obnoxious at all," I sniff, then glance towards my new friend. "What kind of service?" I ask next, my stomach turning sour.

Fly doesn't answer, which tells me everything I need to know.

"Well," I say with a frown, "I don't care who they are or how powerful they may be, there's no way in hell I'm being their thrall."

Chapter Twelve

B riony

"Are you crazy?!" Fly asks. "Did you bump your head as well as twist your ankle? Or did you not hear what I said? If you're a thrall, you're untouchable. No one can hurt you."

"Except the ones you're a thrall to," I point out.

I know how that goes. I've been a lackey to Muriel for years.

Firestone Academy may have a reputation for being brutal but at least it's my chance at freedom. I won't be dependent or bound to anyone. I will no longer be someone's slave. Least of all a bunch of privileged shadow weavers who will use and abuse me just like my stepmother.

Fly shakes his head. "Do you know how many kids from Iron Quarter didn't make it back from the academy last year? Four. Four kids who were some of the toughest, strongest people I knew. No offense, Cupcake, but you're going to need all the help you can get."

"If it's such a help, then why the hell did some girl nearly kill me out there on the assault course?"

"Hmmm," he ponders. "It's not official yet, I guess. Until it is, maybe some of these kids think there's still a chance the Princes will change their minds and choose them instead of you. Especially if you're dead. I'd get it all official as quickly as you can." He peers over his shoulder as if he expects someone to be coming at us with a knife.

I chew on my lip. "I'm not going to be a thrall. I'll take my chances with the other kids."

Fly harrumphs. "I'd give my right leg *and* my right ball to be someone's thrall – anyone's at all."

"Can we change the subject?" I say. I don't want to fall out with my new friend already and right now I can't see us agreeing about this. I would refuse to be anyone's servant as it is. I most definitely will not be serving shadow weavers. "Where are we going exactly?" Because we're not heading in the direction of our rooms.

"The clinic, of course."

"Uh uh, I don't need any treatment. My ankle will be just fine."

"You're going to have to start accepting help if you want to make it through the next year." He glances at me and I drop my gaze to the floor. "It doesn't make you weak, you know. In fact, if you're crazy enough to refuse the Princes, I'd say our next best plan is to stick together and help each other out."

"It's not that I think accepting help makes me weak, it's just ... it's hard to trust people." Because look what happens when you do! Muriel. Stanley. I trusted them and both of them abused me. And goodness knows who Amelia trusted.

Keeping my cards close to my chest, being wise about who I share my secrets with, is the only way I'm going to survive this place.

"I'm hurt," Fly says, adopting a fake expression of pain. "You don't trust me, Cupcake?"

"I don't know yet," I say honestly. "I want to."

"Fair enough. That is sort of sensible. We probably shouldn't trust anyone in this place. Not even each other." He sighs. "Although that's going to make for a very miserable twelve months."

"Were you expecting anything different?"

He laughs. "No, I suppose not."

Nonetheless, he still drags me along to a clinic, where there is a small line of other students waiting to be seen. Most of them are injuries from the assault course, a few look like casualties from the night before. I wonder just how many kids got hurt that night.

"Now," Fly says, resting his hands on his hips, "can I *trust* you to wait here and be seen? Or do I need to stand guard?"

"It's okay, Fly. You can go. I'll be just fine."

"Good," he says, relief flooding his face. "Because I'm freaking starving and need to find some food." My stomach growls loudly in agreement. "I'll grab you some too. And hopefully," he winks at me, "I'll see you at the next lesson."

"Which is?"

"You think they'd actually tell us?" he scoffs. "It starts at two in the Great Hall."

I nod and watch him go. Then shrink into my chair, dragging my arms inside my sweater and dropping my chin to my chest, closing my eyes and making it clear I don't want to talk to anyone else. Not that anyone in the clinic is talking. Most people are curled in on themselves like I am, one or two look ghostly pale.

One by one the students in front of me are called in to be seen and finally it's my turn.

A nurse in a stiff uniform that once upon a time must have been white, but now, like everything else around here, is gray, calls my name. I hop up onto my good leg and limp towards her. She watches me come, a hand on her hip.

"Let me guess," she says with sarcasm, "period cramps."

I blink at her. "No, my ankle."

"Come on then." She beckons me to follow her. "Let's check it out."

Fifteen minutes later, both my ankle and my ribs are bandaged. The ankle is not broken, just sprained, the ribs, however, are cracked. Not that there's anything the nurse can do about it.

"I'd tell you to rest and let it heal," she says, handing me a bottle of painkillers. "But that won't be an option here at the academy. You'll just have to do your best. Pills will help ... just don't be silly with them." She gives me a knowing look, then sends me on my way.

The bandage on my leg actually seems to help. I can place more weight on my foot and I am definitely not hobbling so much. I just have to hope whatever they have in store for us this afternoon, it isn't anything physical.

I glance up at the clock tower and seeing I have half an hour before the next lesson, I make my way through the maze of towers to my own, hauling my tired body up the staircase hoping to discover the bathroom on my way.

My empty stomach aches just as much as my ribs and my legs and I'm exhausted. I'm in desperate need of food. I'm also covered in mud and dirt, and I smell really bad. Washing is definitely a priority. I don't want to be picked out as the stinky kid, especially as it sounds like I already have a price on my head.

I find the bathroom halfway up the staircase. Unfortunately, there are no clouds of steam billowing from the communal showers. There's just one lonesome girl, a thin towel wrapped around her middle, shivering so hard her knees knock together.

"The water's frigging freezing!" she says through clattering teeth as she darts from the room.

There is a pile of towels set out by a row of sinks, a row of cubicles on the other side of the wall. Some containing toilets and some showers. As I'm short on time, and don't fancy an extra climb up and down the tower, I grab a towel, duck into one of the cubicles, strip off my clothes and unwind my hair. I turn the ancient knob and after a moment of groaning from the pipes, a torrent of water comes gushing from the overhead shower. The girl wasn't lying. The water is so cold I'm surprised blocks of ice aren't tumbling from the showerhead instead.

I grit my teeth, and duck under the water, shrieking despite my best efforts because it is colder than the poles. Balancing on my good foot, while keeping the other out of the water, I scrub the mud from my body and the grime from my hair. There's no soap but at least it makes the ordeal quicker and as soon as most of the dirt is gone, I yank off the water and wrap myself in the towel. It's worn and threadbare and does little to warm me up so I dry myself as quickly as I can, dress again in the tracksuit, then climb back up to my room.

A small fireplace crouches in the corner of my room, but it contains no firewood or coal and no means to light it even if it did.

I strip out of my tracksuit, shivering like the other girl,

my hands shaking and barely able to grip the material, and pull on my uniform.

When I'm done, I turn to my reflection in the warped mirror and confirm I do not have Fly's sense of style. He'd made this uniform look good. On me it looks no better than the tracksuit. The short gray skirt shows off my bruised knees, the long socks are itchy as hell and the blazer hangs from my shoulders. Maybe it will be enough to convince Beaufort Lincoln that I am not worthy to be his thrall. The girl who pushed me from the net would be way more suitable.

I smile at my reflection as I drag a comb through my wet hair and then twist and pin it back as usual.

Yep, the Princes will take one look at me this afternoon and will no longer be my problem.

Chapter Thirteen

B^{riony}

I arrive outside the Great Hall with precisely no minutes to spare but at least I'm not late.

"Briony!" I hear Fly call out and then find him squeezing through the other students to reach me. I cringe as once again it draws everybody's attention my way. "How's the ankle?"

I shrug. "I took some pain meds. So it and me are feeling pretty darn good." I peer at him hopefully. "Just really damn hungry."

"Well, that, Ma'am, is something I may be able to help with." He does a fancy little bow and pulls four bread rolls filled with cheese and ham from his blazer pockets and passes them to me. "I risked my neck swiping these for you," he whispers to me as I grab them from his hands.

"Oh my stars, thank you so much! I owe you big time," I

say, stuffing one into my mouth and the other three into my pockets.

Fly chuckles. "Slow down, Cupcake. You don't want to choke. You've already missed near-death once already today."

I chew aggressively and roll my eyes at him.

Then we notice the line is moving and we're being led inside the hall.

Today, the hall is filled with single desks, all laid out in neat rows of tens.

"Take a seat," a man booms from the raised platform in the recesses of the hall, his form bathed in shadow, no light filtering through the circular window today. "And be quick about it."

I follow Fly along one of the lines, sliding onto a seat next to his and tucking my knees under the desk.

"We should be safe here," Fly whispers as the other students grab their desks around us. "Never grab a seat at the front or the back. It's asking for trouble."

I grin at him. "They do send us to school back in Slate Quarter, you know."

He grins back. "I wasn't sure."

Furtively, I break off a piece of bread roll in my pocket and smuggle it into my mouth.

The shadow weavers are the last to enter the Hall, strolling in like they have all the time in the world and heading straight for the empty rows of desks at the front.

I try not to, but despite all my protests to Fly about my determination to stay away from the Princes – I'm still curious. I can't help it. After all, I'm as surprised as everyone else as to why the hell they would want me as their thrall. I mean, you only have to flick your gaze around the Hall and see there are far better candidates. No matter what their preference is, there is someone better suited to meet it. I don't even come out tops among the scrawny, pathetic girls.

I spot Beaufort right at the back of the shadow weavers and this time I pay attention to who he is with – because I'm assuming they are the magicals he's bound to.

My eyes linger on Beaufort and then move to the man behind him.

I jolt in my seat.

It's the shadow weaver I encountered out there on the path yesterday evening.

He's as tall and broad as Beaufort, but where Beaufort's skin is fair, the other man's is dark. His hair, shorn brutally short, is jet black and his eyes are just as dark. The expression he wears on his face is ominous – like one glance your way and he could turn you to stone.

I shiver and is it my imagination, or does that action attract his attention? His head snaps my way and his eyes meet mine. Dark and soulless.

Instead of turning to cold stone, though, my insides seem to heat, a flush creeping up my neck and into my cheeks.

What is it with the men around here? Did they all take lessons on being moody and broody before entering the academy? Or maybe that's just how shadow weavers are. Maybe the aura of their magic, crackling in the air around them, gives them this sinister persona.

I lower my eyes down to my desk, only daring to raise them again several minutes later, just in time to catch sight of the third man. He couldn't be more different to the others. A white mop of long locks sprawls from his head and a wild smile stretches across his face. His teeth sparkle white and perfectly straight and there are actual dimples in his cheeks.

However, his baby-faced appearance ends there. Tattoos crawl out from under his shirt and twist up his neck, in ominous patterns. A heavy silver chain hangs around his neck.

I can't discern the color of his eyes over the distance, but I can see they're brimming with mischief as he flicks his gaze around the Hall taking everyone in. When his eyes land on me, he doesn't scowl like his friend did, instead his smile stretches even wider and he winks at me. It's so damn flirtatious my cheeks burn even hotter.

My insides do something similar. Men were never this hot back in Slate Quarter. And the men in Slate Quarter never looked at me like that. It's been a long time since a man looked at me with anything but revulsion. I'd forgotten what that felt like.

I bite down hard on my lip.

I don't want to be admiring shadow weavers. I don't want them to make my insides spin.

I hate them. I hate them all.

"So kind of you weasels to join us," the voice of the teacher bathed in shadow booms, his form still hidden. There are several shocked gasps from around the Hall and one or two giggles. Shadow weavers are the elite among us. Sure we may bitch about them in hushed, secretive tones behind their backs, I've never known anyone to insult them to their faces. I swallow, expecting there to be some rebuttal – for the shadow weavers to jump to their feet in outrage, to fling magic at the hidden teacher. But most seem unconcerned. They slouch in their chairs, one or two yawning as if being dragged to the academy is one giant inconvenience and bore.

"Then let us begin," the voice booms and immediately a booklet and a pencil appears on the desk in front of me.

"You have three hours to complete the questions in this booklet. There will be no talking."

The man clicks his fingers and an hourglass timer the size of a horse appears, suspended in the air at the front of the Hall. It tips over and the grains of sand inside begin to seep through.

Tearing off another piece of roll from my pocket and popping it into my mouth, I print my name on the front of my booklet and then turn over the first page, running my eyes down the questions. It's all logic questions – a mix of mathematical and lateral thinking. I twist the pencil around in my fingers and then tackle the first question.

Around me I can hear the scratch of hundreds of pencils, the occasional scrape of chair legs against the floor or a huff of agitated breath. I keep my head down and focused on the paper. I'm going to give these questions my best shot. Even though I know it will make no difference, that my fate is Slate Quarter no matter what. I'm still going to try. I know I'm smart enough to make it into Granite Quarter – even if I don't trust the system and have no expectation at all that I'll make it there when this year ends.

Several of the questions make my brain hurt and my vision multiply; some I don't even attempt, but by the time that last grain of sand filters through the hourglass and a bell clangs loudly above our heads, I've tackled all the questions I can.

Before we've had a chance to lower our pencils, they vanish from our hands along with the booklets from our desks.

"You are dismissed until your next lesson tomorrow morning," that mysterious voice booms.

All around me, students hurry to push back their chairs and climb to their feet, rushing for the door and freedom. I glance at Fly and without a word spoken, we agree to wait until the crush is over and everyone else is gone. I don't want to bump into the Princes again or the murderous brunette or anyone else with murderous intentions for that matter.

"Did you not hear me," the voice booms, "you're dismissed!"

We both jump to our feet and as fast as we can – given I have an injured leg – hurry out of the Hall.

"Jeez," I say once we're outside again, "who was that? Was it the Headmaster?"

"I don't think so," Fly says, peering back over his shoulder. Behind us the candles have extinguished and the Hall is now a dark cavernous space. It's creepy as hell. "The Head is known to be a recluse. He hardly ever shows his face. Madame Bardin pretty much runs the academy."

"Then who was that?"

Fly shrugs. "If I had to hazard a guess, someone we don't want to get on the wrong side of."

Chapter Fourteen

B^{riony}

I finish the rest of my cheese and ham rolls as we walk (or in my case hobble) back towards our rooms. The bread is a little stale, the cheese bland and the ham hard, but stars, it tastes so good I can't help making little moaning noises as I chew.

"That really is pretty pornographic, you know," Fly says, eyes flicking towards me. "If you're trying to seduce me it isn't going to work. Firstly, because I don't want to have my skull smashed in by the Princes." I scoff at that. "And secondly, you're not my type, Cupcake."

"What is your type?" I ask out of curiosity.

"Hmmm, I'm not really that fussed, just as long as he's smart, handsome, built like a brick house and has a large–"

"I get the picture."

He chuckles. "You don't like big dicks?" he asks me. I roll my eyes. "What is your type then? Do you prefer girls?"

"I don't know. For the last few years, I haven't liked anyone at all really."

"No hotties back in Slate Quarter then?"

I don't answer that. I'm sure he'd consider Stanley to be a catch. He also turned out to be a backstabbing bully.

Fly examines my face. "It would be hard not to be into at least one of the Princes."

"Humph," I reply.

"You have to admit they're hot."

"I don't have to admit anything."

"I'm going to take it that you do. You'd have to have seriously unusual taste to find them unattractive. They're probably the best looking boys at the academy – trust me, I've been checking."

"You have?"

"Of course," he sighs, "a man can dream." His eyes flick to mine. "Being the Princes' thrall would hardly be a chore, would it?"

"We're not talking about that. I already told you, it isn't happening."

"I have a feeling you won't get a choice in the matter, Cupcake. I know guys like them, and they don't really take no for an answer. They always get their way in the end."

"I also know guys like that lose interest pretty quick. I bet they've already picked out a different, better thrall and haven't given me a second chance."

Fly sighs. "You're probably right."

I glare at him. I wasn't expecting him to agree so easily with me.

"So," Fly says, "we're free until tomorrow morning – at least I am. You have somewhere you have to be at 7pm."

"Not happening!"

"Well then, what do you wanna do?"

What I want to do is get up into Amelia's old room, but I daren't try again so soon after yesterday's attempt.

"Stuff my face and then sleep for twelve hours straight," I say, instead.

"You don't want to check out the campus? See what's going on?"

I shake my head. Definitely not.

"I may have to reconsider this friendship, Cupcake, if you're gonna be this dull."

"I completely own up to it. I am dull and boring and ordinary. There is nothing special or exciting about me at all."

"Hmmm," Fly says, "you see, I'm not so sure about that. A boring person wouldn't say that."

We join the line at the canteen, collecting up a tray and moving slowly along the line.

It's then I notice something strange about the canteen. Something I failed yesterday – in my desperate rush to consume food – to notice.

"Where are all the shadow weavers? Do they not need to eat? Do they live off the air itself?"

"Did you really think they'd be eating with commoners like us?" Fly says.

"I guess not. Where do they eat, then?"

"They have their own private dining room."

"Of course they do."

"You would probably be allowed there as their thrall."

"I'm going to ignore that comment." I change the subject again and we talk about the test we just took in the Great Hall. "It made my head ache," I confess.

"Mine too," Fly says, resting his fork and knife down on

his plate and pushing it away. There's still a good third left on his plate.

"Can I have that?" I ask.

He nods. "I didn't find the test too bad," he says. "Better than any physical test anyway." He darts his gaze around the canteen, then leans really close and whispers, "I'm hoping they'll assign me Granite Quarter."

"You don't want to go back to Iron Quarter? To your family?"

"No," he says simply. "I don't really belong there. My two elder brothers – they're these massive, talented jocks – both captains in the army now. My dad's a major general. My mom an ex-athlete. They belong there. I don't fit in. Granite would suit me better."

"You don't fancy Slate?" I tease.

"Tell me about Slate," he says, resting his elbow on the table and his chin in his hand. I describe it as best as I can. The cold, the misery, the hopelessness. "Yeah," Fly says. "I'll give that a miss. Where do you hope to end up?"

"Me?" I scoff. "I'm not delusional. I know where I'm headed. Straight back to Slate."

"You might–"

"No, I won't. I know how the system works."

Fly's silent for a while after that, watching me eat, then he asks me the dreaded question, one I was hoping I could avoid. "How about your family?"

"What about them?"

"I don't know. What do your parents do? Do you have any brothers and sisters?"

"I have a dad ... and a stepmom."

I don't tell him about Amelia. It's too painful. I don't want him looking at me with sympathy in his eyes. And if I'm honest, as lovely as Fly seems, I don't know who I can trust. What happened to Amelia is a secret I intend to guard.

After I've eaten so much food my belly is actually bulging, we walk back through the campus towards our rooms. Music plays out from somewhere above us and laughter spills out from some of the towers.

"Are you sure you don't want to go exploring?" I shake my head. Fly glances up at the clock tower. It's ten minutes to seven. "And you're really not going to go meet Beaufort?"

"Nope," I say, reaching the bottom of our staircase. "I'm going straight to bed."

Chapter Fifteen

Beaufort

The shadow weaver common room at the Firestone Academy is something of legends back in Onyx Quarter and I have to admit the place does live up to the hype. The room sits right at the top of one of the towers and once upon a time was an observatory for stargazing before our kind claimed it as our own. The glass roof and large panoramic windows still exist though, lending views over the entire academy and out over the land beyond. Inside, a large fire roars in a central fireplace, velvet armchairs and chaises are scattered around and golden chandeliers provide flickering candle light. Below our feet, smooth black onyx covers the floor, reflecting back the light.

Nearly all the shadow weavers are here tonight for the inaugural party, all draped in their finest clothes from home with a lot of skin on show. Most of the men wear their shirts unbuttoned nearly to their navels and several of the girls are dressed in skimpy dresses that leave nothing to the imagination.

I search the crowd. Thorne won't be here. He never comes to events like these. Dray went out running this evening, but he must be here somewhere. He wouldn't miss a party if his life depended on it.

In fact, in the next moment, my bond brother is bounding up to me, usual manic smile pinned on his face. He's always in a good mood after a run. The sulk from the day before is over.

"Want a drink?" he asks me, slapping me on the shoulder and motioning to the bar in the corner, a collection of multicolored bottles set out for us to help ourselves.

"Sure," I say.

We step that way, and Dray proceeds to unscrew each bottle, sniffing the contents until he finds one he likes and pours a slug into one glass and then another. He hands me his and then clinks his glass against mine.

"Is it me," he says, bouncing on his toes, eyes scanning hungrily over the small crowd of people, "or did everyone just get a whole lot hotter? Did you see Elaine? Man, her tits. They must have doubled in size since we last saw her." He shakes his head.

I follow his gaze. He's right. Everyone did get a lot hotter. Filled out in all the right places. Tightened up in others. However, I'm not interested. Which is damn strange. I'm not like Thorne. I've always been as keen as Dray to sample the goods offered up to me on a plate – especially when the goods offered are so damn hot and so fucking tasty.

But tonight, there's no spark of arousal, no desire to go out and hunt down pussy.

No, none of the women here pique my interest.

Not in the way the Slate girl does.

The Slate girl who failed to turn up at our room as I commanded.

I grip the glass tightly in my fist and take a slug of my drink, the alcohol stinging the back of my throat and warming my gullet.

"If you're going to–" I start to warn my brother.

"I got a name," he says quietly with an even bigger grin on his face.

"What?"

"I got you a name. Her name. Little Miss No-show." He takes a long sip of his drink, peering over the rim of his glass at me with mischief brimming in his eyes. He knows I'm as impatient as hell and he loves to tease me.

Once he's swallowed, he takes his time licking his bottom lip, fiddling with his lip ring, and I'm tempted to grab the lapel of his jacket and shake the information out of him.

"Are you going to tell me?"

"So, you are still interested, even though the little brat failed to show up as asked?"

"I'm even more interested *because* she didn't turn up," I growl.

"Yeah," Dray says, eyes twinkling, "me too."

"So, what the hell is her name?"

"Briony," Dray says, "Briony Storm."

"Storm?" I repeat, frowning. It's an unusual last name and yet it stirs something in the back of my mind. Like I've come across that name before. Or is it just ...

"I have a feeling our little brat could be stormy by name, stormy by nature. Maybe this could be fun after all," Dray says.

"So you're now in favor?"

"I don't have a choice," he answers, "so I'll make the best of the situation. And," he tips the rest of his drink down his throat, "have some fun in the meantime." He winks at Dahlia, slams his empty glass on the bar top and goes to stalk off in her direction. I grab ahold of his arm and stop him.

"How about the black eye? Did you find a name for that too?"

"Possibly," he says, "some kid called Stanley."

"Stanley," I repeat, committing the name to memory.

I let go of Dray and he walks away, leaving me on my own.

Not for long though. It doesn't take two minutes for Henrietta Smyte to slide up alongside me. She is the taller of the twins, her straight red hair falling in curtains around her pale pointy face. She's wearing an ivory dress that, against her pale skin, makes it look as if she's wearing nothing at all.

"Why the long face, Beaufort?" she says. Her lips are painted a blood red to match her hair and it leaves an imprint on the rim of her glass as she takes a sip of wine, probably in a manner she believes to be seductive.

"My face is the same as it always is," I grunt. Henrietta and I were an item last year. She wasn't happy when I ended things. She's been trying to manufacture a reunion ever since. It's not going to happen. The girl is vain and boring.

"Did your little thrall not live up to your expectations?" She laughs, high and shrill, making my teeth hurt. I've always hated it. "Was she a disappointment? Any one of us could have told you that. I mean, Beaufort, a girl from the Slate Quarter, what are you thinking?"

"I'm thinking I don't have to explain myself to you, Henrietta, or anyone else for that matter."

I'm not going to tell her our thrall never even showed up. That would set the girl purring with delight.

"Our thrall is an absolute dream. So obliging, so willing, so good with his hands." She curls her tongue up inside her mouth and steps a little closer. With the bar behind me, I can't step away, instead I draw myself up to my full height. "I'd be happy to share." She places her hand on my chest, sliding her fingers across the soft cotton.

I snatch her wrist and yank her hand away.

"Go bother someone else, Henny," I say in my most bored tone, pushing her away.

She snaps her arm forward, tossing a bolt of magic right at me, I block it with the swing of my arm and it explodes right in front of my face.

I take a step towards her, lifting my hand. My magic crackles in warning.

The common room is silent, everyone suddenly staring our way.

"Careful," I warn her.

She sneers at me, tosses her head like an irritated mare, and saunters away, probably to try to sink her claws into some other poor unsuspecting soul.

I glare at all those still staring my way, and they drop their eyes in alarm.

Then I'm striding right out of the common room, my body broiling with annoyance.

Because both Dray and Henrietta are right.

Our thrall is a brat and a disappointment.

Why her?

Why the fuck her?

Chapter Sixteen

B riony

Today, we're having our lessons in the main part of the academy – a collection of connected buildings that crouch in the center of the ring of towers. They've split us into eight groups and by some kind of miracle I'm with Fly.

I wasn't expecting to make any friends here in the academy – I haven't had any friends for years. But now I have one, I find I'd rather be in his company than without it. Especially as I haven't forgotten his comment about having each other's backs. Fly may not be some kind of muscle man and I am definitely not terrifying enough to deter anyone from murder (as demonstrated yesterday) but there is safety in numbers.

Our very first lesson turns out to be in a room down in the cellars. We follow the other students down a dark set of steps, the air becoming gradually cooler and danker, and into a room I'm convinced used to be a torture chamber, chains still hanging from the stone walls, no natural light at all and rickety wooden benches lined up in rows.

"Well, this isn't creepy," I mutter to Fly.

"Do you think our next lesson involves thumbscrews and the rack?" he whispers.

"I wouldn't be surprised." I laugh, a noise that is cut off at once by a booming voice.

That same booming voice from yesterday.

"Sit down and shut your mouths."

I swing my head in the direction of the voice and find, once again, the owner lurking in the shadows at the front of the room. It's impossible to make out his form or his face and it seems he has no intention of making himself seen.

I take a seat on one of the middle benches, shuffling along as others join us. Unlike the canteen, it seems the shadow weavers will be slumming it down here with us. Five enter the room after the rest of us and send a few kids sitting on the front bench, scurrying away.

I scan my eye along them. The Princes aren't with them and my shoulders relax in relief. The feeling lasts less than one minute because three of the shadow weavers are glaring my way. A set of twins, pale with long red hair and another girl too – this one darker skinned, with spiky hair dyed a myriad of colors.

I flick my gaze away from them and towards the mysterious man at the front of the classroom.

"We want all of you to have a fair chance at the academy," he begins, I repress the urge to snort. "Some of you have not had the same advantages that others have benefited from. In order for us to spot true talents and true abilities, not only will you be tested here at the academy, but you will also be taught."

There's some dramatic sighing from the front row as if this is extremely tedious to the shadow weavers.

"You never know," the voice says dripping with sarcasm, "you may be surprised. You may actually learn something new." The man's feet scuff on the stone floor. "Who among you can weave magic from the shadows?"

Unsurprisingly, the arms of those in the front row shoot up, everybody else's remain lowered. The shadow weavers glance over their shoulders at the rest of us, smirking, scoffing and generally being obnoxious. Fly mutters something rude under his breath beside me.

"Well, I am here to determine whether others among you may possess the gift but are unaware," the man says.

Several of the shadow weavers laugh out loud at this.

"Did I say something amusing?" the voice asks quietly but with a venom that makes my blood run cold.

One of the twins lifts her nose into the air. "Everyone knows that's impossible."

"Do they?"

"Yes," her sister says with confidence. "The ability of shadow weaving is passed down from generation to generation. It's inherited. You have to possess the power and the ability in your blood. Ordinaries like them," she says with a sneer, "could never possess such a power."

"That's what is believed."

"That's the facts," the spiky-haired girl says.

"Nonetheless," the voice says, "we must ensure there are no others who possess such a talent."

"Right," a shadow weaver boy who is so stacked with muscle, he looks more troll than human, says, "can you losers do this then?"

He flings back his arm and launches a ball of fire right at the rest of us. Several kids scream, ducking down low, as it skims over our heads and hits the far wall, bursting into a thousand sparks.

"Or this," one of the twins says, lightning streaking between her palms before she hurtles it our way. There's more screaming, more students diving out the way in front of me and then the lightning is streaking right towards my face. I've no time to move and if it wasn't for Fly, knocking me off the bench and onto the floor, it would have hit me right on the nose and scorched a hole in my face.

I groan, sprawled out on my stomach, my legs akimbo.

There is laughing from the front of the room and when I lift my head, I see the twin smirking right at me and I know right then and there.

It was deliberate.

That strike was meant for me.

So much for fading back into the background.

"Enough!" the voice roars, the walls shaking and the benches rattling. Then the shadow weavers are forced down into their seats by an unseen force. They struggle against it, but they are unable to fight it.

"I didn't ask for practical demonstrations. You are here to learn. And the first thing you will learn is how to feel the magic in your blood."

"This is a waste of time," Fly moans, suppressing a yawn, as the voice delivers an explanation on how to determine if magic resides in your veins, how best to coax it out, how to feel for it when needed. But I'm all ears, taking it all in. It's fascinating. I know so little about magic and shadow weavers and I realize now that that is a mistake. I need to learn everything I can.

After all, if I hope to find answers, I need to pay attention.

Two hours later, we're dismissed out into the freezing cold corridor and making our way up the stairs. I'm halfway up those steps when I pat my pocket and realize I have lost my pen.

"I forgot my pen," I say, stopping in my tracks and causing those behind me to bump into me. Several swear at me and push past, knocking against my shoulder as they do. Fly plasters himself flat against the wall and lets them pass. "It must have fallen out of my pocket when I fell off the bench."

"You want to go get it?" Fly asks, peering back down towards the classroom.

"Yes," I say, "it belonged to ..." I trail off.

"I'll wait here," Fly says, obviously not keen to enter that classroom again until we have to. "That room gives me the creeps. Just be quick, okay? We don't want to miss out on all the good lunch choices."

The classroom gives me the creeps too and I'd prefer it if Fly came with me, but it's a new friendship and I don't want to seem needy or pathetic.

I trot back down the empty staircase and push against the heavy door with my shoulder, stepping inside.

"Knock before you enter!" a voice roars in anger – that same mysterious voice from before – and I freeze to the spot. Only one candle remains flickering in the room and it takes my eyes a few seconds to adjust to the gloom. Then I make out a man standing in the middle of the benches, my pen in his hands.

He's huge, although his well-built frame is contained within a well-cut suit, a dark cloak hanging from his shoulders. His face is chiseled, his nose aquiline and his thick dark hair swept back from his face.

I stand there in shock, my mouth hanging open, my mind whirring. Because I know this man and yet I don't. He is like an image of a man I once knew – but the details are slightly different – his figure more muscular, his cheeks no longer hollow, his brow heavier, his clothes more refined and his eyes – the eyes are completely different … and yet he looks so much like him.

He stares back at me and for a moment I think he is as shocked as I am. Then the shock fades away, more anger erupting over his features.

"You do not enter a classroom – any room in the academy – without knocking first. Without seeking permission to enter."

"I-I-I'm sorry," I stutter, unable to drag my eyes from his familiar face.

His skin is different too. The man I knew had sun-kissed skin. This man is pale as marble.

"What do you want?" he says, with obvious annoyance.

"M-m-my pen," I say, gesturing to the one in his hand. "I dropped it."

He turns it over in his fingers, then holds it out to me.

Like the other shadow weavers, there is an aura of magic about him, crackling in the air. But it's different from theirs, cold where theirs is hot.

With a little reluctance – because the dude is hugely intimidating – I step forward. I reach out my hand to take the pen and in that moment an expression flickers over his face – one of amusement. It's so similar, so unique, I know it is him.

"Fox Tudor!" I blurt out.

He jolts and the pen falls from his hand and clatters to the floor, rolling across the stone towards me.

I reach down and scoop it up from the floor and when I stand to face him again, his brow is furrowed.

"Professor Tudor," he corrects.

Now my mouth really does fall open, so wide he probably sees right back to my tonsils.

Fox Tudor was a golden boy back in Slate Quarter – *the* golden boy. Good looking, clever, athletic and charming. The full works. Everyone said he was destined for great things, so when he didn't return home from the academy, nobody was surprised. I always assumed he'd ended up in Iron Quarter, or perhaps Granite. I never for one second considered he'd be here – at the academy, teaching. Teaching magic!

How? How could that be possible?

"They're wrong," he says, as if reading the thoughts in my head. "There are other ways to acquire magic in your blood." There's a bitterness in his tone. One I can't understand. He can wield magic – strong magic – I saw him force those shadow weavers down into their seats. He escaped Slate Quarter. He has a position at the academy itself. What could he possibly be bitter about? The crooked odds have somehow worked in his favor.

"You're Amelia's kid sister," he says, observing me with as much interest as I am observing him.

"You knew her?" I say, way too eagerly.

He shakes his head. "No, not really, she was a few years younger than me."

My own brow furrows, trying to do the math. I was just a kid – a young one when Fox Tudor set off to the academy. How old would Amelia have been? Fifteen, sixteen? Did he really not know her?

"How ... how are you here?" I blurt out, unable to help myself.

"Is it so hard to believe," he says, "Miss ... Miss ...?"

He doesn't know my name, and yet something about the way his eyes flick away from mine, tells me he does, that he's pretending he doesn't.

"Storm."

An expression flickers across his face. One I hate. "Fergus's daughter."

"I'd better go," I say, scurrying backwards. "I'm sorry for barging in like that."

"You need to be careful," he says slowly, watching me as I back out of the room.

"Wh-what?" I say, my blood running cold. Why do I feel like that's a warning?

He points to his own left eye and then his ankle, mirroring my collection of injuries. "You need to be more careful. Watch your back."

Chapter Seventeen

B riony

"Jeez, Cupcake, what took you so long?" Fly says as I join him back out on the stairwell. "I was beginning to think you'd been chained to the wall."

"Huh?" I say, my mind still back there in the classroom.

Fly looks at me funny. "I said, what took you so long?"

"I couldn't find it," I say, unsure why I'm lying to my new friend, why I'm not telling him about the strange encounter with our new professor. "Come on then," I say, pulling Fly up the stairs, "all the good food will be gone if we hang around any longer."

"You're very food motivated," he observes.

"You have no idea," I tell him.

In the canteen, we join the back of a long line. Fly gives me a knowing look.

"By the time we get to the front, all that's going to be left is crumbs."

"Sorry," I say, fingering my pen in my pocket and reliving that strange encounter in the classroom.

I can't believe our professor – gruff, powerful, grumpy as hell – is Fox Tudor – Slate's golden boy, the boy who was always quick with a smile, who could make even the most somber of people laugh, who nearly everyone was in love with – young, old, female and male.

I'm still lost in my thoughts, when Fly nudges me on the arm.

"What?" I say. He jerks his chin towards the seating area of the canteen and I see everyone else has fallen quiet and is staring that way too. "What is it?" I whisper to Fly, unable to see what all the fuss is about.

Fly jerks his chin again and this time I realize everyone is staring at a person. One person in particular. He's not particularly tall and is as skinny as I am but he has the kind of face you only see in paintings – paintings of angels. I kinda understand why everyone is staring his way, but I also don't get it. Sure, he is beautiful. But he's not the only one.

"I don't get it," I whisper again to Fly, "did he do something or–"

"His collar," Fly whispers back.

His collar?

My gaze drops to his neck and sure enough he wears a band around his throat. Although I'd hardly describe it as a collar – more like a choker crafted from golden silk.

"It's very pretty ..." I murmur, although I still don't understand why that is causing everyone to stare.

The boy walks through the canteen, seemingly oblivious to everyone's staring, his head held high, a little entourage scuttling along behind him.

Fly watches him exit the building, then drags his eyes back to me. He looks at me.

"You don't know what that was, do you?" His brow crinkles. "I still don't get how you're so clueless about all this." I shrug. Maybe I would know if my sister had come home. If she'd sent me more letters. All I do know are the bits and pieces I learned from Muriel and most of that focused on the hardship and pain. Two of Muriel's most favorite subjects. "It's a thrall collar," Fly says.

I guess Amelia was selective about the information she did send me.

"A what?" I say, an unease rumbling through my body.

"A collar given to a thrall by their protectors. It symbolizes they are taken and, more importantly," he says, giving me a knowing look, "protected."

"That is really sick," I say, frowning. I knew the realm and the system were messed up. I knew the academy wouldn't be fair – that it would be biased and corrupted. That the shadow weavers would live in luxury while the rest of us slummed it. I guess I had no idea just how twisted it would be.

"He didn't seem too unhappy about it," Fly says longingly. "He seemed to be reaping the benefits."

"I'm not some possession a group of over-privileged boys gets to own!" I spit out. Fly's eyes go wide as if I've said something truly outrageous. "Just because they grew up somewhere special, just because they can do a few magic tricks, just because they're quite pretty to look at, they think they can stroll around with sticks up their asses treating everyone else like dirt and acting like giant assholes and obnoxious dicks." Fly lifts his eyebrows at me and glances over my head. "What?" I say, irritated that my new friend doesn't seem to agree with me. "They are and

I'd rather eat pig shit than have anything to do with them."

"Erm, Cupcake ..." Fly splutters, pointing as inconspicuously as he can behind me.

I peer over my shoulder and right at the broad chest of a shadow weaver. My cheeks burn as I lift my gaze into the pissed-off face of Beaufort Lincoln.

"Cupcake?" he spits in disgust.

"Just a friendly nickname," Fly mumbles, "we're not ... I'm not ... she's not my type ... and even if she were ..." He trails off as it becomes clear Beaufort isn't listening, he's too busy glaring at me.

"Assholes and dicks are we?" he snarls right at me.

"Pretty ones," Fly points out.

"Is that why you didn't come to our rooms as you were asked?"

I go to open my mouth and tell him, yes, that's exactly why, but in that moment, he glances over my shoulder, probably spies everyone in the canteen now looking our way, grabs my wrist and, before I can protest, hauls me out of the building.

Outside, the weather has turned stormy, the wind whipping around the buildings, driving dead leaves along the pathway and stinging against my face.

I attempt to yank my arm from his grip. I try to dig my good heel into the ground. But he's twice my size and about ten times stronger and in the end I admit defeat and let him take me, complaining instead.

"Hey, my leg. You're hurting me." He pauses, gazing down at my ankle.

"You hurt your ankle? How? It wasn't–" His expression darkens.

"No, I sprained it during the assault course."

"Why hasn't it been healed?"

"It's been bandaged. A sprain takes time to heal."

"Not if magic is used. Why didn't you go to the clinic?" I look at him blankly and he scoffs in annoyance. Then motions with his fingers. "Give it here."

"Give what–"

"Your leg." He crouches down and before I know what he's doing he has my ankle lifted into the air, his hands wrapped around my leg.

I peer down at him – his blazer stretched across his broad back, his hair thick and dark.

A warmth radiates from his palms, a warmth that spreads from the injured part of my ankle, right along my leg, up my thigh and towards my …

"What the hell are you doing?" I cry, trying to yank my leg away.

"Healing your leg," he says, not letting go. Instead, he closes his eyes, his mouth moving silently and I notice how full his lips are.

More heat, a tingling sensation. I bite my lip because … because it feels good. Really very very good. The kind of sensation you could close your eyes and sink right into. I peer down at him some more, his large body crouched before me, his strong hands wrapped around my ankle, his handsome face taut with concentration. Something flutters low in my belly. It's … really damn pleasant.

He releases my leg. "There, try it."

Swallowing down whatever the hell I was just feeling, I rest my weight on the leg. No shooting pain. No cramping. Not even a slight ache. I have to admit, it's as good as new.

"Thank you," I mumble reluctantly, unable to meet his eyes.

"You're welcome," he says, standing to his feet.

He hesitates, then takes me by surprise a second time. Cupping my face in his hand. For the briefest of startling moments, I think he's going to lean down and kiss me, press that full mouth of his against mine. My belly flutters all over the place.

But then he brushes his thumb under my eye.

"I should have done that before," he murmurs, before marching us around a corner and off the path.

"Where are we go–"

"Somewhere we won't have the entire academy listening in to our conversation," he snaps.

He backs me right up against a wall, planting his hands either side of my head and leaning in towards me.

"I'm going to miss my lunch!" I protest because I don't know what he's going to do – if this time he really is going to kiss me – and I don't know what else to say.

"Thralls are given the privilege of eating in the shadow weaver dining hall."

"Is that meant to entice me?" I spit.

"Entice you?" he says, top lip curling. "It's just a fact. You know what else is a fact?" I glare at him. "You failed to show up when summoned."

"Summoned?!" I say in outrage.

"I told you, seven o'clock in our rooms. It was an instruction, not an invitation."

"Well, maybe it should have been an invitation and then maybe I would have come. You know, you didn't even ask my name. You didn't even give me yours."

"You don't know my name?" he scoffs, like that's the stupidest thing he's ever heard.

"Oh, I suppose I should, should I? Because you're so fucking special."

He raises an eyebrow. "Yes, I am. So if I tell you to be somewhere, you damn well be there."

"I don't want to be a thrall. Anybody's thrall. Least of all yours!" I push at his chest, my hands meeting a solid wall of muscle beneath his blazer, a solid wall of muscle that does not move. That something in my belly flutters all over again. Why the hell does he have to be so hot? Why the hell does he have to smell so good?

"You just said you don't know who I am," he says, scowling, his face inches from mine.

"Oh, I know enough. I know what your kind is like."

"My kind?" His frown deepens, cutting heavy lines between his brows. "You mean your betters. Strong, powerful, elite."

"Yes, your kind. Cruel, callous and conceited."

"You know a lot." I scowl at him, lifting my chin in defiance. "Then you should know this: you don't get a say in this. So be at our rooms at 8pm tonight, understood?" Those silver eyes meet mine and his magic hisses in the air.

I want to tell him to go to hell but in that moment, trapped by the cage of his strong arms, his magic fierce and threatening and his eyes even more so, I can't find my voice.

He pushes off the wall and strides away.

Only when he's almost around the corner do I find my voice again, calling after him. "No, no way."

But the wind howls, carrying my voice away and I doubt he even hears me.

I lean back against the wall. My heart pounds in my chest, and my stomach won't stop fluttering.

I close my eyes and catch my breath.

It's been so long since anyone touched me with anything close to kindness, with gentleness, with care. I'd forgotten how good that could feel.

I can still feel his touch against my ankle, against my cheek.

I shake my head.

Shadow weavers aren't kind. They aren't gentle. They are cruel and they are selfish.

And as one of the most powerful, Beaufort Lincoln will be one of the worst.

Unfortunately, he hasn't lost interest. In fact, he just healed my ankle and told me to come to his rooms again.

But, so what?

If this comes down to a battle of wills, he's going to learn just how damn stubborn I can be.

Because there is no way, no way in hell, I am going to belong to anyone – let alone a shadow weaver – let alone three of them.

Chapter Eighteen

Beaufort

I storm along the pathway, my magic sparking in my fingertips, crashing through my veins, my blood red hot.

How long has it been since someone defied me? Since they refused me? Since they looked me in the eye and told me, no?

I don't remember. I wonder if anyone ever has.

And fuck, it makes me hot, makes me hard. Makes me want that little scrap of a girl – with her fierce eyes, spitting at me like a wild cat who might lash out and bite.

I may not admit it to anyone – maybe I've hardly admitted it to myself – but I've harbored the same doubts Dray has. I know what I saw in that flash of a vision – streaking past my eyes the moment our gazes connected – but nonetheless, I've wondered, why her?

Why some pathetic nobody from the furthest, most rotten, hopeless shithole in the realm.

It makes no sense.

Now, I'm beginning to see the appeal. To understand it.

My lips curl up into a smile and I run my tongue against them.

Her lips are soft and plump. Okay, they were pursed together, set into a downward frown. It makes them all the more tempting. I'd like to taste them. I'd like to drag them through my teeth. I'd like them wrapped around my cock.

I could have a lot of fun with her. *We* could have a lot of fun with her.

I forget the bad mood I've been brewing all last night and all this morning and stride towards my next lesson with a bounce in my step – some history class, apparently we need to know about the history of our realm, as if it hasn't been drilled into us all since the moment we took our first breath.

I sit beside Dray, hardly aware of what the old dude with his scruffy beard and tweed suit is droning on about, focused on the visions I'm creating in my head – visions of exactly how I'm going to play with our little thrall tonight.

Because for all that defiance and spiteful attitude, I have no doubt, no doubt at all that she will come tonight.

Yeah, she's had her little fun – played at being the brat. But she knows who we are. She knows how powerful we are. She knows what a fucking honor it is to be chosen by us.

She will be there.

"Why are you in such a good mood?" Dray says, leaning closer towards me, his nose suddenly twitching. "And what the hell is that smell?" He takes a deeper inhale, his eyes spinning in their sockets and his eyelids drifting shut. "Fuck, that shiiit smells goooood."

"The girl," I tell him, probably wearing a smug grin on my face.

Dray's eyes flick open and he stares right at me. "The girl?" He studies me. "You're serious?"

I nod. "We had a little chat about her disobedience."

"That sounds fun," Dray says, left leg bouncing with excitement.

"Yeah," I say, rubbing at my chin. "It was."

Dray leans towards me and sniffs again. "Her scent ..." he says, as I push him away from me, "it's fucking amazing. Smells just like ..." He groans.

"I told you," I say. "She's the one."

"With a scent like that," he says, rolling his shoulders and fidgeting on his chair. "She's coming tonight?"

"Yeah," I say. "She'll be there."

Except eight comes and goes.

I'm waiting patiently in my study for the knock on our door, distracting myself with some reading – some reading I've barely looked at, because, shit, I'm impatient. I want to see her again.

But there's no knock.

More and more minutes pass.

The excitement I was feeling curdles in my gut, anger filtering through my veins to replace it. I glance at the clock on my mantel again. 8:30. She isn't just late. She isn't coming.

My hands curl into fists on my desktop.

I was wrong about her. This isn't fun – some clever act to rile us up.

The little brat is for real. And this is fucking disre-spectful.

Does she know how many of the losers out there would kill to be in her shoes? The things they would do to be given half a chance? Does she realize who the fuck she is dealing with here?

She's about to find out.

I yank open the bottom drawer of my desk and pull out the pages of neatly typed text I was given yesterday, fastened together by a staple in the corner. These are the names of all the new students at the academy. Their names and their rooms.

I flip the pages until I reach surnames starting with S, then run my forefinger down the rows until I find her name.

Storm, Briony Mae. Date of Birth 23rd April. Born: Slate Quarter. Room: 10, Old Tower.

I stare at that information for several minutes, then slam the pages shut, grab my jacket from the back of my chair and step out into the night. The wind churns violently, flapping the tails of my jacket and whipping my hair around my face. I lower my head against it and set off from the front of the academy where the towers are shiny and new, towards the far side where the towers are much older, their upkeep clearly not a priority.

I meet one or two other students out on the pathways, heads also bowed against the storm, hurrying this way or that, eyes darting at me in curiosity. Those looks of curiosity become even more apparent the closer I draw to her tower and the more rotten the buildings grow.

Her tower has definitely earned its name, the oldest and most decrepit by far. It must have been built at least a millennium before and it's a miracle it's still standing. I climb the narrow stairwell, a few doors creaking open as I pass, people peering out. They'll be whispering about this tomorrow.

It makes me even angrier. She's making a laughing-stock out of us. Once, I can over look. I can dismiss it as a bit of fiery fun. But twice. I can see Kratos and his brothers laughing at me now. Can see the Smyte twins sneering.

I growl under my breath as I reach the final floor.

For one brief moment, I consider hammering on the door. Then I dismiss that, raise my hand and hurtle magic right at the locked doorway. It buckles and slams open and I catch sight of her, curled on top of her bed, gaping at me in horror.

I don't wait for an invitation, I stride straight inside and slam the door behind me.

"What the hell are you doing?" she shrieks, leaping off the bed. She's dressed in just a t-shirt, one that barely skims the underneath of her ass, a lot of freaking bare leg on show.

"You're late," I growl at her. "Don't you have a fucking watch?"

She lifts her chin like she did when I backed her soft body against the wall. Fuck, it was hard not to press my body against her then, it's even harder not to do it now. Not to slam her onto that bed and cage her again.

"No, I don't have a watch."

I snatch up the sleeve of my jacket, and snap off my own wristwatch, flinging it on the mattress that stands between us.

"Well, you do now."

Her eyes dart down to the watch.

It's made from rare rose realm crystals. It's probably worth more than all her possessions combined, which, by the looks of this bare room are few and far between.

"I told you before," she says calmly, "I don't want to be a thrall."

"Because?" I say, humoring her.

"I'm not some thing to be owned and ordered about."

"You seem to have this perverse idea of what a thrall is, sweetheart. It's a fucking honor. A privilege."

"Ha," she snorts. "You can wrap it up in all the pretty little velvet collars you like. I know what it is. And I am not interested."

I take a step forward.

"And I am sorry you seem to believe you have a choice in this matter."

"Can't you just pick some other girl or boy?" she says in frustration. "I mean, why the hell do you want me anyway?"

"Because I do," I say. Maybe I could convince her if I told her the truth. But I don't trust her enough to tell her. Dray and Thorne are the only ones who know about the visions. And I'd like it to stay that way. "And I always get what I want."

"Not this time," she says, crossing her arms over her chest.

Now it's my time to snort. "Like I said, you seem to think you have a choice. You don't. I've made up my mind. You are going to be our thrall – for the twelve months we're at the academy. Maybe," I say, my gaze traveling down her form with heat, "for longer if we choose."

"Longer–" she cries, but I cut right across her.

"So, we can do this one of two ways. You can come willingly, like a good little thrall. Or you can come kicking and screaming. It makes no difference to me. I'll happily drag you across the academy for every other student to see if that's how you want it to be, sweetheart."

"Drag me?" she scoffs, examining me and reading how deadly serious I am. "You wouldn't?"

"You wanna try me and find out?"

She shifts her weight from one foot to the other, a little less sure of herself now.

Behind us, the handle of her door starts to turn and I raise my hand, forcing my magic against the door to hold it shut.

The door rattles in the doorway and then a voice calls out: "Cupcake, are you okay in there?"

I frown at her. "Him again. Is this the reason–"

"No–

"–because let me make myself clear. It's just us. No one else. No one else gets to touch you."

"Are you fucking serious?" she says.

"Deadly. Now, I'm giving you one last chance to show you can behave and to do as you're told. You come to our rooms as instructed tomorrow evening. If you don't ..." I warn. "Do you understand?" I ask her. After all, I thought I'd made myself fucking clear earlier today and that didn't prove to be the case. I want to be sure this time.

"What? You're not going to drag me there now?" she says with a whole heap of sarcasm. Maybe she really is ignorant of what we can do. Maybe she really is unaware of just how powerful I am. If not, she has some serious balls for such a small scrap of a girl with no fucking powers, plus an only recently healed black eye and ankle.

"No, I want you to come willingly like a good little thrall, *Cupcake*," I say, my eyes lingering on where I healed the bruising around her eye socket.

I release my hold on the door and that tall skinny boy with far too much attitude comes tumbling into the room.

"Touch her," I say, bending over him and getting right into his face, "and I will kill you."

Then I storm out and go to take my bad mood out on someone who most definitely deserves it.

Chapter Nineteen

Briony

"I told you," Fly says, picking himself up off the ground and brushing himself down. "I told you they wouldn't move on."

"Yeah," I say, flopping down on the bed.

"Guys like that aren't used to people saying no to them," Fly says, perching on the side of the bed beside me, then glancing down at the mattress. "You think he'll skin me for sitting on your bed?"

Carefully, as if I'm just trying to get comfortable, I adjust the pillow, ensuring it's still hidden. I'm lucky Beaufort was so angry with me he took no notice of what I was cradling in my lap.

"Jeez," I say, blowing out air from my cheeks. "I have no idea. He's ..."

"Hot, handsome, powerful, rich?" Fly offers.

"Intense," my eyes flick towards the stairwell, "and an asshole."

"One who hasn't forgotten about you. In fact, your refusal and reluctance has probably made him all the more determined." Fly reaches out his hand to comfort me, then snatches his hand away, seeming to remember Beaufort's warning.

"Seriously," I say, "I don't think that's what he meant by *touch* me (misogynistic piece of shit). And secondly, how would he even know?"

"He's a shadow weaver. He probably has ways. Magic and stuff." He peers around the room with suspicion, and I follow his gaze around the room. Is he right? Could Beaufort be spying on me? I dismiss the idea. He would already have questions for me if he did. Fly looks back at me. "What are you going to do?"

I shrug. I'm not stupid. I don't have a death wish. And I know when I'm beat.

I want my answers. And I'm not going to get them with an angry shadow weaver chasing me around the academy.

"I guess I'll be going round to their rooms tomorrow."

"Really?" Fly says with mischief. "I was beginning to suspect all this protesting about not wanting to be the center of attention was a lie and secretly you crave it. I thought the idea of being dragged across the campus by the hottest man in the academy might actually appeal." Fly flops back on my bed. "I think I may add it to my long list of fantasies."

"He isn't the hottest man in the academy."

"Oh Cupcake, I think he is."

My mind flashes back to Professor Fox Tudor and I'm really not sure Fly is correct. Although, perhaps there isn't much in it. I hate to admit it, but they are both extremely good looking.

That doesn't make this situation any better.

I flop back on the mattress beside him and stare up at the ceiling. A sense of fear prickles across my skin.

"What do you think they're going to make me do?"

Out of the corner of my eye, I see Fly turn his head towards me, that same look of mischief on his face.

"My advice, Cupcake, go with the flow, maybe even embrace it, and you may find you actually enjoy yourself."

I shake my head. "No," I say. "These are shadow weavers."

He doesn't know what they're capable of. He doesn't know how dangerous they can be.

Once Fly's left my room, I retrieve the object from under my pillow and carefully hide it back in the base of my cupboard.

I'm going to need to be more careful.

Chapter Twenty

T horne

There's a firm knock on my door.

I roll over, pick up my gloves from my night stand and tug them onto my hands.

"Come in," I say.

Beaufort opens the door and leans against the door-frame. His brow is drawn over his eyes in thunder.

"You wanna come have some fun?" he asks.

"If you're talking about the girl–"

"No, I'm talking about teaching someone who deserves it a lesson."

I sit up straight on my bed. "Who?"

"The scum who gave her the black eye."

I swing my feet to the ground and curl up, flexing my fingers inside my gloves, and pulling a shirt over my head.

"Lead the way."

He nods and I follow him down the staircase. "Where's Dray?" I ask. I'm sure he wouldn't want to miss this.

"Out with his little buddies somewhere," Beaufort says.

"Shouldn't we wait–"

"Can't," Beaufort says, grinding his teeth. "It has to be now."

I sense his magic in the air – fierce and angry and close to boiling over – and I understand.

"Who is he?" I ask, as we step out of our tower and into the night.

"Some piece of scum from Slate Quarter."

We make our way along the weaving pathways, the clouded night sky blocked from our view by the towers above, the wind whipping after us. It's late and there's no one else out, most of the windows we pass, dark. We walk to the east of the academy, to the tower blocks where most of the commoners have their rooms.

It's noisier here. Someone playing music. A few people shouting. A couple of peals of laughter.

"It's this one," Beaufort says, pointing to a plain-looking tower. We push back the heavy wooden door and find a group of boys, lounging about in the entranceway, passing around a joint.

Their conversation cuts short and they turn to stare at us, the spliff hanging limply from a short boy's mouth.

"Any of you Stanley from Slate?" Beaufort booms.

They all glance at each other and shake their heads.

Beaufort takes a menacing step forward. "Are you sure about that?"

"He's up in his room with some girl," the boy with the joint says.

"Number?" Beaufort asks, although I'm sure he already knows it.

"Seven."

Beaufort nods, then holds out his hand.

The boy hesitates, then passes him the joint hurriedly.

Beaufort twists it in his fingers, examining it and sniffing the smoke. Then he brings it to his lips, clamps it in his mouth, and inhales deeply, eyes open and not leaving the group of boys in front of us. The spliff crackles, the end glowing.

Holding the smoke in his lungs, he removes the spliff, then lets the smoke curl like a snake from his lips as he passes me the joint.

I look at it. It's barely a butt. I take a couple of puffs on it, the weed making my head buzz – a buzz that matches the anticipation in my veins.

When I'm done, I drop it to the floor and crush it into the stone floor with the heel of my boot.

Then I'm following Beaufort up the stairs, the boys still silent below us as if they daren't speak.

Room seven is the first on the left.

Beaufort rests his ear against the door. "He's in there," he whispers, disapproval written all over his face. "You ready?"

I nod.

Beaufort takes a step backwards, lifts his arms and blasts the door clean away, the piece of wood flying from the doorway, through the room beyond and crashing against a window, glass and wood splintering everywhere.

My friend always likes to make an entrance.

A high-pitched scream issues from inside the room and when we step inside we find a couple in bed together, both scrambling around for clothes.

We don't give them the chance to find any. I march straight over to the girl, some curvy thing with big blue eyes, grab ahold of her upper arm and drag her from the bed. She's wearing panties and nothing else.

"Out!" I order her, flinging her in the direction of the door. Covering her tits with her arms, she scurries away, leaving the boy I assume is Stanley scrabbling to pull on a pair of boxers.

"What the hell," he mutters.

He's tall and built with a little muscle. Not as lean as most of the kids from Slate Quarter. Probably stronger than them which is why he's been throwing his weight around. Although why the fuck he'd hurt our girl, I can't understand.

"Stanley?" Beaufort asks him.

"Yeah," he says, pulling a shirt over his head and trying to stand up tall as if he isn't intimidated by us, when it's clear he is.

My bond brother lifts his hands again and this time sends the asshole flying across the room and smashing into the broken wood and glass.

He hits the debris with an *oof*.

"Hey man, what I–"

Beaufort sends another blast of magic hurtling towards him, hitting him right in the belly. He groans, folding over in half.

"I don't know what this is about but I–" he mutters.

Beaufort isn't in the mood for talking. He targets him with a volley of vicious magic. It's not enough to kill or maim. It is enough to hurt – possibly scar. The boy jolts around on the floor, moaning and groaning with every impact, curling up into a tight ball.

Beaufort stops, his shoulders heaving. He turns and looks at me.

"Want a go?" he asks.

"Yes," I reply.

I walk over to the far side of the room, splinters of glass crunching under my boots, and grab hold of the boy by his neck. His eyes are swimming around in their sockets as he struggles to focus on our faces.

"Know who we are?" Beaufort asks him.

"Yeah, but I don't know what–"

"The girl," he says, as I squeeze his throat, "you don't touch her ever again."

"The girl?" his brow crinkles in genuine confusion. "That girl just now?"

"Briony Storm," I tell him, liking the sound of her name in my mouth.

"Briony!" he says, eyebrows leaping up his forehead and a smirk forming on his lips. "This is about Briony? Man, she's not worth–"

I swing back my fist and slam it right into his mouth. Despite my gloves, I feel a tooth crack against my knuckles and when I withdraw my hand, his mouth is full of blood.

"The black eye," Beaufort growls from behind me. "You gave it to her. Only seems right that we repay the favor."

I hit the boy again, this time right against his cheekbone. Tomorrow he'll have a shiner blacker than the depths of night and everyone will know who gave it to him.

Chapter Twenty-One

B riony

I don't sleep nearly as well as the previous night. There are too many thoughts spinning around my head and even lying in an actual bed with a mattress and covers isn't enough to lull me into sleep. Which means, despite no longer having an injured ankle (or ribs – it seems Beaufort may have inadvertently healed those too), I am not in the best shape for our first lesson the next morning. More torture with the gruesome twosome. At least this time, that torture consists of running. Something I am not so bad at. In fact, I'm pretty fast. I'm just not sure I'll be that fast today after a night of no sleep.

We assemble on the field in our dull gray tracksuits, the shadow weavers in their shiny black ones, the cold morning mist swirling out in front of us and listen as the more talkative of the twins explains the route our run is to take and informs us that the girls will be running first.

I glance towards Fly, giving him a little pout of disappointment – running along with Fly would have made this morning a million times better – then flinch when I catch sight of the brunette who tried to kill me. I haven't seen her since, but today it's impossible to miss her. Around her neck sits a golden collar – just like the one that boy was wearing yesterday. She's smiling smugly, a crowd of admirers forming around her.

For a minute I think ... but then I glance towards the shadow weavers and find the Princes all glaring at me. I jolt and avert my eyes.

Okay, so the situation hasn't changed. Someone else has obviously claimed that girl as their thrall.

"Look," I whisper to Fly, nudging him in the ribs, "that's the girl who pushed me off the net. Hopefully that means she'll no longer have murderous intentions towards me."

"Hmmm," Fly says, peering her way. "That's Odessa Gunvald. She's from my Quarter and she's a giant bitch with constant murderous intentions. I'd watch your back when she's around."

"Great," I mutter, then along with the other girls, shuffle towards the start line.

The other twin lifts his arm, then trumpets on his whistle, and we're racing away.

It's hard to know what tactics to employ – especially when my brain is too tired. Do I set off fast – lose the others and run this race in peace but risk running out of puff pretty quick? Or do I slump along at the back and risk being trampled by the crowd?

In the end, I decide to run my own race at my own pace which means I'm racing away from the other girls from

Slate and Granite Quarters but am hot on the heels of those from Iron. The shadow weaver girls shoot ahead, soon out of sight entirely. It's not long before the academy is out of sight too as we jog down a slope, across rough ground and out towards the woods we'd trudged through the night we arrived.

The field is so spread out now, I can no longer see the girls behind me and lose those in front as they squeeze through a gap in the fence and duck under the trees. I follow them, the ground soon a carpet of dead leaves, fallen branches and snapped-off twigs. I run through the debris, ravens cawing above me, five minutes into the depths of the wood when I find my way blocked by five girls.

At first, I assume something has happened – someone is injured or hurt. Then I conclude they must be taking a break – perhaps choosing to bunk off the lesson.

Then I realize, no, they're waiting for me.

I slow up warily, coming to a halt a few feet away from them. In a flash, they're forming a circle around me, hemming me in. I try to calm my breathing, resting my hands on my hips and adopting my blank expression.

"What the hell do you think you're doing, Slate scum?" the girl immediately in front of me says. Like the others she's athletically built and she's tied her black braids away from her face. "Are you trying to beat us?"

The girl beside her, a little taller, thighs strong and thick and about twice the width of mine, tosses her head. "Do you think by running fast they're going to let a little shit like you into our Quarter?"

The other girls laugh.

I don't say anything. I learned long ago that it only antagonizes them – makes the beating twice as hard.

Because I'm pretty sure that's what's coming. Like everyone else in my life, they want to teach me a lesson.

Yeah, just when I'm injury free, it looks like I'm about to get a host of new ones.

"What?" the first girl says. "Cat got your tongue? Or are you dumb as well as stupid?"

She smiles at me and a weight hits me violently from behind. I try my best to keep my footing, but I stumble down onto my knees and the girl from behind me takes a fistful of my hair. She shakes me as the first girl aims a kick at my recently mended ribs.

I struggle against the hand gripping my head and try my best to climb back onto my feet, but another kick – this time to my stomach – has me doubling over and gasping for air.

"Stay away from us. Keep to your own kind. Do you understand?" the taller girl hisses.

I close my eyes, flinching in anticipation of the next strike, but then a noise cuts through the trees.

A loud bark, followed by the thundering of paws hitting hard ground.

I open my eyes, I can't twist my head around because the girl still has a grip of my hair, but I can see the girls in front of me are peering over my head and off into the distance.

"What's that?" the first girl asks.

"A wolf!" one of the girls behind me says.

"A white wolf!" another says, as the ground underneath us seems to vibrate with the coming beast.

The tall girl looks down at me in shock.

"Shit, she's not ..."

"Fuck!" the girl gripping my hair says, releasing her fist and sending me tumbling into the dirt.

And then they're off, scattering through the trees as the

pound of those paws comes dangerously close, so close I can smell the beast, can hear its panted breath.

It's too late for me to run. Instead, I stay as still as I can, face down in the dirt. Maybe it won't see me and will take after those other girls instead.

Except I'm not that lucky, because in the next moment, I hear the wolf come to a skidding halt and then it's padding softly towards me.

There are many ways I imagined dying at this academy – especially after my fall from the net. None of them involved being mauled by a wolf.

I try to calculate how far behind the other runners must be, whether they'd even help me if they reached us in time.

Without moving my head, I glance around, searching the dirt for a weapon – a rock, a stick, anything at all. However, there's nothing big enough to fend off a giant wolf.

I curse myself. Day four and I'm already tapping out. All those plans I had, all those promises I'd made to her in my heart. All of it's come to nothing.

I hear the wolf sniff the air, padding closer and closer, its breath coming in loud huffs.

And then it stops. I pray it rips out my throat – at least that will be quick.

But nothing happens. For several seconds the world is as still as I am and then suddenly I feel something wet and slippery hit my ear. I jolt, expecting the sharp cut of teeth to follow. They don't, just that wet slippery object again.

A tongue!

The wolf's tongue.

He's licking me, drawing his tongue over my ear and my cheeks, under my chin. He pants excitedly and I'm reminded of Baxter, my old dog from home, how he'd jump up and lick my face whenever I returned home or whenever I needed cheering up.

Is this the same? Or is the wolf simply sampling me before he devours me completely?

I decide I have nothing to lose.

I roll over and sit up, and the wolf comes charging at me, his tail swinging side to side in excitement. He licks my face again, then at my hair that's come loose from its tie.

I can't help myself – I miss Baxter, about the only thing I do miss from home. And so I bury my hands in the thick fur around his throat and stroke him.

"Well, you're a handsome fellow, aren't you?" I coo, as the wolf attempts to lick at my hands. "And I don't think you realize, but I owe you one. You just saved me from a beating."

The wolf stops licking at me, and gazes off through the trees, sniffing at the air. I take the opportunity to stroke up his head and along his fluffy ears.

He's about three times the size Baxter was, and Baxter was a big dog – one my dad brought home with the intention of making a guard dog (not that we had anything to guard). Fortunately, he proved to be a big softie – just like this wolf.

"You look pretty terrifying," I tell the wolf, as I rub at his sternum, his eyes drifting shut in pleasure, "but you're really a big softie, hey?"

The wolf opens his eyes and snarls quietly at me as if he understands and doesn't like that observation.

I laugh and raise my hands.

"Sorry." I giggle.

He butts his snout against my right palm, demanding more petting. I oblige and he takes the opportunity to give me a good old sniff, starting at my neck and making his way right down my body, burying his face right into my crotch.

"Hey," I say, pushing at his snout, "that's a little bit too forward. We only just met."

The wolf, however, doesn't take too kindly to that, growling at me and rubbing his nose right between my legs.

I scramble up onto my feet.

"Bad wolf," I tell him, knowing that this wolf might turn on me any second. He's a wild animal after all – not tame like Baxter.

The wolf ducks his head in an attempt to capture my pant leg between his teeth, but then something obviously captures his attention. His ears twitch. He lifts his head. His ears twitch some more, then he's tipping back his head and howling. The noise is deafening, thundering through the forest.

I swing my gaze around, trying to determine what's bothered him, but then he's off, chasing through the trees, leaving me alone with my newly bruised ribs.

Chapter Twenty-Two

D ray

As usual, I'm the first over the finish line and the first to hit the showers. The shadow weavers' wash room is separate to the commoners'. I'm also betting it's a hell of a lot nicer – more a hammam than a locker room, with scented steam drifting through the large open space; the walls, floors and ceiling tiled in a decorative green and the lighting dim. It makes the place feel as if you're walking on the sea bed.

Under the circle of showers that hang in the center of the room, I wash away the grit, grime and sweat from my body, reliving that run. Reliving one part of it in particular, closing my eyes and letting the scene play out against my eyelids. My cock's rock hard and standing to attention between my thighs. I wrap my hand around it and run my fist up and down.

"Fuck," I mutter into the water, letting it run down my body like a soft caress.

I pump my cock in my hand, but as my balls tingle and begin to tighten, I stop, biting down hard on my lip – so hard I probably draw blood.

I want to save that for tonight.

I smile. Yeah, tonight is going to be fun.

My cock's not happy about it, dribbling pre-come into the water and twitching in agitation.

I cut off the shower and march over to the plunge pool. I dip my big toe into the water. Ice-cold. This is going to hurt. I smile to myself and jump right in – the cold water hitting my body like a thousand sharp knives. I go right under, the water soaring over my head, and my feet hitting the bottom of the pool. I kick off and shoot right back to the surface.

"Shit, yes!" I mutter as I break through the surface and shake the water from my eyes and my face.

I remain in the water even though it makes my lungs ache and my skin sting as the rest of the shadow weavers begin to trickle in – Beaufort one of the first. Thorne is faster – only a little slower than me, but he'll have gone back to our rooms to shower in private.

I drag myself out, not bothering to tie a towel around my waist – the other dudes can look if they want to feel fucking inferior – and stride to the hot, bubbling pool. I slide into the warm water, groaning with a different kind of pleasure, and lean back against the side, big-ass grin pinned to my face.

Beaufort, soaping himself under the shower, examines that grin, shakes his head and turns his back on me.

He says I'm too easy to read. That I wear my emotions written all over my face. What do I care? I have nothing to hide.

Beaufort isn't the only one who notices how smug I'm looking.

"What you grinning about, Eros?" Kratos calls across the bathroom, washing his meager-looking cock under the water. "Like something you see?"

"I'm not sure," I say, "I can't exactly see it from over here. Too small."

The other boys cackle and Kratos scowls at me.

"I wouldn't be looking so fucking pleased if I were you," he sneers. "I saw that girl out there on the field – still no fucking collar around her neck."

"There's no rush," I say, leaning back against the side of the pool and closing my eyes like his words don't grate me when really they fucking do.

"You choose the ugliest, skinniest freaking girl in the academy from the actual shithole of the realm and even she doesn't want to be your thrall. It's fucking hilarious." He laughs, his brothers chuckling along too – although none of the other boys are brave enough to join in with him. Several drop their gazes or look away, not wanting to get involved.

I open my eyes and grin even wider.

"Ahhh Kratos," I say, "haven't you figured out by now that it's no fun if they hand it to you on a plate, if they drop to their fucking knees before you've even asked? Where's the fucking fun in that?"

"Really?" Kratos says smirking at his brothers. "I've been very happy with how willing our little thrall has been to drop to her knees. We all have."

"The mouth on that girl," Prentice mutters, biting his goddamn fist.

"Yeah," Beaufort says, yanking off his shower and walking over to join me in the hot tub. "I hear that mouth's been busy all around the Iron Quarter."

"Fuck you," Kratos says, striding out of the shower towards us.

"With that cock? No thanks." I laugh.

He raises his hand but his brother, Nathan, catches ahold of him and pulls him backwards.

Beaufort stands, his body tense and his magic loud and dominant in the bathroom.

"Get the fuck out of here, Kratos," he orders.

Kratos glares at him but doesn't resist as his brothers haul him away.

Beaufort waits until he's gone, swings his gaze around the remaining men, all barely daring to breathe, and then sinks down into the water.

"He's getting too fucking big for his boots," I mutter.

"His mouth has always been bigger than his mettle," Beaufort says. "He's no threat."

A year ago the Hardy brothers challenged us and we wiped the floor with them.

"Yeah," I say. "But it's not going to stop him from being a fucking nuisance."

Chapter Twenty-Three

Briony

I've lived all my life in Slate Quarter where there's snow on the ground for six months of the year and yet the academy changing rooms where we're sent after our cross-country run, must be the coldest place I've ever encountered. I shiver, my knees actually knocking together and my teeth chattering and I haven't even stripped out of my gray tracksuit. At least it means no one is hogging space under the showers. Everyone is determined to wash as quickly as they can, squeaking and squealing in pain as they do.

I've no intention of joining them. Not because I'm scared of a bit of cold water – the water in our bathroom back in the tower is just as cold – but I refuse to strip down and walk around naked like all the other girls.

Instead, I hover in the corner, carefully removing one garment as I whip on another.

The girls I encountered on the run are already dressing too. I see them glancing my way and whispering, but they make no move to bother me again. For some reason, that encounter with the wolf appears to have spooked them. If they'd actually seen what a softie he was – if not a bit of a perverted softie – I doubt they'd be leaving me alone.

Unfortunately, there are plenty of other girls in this changing room and some are more than happy to torment me.

The brunette – Odessa – being one of them.

"Oh my god," she says from the showers as she scrubs scented shampoo into her long, thick hair. Her golden collar glistens under the water. She hasn't removed it to shower – I assume so everyone can admire it. "Do you see that? The piece of scum from the Slate shithole isn't showering!" She glances my way and adopts a patronizing tone. "I know you come from a pig sty where people are happy to stink of shit and washing and cleaning doesn't exist, but here at the academy we don't want to smell your stench."

Usually, I'd ignore bullshit like this but the other girls are all looking at me with disgust and I do have some pride.

"I'm going back to my room to get washed up," I say, buttoning up my shirt as quickly as I can. I don't want to get in a fight with Little Miss Murderous Intentions. But obviously, I don't have a say in the matter.

"Why? Are these changing rooms not good enough for you?" Odessa says, washing the soap from her hair, a train of bubbles sliding down her shoulders and between her breasts. Breasts that, I hate to admit, are pretty damn perfect – no wonder *she* has been claimed as a thrall. "Or maybe she's got something to hide." She snaps her head down and glares at me. "Maybe under all those layers of baggy clothes, she's hiding something." Inadvertently I jerk, my heart beginning to hammer in my chest. How does she know? "Maybe she's a freak." Her lips curl into an evil smile and I know this is not going to end well. "I say we find out." She glares at her new band of admirers, who all look back at her with incomprehension. "Well, go on," she says, "what are you waiting for? Let's strip her down."

I glance towards the group of girls from the woods. They whisper to each other and then dart out of the changing rooms. I guess they've had their fun tormenting me and are happy to leave me in Odessa's hands now.

I swing my gaze back towards the showers. The girl joined to Odessa's hip comes striding my way. She is huge – at least six feet tall and muscular to boot. I consider bolting the way those other girls did, but stupidly I picked the corner furthest away from the doorway to cower in. I'm trapped. I blame the tiredness and all the distracting thoughts in my head. I'm not usually so careless.

"You heard Odessa," the tall girl says. "Strip! Unless you want *me* to strip you." She grins menacingly. One of her front teeth is missing and she has tattoos printed over her knuckles.

"I'm not stripping," I tell her, lifting my chin in defiance. "If Odessa's so desperate to see me naked, she'll have to try harder at wooing me first. You know, ask me out on a date, buy me some flowers."

"Is that what you're hoping the Princes are going to do, Slate scum?" Odessa asks, coming to stand next to her friend. She's still naked and I notice her bush is just this neat line of curls and her ass is round like a watermelon. If I'm being fair, I can totally understand why she's pissed that the Princes have chosen me and not her. It makes no sense. "Woo you?" She laughs. "That's not how it works. You're scum and they're going to treat you like scum."

"Yeah, but they'll be treating *me* and not *you*," I say, unable to help the words from slipping out, even though I know better.

I'm rewarded with a fist to my face. My second beating of the day. And Fly said being picked out as the Princes' thrall would keep me safe.

My nose cracks and pain ricochets through my face, tears flooding my eyes.

I blink, my vision multiplies, and I feel blood slide from the mess that is now my nose and drip down the front of my uniform.

"Strip!" Odessa's friend growls, her fist hovering dangerously close to my face again.

"No!" I say, my voice coming out funny on account of my smashed-up nose.

"I don't think you understand how things work," Odessa says, placing her hand on her hip. "The Hardies are the second highest-ranking shadow weavers in the academy and I am their thrall which means I outrank everyone in this locker room. Including you. You have to do as I say."

"But the Princes outrank the Hardies," I say, hating myself for resorting to this, but wanting to emerge from this bathroom alive. Because I won't be like Amelia. I will survive this. I will. "And I am their thrall."

"Funny," Odessa smirks, "I don't see no collar. Do you Helene?"

"No," her friend says, "I figure they've changed their minds about you, come to their senses."

Odessa titters. "Probably, I mean look at her." She runs her fingers through her wet hair.

"Maybe the Princes will end up claiming me too. Maybe they'll share me with the Hardies and I will have twice as much fun." Her eyes glaze over as if she's picturing the scene in her mind.

"Errr, Odessa?" her friend says, jerking her out of her daydream. "You want me to strip her clothes off?"

Odessa's lips curl again. "Ewwww, no. I won't be able to eat my lunch if I see that thing naked. Come on," she nudges her friend, "she's learned her lesson."

The giant friend smirks at me and I take my opportunity to dart away before she decides to smack me again.

I head for the bathroom, meeting another girl shuffling out of a cubicle as I duck in.

"Oh no, gosh!" the other girl cries out, hands dashing up to her mouth in alarm when she catches sight of my face. She's small – smaller than me with big round glasses that amplify her auburn eyes and the freckles scattered across her face. "Are you okay?"

"Yes ... actually no," I say, grabbing a handful of tissue for my bloody nose and walking over to the mirror. It's worse than I thought and I wasn't expecting it to be pretty.

"Can I help?" she says, hovering around me.

I glance away from my reflection and towards her face. Is she serious? She looks genuine.

"I don't know. Do you know how to fix a broken nose?" I say.

To my surprise, she nods. "Both my parents are doctors in Granite Quarter. You pick things up."

"There are a lot of broken noses in Granite Quarter?" I ask. The Quarter is known for its scholars and academics. Unlike the other Quarters, I doubt there are many fist fights.

"You'd be surprised."

I examine her as I dab at the blood. What are my choices here? Head back to the clinic, wait in line and miss lunch yet again. Or seek out Beaufort Lincoln and ask him to heal me with his magic.

Yep, I definitely won't be doing that and as my stomach growls hungrily, I decide it's worth the risk.

"Okay," I say, "if you would fix it, I'd be grateful."

"It will hurt," she says with an apologetic grimace, "and it is going to be swollen and probably every color under the rainbow, but it will be straight."

I take a deep inhale of breath. "Right," I say, turning towards her. "Do your worst."

She takes me by the arm, leading me into one of the cubicles and making me sit on the toilet, then she peers at me through her glasses, pinching her tongue between her teeth.

"How did you do it anyway?" she asks, touching my nose with her fingertips. I wince even though she's gentle.

"Someone's fist met my nose," I say.

"You're a bit ... weedy to be getting into fights, aren't you? No offense. I mean I'm pretty weedy too."

"I'm not weedy," I say, definitely taking offense. "Okay, so I'm not all muscle like the shadow weavers and the kids from Iron Quarter. I'm lean, but I'm pretty strong when I want to be."

"I've been trying my best to stay out of trouble."

"I've been trying to do the same," I sigh, "just not very successfully."

The girl grips my nose with her fingers. "Ready? After three. One ... two ..."

She yanks my nose back into place and I howl, white light streaking across my vision. It hurts way more than the punch did.

"Stars!" I cry out.

"Sorry," she says, "but that looks much better."

Blinking away tears, I hobble back towards the mirrors and peer at my reflection. "I'll take your word for it," I say, splashing water on my face and washing away the blood.

"I'm Clare by the way," she says, cleaning my blood off her hands.

"Briony," I say.

"You're from Slate Quarter?" she asks.

"Yeah," I say. "How'd you guess?"

"I think the Slate kids are being targeted the most by the bullies," she says matter-of-factly. "Are you going to the canteen to get lunch? If you are, we could go together."

"I thought you were trying to stay out of trouble? I warn you, all I seem to be able to do successfully since arriving at the academy is attract trouble."

"I haven't really made any friends since I got here," she says, again matter-of-factly. "And it sucks being alone."

I should be insulted but I have a feeling Clare is one of those people without a filter. It makes a change to all the two-faced people telling you one thing and meaning another.

"Didn't you come here with any friends?"

She adjusts her glasses. "Yes, my best friend Pippa but she's been at the clinic since the first night."

"Shit," I mutter, "I'm sorry."

"Yeah," her eyes drop to the floor, "I don't think she'll be out any time soon."

"Stars, this place sucks," I mutter. She nods in agreement. "But at least the food is decent."

"You think the food is good?"

"Well, edible, which is a lot more than can be said for the food at home."

My new friend (because I'm assuming that's what she is) looks at me with a mixture of shock and sympathy.

"I need to go back to my room to clean up, but I'll see you in there." Disappointment flickers across her face and I figure she's thinking I'm going to blow her off. I take her hands in mine. "Thank you. For my nose." I attempt to wrinkle it and wince in pain. "It's the nicest thing anyone's done for me in a long time."

That's if you discount Beaufort Lincoln healing my ankle, which I totally am.

Chapter Twenty-Four

B riony

Fly and Clare gaze at each other across the canteen table with suspicion, probably thinking they have nothing in common. But they have me. And as I haven't had a single friend for a long time, I really like the idea of having two. Maybe that's just greedy, but I'm determined to make it happen.

I try a number of different conversation topics, searching for something they are both interested in: healing injuries, making the drab uniform look good, our likely trials and upcoming lessons. It isn't until Fly makes some off-handed comment about my plans tonight that they find common ground.

"What are you doing tonight?" Clare asks, breaking apart a bread roll. "I've spent my last three evenings staring blankly at the ceiling."

"Oh man," Fly mutters, "me too. We need to find something better to do."

I keep my eyes fixed on my creamy pasta, hoping the conversation will move on and I won't have to answer Clare's question.

The conversation doesn't. It stalls right there and when I peek up, I find Clare peering at me with curiosity and a knowing smirk hovering on Fly's face.

I sigh. "Going to see the Princes," I mumble as quickly and as quietly as I can.

Clare blinks at me behind her glasses. "The Princes? As in *the* Beaufort Lincoln Princes?" Fly nods enthusiastically. "As in the shadow weavers?"

"Yes," I say with a lot less enthusiasm, "them."

"Why?" Clare says, forehead wrinkling in confusion.

I shuffle pasta around my plate. Seeing I'm not going to answer that for myself, Fly fills her in.

"They've chosen Briony as their thrall."

Several emotions wash across Clare's face: astonishment, amazement and admiration.

"Oh my gosh! I can't believe I didn't recognize you. It was probably–"

"All the blood and busted-up nose?"

She nods. Then shakes her head. "I can't believe I'm eating lunch with the Princes' thrall." She gulps. "I can't believe you let me fix your nose!" She drops the remains of her bread roll onto her plate. "You should have gone to the shadow weaver healers for that."

"I'm not their thrall," I whisper, eyes shifting around to check no one is listening into our conversation. Luckily, the canteen is more concerned with the actual thralls present this lunchtime. There are five in total, each wearing their golden collars, each surrounded by a posse of admirers. "And I have no intention of being their thrall."

"Why?" Clare says in even more astonishment.

"Exactly, why?" Fly says.

"I mean, do you have any idea of the benefits that come with being a thrall?" Clare asks.

"She does. I've told her."

"I'm not interested," I say.

"But they're so–"

"Hot?" Fly says, grinning.

Clare's cheeks burn. "Well, yes, they're very attractive. And powerful. And well connected."

"Well hung too from what I've heard," Fly says.

I stab a piece of pasta onto my fork and fling it at Fly's head.

"Hey," he says, "less of the violence."

"I don't want to think about their dicks," I mutter.

"No, I can imagine that would be quite intimidating. Especially when there are three of them," Clare says.

"Three of them," Fly says, waggling his eyebrows, "that's like my ultimate fantasy."

"Mine too," Clare says, stuffing a piece of bread into her mouth. Fly and I both stare at her. I don't think either of us were expecting that.

"Really?" I say, now staring at them both as they nod.

I haven't had a lot of time or space for fantasies. And my experience with Stanley put me off boys, men, and sex. I've tried to push that part of myself aside, buried it away and refused to acknowledge it. It only got me hurt after all, and I don't think anything has changed. Even if the way Beaufort touched me stirred something long dormant inside me. That was a slip up. Next time I'll do better. I'll be prepared.

"Anyway," I say, "I'm not going to have to worry about

any of that. If they wanted some sex bunny, there are much better and more willing candidates." I roll my eyes. "They probably want me to scrub their toilets. Which is why I'm not interested."

I was Muriel's slave for five years, as well as her punching bag. I didn't have a choice back then. I was young with nowhere to go. I'm not going to let that happen again.

"I'm pretty sure they already have someone to clean their rooms," Clare says factually.

"I guess you're going to find out tonight," Fly says.

"Yeah," I say with absolutely no enthusiasm. "I guess I am."

The next lesson is an algebra one which leaves me to mull in my thoughts and that conversation. I come to the realization that I'm pretty damn scared about tonight – actually pretty terrified. But I survived all those years with Muriel; I survived all the ridicule and bullying Stanley put me through; I survived the first night at the academy plus an attempted murder and a punch to the nose. I can survive this too.

I'm going to have to. Because I made that promise to Amelia and I'm going to keep it.

I skip dinner – partly because I'm too nervous to eat and partly because I'm not sure I can cope with Fly and Clare discussing my upcoming evening in detail.

Instead, I head for my room and after I've checked on my bag, I tackle the most pressing issue – what the hell am I going to wear? Of course, it shouldn't be an issue or a question. I should grab the first thing I find in my wardrobe and be done with it. But as usual my pride is niggling at me. I don't want to turn up at their rooms looking like I've just been dragged from the Slate Quarter. Problem is all my clothes say exactly that. Most of them were hand-me-downs from my sister or bought from one of the many thrift stores – filled with unwanted clothes imported from the other Quarters. All my clothes have been mended – patched up or sewn back together numerous times.

As the clock tower strikes seven o'clock – the gongs vibrating right across the academy – there's a knock on my door, followed by a voice.

"How you getting on in there, Cupcake?"

I open my door, still dressed in my uniform, to find Clare with him in the doorway.

"Fine," I tell them both.

"Oh," they both say in unison.

"What?" I say, resting my hand on my hip.

"We thought you'd be getting ready," Clare says.

"We assumed that was the reason for ditching us at dinner."

Is it bad that I'm regretting introducing them to each other? Seems I neglected to think through the consequences. The consequences being their ability to gang up on me.

"I've been trying," I say dramatically. "I have nothing to wear. Maybe I should just go in my uniform."

We all stare down at the shapeless gray garments hanging from my frame.

"You must have something," Fly says, strolling towards my wardrobe. I launch myself in front of him and block him off. I do not want him rummaging around in there.

"Trust me, I don't."

Fly and Clare look at each other.

"It's fine," I say, not liking the pity I can see in their

eyes. I don't need sympathy. I'm perfectly happy with who I am. "I'm going to be scrubbing toilets, remember? My uniform is probably the best thing for the job."

"Like I told you, the shadow weavers have people to do that for them," Clare says, sliding her glasses up her nose. "I think you ought to wear something else."

"Agreed," Fly says.

"I might have something you can borrow," Clare taps her fingers against her chin, "I'm smaller than you so it might be a bit short and tight–"

"Perfect!" Fly says, clapping his hands. "Straight men love short and tight."

"Urgh," I say, sticking my tongue out at him. I turn to Clare. "That's really kind of you but–"

"Come on," she says, beckoning us to follow her, "let's go look."

Clare's room is in a tower a million times better than ours.

"Jeez," I say, peering up at the walls which aren't crumbling and the windows which actually let light through. "You must have come in quite quickly that first night."

"Yeah," she says, her face morphing a green color, "I don't know how. I guess I got lucky."

She rests her hand on the entrance door, then hesitates. "Just to warn you, there is usually a group of idiots hanging out, smoking and drinking in the entrance way. Best to keep your heads down."

"Smoking and drinking?" Fly says hopefully.

"We're not going to get invited," I tell him. "You know that."

He shrugs and Clare opens the door. Sure enough we're greeted by a haze of smoke and through it I spy four or five guys lounging about by the stairwell: three sitting on the steps, two resting against the banisters.

I nearly jump right out of my skin when I realize one of them is Stanley.

Stanley with a face that is even more busted up than mine.

"Oh my goodness," I blurt out. "What happened?"

He jolts and peers up from the cup he was staring into. He jolts a second time when he sees it's me standing in the entrance way.

For a moment, we both stare at each other and is it my imagination, or is his expression different? Usually, it holds nothing but contempt and disgust – like he can't quite bring himself to accept that once upon a time he slept with a girl like me. The expression on his face today is different. Fearful perhaps? No, that can't be right.

"Nothing," he mutters, although by the way the boys gathered around him all glance at one another, it must have been something. "What happened to you?"

I lift my hand to my nose. I'd almost forgotten about it. "Well, it wasn't you for once," I say, sneering at him.

Stanley's gaze drops down to his shoes and the entrance hall falls into silence, everyone staring at me, then Stanley, then back to me.

Eventually Fly says, "Come on, we'd better get moving. You're running out of time."

Clare beckons us forward and the boys squeeze out of our way without protest as we climb the stairs.

As soon as we're out of earshot, Fly hisses, "What the hell was that about?"

"We used to date," I tell him simply, "if you can call it that."

"He is your ex-boyfriend?" Clare says in amazement, peering down the stairs the way we've just come.

"It was a long time ago. We were just kids, and he didn't look like that back then."

"I bet he didn't look too different," Fly mutters.

"He was also the one who gave me the original black eye," I explain.

Fly frowns and follows Clare's gaze down the stairwell. "Shithead. I wish you'd told me earlier. I'd have–"

"He's massive, Fly. You would not. Anyway, it seems he's had a taste of his own medicine."

Is it bad that I can't help smiling about that?

"Your life seems really complicated," Clare says, shaking her head.

"Are you regretting helping fix my nose and eating lunch with us?" I tease.

"I don't know," she says uncertainly, "ask me again in a week."

"I've known her three days longer than you have and I can honestly say it's not so bad. Although, as you've seen, she does eat with her mouth open."

"I do not!" I protest.

"Cupcake, you do. Along with the talking to yourself."

"I'm beginning to see why you have no other friends," I mutter and he gives me the finger.

"Were your friends hurt on the first night as well?" Clare asks.

"Nope, we just don't have any," Fly says. "Me because I don't exactly fit in in Iron Quarter," he sweeps his hand down his frame in way of explanation, "and Briony because ..." He frowns. "Actually, why don't you have any friends?"

"Because I murdered them all," I say coolly.

"I don't know whether to believe her or not," Fly whispers to Clare. I give him a menacing look. "You look just like Odessa – so, yeah, I think you did."

"Odessa?" Clare asks as she unlocks her room.

"It was her friend who broke my nose," I explain. "It's not the first time she's tried to kill me."

Clare turns around and stares at me. "Maybe I am regretting being your friend. Seems dangerous."

"Not if she becomes the Princes' thrall," Fly points out.

"Is that why you're so desperate for me to do it?" I ask, following Clare into her room. It's also much nicer than mine and Fly's. The sheets and blankets look newer, the mattress actually made of something other than straw, and there is a desk in here as well as a window seat, a wardrobe and a chest of drawers. Clare has obviously attempted to brighten up the place too. There are at least five potted plants dotted around the room.

"Yep," Fly says. "There has to be some benefits to being your friend."

"Other than my wonderful personality?"

"You have one?" he deadpans and I stick my tongue out at him again.

"Right," Clare says, flinging back her wardrobe doors. "Let's see if anything in here is any good."

"Woah," I say, taking a step forward. She must have ten times the number of clothes I have, and while they aren't made from the exuberant materials the shadow weavers wear, they are colorful and new looking.

Fly pushes past me and starts to rummage through the hanging garments, tossing a few over his head and onto the bed.

"Try those on," he instructs.

I pick a blue dress up from the pile. It has a high back,

little capped sleeves and probably reaches to below the knee on Clare.

"This looks nice," I say, gathering it up in my arms. "Thank you so much, Clare." I walk towards the door.

"What are you doing?" Fly screeches.

"Taking it back to my room to get ready."

"Uh uh. We need to see it. And you need to try the others on too so we can judge what's best."

I hold the dress to my chest. "I don't think we need to–"

"Don't be silly, we do," he insists.

I hesitate. I really don't want to undress in front of them. I peer towards the door.

"Are you worried about us seeing you naked?" Fly laughs. "Cupcake, we already went over this, you're not my type."

"I know, I'm just ... shy."

"Are you?" Clare says, unconvinced.

"Yes, I'd rather try this on in the privacy of my own room."

"No need," Fly says, grabbing Clare by the hand and spinning them both around. "We won't look. I'll even cover my eyes, see?"

I hesitate again, then quickly as I can, strip out of my uniform and tug on the dress.

"Are you done?" Fly asks impatiently.

"Errr, yes," I say, smoothing down the skirt that falls right above my knees.

"Ooo," Fly murmurs, turning around to face me again. "That color suits you. It would look even better if you took down your h–"

"No," I say.

He shakes his head and leans towards Clare, saying in a faux whisper, "She has a thing about her hair too."

"Why?" Clare asks, blinking.

"I don't have a thing about my hair, I just prefer it up, that's all."

Fly rolls his eyes, then yanks Clare around again. "Right, try on another."

"But you said this one looks good."

"Yes, and the others could look better."

I know I'm not going to win this battle, so I strip again and try on one of the other outfits he's flung on the bed.

Five outfits later, we're all in agreement that the blue dress is the best.

"It's pretty, and a little bit sexy," Clare says, "without being too sexy."

"Yeah, it doesn't make you look desperate," Fly agrees.

"I'm not," I remind him, wondering if the uniform was better after all. I glance down at the dress. "Does it look like I'm trying too hard, like I'm making an effort?"

"I have a feeling boys like the Princes would like that," Clare says.

"Yeah," I say; the problem is, I think they would.

Chapter Twenty-Five

B eaufort

This time I'm waiting by the door at eight o'clock.

If the little brat isn't knocking at our door exactly on time, I'll be keeping my promise and marching right over to find and drag her here.

I can tolerate a certain amount of disobedience. I can even find it a turn on. But this has gone too far.

Luckily – or maybe unluckily – was the idea of dragging her here turning me on? As the clock in the lounge chimes eight, there's a light rap at the door. Even though I'm standing right there, I don't answer the door straight away. She kept me waiting. Now I will keep her waiting too.

I count to one hundred in my head, then step to the door, pull it open and immediately my hackles are rising, the shadows inside me hissing.

"Who the hell did that?" I boom, staring straight into

her messed-up face. Her nose is swollen and dark bruises circle under each of her eyes. It looks fucking painful.

"Who said anyone did it?" she says, frowning. "I fell over."

"Onto your nose?" I spit in disbelief.

She shrugs.

"Were you pushed?"

"No, I tripped."

I take her wrist and yank her into the hallway. Immediately her head tips back and her bruised eyes widen.

"This is your room?" She gasps.

"This is the hallway," I tell her, wondering whether knocking her head has messed up her mind.

Her brows wrinkle. "There's more?"

"Of course there is more," I say, pulling her into the kitchen.

"This ... this belongs to you?" She swears under her breath.

I glance around at the room again. There's nothing particularly special about it. In fact, I've hardly been in here since we arrived. "Yes." And then I understand. "This entire tower belongs to us. All of it. Every single room in it."

"Us?"

"Me and my brothers. The three of us."

"I—"

"Sit down," I say, pushing her into one of the velvet-covered chairs that ring the walnut table in the room. "Why didn't you come and find me to fix your face for you?"

"It's already fixed," she says, eyes still taking in the room.

"Doesn't look fixed to me," I growl, hooking my forefinger under her chin and lifting her face to mine. Her skin is soft against my fingers – soft and fragile and from this angle I can see the pulse leaping in her throat. I can imagine our collar wrapped around that throat.

Her eyes – a deep green – meet mine for a fraction of time, then dart away.

"Are you going to tell me what really happened?"

"No," she says.

"Was it that loser again?" I growl lowly and I swear the sound makes her shiver.

Fuck, I like that. Could I make her shiver in other ways too?

Her eyes narrow. "Did you–"

"Yes, and this ends now. I will hurt anyone who hurts you. In fact, I will fucking kill them. If anyone tries to hurt you, you make that abundantly clear to them."

As usual, she says nothing.

"So tell me, who did this to your face?" I say.

She clams shut her mouth. The girl is fucking stubborn.

"You realize I will find out?"

She glares at me.

"Fine," I say, unable to help but glide my thumb along her jawline. Then I'm closing my eyes and urging the shadows from my veins, along my hands and my fingers to her face. I shiver myself when my magic connects with her skin, a tingling manifesting along my flesh.

I swim the shadows up to the injured tissue, calming and soothing it, returning it to normal. It must feel good because the tension in her jaw lessens and a soft sigh issues from her lips, her breath whispering across my face.

When I'm done, I open my eyes and examine her face. The bruising and swelling have gone and the color has returned to her cheeks. I keep holding her face in my grip and she stares up into my eyes, her pupils blowing wide.

It would be so easy to kiss her now, to drag her onto my

lap. To take everything from her. But for some crazy reason, I want her to want this. I want her to want me.

"Better," I whisper. It's only now that my gaze meanders its way from her face and down to the rest of her body. She's wearing a thick winter's coat that I don't recognize from before.

With some reluctance, I let go of her face.

"Take off your coat." Alarm radiates across her features. I huff. "I'm not asking you to undress, sweetheart. But it's warm in here."

She swallows and I watch as she undoes the large buttons and shrugs the heavy garment from her shoulders. It's erotic, like she really is stripping.

What the hell is wrong with me?

I'm acting and thinking like some inexperienced virgin.

I've had girls strip for me. *Really* strip for me. This isn't the same. And yet I'm fucking turned on. Even more so when I discover what's under the coat.

No, not lacy underwear. No stockings or corsets.

Not even the fucking awful academy uniform or the clothes that were no better than rags that she showed up in five days ago.

No, just a plain blue dress. Nothing special, not like the slinky things the girls wore to the common room party.

But it still has my blood heating. It's the way it hugs her frame, revealing curves I had no idea the girl possessed – fuck, tits I had no idea she possessed. I realize she's not as skinny as I thought. She's lean. Muscle and bone. An active girl.

The dress is also short: a strip of bare thigh flashing my way.

"You understand what's required of a thrall, right?" I say, my voice heavy in my own ears, like it's laden with lust.

Why the hell do I find this girl so fucking attractive? Is that part of it? The reason?

I wonder if that flash of a vision was even real – if I created it in my own head simply to give myself an excuse to lay my hands on her.

"No," she says obnoxiously, making it clear any cooperation is going to be given reluctantly. Fine by me, I can play that way too.

"It's pretty simple really. We give the orders and you follow them."

"I don't want to be a thrall."

I sigh dramatically, pull out a chair and sit myself down, leaning forward with my forearms resting on my knees so I'm eye-level with her. "It doesn't matter. You're ours now. And you're going to do as we say."

"I'm not," she says simply.

I decide to humor her. "Why not? Why are you so dead set against this?"

I mean, we're the most powerful shadow weavers in the academy. Not only can we offer her protection (which let's face it given the number of injuries the girl has already picked up, she needs), by being our thrall she also gains access to privileges other ordinary kids in the academy could only dream of.

She tilts her head to one side.

"Would you want to be someone's slave?" I sniff at the insinuation. She grins at me like she just won a point in a game. I frown back at her.

"A slave and a thrall are not the same thing."

"Really? Because you just said I'd have to do anything you asked."

"Slaves don't have their faces healed by their masters. Slaves don't get to dine with their masters or hang out with their masters. They're not given gifts. They're not ..." I shift my chair forward and graze my knuckles against her bare knee, "pleasured."

My magic crackles with excitement. The shadows inside me wants me to touch her more. A fuck-load more.

I slide my tongue along my bottom lip. It wants me to taste her too.

I bet she'd taste all stubborn. All stubborn and innocent. I bet she's never even been with someone before.

She presses her legs together, denying me access further up her thighs. But is it my imagination or does she rub those thighs together?

Is she fighting this? Under all this stubbornness, does she feel it too?

"A gilded cage is still a cage," she whispers.

"The whole world's a cage," I tell her. "Better to be inside a golden one than one made of shit."

Her brow crinkles.

"You're not caged," she hisses, swinging her gaze around the kitchen as if this place demonstrates that. "You have everything you want."

"Yes," I say, "and that includes you."

She shakes her head slowly. "Why me?" she whispers. "You could have anyone you wanted."

"We want you."

"Is it because ..." Something flashes in her eyes. Some-thing genuine. Something real.

"Is it because ...?" I prompt, wanting to capture what-ever that was.

She bites her lip as if to stop herself from saying the words.

I take hold of her chin again. "Tell me," I say, the

shadows dancing around us, enticingly. It makes it impossible for her to drag her eyes from me.

She closes them instead.

"Tell me," I whisper again, more gently this time.

"All my life people have wanted to break me. Is that what this is? Is that what you want?"

I can feel her trembling.

Have I got this all wrong? The defiant attitude. The bratty persona. Is it all an act?

She opens her eyelids and stares at me, her gaze now steely. "Because if it is, then you can go to hell. I will not break."

I let go of her chin and chuckle.

Yeah, it's no fucking act.

And I'm bored with this now. I'm done with arguing.

Right on time, there's another knock on the door. This one is more firm. I keep my eyes trained on her face as hers slides in that direction. We hear footsteps, the door open and voices.

Then Dray calls out for me from the hallway.

"Beaufort?" He comes to stand in the doorway, leaning on the doorframe chewing gum, Thorne right behind him. They both peer at the girl. A wolfish grin spreads across Dray's face, while Thorne just glares at her with a disdain.

It's clear while Dray is coming round to the idea of the girl, Thorne is not. He turns his head away and walks right out of the kitchen without saying a word.

She scowls at his retreating back and Dray winks at her, then turns to me. "Are you coming?"

I push back my chair and stand up.

"We have guests," I tell her. "I'm going to go and be with them now. And you can stay here."

"You're leaving me here?" she says with a little outrage. "You forced me to come over here and now you're leaving?"

"Funny," Dray says, "I thought she'd be pleased."

"I ... I am," she mutters. "And I'm going back to my room."

She starts to stand up and I push her back down into her seat. "No, you're staying here until we return."

"In the kitchen? While you hang out with your friends? Erm, no!"

"Now," I say, "if you were a thrall, we'd invite you to join us, but as you're not ..."

"I'm not staying here."

"You are," I wave my hand through the air, weaving shadows around the room that will keep her here and then I walk to the doorway.

"You're such an asshole," she snarls

"Ahh, you have no fucking idea, little one," Dray says, blowing a bubble with his gum that bursts with a bang. "Make yourself at home."

Chapter Twenty-Six

B riony

The door slams behind them and then I'm alone in the kitchen. Okay, it's a really nice kitchen. The nicest kitchen I've ever been in. Possibly one of the nicest rooms I've ever been in full stop – glistening marble worktops, expensive-looking gadgets and polished floor.

It doesn't really matter. I'm still locked in.

Or so they say, anyway. I decide it's best to check. I walk to the door and try the handle. It's locked and a thin wisp of shadow curls around my wrist, making my skin tingle with pleasure. I shake my arm, trying to detract it, but it only slides further up my arm.

I swipe at it with my other hand, trying to dislodge it. My fingers simply float straight through the misty shadow.

I jump away from the door, shaking my arm more

violently and the shadow slides down my arm and glides back towards the door.

"Asshole," I mutter, assuming the window will be guarded in the same way.

I'm guessing this is punishment for not playing along. If it is, it's a pretty pathetic punishment. Nothing compared to the ones doled out by Muriel. It still sucks. My room may be dingy, cold and damp compared to this room but at least I have Fly across the hallway to talk to, plus a book to read and I can keep guard of the package hidden in my wardrobe. All I have in here is kitchen gadgets and food.

Food!

I swing my gaze around, finding a small larder door at the back of the room. As I stalk that way, I hear laughter and voices radiating from elsewhere in this tower – a tower that these three men have all to themselves.

As I pull back the door, I find a small room laden with food – so much food it has my stomach aching and my eyes watering. This is too much for three people – even three very large people who must burn through food at a rate of knots. I think of how little fills the meager pantry back at my home in Slate Quarter and for a moment I have the desire to smash this all up. However, my stomach rumbles in protest at that idea and I decide I'll have myself a little feast instead. May as well make the best of this situation while I can and I did skip dinner.

I laden my arms with as much as I can carry – bread rolls, whole slabs of cheese, cured meats, jars of pickles and sweetened fruits.

Then I carry it back to the table and go in search of a plate and cutlery. The cupboards are full of pots and pans and at least three different types of dinner services as if these guys are going to be hosting dinner parties every day. I pick one plate made of fine bone porcelain, an intricate flower design hand painted across its surface and take it over to the table, staring at it the whole time. This plate in itself is probably worth more than my dad makes in a month. Again I have the desire to smash it into a thousand pieces. Again my stomach protests and I sit and make myself the biggest, most decadent sandwich of my life.

As I hold the thing between both hands and bring it up to my mouth, I wonder if I'm doing the right thing. I don't mean eating the sandwich, as I sink my teeth into the fresh white bread, I conclude this was the best decision I ever made.

No, I mean about the Princes.

Fly and Clare both seem to think I'm mad for not accepting my fate as a thrall.

Beaufort certainly seems to agree. Not accepting my fate has led me into an awful lot of danger.

I lower my sandwich to the pretty plate and lean back in the chair, closing my eyes.

It would make sense. Just do as they say. It's only a goddamn year. And can it be any worse than what I've endured back home?

I could eat food like this every day. Maybe I could even live in this palace of a tower. They'd protect me.

Sure, there'd be things I'd have to give in return. Things I'm not sure I even understand. But wouldn't it be worth it?

But then Amelia's face comes floating into my head. So like mine. Only painted with hope and excitement. Believing, truly believing things could change.

I can't betray her like that. I can't let her down.

I open my eyes, pick up that pretty plate and sling it across the room.

They took her from me. And there's no way – no way in

hell – I could trust them. No way I'll be anything but a spitting hissing hellcat to them.

When I've stuffed as much food down my throat as I can stomach, I decide I'm going to show them just how much of a hellcat I can be. I start with the crockery. It pains me – the plates and bowls are beautifully crafted and obviously hand painted with care, most probably by some poor bastard back in Slate Quarter. I do it anyway. Hurtling plate after plate, bowl after bowl at the walls and the floor.

It proves to be pretty cathartic. I imagine I'm tossing the plates at Odessa's head, at Stanley's face and at the fleeing back of those Iron Quarter girls. Once I'm done, I start on the glasses and then the cups. The pots and pans turn out to be unsmashable but throwing them at the floor does dent and bend them out of shape and I manage to snap all the wooden spoons and cooking implements in half.

I make my way through every cupboard until the only thing left to damage is the remaining food.

I can't bring myself to do that though. It's just too damn wasteful, besides all that destruction has worn me out – especially after the lack of sleep last night and the run this morning.

I listen out for the clock tower and after a while I hear it ring out eleven o'clock.

I smother a yawn, then spot a cushioned seat under the window.

I was hoping to be awake to witness their expression when they discover my trail of destruction, but my eyelids have other plans and wrapping myself up in Clare's coat, I curl up on the seat, falling asleep with a sly smile on my lips.

I'm going to make them regret they ever chose me.

Something stroking my cheek wakes me later.

I blink awake, my mind taking several minutes to remember where I am.

For a moment, I think it's Baxter's soft head snuggled against mine. Or my sister climbing into bed with me. But soon I realize it isn't.

I'm not back home, or snuggled up with Baxter out in the woods somewhere, not even in my new room at the academy.

No, I'm in the kitchen in the Princes Tower. A kitchen I have destroyed.

And that softness against my cheek is a hand.

I peer up into the face of Beaufort Lincoln.

Before I went to sleep, trashing the room they locked me in seemed like a really clever idea. Now faced with the imminent consequences of their disapproval, I'm less sure.

Except he doesn't look angry, he looks pretty amused.

"Did your little temper tantrum wear you out, sweetheart?" he says, still stroking my cheek.

I snap up to sitting and jerk my head away from his hand.

"It wasn't a temper tantrum," I snarl.

"Looks like it to me," he says, jerking his head towards all the mess I've caused.

I smile sweetly at him. "Just a little gift from me to you, to thank you for your wonderful hospitality."

"Very thoughtful of you, sweetheart. I understand this is

how you may like things back in Slate Quarter, but I preferred it the way it was."

He sweeps his hand in the direction of the room, and just like before shadows race from his fingertips, curling across the room and engulfing the mess of smashed-up plates, bowls, cups and glasses.

I watch in amazement as the shadows weave the destruction back together, piling the plates neatly on top of one another, stacking the glasses, and returning everything to their shelves.

"Ahhh, and I see you did enjoy our food." My cheeks burn in annoyance. "You're free to help yourself to anything in the pantry any time you like."

"No, thank you," I say. I swing my legs to the floor, ignoring the way my knees brush against his. "I'm going home."

"Not yet," he says, grabbing ahold of my wrist, his fingers curling around my skin, his magic making it tingle. Tingles that race right up my arm into my chest and down into my core. Those are tingles, right?

Despite myself, I freeze.

"I have something for you," he says.

"I don't want anything of yours. In fact ..." I reach into the pocket of Clare's coat and pull out his watch, thrusting it at him.

He takes it, examines it and then straps it back onto his wrist without comment.

"It's not mine," he says. "It's a gift."

"I don't want ..." My words fade away as he reaches into the pocket of his pants and, tantalizingly slowly, pulls out a golden collar.

It possesses a shine, a light, of its own, the threads

expertly and intricately woven and the effect both delicate and dazzling.

It's more beautiful than any of the collars worn by the other thralls. A million times more beautiful. My fingers itch to reach out and touch it – to stroke my fingertips down the exquisite threads.

But it's a trap. One I don't intend to walk into. He can offer me all the gold and jewels in the realm and I would still refuse to be his, to be theirs.

They are my enemy.

"I don't want it," I tell him, tearing my eyes away from it.

"Really?" he says with sarcasm, "because you seem to like it."

"You're mistaken."

"You don't like the way it looks." He draws it over his hands and it slithers like a grass snake. "It was made by the finest craftsmen in Onyx Quarter. It's made from the threads of velvet silkworms."

"Then give it to someone else."

"It's meant for our thrall. For you." He holds it up to my throat and once again I can't resist the temptation to let it rest there, his touch electric against my skin, the collar warm and seductive. His eyes fall dark. "That looks damn good," he growls.

My heart beats ferociously in my chest. The warmth and the magic from his body is palatable and he smells of orange and cedar. A scent so different from everything back home.

My cheeks warm, the beat of my heart jumps to my throat. It would be so easy to close my eyes and let him tie this collar around my neck.

I duck my head away.

"I told you, I don't want it."

He considers me for a moment, then obviously decides to change tactics. "It will keep you safe."

"I don't need the three of you to keep me safe. I can look after myself."

"You know you can't win at this little game of yours, right?"

I stand up and storm towards the door before he can stop me.

"Make sure you're back here again, same time Saturday night."

"We'll see," I tell him.

"Yeah," he says, "we will."

His words irk me but I resist the urge to snipe back and keep walking out of the kitchen and into the hallway. The light is extinguished out here and as I walk towards the door, I almost don't see him lurking in the darkness. The third Prince. The third shadow weaver. Thorne.

He's watching me with that same look of disdain painted all over his face. Beaufort might be insistent that he and his brothers want me but it's clear as day that Thorne does not. Everything in his expression tells me how much he despises and loathes me. A commoner. A Slate girl. Clearly not worthy of a man like him.

"Don't worry," I snap, "I'm going. I don't want to be here any more than you want me here."

His face doesn't alter and he doesn't say a word.

I toss my head in annoyance and stride right out of the door.

I won't be back.

Chapter Twenty-Seven

T horne

I watch from the window as the little thing dashes out of the tower and scurries away.

Beaufort has always enjoyed playing with his prey. I remember as a kid how he'd go scavenging out in the palace gardens for insects and small creatures – collecting them up in glass jars and making homes for them in discarded boxes. He never hurt them – never tortured them like some kids did. But he didn't let them go either. They were his pets. His playthings.

He didn't like to share back then either. Given his status in the realm, he didn't have to.

Things are different now. Fate has tied us together and we're bound to share for eternity.

That includes the girl.

A girl I have an aching desire to protect.

Is that fate again? Dictating my actions? Manipulating my emotions?

It doesn't matter either way. The desire is too strong to ignore.

Knowing both Beaufort and Dray are in their rooms – our guests long departed – I step out into the night unseen.

Someone – probably more than one person – has been using the girl as a punchbag. Every day she has a new injury. It ends now.

I will no longer let that happen.

I will be her private protector. Her shadow. Blending unseen into the darkness.

I follow her through the cobbled pathways that weave between the towers of the academy, treading silently on the ground, hiding in the dark. Perhaps she senses me. Three times she peers over her shoulder and once she stops completely, spinning around.

But if she does sense me, she doesn't see me, and each time, with a puzzled brow, she continues on her journey.

Beaufort told the both of us that the girl has been given a room in one of the old decrepit towers. But until I see it for myself, I have no perception of just how bad it is. Though the tower itself is solid and sturdy, its roof is thatched and will be little relief against the howling wind that sweeps the moor. The windows were built for battle not for students, long slits for archers and not for light. I imagine the place is cold, damp and dark.

The girl should come and live with us. We have empty rooms. Rooms that – while nothing in comparison to our chambers back home – are luxurious compared to this.

Although, as soon as the thought occurs to me, I dismiss it. It can never be. It is too dangerous.

At the base of the tower, she tips her head back and peers right up to the sky, blowing on her cold fingers. She stands there looking up at the sky, her lips moving as if she's talking to herself – or maybe the heavens themselves. I can't catch the words above the blustering wind. Then she closes her eyes, her face crinkling in pain. A pain I recognize – one I've seen before.

I've been watching her these past few days and this is a face she's kept hidden beneath the scowl of defiance and indifference.

I wonder what it is that has hurt her. Whether it's her very existence – a nothing girl who's endured the hardships of the Slate Quarter. Or whether it's something more.

She drags her eyes from the sky and, with a heave of her shoulders, leans against the heavy door of the tower and steps inside.

I hesitate for a moment – she's safely home, there is no need for me to follow her any further. I pass inside, following behind her as together we climb the narrow staircase. She trails the fingertips of her right hand over the rough wall as she climbs, humming a tune under her breath that I don't know. Her voice is soft – would her touch be as soft? As gentle?

I trail my own fingers over the path of hers, catching only a glimpse of the feel of the stone through the thick leather of my gloves.

We climb right to the top of the tower. There are two doors off the landing and she stops at the first and raps her knuckles quietly against the woodwork. A male voice from within instructs her to enter and jealousy erupts out of nowhere and charges through my body. I want to grab her by the arm and tug her away. I want to batter my way into that room and strike whoever waits inside.

But then as quickly as the red mist rises, it disperses. The boy who waits inside is her friend. Harmless, pathetic. No challenge to us.

Tracking inside to listen to her conversation with her friend is unnecessary and contemptuous. It is also tempting beyond belief and so I slip inside the room with her, careful not to let my body brush up against hers, and linger in the corner of the room. It is as bare and cold as I predicted – almost no furniture and the few pieces that there are, old and worn.

The boy sits on his bed reading a book and the girl comes to sit on the end, tucking her feet up under her and wrapping part of his blanket over her lap.

The boy closes his book and rests it down on the mattress, eyeing the girl with interest.

"I didn't think you'd be home tonight," he says, leaning forward eagerly. "What happened?"

She shrugs. "Not much."

"Uh uh." He wags his finger at her. "Don't pretend like you don't want to tell me when you're here knocking on my door. Come on, out with it, spill the beans."

"You'll be disappointed. Nothing much happened. They locked me in the kitchen all evening while they went partying with their friends."

"You're kidding me?"

"They're shadow weavers," she says with contempt. "What did you expect?"

"Something more interesting than that," he says, flopping back against the metal bars of the bed frame. "You haven't even got a collar. Did they change their minds about the whole thing after all?"

"Unfortunately, no," she examines her fingernails,

biting at one, "and Beaufort offered me their collar. I refused it."

"Ahhh," the boy says, grinning, "so something did happen."

"Not really. Besides, it's clear they're in disagreement about me being their thrall."

"Really?"

"Thorne Cadieux wants nothing to do with me. He looks at me like I've rolled around in shit."

"You do smell pretty bad."

The girl rolls her eyes, and he tilts his head. "You're not telling me the whole story. I notice someone fixed your nose."

"Beaufort."

"That's becoming a habit."

She touches her nose and frowns. "I hate him. I hate them all. I don't want anything to do with them."

"And do you think they'll give a shit about what you want?"

She scoffs. "No, shadow weavers, remember? When have they ever cared about anyone but themselves?"

I stare at her face. There's none of that pain now. Just bitterness and hatred, pure hatred.

I've always been led to believe that the subjects from the other Quarters love us – that they admire and revere us. The shadow weavers. The beings that keep the realm peaceful, that protect us from the dangers and the threats.

My assumptions have only been confirmed since we arrived at the academy. The other students have looked at us with awe and admiration, have practically kissed the earth we've walked on.

Any other student would probably give the life of their own grandmother to take the girl's place and be our thrall.

But not her. She doesn't want it. She doesn't want us.
She hates us.
I slink away.
Not us, me.
The monster.

Chapter Twenty-Eight

B riony

The next day sees our first lesson with Madame Bardin.

To my surprise, Fly is twitchy as hell about it.

"What's wrong with you?" I ask, as we walk along the pathways towards her classroom, Fly biting his nails down to the nub.

"We got on her wrong side right from day one, Cupcake. I have a bad feeling about this."

"You really think she's going to be that bad?"

"I've heard some girl talked back to her and she turned them into a rat."

"That sounds like a rumor," I say skeptically, then seeing the fear on Fly's face add, "Forever?"

"For a week."

"Ahh, well," I say.

"You'd like to be a rat for five minutes, let alone a whole week?" he screeches.

"No, I suppose not."

After Fly's warning, I was kind of expecting Madame Bardin's classroom to be similar to Professor Tudor's – down in some torture chamber somewhere. Or, considering the nature of her discipline, some kind of laboratory with boiling test tubes and simmering vessels. It is neither. Her classroom is situated in one of the more ornate academy buildings, and though it is dark and dingy like every other room in the academy, it has a luxurious feel about it: heavy velvet curtains draped around the window, a crystal chandelier suspended from the ceiling and elaborate pieces of art housed in gilded frames hanging on all the walls.

Madame herself wears her usual black gown, heeled boots and red lipstick. Today the gown is particularly low cut and she looks more like she's heading out for a dinner party than about to conduct a lesson.

"Be seated," she says from the front of the room, one hand resting on her hip.

As usual the shadow weavers grab the seats at the front and she greets them all by name, ignoring the rest of us completely.

"Alchemy," she says, when we have all taken our seats, "is an art form, not, as many of you have no doubt been led to believe, a science. Only a truly great creative possesses the vision necessary."

She smiles at the shadow weavers with admiration and they all seem to grow about three inches in front of our eyes.

She's just about to open her mouth to start speaking again, when the classroom door swings backwards and Dray Eros walks through. He has his blazer slung over one shoul-

der, his shirt sleeves yanked up his arms, most of the buttons of his shirt undone and he's chewing gum.

I peer at Fly. Dray Eros hasn't been in any of our classes so far but this one he seems to be joining.

He slides his hand through his long white hair, ruffling it so it's even messier, and, ignoring everyone else in the room, strides towards a desk at the front of the room. He glares at the boy already occupying the seat, and the boy hops up immediately, scampering to the back of the classroom without a word of complaint. Dray slings his jacket onto the back of his chair, and flops down into the now vacant seat.

Everyone in the classroom gapes at him.

Madame Bardin has a notorious reputation. Madame Bardin made it clear on the very first day that she won't tolerate tardiness.

I wait for her to unleash this temper we've all heard so much about. Or at the very least give him a taste of her wicked tongue.

Instead, she gazes at the latecomer as if he is sunshine itself, forcibly dragging her eyes away from him to reconnect with the rest of us.

"However," she continues as if there was no interruption at all, walking through the rows of desks, "there are some acts of alchemy that don't require creativity or magic. Acts that even the most pathetic of you should be able to manage." She peers at me and the other Slate Quarter students huddled at the back of the classroom, pressing her hand to her stomach like the sight of us all makes her physically sick.

"And so," she says, waving her hand through the air, small cauldrons appearing on the desks in front of us, "today we will see if you are indeed capable of brewing such concoctions." She clicks her fingers and a pile of ingredients plus a piece of paper with a list of instructions appear by our pots. "You will work in silence. Begin."

I peer down at my equipment. The cauldron is cracked all down one side. The metal utensils are bent out of shape and I'm pretty sure most of these ingredients are rotten. Around me the other students are looking just as doubtful. One boy raises his hand.

"Is there a problem?" Madame Bardin asks sweetly, her mouth curved into a pleasant smile. However, her magic hisses and swirls around her, and the boy leans away and shakes his head.

Madame strolls back to the front of the classroom, immediately engaging in conversation with the shadow weavers. I see their equipment looks brand new and made of far more advanced materials. Their ingredients also look fresher and there are a lot more of them.

I check my list; yep, I don't have half the things we're meant to. I'm guessing we're being set up to fail here.

I shrug off my own blazer, pull back my sleeves and follow the instructions, improvising and adapting as best I can. Every so often I can't help gazing to the front. Most of the shadow weavers are half heartedly stirring cauldrons, or dumping ingredients into their pots, using their magic to mix and simmer the concoction.

Madame Bardin sashays around their desks, lending guidance and advice, leaning into them as she does, her hands resting on their shoulders, or stroking down their arms.

Maybe she's just a tactile person, but it doesn't seem entirely appropriate, especially the way she lingers over

Dray, leaning right over him and offering him a flash of her impressive cleavage.

Discomfort bubbles in my stomach. Is that jealousy? Am I jealous?

No, definitely not. I hardly know Dray Eros. And what I've seen of him, I don't like. Arrogant and self-conceited.

As if he hears these very thoughts in my head, he turns right around in his seat and rewards me with one of those infuriating winks of his. A wink that makes my knees involuntarily weak.

How the hell does he do that? How does he succeed in making one look so devastating?

I avert my gaze and spend the rest of the lesson with my eyes fixed on my concoction. The instructions say we should have formed a thick treacle that can be used for healing wounds. Mine is a thin liquid that smells of pig shit.

Madame Bardin struts around inspecting each of our results and informing us in no uncertain terms that we are stupid, untalented and beyond hope. All of us except the shadow weavers of course. The praise she heaps on them is almost embarrassing and I can't get out of the classroom fast enough, even if I do find Dray Eros lingering by the exit waiting for me.

He leans with his back and one boot against the wall, chewing his gum languidly. When he sees me his eyes light up and he pushes off the wall and shoves Fly to one side, taking the position next to me.

"Caught you looking, little thrall," he says.

I keep my gaze trained ahead. "I don't know what you're talking about."

"You don't, huh?" He chuckles, ruffling his hair like he did earlier and letting the locks fall across his face. "Tell me, did you like what you saw?"

I glance towards him and his eyes flick around my face with excitement.

I give him my most unamused and unimpressed look. One I hope conveys my message.

"No," I say firmly, then reaching behind me, I grab Fly and stride away.

Chapter Twenty-Nine

T horne

They have us lined up as usual along the perimeter of the academy, boys on one side, girls on the other, the ancient towers looming behind us and icy mist swirling over the moorland in front of us.

I stand with my brothers at the head of the line, the other shadow weavers right alongside us, and gaze straight ahead, vision lost to the mist, oblivious to the surrounding chatter. Every so often, I swing my head around to peer along the line to where the other students stand and wait, the pathetic forms of the kids from the Slate Quarter right at the end of the line. Eventually I spy her, dressed in the oversized gray tracksuit the other students wear, the sleeves rolled up and her hair, as always, scraped back tight against her scalp. I watch her, my skin seeming to tingle in response to her vicinity, my magic prickling the air.

I ball my hands into fists, lift my chin and stroll down the line.

"Hey," Dray calls out, the amusement clear in his voice. He'll never understand me, just like I'll never understand him. "Where you going?"

I don't reply. I walk the line, glaring into the face of every student I pass. Several step backwards in alarm, others drop their eyes to the floor.

When I reach the girl, I halt and spin back around to face the students. No one has missed my march down the line. Everybody is watching.

"Listen up," I bellow, using the magic in my veins to amplify my voice. And they listen. They listen because I rarely speak. "This girl here," I jab my finger at her, "she's ours." I don't look at her face. I don't need to. I can imagine she's scowling. Maybe even about to argue with me. I don't give her the chance. "She's our thrall and under our protection."

"I don't see no collar," some wiseass mutters under his breath, probably thinking I wouldn't hear.

I shoot my arm out in front of me, sending shadows soaring his way. They strike him on the chest, wrapping him in a darkness that squeezes the air from his lungs and has him choking. I leave him spluttering and groaning and address the crowd.

"If anyone harms one hair on her head – if you so much as touch her belongings, look at her funny, mutter under your goddamn breath in her direction, I will sear the fucking flesh off your bones and scatter what's left of you out there for the ravens to feast on."

I lower my arm and slowly the shadows retreat from the boy writhing on the floor and gasping for air, back into my body.

Then I march right back up the line and reclaim my place beside my brothers.

"That was fucking dramatic," Dray mumbles.

"It was fucking necessary," I hiss.

The girl is ours and no one touches her.

Chapter Thirty

B riony

My cheeks blaze hot as I watch Thorne Cadieux march back up the line to his own kind.

The man has said not one word to me, has stubbornly avoided making eye contact with me, making it abundantly clear that while Beaufort may have chosen me as their thrall, he isn't happy about it. In fact, he despises the idea.

And yet, here he is declaring to the entire academy that I am theirs, that he'll kill anyone who harms me.

Which just goes to show how out of touch and dumb these men are. Do they have no idea how the real world works? No idea that saying all that bullshit grew the target on my back tenfold? Everyone seems to hate me already, now they'll hate me even more.

I can hear them whispering all around me and taste the animosity in the air.

Hot tears of frustration prickle behind my eyes and it takes all my strength not to give into them.

"Is everything okay?" Clare whispers in my ear, sliding up alongside me.

I shake my head. I'm too darn frustrated to speak. That and I don't trust my voice not to break.

"What's wrong?" she asks.

What's wrong? *What's wrong?!*

What's wrong is that nothing is working out the way I planned.

I want to melt into the background and disappear and now there is no doubt that everyone knows who I am.

I want to stay as far away from shadow weavers as I can and yet three of the most powerful want me as theirs. Even Thorne, who I was convinced disliked me.

I want to hate and despise them with every bone in my body and yet, I can't deny I feel some strange attraction to them. One that whispers through my body whenever they're close to me.

Dray outside the classroom. Thorne just now standing next to me in front of the line.

Why?

They represent everything I loathe.

The gruesome twosome come striding out onto the field, whistles hanging around their necks, sinister smiles pinned on their faces.

"We're racing again," the slightly taller one declares. There's some moaning. My legs still ache from the last run and I bet I'm not the only one.

"Gentlemen first today," his twin declares before blowing his whistle.

I stand alongside Clare and watch as the men race away

into the mist, Beaufort, Thorne and Dray at the front of the pack, fast, powerful and agile.

If I didn't know they were bond brothers, the closest of friends, I'd never have guessed it. Their demeanors and their looks are so different. Beaufort smart and pristine, his hair styled perfectly, his tracksuit zipped right the way up to his neck, his gait controlled and powerful.

Dray's appearance is so laid back, it's verging on horizontal. His tracksuit hangs open and his shoelaces are untied. However, despite the casual persona, there's an eagerness in the way he runs, an excitement, an energy that can't be contained.

Thorne is impossible to read. His face is blank most of the time and though he looks more put together than Dray, there's still a scruffiness to him – stubble covering his cheeks and chin, his hair shorn in that haphazard manner. And then there are those gloves he always wears, like he doesn't even want his hands to give him away.

In a couple of seconds, all three are lost to the mist. It's so thick today, it's like pea soup, swallowing them up into its depths.

I wonder how the hell we'll find our way through.

I guess I'm about to find out because in the next minute, the whistle is blown again and we're off.

"You don't have to run with me," Clare says, her cheeks already puffing and her face red.

"It's fine. I'd like the company. Unless," I say, "you're worried running with me might land you in trouble."

"Are you kidding?" she pants, "after what Thorne Cadieux just did, no one will ever touch you again."

"Hmmm," I say, "I'm not so sure about that."

"If you'd accepted the collar," she says, stumbling slightly, "you'd definitely be safe."

"How is a collar any different from Thorne's warning?"

"Well, it has magical properties I guess," Clare says musing on the question.

I slow my pace, so she can catch me again. "Magical properties?"

"Yeah, I mean, I don't know what they are exactly, but they protect the thrall from danger."

"Bullshit, I bet there is no magic."

"That's what people ..." she raises her hand, struggling to catch her breath, "say. Honestly, Briony, please just go ahead, trying to keep up with you is going to kill me."

"Really? I'm going slow."

She gives me a little push. "Please just go."

I blow her a kiss and leave her to suffer in peace, picking up the pace and racing through the mist and across the moorland, hoping I am running in the right direction. It certainly *feels* like I am.

The air is dank and cold, the tip of my nose and my toes freezing, but it feels good to be out here, pummeling the earth with space to think.

I'm so damn irritated about last night, seething about that bullshit display just now and confused, really damn confused. A confusion I can't even understand, that I can't pinpoint.

I need to find a way out of this situation. Trashing the Princes' kitchen didn't work, being bratty and bitchy didn't work either. I need a better plan. I just haven't come up with one yet. One that has them leaving me alone.

The mist is so dense, I don't meet any of the other runners out here, I don't even hear them. It makes me uneasy. It would be damn easy for someone to jump me right now, and, despite Thorne's pretty sinister warning, I'm not sure how the hell he thinks he'd prevent it.

However, I make it right the way to the trees without being attacked. Waiting for me under the first few branches is not a group of girls with vengeance or murder on their minds, but a giant white wolf. Sitting all primly and properly, as if he's been waiting for me. And maybe he has been, because when he spots me, his ears perk up on the top of his head and his tail thumps the ground in excitement, then he's leaping onto all fours and bounding towards me.

"Hello, fellow," I say as he barrels into me. "I didn't think I'd see you again." He licks at my hands. "Come to protect me from those girls? Actually, they haven't been bothering me. It's Odessa I need to worry about," he makes a cute little bark, "yep, she's already tried to kill me and broken my nose and I haven't even been here a week."

I lean over to stroke him and he buries his snout in my crotch and has a good old sniff.

"Yeah, I probably stink. I'm actually in the middle of a run. One I should probably be continuing."

Although the affection – even if it is from a wild wolf who could probably maul me to death at worst, at best will be giving me fleas – is nice, I miss Baxter. I miss our snuggles. I miss how happy he always was to see me. He is the one thing I do miss from home.

Is that why the Princes are having this strange effect on me? A bit of tenderness from Beaufort and my insides seem to be spinning. Is it because it's been so long since anyone touched me like that?

The wolf whines.

"I know," I say with a sigh, "this is nice, huh?" I rub my knuckles against his broad sternum, feeling the compact muscle that lies beneath his fur. "But you probably have a pack for kisses and snuggles. Where are they?"

The wolf slurps his long tongue over my hand, then jumps up and drags his tongue over my face too.

"Okay," I laugh, "maybe just a tad forward. This is only our second date, remember?" I stroke his ears. The wolf obviously doesn't understand, he licks me several more times, then drops back down and buries his snout right between my legs again.

"Jeez," I say, trying to push him away, "that's a bit personal, boy." He keeps his nose at the apex of my thighs, having another good old sniff. His warm breath heats my most intimate of places and then he darts his tongue out and licks there too. "Right," I say, "and now I really do have to go."

He whimpers as if he doesn't like that idea, but then drops down on his stomach and rests his head on his paws. He is a huge scary wolf with razor-sharp teeth and even sharper claws and yet he looks adorable. It is very hard indeed to turn away and start running again.

I don't even bother with the changing rooms this time. I head straight back to my tower, diving into the freezing cold shower in the bathroom and then returning to my room to get changed.

By the time I'm dressed, it's lunchtime. I consider skipping it. Walking into the canteen alone because Fly and Clare are probably already there, is not appealing. Everyone will be gossiping about me. I've been invisible for so long, being thrust into the glaring-hot spotlight like this is alarming to say the least (as well as dangerous). But I'm going to have to suck it up because after that run, I'm famished.

It's worse than I predicted. The canteen falls deadly silent as I enter and you could hear a pin drop – in fact you could hear the head of a pin drop.

Luckily, I have two new friends – who may not be good for snuggles – but can be depended upon to help me out.

"Briony!" Fly calls from across the room. "Over here! We got you some lunch and saved you a seat."

I could lick his face because it's a seat right in the corner which means, although I still have to walk across the canteen with everyone staring, at least I can hide away once seated.

"You're popular," Fly says, with a wink, pushing a bowl of soup towards me as I take the spare seat.

"I'm not sure that's what I'd call it."

Clare gazes around the room. "I don't understand why more people aren't sucking up to you."

"Yeah," Fly agrees, "Odessa, Julian and Gillian all have little bands of adoring fans."

"I have you," I say, smirking.

"Cupcake, don't get a big head. We adore you, obviously, but not in an unhealthy or self-serving sycophancy way."

"Trust me, I'm not getting big-headed. Although, I do have one fan."

"You do?" Clare says, pushing her glasses up her nose, her face still flushed from the run.

"Yep," I say, unable to stop from smiling, "although he's a little unusual. Not strictly a student."

"Oh my god!" Fly gasps, hands flying to his mouth, "a teacher?"

"No," I say, "a wolf."

Fly's hands fall away from his mouth and my two new friends stare at me, unblinking.

"A wolf?" Fly says flatly. "What kind of wolf?"

"I have no idea," I say, moving lumps of vegetables around my bowl with my spoon. "He lives out in the forest.

Today's run is the second time I've met him. The first time he saved me from an ambush. He's really friendly."

"I bet he is," Fly mutters.

"What does he look like exactly?" Clare asks, eyes flicking to Fly.

"He's gorgeous. Really beautiful. And big for a wolf. There are wild wolves out in Slate Quarter. Sometimes when the weather is really bitter, they venture closer to the town. They are always quite scrawny. This wolf, he's huge, and his coat is like snow – pure white."

"Oh Briony," Fly says, dropping his cutlery down on the table.

"What?" I say. "I like animals, okay? And he wasn't aggressive. He made me feel safe."

Fly and Clare exchange glances again. "Should I tell her or should you?" Fly says.

"I will," Clare adjusts her glasses. "Briony. He isn't a wolf."

"I know what a wolf looks like, Clare."

"There are no wild wolves out here in this part of the realm," Clare says. "There haven't been for hundreds of years."

"Well, you can ask the girls who tried to ambush me. I'm not seeing things."

"He's not a wolf. He's a shifter," Clare says.

"And by the sounds of things, Dray Eros," Fly adds.

I nearly spit my mouthful of soup out across the table.

"What?!" I shake my head. "No ... no ..."

"Yes," Fly says. "Possibly one of the other shifters but I've heard Dray's wolf is pure white like you described."

"But ... But ... he sniffed my crotch," I mumble, my face now as flushed as Clare's. "Oh my stars, he licked it!"

Fly roars with laughter. "That perverted son of a bitch."

"I don't think you should call him that," Clare whispers nervously.

"Well, he is!" I say pushing my unfinished bowl away. I no longer have an appetite. "I can't believe that was him." I groan and bury my face in my hands. "I petted him like a dog."

Fly keeps right on laughing. "I bet he loved that."

"Why was he even in his wolf form?"

"I guess he likes to run that way," Clare says.

"And are there other shifters?"

"I hear there are a handful among the shadow weavers. All of them male. There are no female shifters in this year group."

"And ... are they all wolves or are you going to tell me that raven that nearly shit on my head this morning was also some asshole shadow weaver?"

"As far as I know, only wolf shifters, but I guess, in theory, there could be others." She chews on a piece of bread. "Although not the ravens. They belong to the academy – story goes they've been here since the first foundation was laid."

"They give me the creeps," I say.

"Me too," Fly agrees. He shivers, then begins to chuckle again. "I can't believe you got it on with a wolf."

"I did not get it on with a wolf."

"That is definitely how rumors start," Clare warns.

Chapter Thirty-One

B riony

We're due another lesson down in the dungeons after lunch and I don't know how I feel about it. Part of me is excited to see Fox Tudor again. He knew my sister. He remembers her. He may know what happened to her. He may have information.

Then again there's something about him which makes the hair on the back of my neck stand on end. He's so different from how he was before. Is that the academy? Has it slowly worn him down – made him that bitter, grouchy man? I don't see why. I've never heard of someone from the Slate Quarter being awarded a job at the academy. I also had no idea Fox Tudor – the golden boy from our Quarter– had magical abilities; strong magical abilities. You'd think news like that would be all over Slate Quarter.

As we shuffle into his classroom later that afternoon, he's hanging back, lingering in the shadows once again, almost invisible. I strain my eyes to try and make him out but all I seem to see is his eyes glowing in the darkness.

"Why'd you think he keeps hidden?" Fly whispers into my ear. "Do you think he's some hideous beast with boils and weeping sores?"

"Anything but," I mumble. Fly peers at me with curiosity but he doesn't get a chance to quiz me.

"Sit," the professor commands us all. I grab my space on the bench beside Fly. I'm way more invested in this lesson than I was before. About a million times more. Fox Tudor was special back home – talented, good-looking, popular. But he was just an ordinary boy from ordinary parents. Just like me. Just like my sister. And yet somehow he has the ability to weave the shadows.

In the previous lesson, everyone was so determined that shadow weaving power could only be inherited. And yet a boy from the Slate Quarter has that power.

"Last lesson," he says, "we talked about feeling for the ability to wield shadows in your blood. This week we are going to see if any of you can find that ability and can use it."

Just like last time, there is more groaning from the shadow weavers in the front row.

"Can't we be excused from this bullshit?" one of them asks. He's one of Odessa's protectors and I think his name is Kratos.

"You have no desire to help your fellow subjects identify such a power?"

"What's the point? We all know those losers don't have any."

"The realm can always benefit from more shadow weavers," the professor continues. "If there is even one among the students, we can not afford to miss them. After all, the safety and stability of our realm depends on it, does it not?" To my ears, his voice appears to drip with sarcasm. But maybe that's just me, because everyone else nods enthusiastically like this is the gospel truth. "Pair up," he instructs, "and listen to my instructions."

"Wanna be my buddy?" I ask Fly.

"Hmmm," he says, scratching his chin, "you smell a lot like wet dog." He winks at me. "Or is that wolf?" he whispers.

I elbow him in the ribs. "Beggars can't be choosers."

"Fine," he says, teasing me. "But if you do have any shadow weaving abilities, do not blast me with them."

I smile half heartedly. "As if."

"When you're ready," the professor snaps, and I can't help but spin round in my seat to face the front.

"The first and hardest step is to beckon the shadows out of your blood and into the air. Once you've conquered this part, wielding the shadows is relatively easy in comparison, although some have more skill in it than others."

"Beckoning the shadows from your blood is not hard," one of the Smyte twins sniffs. "It's as easy as breathing."

"Did I ask for your opinion, Miss Smyte? I'm not sure what gave you the impression I'm at all interested in it." Next to me, Fly snorts in amusement. "For a shadow weaver who has been wielding all their life it may be easy. But for a shadow weaver who has never done this before, it is the most challenging first step."

"How do we do it then?" a girl from the back row asks.

"If you have a question," the professor says with irritation, "raise your hand." The girl hesitates, looks around, then lifts her arm. "Yes?" the professor says, and the girl repeats her question. "It isn't something I can instruct. If you have the ability, you will have to work that out for yourself." Another two hands shoot up into the air. "Enough discussion!" he booms, making us all quake in our seats. "Work with your partner. See if you can achieve this."

Of course, the shadow weavers don't need to work at it. They're chucking shadowy balls of magic up into the air and lounging about on the benches, yawning and otherwise being obnoxious.

It's pretty intimidating for the rest of us, especially when they start to heckle us from the front row. Something the professor ignores. In fact, if his presence wasn't so oppressive I'd assume he'd left the classroom all together.

"Oh my stars," one of the twins drawls, "look how pathetic they are."

"They really think they can do this," her sister replies. "It's so pathetic. They're so desperate to be like us."

"Not going to happen, losers," Kratos calls out.

"If the professor was actually serious about finding shadow weavers among us," I mutter to Fly in frustration, "he could at least give us a fighting chance and tell these idiots to shut up."

My hands still raised in front of me where I've been trying to 'feel' the goddamn shadows, I peer towards the front of the classroom.

I catch the glint of the professor's eyes in the darkness, and if it wasn't so ridiculous, I'd bet my next five dinners he was staring right at me. I hold his gaze in mine for a fraction of time, and I wasn't joking about his presence being oppressive. It's powerful and dominant and I have to look away before something inside me explodes.

I turn my attention back to my friend.

"Why would he waste his time?" Fly says in response to my question. "They're right, aren't they? None of us can weave shadows. It's pointless."

"But ..." I glance back towards the shadows. Does nobody else but me know who he really is? Where he comes from? And why doesn't he tell them all? Prove to them that shadow weavers can come from the shittiest of places – even the Slate Quarter. "Why are we even bothering then?" I slap my hands down into my lap. "I'm giving up."

"Miss Storm," the voice booms from beyond. "Did I instruct you to stop?"

"No, you didn't," I reply. "I made the decision myself."

A stunned silence grips the classroom. I'm guessing it's pretty shocking to hear one of the ordinaries talk back to a teacher. Especially an ordinary from the Slate Quarter.

"I beg your pardon," he says quietly, his voice full of venom, venom that has me trembling.

Yeah, maybe I'm not feeling so brave about that little quip. But I've stuck my neck out now and my stubborn streak always gets the better of me.

"I said, I decided to stop. I can't do it. There's no point in continuing."

"You always give up so easily, do you?"

His words hit me square in the chest. I lift my chin. "No."

"Urgh," one of the twins says from the front, "can you believe her? It's because the Princes have chosen her as their thrall. She now thinks she's someone special. That she can go round doing what she wants and saying what she thinks. That's not how being a thrall works, Slate scum."

I have to say, despite what I told Clare, I'm a little taken aback by the Smyte twin's boldness. She just insulted me to my face. Not whispered words out in the middle of nowhere with no witnesses. No, words uttered in a classroom full of students. She's obviously not afraid of Thorne Cadieux. Or perhaps she believes herself to be untouchable. A belief that is probably fact.

"A ... a ... a ... thrall?" the professor says, sounding utterly confounded. "Her?"

"I know. What the hell are those men thinking?" the other twin sniffs, throwing me her most evil of looks.

"But she has no collar?" He sounds just as astounded. Is he worried about offending me and by proxy, the Princes? And if he is, why? He's a professor. A powerful shadow weaver. They're only students – okay they are shadow weavers too, and, from what people tell me, they come from powerful families, but I can't imagine Fox Tudor being cowed by anyone. Not then and certainly not now.

Henrietta shrugs.

"Thrall to the Princes?" he repeats.

"Yes," she says.

"No," I say, meeting his glowing eyes across the distance.

There are some shocked gasps in the classroom and beside me Fly groans, then whispers, "Briony, don't. It isn't going to end well."

But I don't care. They've had their little shows of public declarations. Now it's my turn. I am not their thrall. I've never agreed to it.

I wait to be interrogated further but I'm saved by the tower bell signaling the end of the lesson.

Like everyone else, I go to gather up my belongings.

"Miss Storm, please stay behind. I'd like a word."

"Oh shit," Fly whispers.

I shrug like I'm not afraid of the professor. Would I have

been afraid of Fox Tudor? Probably – sure he was charming but I've learned many times that charming can be deceptive. I would still have been wary of him. Now he's an intimidating professor who likes to lurk in the shadows, I am definitely afraid of him plus the punishment he is likely to dole out for answering back. I try my best not to show it though, waiting on the bench for all the other students to leave with that same passive expression glued to my face.

The heavy door slams behind the last student and, I concede, I'm more than just scared; I'm terrified.

The professor steps out of the shadows and into the feeble light of the lamps, moving across the stone floor silently until he's standing before the first row of benches.

He's as pale as before, his eyes that strange glowing color, but just as strikingly handsome as before, his suit just as immaculate.

"Why does Henrietta Smyte believe you to be the Princes' thrall, while you deny it?"

My brow creases in confusion. I thought I was going to receive a berating, not a further grilling. Although, perhaps, the grilling is to help determine whether he should proceed with the berating.

"I'm not denying anything. I simply don't agree with the statement."

"That you are their thrall?" I nod. "Then why would Henrietta believe otherwise?"

He stands with his hands on his hips in a menacing fashion and even though he's several feet away, he still seems to crowd over me.

I stare into those strange eyes of his. I have questions of my own and maybe if I'm a little more cooperative he might help me. Then again, this is the one topic designed to rile me up.

"Why? Does it matter?"

He's a little taken aback by that, burying his hands in his pant pockets. Then he collects himself.

"How about I ask the questions and you answer them like a good student?"

"And if I don't want to?" I say, unable to help myself, despite how afraid of him I am.

I've been afraid before, very sure I'm in for a beating. Even when I've known it to be foolish, there have been times when my mouth just can't help from running.

He pulls back the first row bench, sliding it easily despite how heavy it must be and seats himself down in front of me, resting his forearms on his thighs and leaning in closer.

"You have a sharp tongue for a girl from the Slate shit-holes ... you're different from her." His glowing eyes skip across my face. "Although you have the same hair. Of course, she always wore it down."

I sit up straighter, shuffling forward on the bench. "So you do remember her? Were you here at the academy when she was here?"

A slow smirk forms on his plush lips. I've walked straight into a trap. "How about you answer my questions and then I'll consider answering yours?"

I sigh and lean away from him. Can I trust him? I don't think I should be trusting anyone. I suspect Amelia failed to keep her own secrets guarded and look what happened to her.

Fox remembers that Amelia and I looked alike, but then again, we were sisters, that could be a lucky guess. Is he dangling this titbit in front of me as a way of persuading me to talk when really he has no information at all?

I try to read his face. I can't tell. He's like a closed book.

"It's simple really," I tell him. "They want me to be their thrall. I don't want to be."

The smirk fades from his face and his expression hardens.

"Why?"

"Professor," I whisper, "if you knew my sister you'd know why."

He holds my gaze unblinking and I can't read if he's bluffing or not.

"I mean," he says finally, "why do they want you as their thrall?"

"I ... I honestly don't know."

"There must be a reason." Maybe if I was some other girl – one who hasn't been dragged here from the shithole of Slate Quarter, one with abilities and talents, connections and personality, beauty and sex appeal, I'd be a little affronted at the fact the professor can't understand why they have chosen me. But I know what I am.

"I'm as mystified by it as you are."

He nods, his eyes sliding over my face again like he's trying to see under my skin to the girl beneath.

"You don't have to accept," he growls. "There are no rules which dictate a thrall is obliged to take up the position."

"That's not what everyone else seems to think."

"People think a lot of things that are false. It is your choice."

He doesn't need to tell me that.

He stands up as if that is the end of the conversation, but I haven't forgotten our bargain.

"You didn't answer my question before. Were you here when Amelia was here?"

"I wasn't."

"But do you know what happened to her?"

"No," he says decisively, but this time there's a slip, one I can't quite describe – a flash of something I find hard to recall once it's passed. Was it a flash of the eyes? A twitch of his cheek? I don't recall. I just know he's lying.

Chapter Thirty-Two

F^{ox}

The girl slams the door closed behind her.

I let my head tilt backwards and I inhale, the air sliding through my mouth, down my throat and deep into my lungs.

I groan.

The girl smells like sin. Like everything I've tried to forget. Delicious, succulent, gratifying.

I run my tongue over my teeth and then my lips, catching just a taste of her in the air.

Fuck, I'd like to taste her for real.

Fuck, I've been dreaming of it ever since that first fucking lesson.

I'd hoped my mind had deceived me – that her scent wasn't as tantalizing as I remembered; that I'd made it more than it was in my mind.

But it's more tantalizing. Tempting. Troublesome.

I groan again, flip my head forward and scrub my hands down my face.

I need to get a grip.

I can't be sniffing the air like some obsessive hunting dog – even if the urge to hunt her down is strong and real.

I snap up onto my feet and march to the back of my classroom. There's a door at the back, hidden in the gloom and I pass through into my private quarters.

It's not much of a living quarters: a bedroom and a room for study. It's still a lot grander, much bigger and more refined than anything I had back home.

Home.

Even the word makes something in my long ago dead heart pang – despite the time that's passed, despite the hell-hole that place was.

One wall of my study is dominated by a bookcase – a piece of furniture they say belonged to one of the first scholars at the academy. It reaches from the floor right up to the low stone ceiling and on its shelves are the volumes I've collected, the bottles of potions I've brewed and the artifacts I've accumulated.

I don't need to search for the book. I reach up and drag it down from the shelves, letting its well-worn pages fall open on my desk.

The girl.

Not just any girl.

Amelia Storm's sister.

I remember Amelia vaguely from home – see her face in her sister's. I was gone by the time Amelia joined the academy, but I recognize the name. Why? Why do I recognize that name?

Something happened to her. Something unusual.

Why the hell would the Princes want her little sister for their thrall? Why would they want Briony?

Is it because they know?

I wipe at my brow.

No, that's impossible. They couldn't possibly. There must be another reason. The Princes could have any girl or boy they wanted. They are the most powerful shadow weavers in this year's intake – fuck, they're probably some of the most powerful shadow weavers in the entire realm with wealth, privilege and connections too.

Why would they choose somebody from the weakest Quarter of all?

The book on my desk lists every student that has passed through the academy, where they came from and to what Quarter they were assigned at the end of the year. It also records any major or unusual events that occurred during the year, school prizes, and school records.

Amelia Storm is several years younger than me. I flip to the year I spent in the academy. Without intending to, I let my eye stray down to my own record and the picture that rests by my name. It makes me gasp. It's been a long time since I stared at my own face. I was so young back then, so confident, so hopeful. I believed the world would see my fucking brilliance and reward me accordingly. Fuck, I was naïve and stupid, like every other kid that passes through here. Deluded, they are all deluded – happy to swallow the dreams the realm feeds them whole.

Not Briony though.

Something tells me she isn't blinded by all the promises. Something tells me she sees through it all.

I look at my face with a detachment – like the boy staring back at me is a stranger, not me at all. They said I was beautiful. Maybe if I hadn't been, maybe if I'd owned more of an ordinary face, none of this would have happened.

I drag my gaze away from that picture and flip forward through the book, running my eyes down each year group, searching for an Amelia Storm.

I find her four years later in the records, right at the end of the listings of students.

I was right about her face, about her hair. She wears it loose about her shoulders, flowing in waves. She's beautiful. Eyes full of hope like mine were. Not hard like her sister's.

I read the details printed by her name. Details of her parents are given – Annie, a housewife. Furgus, a laborer at one of the factories. Home: the low district of Slate Quarter – out on the outskirts, near the forest. The shittiest part of the shittiest place in the realm.

As I expected then, no money, no name – not even back in Slate Quarter.

My gaze slips over the words and then I halt.

The next few details have been scrubbed out of the book. Information about this girl was added and then removed – the words blacked out with shadow magic – impossible to read. My eyes continue along the line and then halt again. There's one more detail that has been added about the girl's sister. One detail that remains. This has not been scrubbed out.

Amelia Storm died at the academy nine years ago.

Chapter Thirty-Three

B riony

A note hangs from a pin on my door, one from Fly telling me they're hanging out in Clare's room. I check my bag at the bottom of my wardrobe. I change out of my uniform and into my own clothes, then jog down the staircase, peering up at the clock tower as I step outside. There's another hour until dinner time and another two until I'm meant to be back at the Princes' rooms.

I haven't decided if I'm going there tonight. I don't think Beaufort's threat of dragging me there kicking and screaming was an empty one, but I don't like my hand being forced. I suspect my best bet is to keep turning up. Keep being a brat, a disobedient little thrall and eventually they'll give up. Because I'm certain my resolve is tougher than theirs. I wasn't the one born with a silver spoon in my mouth after all. I've had it a lot tougher than those dudes and that has to count for something.

Clare has an old gramophone set up in her room, and when I step inside I find my two new friends poring over her record collection, discussing musicians, singers and bands I've never heard of. Not that we didn't have music out in Slate Quarter but few people could afford a luxury like a gramophone or a radio – certainly not us who could barely afford bread or the mounting bills my father racked up at the tavern.

"Hey," Fly says, as I settle down on the rug beside them both. "You're still in one piece then? I was worried he'd chain you to the wall and break pieces off you."

"You really talked back to Professor Tudor?" Clare says in wonderment. "You're crazy. That man is terrifying – and you can tell that just from his voice."

"The shadow weavers talk back to him all the time," I point out.

"Yeah," Fly says, "because they know no teacher will ever truly punish them. Not when their parents will be here in a flash causing all sorts of shitstorms."

I shrug. "I'm not sure Professor Tudor would be intimidated by any parents."

"Yeah, but I bet he's intimidated by Madame Bardin. And she does care what the parents think."

"You think he's intimidated by Madame Bardin?"

"Fuck yes," Fly says, shivering, "doesn't she give you the creeps?"

"There's something about her," Clare agrees. "Like she could suck out your soul."

"So what punishment did he dole out?" Fly asks, searching my body for any obvious signs of injury.

"None, he, erm, wanted to talk."

"Talk? What about?" Clare asks.

"The thrall business. It seems he at least is in agreement with me. He says there is no obligation for me to accept my fate as a thrall."

"So you're still sticking to that decision, huh?" Clare says, carefully slipping a record back inside its paper case. "Despite Thorne Cadieux's speech."

"Yep."

Clare stares at me and shakes her head. "I really can't see how this is going to turn out."

"You can't?" Fly rolls over onto his back and leans down on his elbows. "Then you haven't had much experience of shadow weavers, because I'm telling you, they always win out, no matter what."

"You have then?" I ask him. "Had experience with shadow weavers?" He's never mentioned that before. We definitely haven't spoken about it.

"Yeah, they come to our realm occasionally to inspect the troops, or watch the athletic tournaments we put on for them periodically. My mom and dad would often host them for an evening or a dinner – something like that."

"Your parents must be someone special," Clare observes. Fly flicks his gaze to mine then peers down at the floor.

"I guess they are."

"Then–" I start.

"Why doesn't that extend to me?" He smiles ironically. "Like I told you before, I didn't turn out like they wanted. But not to worry, they have two other sons that did."

"That kinda sucks," Clare says.

"I bet your parents are proud of you," Fly says and I can detect the smallest drop of bitterness in his tone.

Clare buffs one of the records with the end of her

sleeve, removing several smudged fingerprints. "Well, yes, I guess they are."

Fly sighs. "That must be nice."

"It is," she says halfheartedly.

"But?" I prompt.

She glances at us sheepishly. "It also comes with a ton of pressure. They're expecting great things from me here in the academy. They like to tell me that frequently."

"I'm not sure mine would care if I never came back," Fly mumbles.

"How about you, Briony?" Clare asks softly.

"Would mine care if I came home or not? Hmmm." I pick up one of the records and examine the decorative case. "My dad would maybe – that's if he's even noticed I've gone in the first place. My stepmom ... I don't know." My first instinct is to think she must be pleased to be rid of me, an extra mouth to feed. Then again, perhaps she misses her punchbag and her little slave, and I never got a lot to eat anyway.

"Your stepmom?" Clara says. "What happened to your real mom?"

"She died. A long time ago."

"I'm sorry," Clare says.

"Don't be. It was so long ago, I never even knew her."

Fly picks a record from the pile. "This one," he says. "It's Saturday night. We need something to lighten the mood."

I can't help feeling he's right because, despite all my protests I know I have very little choice but to show up once again at the Princes' tower and I am not looking forward to it.

No, not one bit.

This time I don't care what Fly and Clare say, I am not getting all dressed up just so I can sit around on my own in the Princes' kitchen. In fact, this time I'm going for the complete opposite effect.

My uniform.

I hope it will say, 'I care about you so little I couldn't even be bothered to get changed.'

Although I wonder if the uniform is as awful as I thought it was, because when Beaufort Lincoln opens the door to me this evening, his eyes snake all the way down my body lingering at the flash of bare thigh between my long socks and my skirt. And I don't know why but that has something fluttering low in my belly.

"I like the outfit, sweetheart." I frown. "You're on time," he says with a smug grin that has me wanting to smack him in the face.

"Not willingly."

"Yeah," he says, taking my hand in his and pulling me inside. As always, his magic tingles against my skin sending those butterflies in my stomach crazy. I try to snatch my hand away but he hangs on to it tightly. "Willingly or not, you're still here."

Unsurprisingly, he leads me back into the kitchen. Is this the only place I'm going to be permitted?

I guess so. I am Slate Quarter scum after all. Not worthy enough to enter any of the other rooms.

A pout forms on my face. I wasn't wrong about these men, about who they are and what they are capable of. Just because Beaufort has been gentle with me so far, means nothing. He's playing with me, leading me into a false sense of security. As soon as he's ready, he'll crush me. Just like the shadow weavers always do with us commoners.

"Seeing as you enjoyed our food so much last time," he continues, "we thought we'd arrange something a little more special this time."

I peer across at the table and can't help but gasp. A feast has been spread across the table; not only the cold meats, cheeses and breads that were here last time but pies and pastries and an array of sweet-looking desserts I've never seen before. In fact, I think there may be chocolate – actual chocolate.

Dray Eros stands by the table munching on something that looks like a pork pie. It's the first time I've seen him since I discovered the true identity of that wolf and my cheeks burn with embarrassment.

"Hey, little thrall," he says, "wanna come a little closer and sample our goodies?"

I glare at him. "No, thank you. I've already eaten."

"Oh yeah," he says, his gaze falling to where my hand remains resting in Beaufort's. I snatch it away and cross my arms over my chest. "What'd you have?"

"Erm ..." That was not the question I was expecting. "Some kind of stew."

"Meat?" he asks.

I shift my weight from one foot to another. "I guess, it was difficult to tell."

Dray laughs.

"You can eat your meals here," Beaufort says. "You can see we have enough."

I shake my head, ignoring Beaufort's corresponding frown.

"I got them to make you up some chocolate mousse,"

Dray says, shoving the last of the pie into his mouth. "It's my favorite. Do you like it?"

"I've never tried it." I snipe. "Chocolate is a luxury in Slate Quarter. One my family can't afford."

Instead of looking suitably ashamed, Dray chews and swallows his pie, and then a huge smile spreads across his face. His eyes seem to twinkle.

"You never tried it? Shit, little thrall, you have to. Sometimes I think it's better than sex."

Beside me, Beaufort snorts.

Dray picks up a large glass bowl filled with a brown substance and one of the silver spoons and walks around the table towards me. He dips the spoon into the mixture, scooping some out and holds it up to my face.

"Try?"

It looks pretty gross, but the smell of it is divine. Rich, velvety chocolate. It makes my mouth water.

But I wasn't won over by a pretty, gold collar. I won't be won over by chocolate either. I stare back at him and refuse to open my mouth.

"Shit, you really are a stubborn little thing." He cackles. "I fucking love it. Now, open wide for me, come on."

I stare right back up at him, into those mischievous eyes. Up close I discover they are a multitude of colors: blues, greens, grays, even flecks of gold.

He cocks an eyebrow and says again, more firmly this time, his magic crackling in the air ominously, "Open."

It's harder to refuse with his magic so threatening, and something more dangerous bubbling to the surface of those eyes, but I refuse, nonetheless.

I am not their thrall. I am not their slave to be commanded and ordered about. I'll keep showing up if I have to but I will not make this easy for them.

"You know I could make you," he says quietly. I adopt that blank expression. "Have it your way then." To my astonishment, rather than blasting me with magic, or forcing the spoon between my lips, another wicked smile breaks out across his face and before I know what's happening, he's landed a large blob of the chocolate mousse right onto the end of my nose. "Right," he tells me, turning around to place the bowl back on the table, "make yourself at home. It's time we left."

"What?" I say in even more astonishment. "Are you locking me in here again while you hang out with your friends?"

"Nope," he says, spinning around to face me. His eyes drop to the mousse on my nose; he grins, looks into my eyes and then he actually leans down and licks the dessert right off. I squeal, jumping backward and he laughs.

"You're such a fucking child," Beaufort mutters.

Dray licks his lips. "Of course, if you wanted us to stay, we could smear this mousse on other places on your body too. Then, afterwards, I'd be happy to lick it off." He winks. "Slowly. In a way that would make you moan."

I swallow. Dray is way more unpredictable and flirtatious than Beaufort and he has heat creeping all over my body.

I keep my face expressionless though and shake my head.

"You have free rein of the place," Beaufort says, ignoring Dray. "Try not to trash any more rooms, okay?"

"Why? What will you be doing exactly?" I ask with suspicion.

"We're going out," Dray says. "Party in the Onyx common room."

"You have a common room?" I snort.

"We do."

"And you want me to stay here while you go off and party?"

"Unless you want to wear the collar, little thrall," Dray says, his eyes falling to my throat. "Then we'd be happy to take you."

"No, thank you," I say.

Beaufort doesn't say another word, walking straight out of the kitchen. Dray picks up his jacket from the back of one of the kitchen chairs and slings it over his broad shoulders.

"Okay," he says, heading for the door. "Have fun then, little thrall and don't get up to any trouble while we're gone."

Chapter Thirty-Four

D^{ray}

"Man, that was fun," I say, bouncing along beside my bond brothers, fuck-off big grin spread across my face.

"You're an idiot," Beaufort mumbles.

"Hey, you've got your ways and I've got mine. Besides," I chuckle, "you shouldn't believe everything that girl says. She likes us."

"Of course, she does," Beaufort snorts but Thorne glances at him and I know he doesn't believe it.

"She does," I say, rubbing at my nose, "I can smell how much we turn her on."

"You smell what you want to believe," Thorne grumbles.

"My nose has never let me down yet," I say, the smell of her lingering in my nostrils. The girl smells so wet – it's frigging obscene.

I tug at the front of my shirt. Despite that run this morning in my wolf form, I'm all gee'd up. It's that encounter with our thrall. I'm a ball of crackling energy. Energy I need to release. Energy I want to release on her. Preferably between those fine legs of hers.

"We shouldn't have left her," Thorne says.

"She's perfectly safe," Beaufort responds, "the tower is enchanted, protected. No one can get in without our say so."

"We could have brought her with us," I say wistfully. I would really have liked to have continued our little game. I was having so much fun.

"Without a collar," Beaufort scoffs.

"She'd be safe with us." Thorne balls his hands into fists. My guess is that Thorne is just dying for the opportunity to beat the crap out of someone. He just needs the right motivation. A little push. Since we got here, the chances have been few and far between.

"Yeah, but I can't be dealing with all the fucking snide comments," Beaufort says.

"There's going to be fucking snide comments no matter what," I point out. "You know today she told an entire classroom full of students that she wasn't our thrall."

"She did what?" Thorne roars.

I grin. Hey presto. Thorne's going to be on the warpath now. And this party probably got a lot more interesting as a result.

"Besides," I say, "what do we care what people say?"

That's the difference between me and Beaufort – the main one anyway. He gives a fuck and I do not. Never have. Never do. I do what the fuck I want.

"She's making us look stupid," he grumbles.

"I like this little game she's playing," I say, licking my

tongue along my lower lip. Beaufort glances towards me, catching my eye and something tells me, no matter what he may say, he likes it too.

I don't think Thorne feels the same way.

For a man with a hell of a lot of complications in his life, he's way more straight forward than us.

"She needs to wear the collar," he grunts.

"Don't you worry, pal," I say, grinning at him. "She'll wear it."

We're silent for the rest of the walk over to the tower and up the magically operated elevator to the common room. I occupy myself imagining how good she'd look wearing that collar and nothing more.

The party's already in full swing and by the look of things everyone is either stoned or hammered – possibly both.

My encounter with our little thrall has quelled any desire I had to get wasted tonight. My blood's already buzzing – I don't need alcohol or drugs.

Thorne glowers at the throng of people in front of us as if every single one of them has personally affronted him. It's going to take one little spark to blow his fuse tonight.

And it looks like that spark is right there in the middle of the room.

Yeah, because dancing right there in the middle of the common room – if you can call that dancing, looks more like dry humping to me – are the Hardies and their cute brunette thrall. She's dressed in a red dress that clings in all the right places, her collar glittering around her throat and from it a golden chain that ends in Kratos' fist. Their hands are all over the brunette, and they're grinding her from behind and in front.

And we get the message, right?

They couldn't be more obvious if they had it written in the air above their heads.

Look at us and our obedient thrall. So obedient she's practically banging us in front of everyone.

Whereas our thrall ...

"Get a room," I call out. It's so transparent. An obvious provocation.

Kratos doesn't look up from where he's sucking on the brunette's neck, offering up his middle finger as way of reply.

It's time we shoved him back in his place.

I lean into Thorne. "I learned something interesting today." Thorne's eyes flick to me. "Seems the Hardies' thrall may be the one responsible for all our girl's injuries."

"How do you know?"

I grin. "She told me herself."

It's the spark I was hoping for.

We can't go after the girl. We have some fucking morals. But the Hardies? They are fair game.

Thorne launches at them and all hell breaks loose.

Chapter Thirty-Five

B riony

Once again I find myself prisoner inside the Princes' tower, while they are out having a good time some place else. Honestly, I don't understand this situation. What is even the point of forcing me to come around?

Actually, I know the answer to that one.

Power.

They want me to know that they are in control, and I am not.

At least I'm not locked in the kitchen this time. The feast is severely tempting but I'm too stubborn to eat it. Instead, I decide I'll go off and do a little snooping. It's a form of entertainment after all and as they haven't even left me with a book, a fair one.

I start on the lower floor. I'm already intimately familiar with the kitchen so I head into the other room. It's a large lounge – large enough for a party and it is set out with armchairs around a roaring fire. The fireplace itself hosts a carved marble mantelpiece and on top of it rests several objects. I pick each one up and hold it in my hands. A carriage clock. A bust. A stuffed raven. Each is heavy and expertly crafted. Objects that must be worth hundreds of coin.

I place them back carefully and turn my attention to the far wall. Several great landscapes hang in heavy frames, old oil paintings that show the four quarters of the realms as well as the academy and the empress's palace. I interrogate them all, sniffing at the one of Slate Quarter because they've made it look a million times nicer than it is. No slag heaps, smog-filled skies, or ravaged forests. The scene is almost idyllic – workers out on the streets on market day, their baskets piled high with food. Yeah, right!

Next, I climb the set of stairs. They aren't narrow or worn like the staircase in our towers. There's an actual banister, carved from oak and each step is polished smooth.

On the first floor I find a bathroom, a study and a bedroom.

The study has barely been used. There are no books, no pens, no ink, no paper. I doubt its owner has even set foot inside.

The bathroom is a little more interesting. I sniff the fancy bottles of soaps – the scents masculine and toe curling, a scent that engulfs me as I step inside the bedroom. A giant bed lies in the center, its frame solid and carved from oak like the banister. There's a wardrobe carved from oak, a chest of drawers, a low chair, two mirrors hanging on the walls and one large full-length mirror standing in the corner.

The man who owns this room obviously loves his reflection. He's also messy as hell. Clare told me they had staff to clean and tidy after them, but there's no sign of that here. Clothes lie abandoned across the floor, over the chair and screwed up on the bed, and more clothes are trying to escape the wardrobe and the drawers. The bed is unmade, the silk covers trailing onto the floor – a floor made from polished floorboards and covered in a woven rug.

I can guess who the owner is but I go and peer at the framed photos on top of the chest of drawers anyway. There are several. An older couple, the man big and burly with snow-white hair. A group of boys, grinning at the camera, their arms slung around each other's shoulders. And the room's owner – Dray Eros, smiling in that manic manner he does and staring off into the distance, like he couldn't sit still long enough just to look at the camera.

The final frame doesn't contain a photo, instead it holds a family crest. Three words printed in the old tongue beneath it. I rack my memory, trying to remember what the words mean.

Pack. Power. Prosperity.

The next floor is laid out in exactly the same fashion: a study, a bathroom and a bedroom. This time the study has been used, although its contents – textbooks, a globe and thick encyclopedia volumes, tell me very little about the occupier. The bathroom has a lot less fancy soaps and the bedroom is almost the exact opposite to the one directly below. In fact, it's so neat, all the objects laid out alongside one another in regimental rows and lines, that I conclude the room belongs to an obsessive. The bed is made so tightly, there isn't a crease on the plain cotton sheets and even the pillows have been carefully placed.

Like the study, the objects tell me nothing about the person they belong to, and maybe I wouldn't know at all if it wasn't for the three pairs of leather gloves lying out alongside one another on top of the chest of drawers.

I hesitate, straining my ears. The Princes won't be back for hours. It's a Saturday night. They've gone out partying. Even still, I do not want to be caught snooping.

The tower's pipes groan and the wind buffets against the walls, but there are no sounds of footsteps or doors opening.

I pick up one of the gloves, intrigued. I've never seen Thorne Cadieux without them. He is always wearing them. I've suspected he may even wear them to bed, probably in the shower too. They're made from a thick, durable leather – certainly not cow hide – and they are lined with several different layers of material. I slide my hand inside the glove and it engulfs my hand completely. The man is huge, it stands to reason his hands would be too. The gloves are even heavier to wear and make my arms ache in a couple of seconds.

I slide my hand back out and carefully lay the glove alongside its twin, lining it up like the others.

There are no photos in this room. No family crests. It is soulless. Rather like the man, I think, picturing those bottomless dark eyes of his.

I climb the stairs to the next floor – halting halfway up, my heart hammering in my chest, because, for just one moment, I swear I hear a sound below me. I peer back down the way I've come, straining to hear again.

Nothing. I'm imagining things.

This floor, I assume, belongs to Beaufort. However, to my surprise, the staircase does not end here. I peer upwards finding there are still several more floors above me.

Once again there's a bedroom, a bathroom and a study.

I step inside his bedroom first. The room is tidy but not

obsessively so. His uniform is flung over a chair, a book rests open on the bed. I turn it over and read the spine. A novel.

Above the chest of drawers hang two oil paintings similar to the ones from downstairs – another landscape of the palace plus a portrait of the empress. I spend several minutes peering up at her face. She was more beautiful in the flesh, more intimidating and intriguing. She stares back at me and the effect is so damn lifelike it makes me shiver.

Not enough to prevent me from drawing my eyes back down to the chest of drawers. I don't know what possesses me, but I can't help but take ahold of the handle and slide the first drawer open. Inside, neatly folded are his clothes, freshly laundered and freshly pressed (probably by that housekeeper). There are a collection of shirts, plus his underthings.

I stare at them, and, before I know what I'm doing, I reach out and touch the soft-looking material with my fingertips.

It has a memory flitting through my mind. My hands braced against his chest, the soft material of his clothing brushing against my skin, his heart pounding under my palms, his scent strong and masculine, his magic sparking in the air.

My skin warms. So does my blood.

I shouldn't be thinking about him like that. He shouldn't have that effect on me.

He's a shadow weaver. My enemy.

Clearly, something is clouding my judgment and warping my mind.

I snatch my hands away.

A mirror hangs above the chest of drawers. I catch sight of my reflection. My cheeks are flaming.

What am I doing?

Dray is the pervert, not me.

I slam the drawer shut, spin around and walk towards the study.

I never make it that far though, because blocking my path is Beaufort Lincoln himself.

Chapter Thirty-Six

Briony

"I ... I ... I ..."

I don't know what the fuck to say. I wasn't expecting them home for hours.

I was not expecting to be caught snooping.

I was not expecting to be caught snooping in his *under-wear* drawer.

"Did you find anything of interest in those drawers?"

"I ... no ... there ..."

"Are you looking for something?"

"Can I go now?" I ask, folding my arms across my chest.

He tips his head to one side, considering me. "Are you stealing from us?"

"Oh, because I'm from Slate Quarter, I'd have to be a thief," I spit.

"You're the one rummaging through my drawers." He crooks his finger towards me. "Come here, little thrall."

I snort. "Err, no."

"Come here and tell me what you've been doing in my room."

I adopt that bored, vacant expression I've perfected, and he huffs and stamps towards me, stopping mere inches from my face. His proximity is intimidating – not just his size, but the way his magic pulsates around him in the air. And then there are his eyes. That strange silver color – mesmerizing like a snake's. Is that why I shiver when he leans in closer?

It must be, right? Because I can't possibly be turned on by him. Him, a shadow weaver?

He's close enough for me to see the bruise blooming across his left cheek bone, the split on his lip, and, as he lifts his hand to slide his fingers around the back of my neck, the grazes on his knuckle.

"Hmmm," he murmurs, his voice low and deep. "I like you in my room."

"Wh-what happened to you?" I say, trying to ignore how good his hand feels gripping my neck. Trying to dismiss the way my heart is pounding in my ears, making me dizzy. Maybe there was some kind of potion in that mousse, because my body is not reacting the way it should.

I hate this man. I hate what his people did to my sister. And yet, the way he cups the back of my neck makes my knees weaken.

"Nothing," he says dismissively, those silver eyes glittering.

I force myself to step away, ducking my head to release it from his grip and taking his hand in mine instead.

Safer, much safer.

I turn his hand over and examine those grazes, unable to help but let my fingertips trace over them.

"It doesn't look like nothing."

"Don't tell me you care," he says with a smirk.

I drop his hand like it just burned me. "Don't flatter yourself."

His tongue wets the slice through his lip.

I can't imagine anyone being capable of giving Beaufort Lincoln a split lip. He's far more powerful than anyone else at the academy – or so he and everyone else keeps saying.

I guess I should be happy he's taken a beating. And yet it has me uneasy.

"But let's just say," he says, "that girl won't be bothering you any longer."

"What girl?"

He tosses his head. "That little bitch the Hardies have taken as their thrall."

All the blood rushes to my head. The room spins.

"What did you do?" I say, my words sounding far, far away.

I think of my sister.

Dead.

Killed.

Did they ...

"I made sure she wouldn't hurt you again." He pauses. "You're our thrall, Briony, and we will protect you."

"What did you do?" I repeat. And to think only moments ago, I was softening towards him. But I was right the first time. He's dangerous. We are nothing to them. "Did you–"

"Hurt her?" His face falls. For the first time, it looks like I may have insulted him. "What do you take us for?"

I stare back at him. What do I take him for? A killer.

Someone who would take a life without a second thought. Isn't that what they're trained to do?

"You know, I was actually stupid enough to think you'd be grateful," he growls, turning his back on me and striding over to his bed. "Go home, little thrall."

I don't need to be told twice. I'm more than happy to leave. More than happy never to speak to him again.

I'm halfway through the door, when he says, "We didn't hurt her."

"You expect me to believe that when your knuckles are grazed and–"

"You don't know how things work between us shadow weavers."

"No," I say, "and I don't want to."

Chapter Thirty-Seven

B riony

The next morning I lie in for the first time in as long as I can remember, only emerging from my bed when Fly comes hammering on the door at 11 o'clock.

"Okay, sleepy head," he says, crashing into the room, "you've slept long enough and I have been dying of curiosity out here. I need to know what happened last night."

"Urgh," I say, wiping the sleep from my eyes and blinking against the dim light. "Nothing happened. It was once again, completely uneventful."

Fly's face morphs from one of excitement, to one of disappointment.

He rests his hand on his hip. "Seriously? Nothing happened? Not even a peck on the cheek or a little hand holding? Nothing at all?"

"Nope, nothing."

I scoot up the bed and Fly flops down on the end. He looks so deflated, I end up scrabbling around for something to tell him.

"I did go sneaking around their rooms."

His eyes light up. "Find anything interesting?"

I consider this. "Err, no."

Fly's face falls again. "Oh, but I did end up pissing off Beaufort Lincoln."

"That's nothing new. I think you've irritated the hell out of him several times already."

"No, this time I really upset him. He basically kicked me out of their tower. I think things may be officially over, once and for all." I grin at Fly.

The relief I feel is indescribable. Things were becoming complicated with those men. I was feeling things I definitely shouldn't have been feeling. Now it's over I can get back to melting away into the background and discovering the truth about my sister.

Fly presses his lips together in disapproval. "Expect to collect some more black eyes, broken noses and sprained ankles then. Without their protection you are fair game. Odessa will probably try to kill you again."

"I don't know about that," I say, yawning and stretching my arms over my head. "That's what we argued about. Beaufort and the others 'sorted her out'," I frown, my arms falling down into my lap, "whatever that means."

"Who cares what it means, if it gets her off your case, that's all that matters." He jumps off the bed. "Right, day off, remember? We can't waste it."

"Have you found anything for us to do?"

"Well ... erm ... no." I flop back down into the bed. "But

I thought we could go off exploring." He tugs me upright. "Come on, let's not waste the day."

An hour later, we're strolling around the academy campus with Clare. The day, as always, is gray and overcast, but it doesn't stop all the other students from doing the same. It seems there really is nothing to do here but walk around aimlessly. That is until we notice everyone else seems to be heading in the same direction.

"Come on," Fly says eagerly. "This could be something good."

Neither Clare nor I are sure about that but we tag along after Fly anyway and find ourselves out by the field. Nearly the entire school is gathered out there too, most sitting on the edges of the field. Some have spread blankets, a couple seem to have carried chairs out here, everyone else either sitting on their coats or standing.

They are all peering out towards the field. I follow their gaze and the blood in my veins runs cold.

Out on the field are a group of shadow weavers. They're playing some kind of game of tag, sprinting backwards and forwards across the field, tossing balls of shadow magic at each other, dodging and twisting away from the balls others send towards them. They're laughing and joking but underneath there's a sense of seriousness about them.

Despite the freezing cold weather hardly any of them are wearing shirts. Even the girls are dressed in sports bras. All of them are damp with sweat, and if the sun was actually shining, they'd be glistening. Among them, right in the center are the Princes: Beaufort, Dray and Thorne. Both Thorne and Beaufort have their shirts off displaying their impressively sculpted chests.

"Let's go," I say, tugging on Fly's sleeve.

"What's the hurry? Don't you want to watch?" he says,

eyes transfixed as he follows the shadows swirl and swerve across the clouded sky.

"No," I say firmly, "I don't."

"It's kind of beautiful," Clare says with awe in her tone.

"It's dangerous," I hiss.

"Because you may have to actually acknowledge how freaking hot those three men are?" Fly rolls his eyes and drops to the ground, Clare taking the spot next to them.

"I'm not hanging around to admire them," I hiss. "It's what they want."

Fly leans back on the grass, making himself comfortable. "I, on the other hand, am more than happy to oblige them by sitting and admiring the eye candy, especially as there is nothing else to do."

"Everyone else is here," Clare points out.

I spin my gaze around.

She's right, everyone else *is* here. Which means ...

"I'm going back to my room," I blurt out, sprinting away before either can question me.

I race back into the campus, along the cobbled pathways until I reach my destination.

Nyneve Tower.

Amelia's tower.

I tip my head back and peer up.

The lights are all out. Hopefully that means no one is in.

Leaning my weight against the door, I step inside and make my way up the staircase. There is no one to stop me this time and I make my way all the way up to room nine without meeting another soul.

I stare at the door. It's plain. Nothing special. The number xx is embossed on the wood along with the new occupant's name.

I reach out and touch the letters, imagining her name there instead.

How many times did she stand just here, unlocking her door, stepping inside?

I glance down at my feet, imagining hers positioned right here.

When I try the handle, the door is locked, of course. But it was worth a try. I give it a shove with my shoulder just in case I get lucky and it gives way. It doesn't.

I yank a pin from my hair and drop to my knees, examining the lock. When you've been locked inside a room as often as I have, with nothing to do but attempt to escape, eventually you learn to pick a lock. It's not as easy as people would have you believe. Of course, the more often you try, the more you practice, the easier it becomes. These days it doesn't take me long and this lock proves to be a simple one. I have it clicking open in less than half an hour, listening out the entire time for anyone returning back to the tower. I got caught out yesterday. I won't be so stupid again.

The room is dark when the door swings open and I stand frozen.

Stars knows why, but my skin prickles. This was the last place she lived. Her final home. It seems almost sacred.

I take a deep breath in, square my shoulders and step inside.

Immediately I'm disappointed. A bed, a wardrobe and a desk. The new occupant's possessions scattered about – some clothes on the bed, books piled by the desk, shoes lined up along the wall.

There's nothing special about it at all. It's just an ordinary room.

Really, I knew it would be and yet I'd hoped to feel something. What exactly? Her presence? Her spirit?

I miss her so damn much. I'm so desperate to see her one last time. To talk to her again. To hold her hand. And I never ever will.

A sob bubbles up in my throat, but I swallow it back down, blink away the tears and go to investigate more closely.

There are no secret panels in the wardrobe. No loose bit of carpet. Nothing under the bed. I check everything twice – just to be sure.

Nothing.

I slump down on the desk chair, more disappointed than I care to admit. This was my only real lead. I have nothing else.

"What happened to you? Why didn't you leave me any clue?" I say out into the open room and it's then my eyes spy something on the surface of the desk. Names scribed into the wood. Scores of them. And among them, hidden in plain sight, my sister's.

Amelia.

I trace my finger over the grooves.

This was one set back. I'm not giving up yet.

Chapter Thirty-Eight

B^{riony}

Monday I wake up with a new determination in my gut. A determination boosted by the fact that today is the day of my very first history class.

Professor Cornelius is a scholar of history – of historical events, facts and records. Which means he must know everything that's ever happened in this academy – every unusual, unique or peculiar event. And if he doesn't, he'd be able to tell me where I could find more information if I wanted to conduct my own historical investigation.

I've neglected Amelia these last few days, and my promise. I've been too caught up in making new friends, navigating my way through this strange new world and generally trying to stay alive.

Professor Cornelius might present me with my first real opportunity in days to actually make some progress.

However, all that hope and excitement vanishes as Fly and I approach the classroom. Waiting at the front of the line is Dray Eros, blazer once again slung over his shoulder, chewing gum in his mouth as usual. Today, it seems he's not just on time, he's early.

After what happened with Beaufort on Saturday night, I am very much expecting him to blank me – either that or give me a piece of his mind.

I'm learning that Dray Eros does nothing that I predict him to do, because when he spots me, he smiles with what looks like genuine eagerness and pushes the boy standing next to him to one side, almost sending him tumbling to the floor.

"Hey, sweetheart," he calls over to me, beckoning with his hand. "I saved you a spot." He points down to the ground right beside him.

I glance at Fly who shrugs his shoulders. I can feel all the other students lined up around us, watching me.

"I'm just fine where I am," I mumble.

"*I* don't think so. I think you'd be a hell of a lot more comfortable resting right here." He tilts his chin back, his eyes full of wickedness.

"Thanks, but no thanks," I say flatly.

He chews on his gum, those eyes flicking all over my face.

Then something catches his attention behind me.

He pushes off the wall and strolls towards me. I take a step back but I'm too slow, he's already slung an arm around my shoulder.

"Hey Odessa," he purrs.

I twist around in his hold and find the Hardies' thrall has joined the back of the line.

Horror is written all over her face and she pales right in front of us, dropping her gaze straight to the floor.

I'm guessing whatever happened on Saturday night, she didn't share the details with her little band of friends. None of them seem cowed like she does and several of them flick their gaze between her and Dray with puzzlement.

"Beautiful day today, isn't it? And doesn't Briony here look fucking amazing? Definitely the most beautiful girl in the school, wouldn't you agree?"

"Erm, yes, Dray," Odessa murmurs.

Fly and I glance at each other a second time. What the hell *did* happen on Saturday? As far as I can tell, she's not injured or hurt. But she is not acting like her usually obnoxious self. They must have scared her half to death.

"Come on, sweetheart," Dray whispers in my ear as the classroom door swings open and an elderly man wearing a tweed suit and bow tie, his hair and beard white and bushy and his glasses so thick it's impossible to see through them, beckons us all inside. "You can come sit next to me."

I duck out of his hold and grab Fly's arm.

"I'm going to sit next to my friend."

"Perfect," Dray says, taking my bag of books from me and swinging it up onto his shoulder, "he'll sit on one side and I'll sit on the other. It's a good idea, right?" he says to Fly, who nods his head mutely, way too scared to disagree. I jab Fly in the ribs.

He coughs, then says, "Wouldn't you prefer to be in the front row with all the other shadow weavers?"

"Nah," he says, spitting his gum into the trash can as we walk into the classroom. "I'd rather be where I can smell her wet-pussy scent."

My cheeks burn so aggressively, I'm surprised I don't set

the classroom on fire, and the little old teacher fumbles with his chalk and blushes too.

"Do you have to?" I hiss as we take our seats, Dray dragging his right up next to mine so there is only an inch of space between us.

"Yeah, I do." He drops down, his right thigh pressing against my left.

"Why are you even in this class? You're not meant to be in this group."

"Wanted to spend some quality time with you."

I shuffle around on my chair and try to ignore him. It's not easy. I can feel the heat of his body; I can see how broad his shoulders are; I can appreciate how sculpted his chest is.

I don't want to be distracted by him. I want to concentrate on the lesson. This is important.

But pretty soon, I realize the lesson is a lost cause. The professor drops his piece of chalk five times in the first two minutes, forgets what day of the week it is and spells his own name wrong on the blackboard.

Nobody can understand a word he's going on about because he keeps hopping from one timeline to the next and in the end nearly everyone gives up, either drawing books out of their bags and reading, or talking quietly among themselves.

I try to listen anyway, even if most of what he's droning on about appears to be ancient history – it's the best option available to me to ignore Dray.

"Some believe it was the firestones themselves that provided those original shadow weavers with their powers. Although other sources ... erm, Peters and Hadrian for example ... or was it Andreas ... indicate that from firestones came dragons. The sources disagree on these points and, of course, many were written centuries after the events –

around the time of Empress Leah – a keen historical scholar. Oh ... no ... perhaps it was actually her granddaughter, Leah the Third." He pauses for a coughing fit that makes several dozing students jerk awake. "Firestones continue to crop up in sources right up until about four hundred years ago. They disappear from the records around the same time it appears dragons died out. Dragon pox – not to be confused with the less harmful chicken, spider and pig poxes – a deadly plague that caused many deaths among humans – and by some accounts dogs too – as well as killing almost all the breeding dragons. The last known dragon was owned by Emperor Gilead and the skeleton is kept in the palace crypt. There are no known remains – partial or complete – of firestones."

"You following any of this, little one?" Dray whispers, leaning towards me, his hand resting on the back of my chair. I shrug. "I didn't see you at the field yesterday."

"Can you be quiet please?" I say as stiffly as I can. "I'm trying to concentrate."

"I wouldn't bother," he yawns, "he's getting his facts and his dates all confused."

"It could be important."

"You a history nerd, little thrall? I can give you your own private history tuition if you'd like. In fact," he leans even closer, his mouth right by my ear, his breath whistling all over my neck and making me shiver, "I could teach you all sorts of things if you like."

I consider stabbing him with my pen just to get him away from me. As I suspect it's a possibility he could stab me right back, I stick to ignoring him. I don't answer any more of his comments and do not respond to the way he's sniffing at my neck.

It's not easy, partly because his presence is disorientating, but also because most of the other students in the class-room are stealing furtive glances our way.

I have never wanted the floor to disappear and the ground to swallow me up more than I have done in this moment and am relieved beyond belief when the bell finally clangs for the end of the lesson. I grab my belongings and dart out of my seat as quickly as my legs carry me. I'm not quick enough though, because I'm only halfway across the classroom when Dray calls out, loud enough for everyone to hear:

"Little thrall, be at our rooms Wednesday night, 8pm. And bring that sweet-smelling pussy with you."

●

I keep my head down for the rest of the day, but it makes no difference. After that little display in history class, everyone is talking about me again. I can hear them whispering as I walk past in the corridors and along the pathways. I even spy one or two girls pointing me out to their friends.

By the time dinner is over, I'm feeling utterly dejected. I leave Fly and Clare chattering away in the canteen and stomp back up to my room.

Amelia's old room turned up nothing. The history teacher is next to useless. And the Princes still want me as their thrall.

Nothing is going to plan.

I go to unlock my bedroom door ready to crash straight into bed and sink into a pit of misery, but as I reach for the door, it pushes open.

My heart leaps into my throat.

I'm sure I locked it. I *know* I locked it.

I swing the door all the way back and gasp, my hands flying to my mouth.

It's trashed. Utterly and completely trashed.

The bed, the wardrobe, all my belongings.

Everything has been smashed to pieces and ripped to smithereens.

"No!" I cry out, racing straight to the wardrobe. "No, no, no, no, no!"

I can't feel it. Is it gone?

I'm in such a panic, I trip over my own feet and struggle to make my stupid lungs work.

The wardrobe door hangs at a funny angle and the paneling has been kicked in. All my clothes have been dragged from the shelves and what remains of them tossed around the room or lying destroyed at the bottom of the closet.

"No!" I screech again, "Please no!"

I toss the pieces of torn up clothes over my head, scrabbling down to the bottom of the wardrobe.

Tears slide down my cheeks and bile rushes up my throat.

How can I have been so careless? Why didn't I keep it somewhere safer?

I find the blanket at the bottom of the pile of clothes.

I close my eyes and cross my fingers and my toes.

"Please," I whisper, "please."

I pull the blanket away, holding my breath as I do.

My bag lies underneath. It's still there.

Of course that doesn't mean the contents are.

I can barely look, my hands trembling as I yank down the zipper and open the bag.

My hands shake even more, as I tip my head forward and peer inside.

Then I slump back in relief, all the air rushing from my lungs.

It's still there, resting at the bottom of my bag.

Whoever did this, they didn't find it.

It's safe.

In fact, as I survey the carnage, I'm certain the perpetrator wasn't looking for my one hidden treasure. They were here to trash my room. To punish me.

And I'd bet my last coin, I know who is responsible.

She would have to have the last word. She'd have to let me know that, even with the Princes protecting me, she'd find a way to get back at me.

Because she'll deny it of course. And there's no evidence it was her. No way to prove she did this.

Odessa.

Chapter Thirty-Nine

Thorne

I'm nearly at the door, when Beaufort steps out in front of me and blocks my path.

"Where are you going in such a hurry?" he says, examining my face.

"Out," I tell him.

"Our thrall is coming tonight. She'll be here in fifteen minutes – if she turns up on time," he mumbles.

"Right," I say.

"You should be the one to greet her tonight."

I stretch and ball my fingers, the leather of my gloves creaking. Beaufort doesn't like to share and yet here he is offering me up his toy. What is his motive?

"Why?"

"The girl is being difficult and Dray's antics aren't helping. You heard about the history class?"

I stare at him. Is he serious?

"Spending time with me will do nothing to persuade her."

My bond brother rubs his fingers through the stubble on his chin. "You don't like her?" He scowls at me. "Is it because she's from the Slate Quarter?"

I scowl right back at him.

"Not pretty enough?" he asks. "Too pretty? Is she not your type?"

"I don't have a type."

"You do," he says, staring into my eyes. "And she is it."

If only he knew how true that was.

It doesn't change anything. Maybe she'll come around eventually. Maybe the others will have her. But I never can.

No matter how much I may want her.

"Thorne," he says, any traces of humor gone from his voice, "I'm asking you to be here when she arrives tonight."

I hold his gaze and nod.

I wait in the lounge, seated on one of the straight-backed chairs, staring into the flickering flames of the fire, watching the smoke twist up into the chimney. My heart pounds in my chest and, despite the heat from the fire, cold sweat trickles down my spine.

The minutes tick by, drumming in my ears.

Just after eight, there's a rap at the door.

I peer over my shoulder, through the hallway, towards the door.

I wait. Maybe Dray will come bounding through and beat me to it. Maybe Beaufort will have a change of heart.

Neither of them appear and reluctantly, I drag myself up onto my feet.

My mouth is dry and I walk the few feet to the door and pause.

I don't have to open it. If I don't, she'll probably turn around and walk away, relieved she isn't required to spend another moment in our company.

But I know what Beaufort's seen. This is our destiny. And I, more than anyone, should know, you can't argue with fate. No matter how strong your powers are. No matter how hard your heart is.

I open the door.

Her pretty green eyes land on me and she jolts.

All my worst fears are confirmed. She's repelled by me.

I flex my hands involuntarily and my magic pulses in the air. She takes a step backwards.

"I ... I came as instructed," she says, trying to sound tough, but I hear the tremble in her throat. I don't just disgust her. She's afraid of me too.

I nod. Then I turn and walk back down the hallway. Behind me, I hear her hesitate, then follow me inside, the door clicking shut.

I don't know what I'm meant to do with her. I peer across at the lounge and then at the kitchen.

The thing doesn't have a lot of meat on her. They say the food in Slate Quarter is worse than pig feed.

I swerve into the kitchen and wait against the wall.

She follows me inside.

"Are you locking me in the kitchen again tonight?" she says, tossing her head in annoyance.

I have no self control. I let my gaze roam down her body, down her fragile neck, to the baggy gray uniform that swamps her frame. I can't help but imagine what she looks like under those layers. The only hint of it is the flash of bare thigh, her skin there smooth and soft looking.

I press my body into the wall as I ball my hands into tight fists.

She harrumphs to herself and drops down into one of the kitchen chairs.

"I can see this is going to be another entertaining evening." She rests her elbows down on the table and leans forward, taking me in. "I don't understand why the hell you keep dragging me here. Especially seeing as you so clearly don't want me here."

I stare back at her, not saying a word.

A crease forms between her brows. "I also don't get why you pulled that little stunt in front of everyone out on the field. Why you said the stuff you did." She tucks her legs under the table, crossing them over at the ankles. She's so small, so tiny. I could crush her in my fist. "Was it a power thing?"

I slip my hands behind my back and force my palms against the cold wall.

She sighs. "If you hate me so much, can't you talk the other two out of this stupid situation? You don't want it," my magic bores into the wall, the plaster cracking behind me, "and neither do I. We could work together. Help each other out."

She examines my face and waits for an answer. My magic crackles and pulsates. Her eyes on my face is the closest thing I'll ever get to her touch.

She sighs again and flops back into her chair.

"Can I just go, please? There is no point in me staying."

When I don't tell her no, she stands slowly to her feet as if any second she expects me to slam her down in her chair. Then with caution, watching me with a puzzled expression, she ventures towards the door.

She's a foot away from me when she passes, close enough for me to reach out and touch her, to hold her. I tense every part of my body. The shadows crash with rage around my veins, my magic hisses angrily and she must feel it in the air, must hear it, because she frowns in displeasure.

"Be back here again on Saturday," I tell her.

She stops. "Seriously?"

My face shows how serious I am.

"Whatever," she murmurs and then she's gone.

I close my eyes. I count to ten and then I follow her outside, trailing her all the way back to her room, ensuring she's safe.

Chapter Forty

B riony

Like the other new students, I fall into a pattern. Up with the seven o'clock bell for breakfast, and ready to begin class at 8:30. I drag myself around assault courses and cross-country routes, sit through lessons learning subjects I'll never make use of back in Slate Quarter, and try my best to disappear into the background – which is hard when everyone knows who I am, when they're all whispering about me. At least none of them are actively trying to kill me right now. Odessa seems content with trashing my room and destroying my belongings – although if she knew she'd missed the one precious thing I own she'd probably have a mega temper tantrum.

The day ends at six and I eat dinner with Fly and Clare, then slump into bed exhausted and ready for sleep.

Before I know it, I've made it through another week and it's Saturday night all over again.

Along with my two new friends, I smuggle my dinner out of the canteen and take it back to Clare's room. We're just settling down to eat, when Fly pulls something out from his jacket.

"Something to get this party started." He produces three tumblers from his pocket – tumblers he's swiped from the canteen, and pours amber liquid into each.

"What is that?" Clare says, her nose wrinkling.

"What is that?" Fly chuckles. "Liquor, what else?"

"Liquor?" Clare's eyes widen. "How did you get that?"

"I may not have magical abilities but I'm extremely proficient at smuggling – a skill I bet is underrated at this stupid academy. Anyway, luckily for you, it means I have several bottles of the stuff swiped from my parents' liquor cabinet. I think it will probably be needed to help us get through the next twelve months."

He hands me a glass and I lift it to my nose and sniff. I can tell by the aroma it's much better quality stuff than the bootleg crap brewed back in Slate Quarter – although I doubt it's as refined as anything available in Onyx.

"I've never drunk liquor before," Clare says, staring into her glass fearfully.

"You haven't? How is that possible?" Fly asks.

"My parents are teetotal. There's no alcohol at home."

"That sounds ... dull." Fly frowns. "I hope you aren't going to be one of those killjoys who likes to preach to–"

"I don't really drink either," I say, although in my case for the opposite reason to Clare's – when you've seen your father become more and more dependent on the stuff just to make it through the day, it loses its appeal.

"Really?" Fly says, surprised, "I'd've thought it was a necessity in Slate Quarter."

"Cause we're all drunks?" I snap.

"I didn't say that." He lifts his glass. "Try it ladies. I promise you, it's good stuff and we deserve it after the two weeks we've had."

I stare down into the glass. I have no desire to become like my dad. But this is different, right? I'm not drinking to drown my sorrows, to try to forget. I'm hanging out with friends – having a good time with friends. Actual friends.

"To surviving our first two weeks," I say, lifting my glass and then taking a large gulp, one that has me coughing and spluttering and my eyes watering.

"Can you call it surviving though, when you've been beaten up so many times?" Fly says.

I stick my tongue out at him. "I'm still here though."

Heart still beating, lungs still breathing. I count that as a win in my book.

"That you are, Cupcake." He smiles at me with affection.

Clare takes a cautious sip, smiling as she swallows the liquor.

"Hmmm, that's actually really nice. I can see why people like this stuff."

"They like it because it makes them feel good," Fly says. "Until the morning anyway. So go slow." He catches Clare's wrist as she attempts to take a much bigger gulp this time. "You don't want to waste your only day off hungover in bed."

Clare groans.

"Which is a good point," Fly says, "how are we going to spend our Sunday?"

"In bed," I confirm.

"Alone or with the Princes?" he says cheekily.

"Alone," I clarify, "and sleeping."

"Urgh," Fly groans. "How about you Clare?"

"Studying. The next trial is only one week away – and I want to be prepared."

"Exactly," Fly says, "one week away. We have tons of time. We should do something this Sunday – after a lie in, of course," he adds.

"We've already established, there is nothing to do here," I say with irritation. Slate Quarter may be a shithole but there were at least parties occasionally.

"We could watch the shadow weavers again?" Clare suggests.

"No." I pull a face.

"I'll find something," Fly says.

"I'd happily stay in bed all day with a good book," I say.

"Err, no," he says. "You did that last weekend. You're not in Slate Quarter anymore, Cupcake. We have to do something entertaining."

I nod, conceding to him. There may have been parties back at Slate Quarter but it's a long, long time since I went to one. Hanging out with friends, doing something fun, actually sounds nice.

Fly and Clare argue over the next record to play and in the end turn to me to pick one. Once it's playing, Fly pours us out another drink and I cross my legs under me and ask a question that's been bugging me.

"What do you think the next trial will be?" I ask. I know that first one was pretty tame. The next is likely to be a lot more vicious.

"Don't know," Fly says, "I'm more interested in the afterparty."

"You're not worried about the trial?" Clare says, biting at her fingernail.

"What's the point? Worrying about it isn't going to change it. What will be will be. I'll give it my best shot, hope I don't end up in a hospital bed and then enjoy the ball afterwards."

"I'm petrified," Clare admits. "I wish I knew what it was going to be. At least then I could prepare." She peers down into her glass, then downs the lot.

"Woah, easy," Fly says, "this is strong liquor. It's meant to be sipped."

"Screw that," I say, following Clare's example and finishing my glassful too. The liquor forms a warm pleasant feeling in my belly and in my chest, and my shoulders feel lighter than they have done for weeks and weeks. It's dreamy – like I'm floating here on the carpet without a care in the world.

"What was that about a ball?" I ask Fly.

"You haven't heard about that? There's a ball held after each trial. A celebration. They hold it in that Great Hall we were in the other day and they are meant to be immense."

"And raucous and pretty notorious," Clare adds.

"Notorious like the first night here at the academy notorious?" I ask, not liking the sound of that.

"Nah, not notorious in the violent kind, more like notorious in the, who's going to end up knocked up this year."

Clare pales. "I don't want to end up knocked up."

Fly cocks his head. "You do know how girls end up knocked up, right? They do teach you brainiacs that back in Granite Quarter? You won't get knocked up if you don't engage in any fucking."

Clare hiccups, then giggles – the alcohol has definitely taken effect. "I do know that."

"Do you have any practical experience?"

She shakes her head.

"Well, if you do want to do that – not that I'm offering by the way, you are not my type – there's birth control to stop you getting knocked up. We can get you some."

"Have you, Briony?" Clare asks, pinching the liquor bottle off Fly and pouring three large measures into the glasses. "Had practical experience?"

Usually I would not answer a question like this, but the alcohol has loosened my tongue.

"Yes, once – well more than once but with one person."

"The cute boy with the black eye."

"He used to be cute," and kind and sweet, "trust me, he isn't anymore."

"Did you like it?" she asks me next. "I'm so desperate to try it."

"You are?" Fly says, laughing.

"Just because I'm a girl and smart, does not mean I don't have needs, Fly Arison," she says, waving her glass in his direction, liquid slopping over the rim and onto the carpet.

"Oh yeah, we all have needs," he nods, "but the only one of us even close to having those needs fulfilled is Briony."

"Do you seriously not find them hot, Briony?" Clare asks. She lowers her voice to a whisper. "I wouldn't be able to help but have my needs fulfilled by those three."

"I do find them hot." The alcohol has *definitely* loosened my tongue because that is not something I've even admitted to myself up until now. "Even though I really really don't want to."

Fly sighs. "Most of the time attraction is something we can't help. The last dude I had a crush on was a serious asshole but I still worshipped the ground he walked on ... he was just too darn beautiful."

"I don't know," I ponder. "If it was just that, I don't think it would be so hard. Sometimes it feels like more ..." I trail off struggling to articulate my thoughts, to describe how I feel whenever any one of them is close. I roll my eyes and change the subject. "How about you, Fly? Do you have practical experience?"

"Some," he says a little coyly. "But mostly just head. I'd be very happy to expand that experience."

"Head?" Clare asks.

"Oh gosh," he says, rolling his eyes. "My poor innocent sheltered little lamb. Do we need a sex ed lesson?"

"What does it mean?" she says, ignoring his sarcasm.

"Sucking dick. Or licking pussy. I've only had experience of the former."

"And you liked it?" Clare asks, seeming a little unsure.

"Like it? I fucking love it. I dream of it. I'd do just about anything for it." He cackles.

"How about you, Briony?" Clare asks. "Have you done that?"

I shake my head.

"Not with the psycho cutie with the black eye?"

"No, that was more of a ..." I shrug, "fumbling in the bushes kind of thing."

"Well, you should learn how. Give a good blowjob, Cupcake, and those Princes will be putty in your hands."

"Uh, no."

"How do you," Clare says, hiccuping, "give a good blow job?"

Fly spins his glass around in his hand, clearly considering his answer. "Hmmm, you got to keep it wet. You can never have enough spit in my opinion. And the head is the most sensitive part, so don't worry about trying to fit it all in your mouth. Then do what feels good, or what they seem to like – suck, lick – and be careful with those teeth."

Clare nods like she's taking notes.

"There's one or two fine specimens here at the academy I'd like to refine my skills on." Fly sighs.

"That boy from the third group is really cute," Clare says.

"The one with red hair?" She nods. "Yeah, he is very cute."

I'm about to ask them who exactly they are talking about, but then the tower clock rings out – eight loud chimes.

"Oh shit," I say, knocking back what's left in my glass and jumping to my feet. I discover standing is a lot harder than it used to be. My legs and my feet no longer seem as stable as they once were and my vision is spinning. I sway, grabbing hold of the back of a chair to stop myself from tumbling. "I'm going to be late."

"So you are going, then?" Fly says.

"Yes, I'm going," I say, walking a route towards the door that is definitely not straight.

Despite all my best efforts, the Princes don't seem to have lost interest. They haven't replaced me with some other thrall. And as much as I'd like to stay here with my friends, if I do I've no doubt Beaufort and Dray will be here to cart me away. Kicking and screaming if they have to.

"I think I'd better take you there." He swings his gaze between me and Clare. "Both of you are a lot drunker than I thought you were. You're both lightweights."

"I've never drunk before," Clare protests as I say:

"I don't really drink."

Fly takes Clare by the shoulders. "You stay here. Don't

go anywhere, okay? I'll walk Briony over to the Princes' Tower."

"You don't want me to come too?"

"No," he says gently, "you stay here and rest. I'll be right back."

Then he turns his attention to me, joining me by the door and offering me his elbow. I'm grateful for it.

"Come on," he says, "we'd better get there quickly. We don't want Beaufort Lincoln out hunting you down."

"You don't?" Clare calls from the rug. "Because that sounds kinda hot to me!"

Chapter Forty-One

Dray

At a quarter past eight – fifteen minutes after the girl should have arrived at our rooms – the bell at the tower door chimes.

Beaufort left ten minutes ago, angry and on the prowl, quite prepared to drag the little brat here by her pigtails if necessary.

I turn to Thorne, sitting beside me in a straight-backed chair and staring silently into the blazing fire.

"I'm assuming that's our errant little thrall. Do you want to answer the door?" He doesn't respond, although his jaw hardens. "I'll take that as a no," I say, jumping to my feet. I really thought after his little performance on the field, he would be jumping at the chance to welcome her inside. But he's back to his usual dismissive, disinterested self.

At the door, I find our little thrall, leaning on the tall, lean boy who is obviously her friend.

"I thought it best I accompany her here," he blurts out before I even say a word. "She's drunk."

I lean against the door. "Is she now?"

"No," she says, finding it difficult to focus on my face. "I'm not drunk."

"You wanna tell me exactly how she got drunk?" I growl.

"No," the boy says.

I can't help laughing at that. "Fair enough." I reach out my hand and take ahold of her elbow. "Come on then, in you come." I drag her towards me and the friend releases her arm.

He hesitates, shifting his weight from one foot to the other, and opening and closing his mouth.

"You got something to say?" I ask him.

"She doesn't want to be here. She doesn't want this."

I have to admire the dude's bravery even if it is idiotic.

"Yeah, she did mention that once or twice."

I pull her through the doorway and slam the door in his face.

I drag her further into the hallway and under the light.

"Shit," I mumble. "You really are fucked."

She squints at me, pupils widening and narrowing before widening again. Her brow descends over her eyes.

"You!"

To my absolute fucking delight, she swings her hand backwards and then slaps me full force across my cheek.

Shit, there's some force to that. I think I even taste the faintest trace of blood in my mouth. She really is wasted.

"Yes, darling," I say with a wide grin because, fuck me, the little brat likes to play. "Me."

"You're a sick pervert!"

I chuckle, rubbing my stinging cheek. That ... wasn't what I was expecting. With my hand still tight on her elbow I guide her through to the kitchen.

"Come on, let's get you some water and you can tell me why exactly I am a pervert."

She attempts to shake me off but my grip is tight, my fingers digging into her flesh. "You know why!"

"Sweetheart," I grin, "I'm not denying that I am a pervert. Fuck," I let my gaze skip darkly down her body, lingering on all the places that turn me on the most, "there are lots of perverted things I'd really love to do to you, but you need to be a little more specific here. Help me out."

Still holding on to her arm, I reach up with my left and take down a clean glass.

"You told everyone in history class that–"

"I'm a very open person. I can't help myself."

"And you tricked me. I thought you were a wolf."

"Did you?" I say innocently. "I have a feeling you knew it was me." I wink at her, something that has the rage boiling even further in her veins – I can feel it. This is hot.

"You ... you ... you sniffed my crotch!"

"Yeah," I say with that grin again. "I did. And, sweetheart, I wasn't lying, your pussy smells fucking fantastic. All wet and juicy and delicious." I slam the glass down on the counter and pull her closer, bending down to whisper right in her ear. "I want to lick that pussy of yours out so badly. I wanna taste it. I want to soak my tongue in your cunt and fuck you with it. I want to find your little nub and play with it. Flick it and suck it and make you come right onto my face."

She stares at me open-mouthed, and I hear the thump of her pulse accelerate. "You really are sick!"

"You think that's sick?" I whisper, letting my lips brush ever so gently against the shell of her ear. I can smell her just as well in my human form as I can my wolf, can smell that wet scent of hers. So damn good! "I'm willing to bet you've never been licked out then, sweetheart, or you'd be jumping up on this counter, spreading open your thighs and begging me to bury my face in your pussy."

"I don't want you to touch me," she says, trying to shake off my grip again. "I want you to keep your hands off me."

"Really? Because you didn't seem to mind my tongue on you when I was a wolf. Do you prefer it that way, sweetheart?" I smile at her again. "That could be fun." Her eyes widen in horror. This is the most fun I've had in years. "You know what else? I think you're lying to me." I sweep my fingers down her arm. "I think the idea of me eating you out turns you on."

"It doesn't."

"Your mouth can say one thing, but your pussy's saying the exact opposite. You have no idea how wet your pussy smells. I bet those panties of yours are dripping and your pussy is throbbing." I shake my head. The idea of it is fucking awesome. "Shit!"

Her mouth drifts open – a little in horror, a little in amazement. Yeah, I caught her out. She can pretend she hates us all she likes. Huh, perhaps she really does. She also finds me hot.

"Unfortunately, as much as I'd like to oblige you right now, it ain't going to happen." She frowns, and am I deluding myself or is there just the slightest hint of disappointment in her scent. "You're drunk. And as perverted as I am," and I am, the girl has no fucking idea, "I prefer my girls fully *compos mentis* and engaged." I drop her arm and slam on the tap, filling the glass until the water is slopping over the brim.

Then I wave my hand over the water, shadows swirling through the liquid, and hold it out to her.

"Here, drink."

She peers suspiciously at the shadows lingering in the liquid. "Did you drug it?"

"Yes," I say and she gasps, "it's going to make you feel better, it's going to make you sober."

"You expect me to believe that?"

"I don't give a shit if you believe me or not. It's your head that will feel like it's been jammed in a vise if you don't drink it."

"You could be trying to drug me so you can–"

"If I wanted to do *that*," I lean my body into hers, "I'd do it. I don't need to fucking drug you."

She scowls at me, but my words decide her; she takes a gulp of the water.

"Good girl." She scowls even harder.

I fucking love this. If she only knew how fucking hard those scowls make me.

"Come on," I tell her. She's incapable of walking in a straight line so I support her elbow as I lead her through to the lounge. It's empty. I guide her down into one of the armchairs next to the fire, draw a stool up close and lift her feet onto it, then wrap a blanket over her lap.

"Comfy?" I ask her.

She continues to look at me with suspicion and takes another sip of the water.

"Good girl," I tell her. "Drink that all up for me. Do you want something to read?" I smirk at her. "Or is the world spinning too much?"

"A book would be nice," she says stiffly.

I walk over to the small bookshelf, run my fingers over the spine and pull out something colorful. I toss it onto her lap.

"Enjoy," I say.

"Enjoy? Why? What are you—"

"It's Saturday night, sweetheart. Party in the Onyx common room." I stand with my hands on my hips, smirking in a way I know infuriates her. "Now, I know how much you wanna come. But you're too fucking drunk. I'm not taking you."

"I don't want to come," she snipes.

"Sure you don't." I head towards the door. "Have fun. Although stay off the booze, okay? You make a pretty pissy little drunk." At the doorway, I pause, peering back at her over my shoulder. "Your pussy really does smell divine."

◈

"She knows about my wolf," I say as I stroll through the academy with Thorne and Beaufort.

"Are you saying she didn't know before?" Beaufort snorts.

I admit, I understand his skepticism. I was fucking surprised myself when the girl appeared to have no idea who I was. I mean, everybody knows who the fuck I am. First-born son of the pack leader, pretty much pack leader myself these days. Everybody – even those living out in the most distant parts of the realm – knows that Dray Eros is a shifter. At least, that's what I thought.

"No fucking idea," I chuckle, "she let me bury my nose right up and personal in her cunt. Man, she smells so fucking goood." I shake my body. "I want to eat her out so badly." Thorne turns his head and glares at me. "Oh come on. You don't want to fuck her with your fingers, get her juices all over those gloves of yours?" I swing back my head, bouncing on the spot. "I'd like to see that."

"Why was she late?" Beaufort asks. He's still pissed about that. Probably even more pissed that I got to spend time with her and not him.

"Drunk," I say.

Thorne halts, even more thunder crashing over his face than usual, actual lightning skipping in the air around him. I take a step back. I don't want to be fried hot dog.

"She was drunk," he growls lowly.

"Yeah, was. I gave her purified water. She'll be sober as a saint by the time we return."

"We should go back."

"No point. The girl needs to sit and sober up."

"We should be watching over her."

"This party will be shit anyway," Beaufort mumbles in agreement.

"This was your plan," I point out. "Deny her our attention until she cracks."

He grunts. "Yeah, and we have to show our faces."

"Anyway, the party was pretty fun last week." I rub my knuckles. "You seemed to enjoy yourself," I say to Thorne.

He glares straight ahead and I shove my hands into my pockets and sigh.

Obviously, it's not going to be as fun tonight. But I have a feeling it could be once we're home again. Because I have a feeling that tonight might be the night that our little thrall finally caves.

Chapter Forty-Two

B eaufort

I squeeze through the heaving bodies, waving at the people who call out to me, smiling at those who reach for me, but slipping from their grips. I make my way to the back of the room and survey the party.

Tonight's party is themed. Many of the students are dressed in togas or colorful robes; several have laurel wreaths propped on their heads. Vines dripping with ripe grapes wind around the room and gold platters hold towers of food; jugs full of burgundy wine stand on all the surfaces.

It's no different from last week's party though. Same people, same music, same gossip, same dull atmosphere. Except tonight the Hardies aren't being so damn blatant. They're huddled in the corner with their brattish thrall still nursing their injuries and hurt pride from last week most probably.

I have no desire to be here. But I have to keep up appearances so the others don't suspect how much our little thrall is getting to me. I don't want them realizing how much her continued defiance has wound me up. We need to keep the façade that we are in control, that everything is just fine.

We are having fun, aren't we? So the fuck what if our thrall isn't with us.

I sweep my gaze over the room. No one else has caused any trouble or attempted to challenge our dominance since we took the Hardies out. I don't think anyone will for a long, long time.

Dray is already dancing with some girls in the center of the room. Thorne is hugging some dark corner somewhere. To the side, the Smyte twins are balancing on either arm of a chair, their thrall pinned between them, his cheeks pink and his eyes glazed.

Henrietta catches me looking at them and obviously mistakes my passing glance as interest. She smiles at me and slithers up onto her feet. I immediately turn my head away. I have no intention of speaking to Henrietta tonight. I don't have the patience for it.

Unfortunately, she doesn't get the hint and is sidling up to me in the next moment, a glass of red wine in either hand.

"You look thirsty," she says, offering me one of the glasses.

"I'm not."

She laughs, placing the unwanted glass down on a side table and taking a sip of her own. She wears a black shiny jumpsuit and her auburn hair is scraped up onto the top of her head and braided over her shoulder. She reminds me of a scorpion. One with a deadly sting in its tail.

"Perhaps you're thirsty for something else. You always used to be." She rests her hand on my arm. "You couldn't get enough."

"Funny," I say coldly, "I don't quite remember it that way."

"You don't remember sneaking into my room, begging to spend the night?"

I snort. "You have a creative imagination, Henny."

She ignores me. Maybe there was a time when I found her attractive, irresistible even – her magic is mesmerizing and powerful. But that time was short-lived. Fleeting even. I've felt nothing but disdain and disinterest for her for months and months now.

"I bet you miss it," she purrs.

I shake my head.

"Especially when you're not getting any from that little thrall of yours."

Despite my best efforts to remain calm, to not rise to the little witch's bait, my shoulders tense.

"Who says we're not getting any? I'm very satisfied with our thrall."

"Well," she says, stroking her hand against my cheek, "it's written all over your face, Beaufort." She laughs again. "I know that look well – I kept you waiting, remember?" A growl simmers in my throat. "And also, the girl's said it many times. She's not your thrall – despite your and Dray's best efforts."

"Watch how you talk to me, Henny."

"Oh," she says, innocently, "I'm only concerned for your welfare, Beaufort. I know it can't be easy for a man like you, in fact it must be crushing."

"It is easy. I'm more satisfied than I ever have been," I lie. I want our thrall so fucking desperately. It's driving me insane. I can't stop thinking about her. Can't stop imagining all the things I want to do to her. I want to end the games and make her ours.

"But the girl is just that. A girl," she hisses. "She'd be such a lousy fuck. You're going to be so disappointed when you finally have her. I don't understand why you're wasting your time."

"I'm not wasting my time."

"We could go back to my rooms right now, if you wanted, Beaufort," she says, sliding her hands down my front, her touch making my skin crawl. "Or we could find a quiet place – you always did like to have a bit of fun like that."

"Not with you, Henny. Not any longer."

Her eyes flash. "Don't expect me to be so obliging when you come crawling back to me, Beaufort, begging for me to take you back. I know you, I know your patience is severely limited. And when you finally lose your patience with that girl, I may no longer be an option."

She tosses her braid over her shoulder and storms back to her sister.

She's right, my patience is limited.

In fact, it has finally snapped.

Chapter Forty-Three

B riony

Turns out Dray Eros wasn't lying to me. Ten minutes after I drink the enchanted water the room is no longer spinning and I'm feeling my normal self.

I don't lose any time. I hurry up the stairs and into Beaufort's study. It was the only room of the three Princes' I didn't snoop through last weekend and the one I think may hold answers for me.

Beaufort has a reputation, one I don't quite understand. Everyone assumes he knows what's happening across the realm and there must be a reason for that.

When I reach his study, I find I'm not wrong. Across his desk lie scores of tiny little scrolled up notes – notes that judging by their size, must have been brought here by raven. Someone is sending him news. What news?

To one side of the desk stands a magnifying glass. I

perch down on his chair and, unraveling one of the tiny notes, hold it up to the glass. The writing is titchy but under the glass it magnifies big enough to read. There are lines of text – one running onto the other. Figures related to the harvest distribution across the realm. Information about a court case in Granite Quarter. Details of troop movements and other meaningless bits and pieces. Nothing I can see Beaufort needs to know or would be interested in. However, among the standard lines of text are meaningless sentences. Ones that make no sense. Pure and utter nonsense.

Code.

I wrinkle my forehead and try to make it out but I've never been any good at that. I pick up the next scroll and the next, finding them all much the same.

It's nothing that will give me answers about Amelia. Not unless I can crack the code. I consider pocketing one of the scrolls and taking it back to Clare to see if she can do it, but I'm worried Beaufort might notice it missing. He's already accused me of stealing once.

I flop back in the chair and rock it side to side, eyeing the drawers that run down the side of his desk to the floor. I try each one. The first three are locked with magic. Not something my pin skills can overcome. The last is unlocked. I draw it open carefully, half expecting it to be booby-trapped. All I find inside are some sheets of paper stapled together in the corner. I draw them up onto my lap.

It's a list of all the students at the academy with details of their Quarter and their rooms. I run my eyes down the details. Beaufort has marked a handful of names with different colored symbols. A couple of the shadow weavers as well students from the other Quarters.

My name. Stanley's. The quieter of the Smyte twins.

Why? What does it mean?

I stare at the names, trying to commit the ones he's marked to memory. Then I return the list to the drawer, close it and scurry downstairs. There's no way I want to be caught snooping a second time.

Back in the lounge, I snuggle under the blanket again and open the book. The fire burns warm right by my toes and soon my eyes are drifting closed.

I wake to the sound of the front door clicking open. I peer through the open doorway and watch Beaufort step through into the hallway and halt outside the lounge. His shoulders rise and fall, and even across the distance I can see the tension riding through his body, can feel the crackle of his magic.

I push away the blanket and climb onto my feet as he swings his gaze my way.

His silver eyes have my heart stopping abruptly in my chest. They brim with something indescribable and they are focused entirely on me.

No one has ever looked at me like that before. With such raw longing, with such blazing heat, with such undeniable need.

We stare at each other and we're back there again, on the platform, the moment our eyes first met. Time sweeping away.

"Enough," he says lowly, and before I have a chance to wonder what he can mean, he's closed the distance between us and pulled me into his arms, and then he's kissing me, pressing his mouth hard against mine, and whipping my breath right away.

I don't know what is wrong with me. I don't understand

myself. But I don't struggle. I don't slap him. I don't tell him to leave me alone.

I melt into him like he is a flame and I am nothing more than wax.

No, I do more than that. As he coils his arms around my waist and drags me closer, I wrap my arms around his neck, bury my fingers in his thick brown hair and press his mouth even harder against mine.

Everything in my body is liquid and heat.

I'm no longer thinking, only feeling.

I am just as needy as he is. Just as desperate for it.

He pulls away and I'm so damn dizzy, I hardly notice him twine his fingers through mine and lead me up the staircase and into his bedroom. As he does, my senses snap back into place.

He's my enemy. They all are. They killed my sister.

"I don't want—"

"I think the lady doth protest too much," he whispers, "I think you do want this. I think you're fighting goddamn hard to deny it."

Dray's words from earlier float through my mind – his description of eating me out was fucking graphic, it also stirred something inside me. Something that's been stirring every time any of them is close, something that's been stirring since Beaufort caged me on the ground. Something I've been trying to repress and control for such a long time.

"I'm not," I say, denying the truth.

"I think you want this so damn badly. The way you just kissed me – you wouldn't kiss me like that if you didn't want this ... I think you're just longing for me to touch you."

He tugs me closer and rests his other hand on my waist. It does feel good to be touched. I can't deny it – even if it's a betrayal – to her, to me, to everything I believe in.

"You could just ... stop fighting. You could surrender." He lifts our hands to his mouth and kisses the end of each of my fingertips. "You could surrender to me."

"Never," I whisper, feebly, weakly.

"Surrender and I'll take such good care of you. I'll make you feel so good."

I shake my head slowly.

"Surrender, little thrall. Get down on your knees and surrender."

I want to fight.

I want to run away.

I don't want to feel conflicted this way. I don't want to betray my sister.

I don't want to feel this way about him.

I want to ... I want to find out what happens if I do give in. If I do as he says. If I stop fighting for just one moment and let go.

If I stop thinking, stop fighting, stop hurting; let myself go and just feel.

Will he destroy me like they did my sister?

Do I care?

My life has been so worthless since she left. So dark and bleak. This sadness has weighed in my heart and for once I want to feel something other than this cold grief.

I want to feel alive. I want to feel Beaufort Lincoln.

And so, I do as the shadow weaver says.

I lower myself down onto my knees, the plush carpet soft against my skin.

He doesn't smirk in triumph. He simply looks at me in wonder; a heat and a desire – perhaps even a reverence – flickering in his pupils.

He doesn't say anything, simply unbuckles his belt, unbuttons his pants.

I know what he wants. I didn't need Fly's little sex ed lesson this evening to work that out.

I watch as he tugs out his cock; stiff and girthy and magnificent in his hand. His foreskin has been cut away and the head of his cock throbs, a long prominent vein running the length of his shaft.

My heart beats in my throat and something swoops low in my belly. I can't deny it now, I am turned on.

On my knees, I'm at his mercy. Maybe I always was. He's stronger than me, more powerful. I've struggled and fought and resisted but a part of me has wanted to give myself up to him right from the first moment he pinned me to the ground.

I must be more messed up than I thought.

He runs his fist up and down his shaft

"Do you want to?" he says, his voice distorted with lust.

I don't answer.

Instead, I cave into that part of me. The part that longs for this, no matter how wrong it is. No matter how dangerous.

I open my mouth, lean forward and take him into my mouth. The taste is salty but not unpleasant, and the skin is soft inside my mouth. I swirl my tongue around his cock-head and he groans above me.

A quiet voice deep within protests at what I'm doing. He's my enemy. His kind took the most precious thing from my life – the only good thing – and ripped my life apart. I shouldn't be doing this.

But the other part – the part I've repressed and caged for so long – wants this so badly. Wants to feel, wants to be felt in return, wants to throw all caution to the wind and feel something more than misery and pain and loss.

I suck on his cock and his fingers tangle in my hair,

yanking out the binds and pins that hold it back, until it falls loose around my face.

"So damn beautiful," he murmurs. "You're so damn beautiful."

My feeble heart flutters, even though I know a boy like Beaufort says that to every girl. That I'm not the first to fall to my knees in front of him and I won't be the last.

"You should wear it down all the time."

My eyes flick up to meet his as I suck him some more, moving my head up and down his shaft, taking him in and out of my mouth.

I've never done this before – only caught glimpses of others doing it at the back of the tavern, out in the woods. I don't know exactly how it works. Yet, the way his silver eyes burn hot, the grunts escaping his throat, the way his fingers tighten in my hair, pulling at my scalp, I know it's good, that I must be doing something right.

And for the first time, I feel like I'm the one in control. That I am the one with all the power – a power that soars through my body. He's at my mercy. He's at my whim. Look what I've reduced him to.

"I'm gonna come," he groans. "Can I come in your mouth, little thrall?"

I wouldn't have expected a man like Beaufort Lincoln to ask. I hold his gaze in mine, my veins singing with desire.

"Hmmm," I moan around his cock and then it's jerking on my tongue, warm liquid hitting the back of my throat. Salty again and earthy.

I choke a little, swallow some, some spilling over my lips and down my chin.

"Shit," he grunts, "shit that looks so ..."

And then he's dragging me up onto my feet and walking us both backwards, back towards the chest of drawers until my back hits the solid piece of furniture. Then, before I know what's happening both his hands are on my waist and he's lifting me to sit on the top of the chest.

"Wh-wh-what are you doing?" I say.

"Returning the favor."

He opens my legs and steps between them. He's no longer hard and I can't understand what he intends to do until his hand is on my leg, stroking the inside of my thigh, making me gasp.

"Hmmm, so soft," he whispers, stroking higher and higher, impossibly slowly, so slowly I realize I'm holding my breath, waiting.

His fingertips hit the gusset of my panties and I jolt. There's an electricity in his touch and it's divine.

I clutch the edge of the chest of drawers, my eyes drifting shut as he leans in, his magic engulfing me, his mouth brushing over the shell of my ear.

"Are you wet?"

His fingers slip inside my panties, along the seam of my pussy lips. My core swoops and a needy pulse beats right there where he's gliding his fingertips teasingly over me. Touching me.

Except he's not touching me. I guess I had no concept of what touching really was. Two years ago with Stanley it had been quick fumbles out in the forest, down in the leaves, against a tree. It had been more for him than me. He'd barely touched me.

"So fucking wet," he groans.

I didn't know what touching was until Beaufort touches me. His thumb circling my clit, his magic sparking against it.

It feels so good, I cry out, my head falling backward.

I grip the wood more tightly as he circles achingly

slowly, slowly and slowly and slowly, a pressure building in my core, my legs beginning to shake, knocking against him.

"Like this," he says, his mouth on my throat. "Come like this, little thrall. Fall apart for me."

I bite on my lip, tears pooling in my eyes.

It's been such a long time, such a long, long time. Nothing in my life has been good or right. I've not wanted to, not desired it. And now I want it so badly.

"Pleeeease," I whine, hating myself for begging but unable to help myself.

"You want a little more, do you?"

He vibrates his thumb over my clit and everything I've been holding back, repressing, caging, hiding, comes flooding from somewhere deep down inside me to the surface, electricity, and pleasure, and heavenly sensations racing in my blood and through my limbs and over my skin.

I feel like I'm somewhere else completely, high above the skies, up with the moon and the stars, soaring in the heavens.

"So ... fucking ... beautiful," he murmurs as I hang there, suspended.

Then I start to tumble back to earth, my body jolting and bucking as I'm hit by waves of pleasure.

I think he'll pull his hand away now. Instead, he's sliding his fingers through my folds and plunging two inside my pussy.

I cry out again, bucking on his fingers, and he fucks me with them, firm and hard. So firm, so hard, I lose control of my senses, my hands leaving the chest of drawers and coming to grip his shoulders instead, my nails sinking into his flesh, wild little noises bubbling in my throat. I rock my hips in desperation, riding his fingers.

I never came when Stanley and I did stuff. He was too

impatient and clumsy with his fingers and I've never made myself come this way either. I didn't think it was possible.

It is.

And Beaufort proves it because, within a couple of minutes, I fall apart again.

"See," he whispers in my ear, withdrawing his fingers from me and bringing them up to his mouth. "See how good it is when you surrender."

And then he's sucking all my mess from his fingers.

"Your virgin pussy tastes so good."

Chapter Forty-Four

B eaufort

One moment there's bliss swimming all over her face, the next that scowl is back firmly in place.

I thought she'd be purring like a contented little pussycat after those two orgasms I gifted her. Instead, she's hissing and spitting with her claws out.

"This doesn't mean anything," she snaps, pushing me away, wiggling down from my chest of drawers and tugging her skirt down her thighs. "And I am not some virgin, so if this is what this is all about, if this is the fetish you shitheads have, you're looking in the wrong place."

"Who?" I boom, unable to comprehend why the fuck I care.

I don't have some fetish. I don't subscribe to the notion that girls have to be untouched, unclaimed. Hell, it's usually more fun when the girl knows what she's doing and I usually don't care where she gained that insight from.

But her …

The thought of someone else touching her has a rage simmering through my veins.

She is ours. No one else's.

"None of your fucking business," she says, attempting to squeeze past me.

I catch her arm.

"Everything about you is my business."

"No, it's not," she snarls through gritted teeth.

I yank her closer.

"You felt how good that was," I whisper, "that's because this is meant to be."

Confusion flickers across her face and for a moment I consider telling her. But how the hell would I explain it? "You are meant to be ours." I take a deep inhale, attempting to calm myself. I don't want to argue with her. I want to take her to bed.

"It's okay that someone touched you before, but no one touches you from now on."

She stares at me in disbelief. "It's 'okay'?" she hisses. "Of course, it's fucking okay. It has nothing to do with you."

"Did you not just hear me say that everything about you has to do with me?"

She pulls against my grip. "Let go of me. I'm leaving."

"No," I say petulantly. I have a taste of this toy – a fucking intimate taste – and I don't want to let it go.

Then she does the last thing in the world I expect her to do. She stamps her booted foot down hard on my own. It takes me by surprise. I howl in pain and release my grip automatically. In a flash, she's slipping out of the door, her light footsteps audible on the staircase.

For a moment, I consider chasing after her and dragging her back. But I've had my fun for tonight. I can afford to let her have her way this time.

I step back towards the chest of drawers and examine the surface; there's a smudge of her arousal there and I drag my fingers through it and bring it up to my mouth, sucking the musky mess off my fingers.

Fuck, a girl never tasted so good.

Fuck, a girl never came so hard on my fingers – never felt so good on my fingers, her pussy tight and warm and convulsing in sweet waves.

Was I telling the truth? Is it because this is meant to be – destined to be? Or is it the girl herself?

She has a pretty enough face, her figure is all right. She's nothing special and yet she turns me the fuck on.

I want to explore more of her, the quiver of her throat, the crest of her breasts, the pert tips of nipples and her ass. Fuck, yes, her ass.

For several moments, I stand there lost in the memory of what just happened, playing it over and over again in my mind. Then, I drag my gaze up to the mirror and stare at my face.

There's a smile on my lips.

I smile even wider.

What a fucking awesome night this turned out to be.

Coming home to get my dick sucked and finger-fucking our little thrall.

I thought the academy would be a bore – I know where I'm going at the end of the year. The trials will be no test for me. And I'm being forced to sit through lessons when there's nothing more to learn.

I changed my mind. It's going to be a lot of fun!

I descend the staircase, finding the other two in the lounge. It seems they also left the party early.

"The little thrall just stormed out of here like someone lit a firework up her ass." Dray tilts his head, examining me as he sniffs the air. "Can I assume you had something to do with that?"

I shrug and yawn. "I fingered her."

Dray bursts out laughing. "Fuck, man, were you that bad at it? The girl looked like she swallowed a hedgehog."

"Trust me, she enjoyed it," I say, smiling to myself.

Thorne gapes at me, then storms right out of the room.

"What's his problem?" Dray sniffs.

"No idea," I say.

Apart from that little display before the run, Thorne has shown no interest in the girl at all. And that display, I suspect, was more about maintaining our reputation and ensuring those at this academy know we're in charge, and nothing at all to do with keeping the girl safe. After all, I had to practically force him to spend time with her this week.

Thorne doesn't give a shit about the girl. He doesn't give a shit about any girls or anyone for that matter.

"Did you make her come?" Dray asks.

"Of course I made her fucking come." I should probably tell him about the cock-sucking but I want to keep something to myself and I suspect Dray will want to pour over the details.

My suspicion is correct.

"What did she feel like?" Dray asks eagerly, stepping closer to sniff the air around me. "What did she look and sound like?"

"Wet," I say, remembering how much arousal I'd found in her panties – a fucking treat I was not expecting.

That was another suspicion that proved correct. She

may be fighting this but underneath all the hissing and spitting and claws, she wants it.

"Wet," he repeats, grinning. "I fucking knew it!"

"And she's noisy when she comes."

Another thing I hadn't been expecting. For a girl who seems to like to disappear into the background, she is noisy, messy and needy when she comes.

"I like that too." He frowns at me. "It's a shame you had to scare her away."

"She's touchy."

"You mean she doesn't jump and lick your ass when you click your fingers."

I suppress a smile. She may not do those things but she did sink to her knees and suck my cock.

"She's broken now," I say, remembering how powerful and all-consuming her orgasm had been. "She'll be back for more."

Chapter Forty-Five

B^{riony}

I wake the next day drowning in a bog of guilt.

Shadow weavers took my sister from me. I loathe them. Detest them. I hate them.

And yet, last night what I did ...

I groan with shame, roll over in my bed and pull the feeble covers over my head, ignoring the clang of the tower bells reminding me I have to be up.

I brushed my teeth three times when I got back to my room last night and yet I swear I can still taste that son-of-a-bitch in my mouth. Plus, I'm a little sore between my legs and my jaw aches.

However, despite all that, I can't deny my skin is still tingling, and my core still prickling, with electricity.

I groan more loudly. That's the worst thing about it. I

can't deny it. I enjoyed what happened last night, even if I hate myself for it now.

It makes the guilt and the betrayal ten times worse, pressing on my chest like a heavyweight.

How could I do this to her? How could I let her down like this?

My sister would have done anything for me – anything. She was the one who looked after me, who looked out for me, who made sure I had clothes to wear, food to eat, a bag packed for school each day. This was long before the days of Muriel, back when father still worked. But without a mom to look after us, Amelia stepped into that role even though I can see now she was still just a kid herself.

When she didn't return from the academy, I made a promise to her – I made a promise to myself – I'd discover the truth. I'd find out what happened to my sister. And what have I done so far? Nothing.

At some point in the morning, there is a light rap on my door.

"Cupcake, are you in there?" Fly whispers through the wood.

"Urgh," I moan in reply.

He pushes back the door and creeps inside. "Not feeling so good this morning? You know the perfect cure for a hangover – fat and grease and bread, lots of bread."

"I'm not hungover," I say from under the cover.

"Really?" he says, the mattress creaking as he perches on the side of the bed, "because you were pretty wasted last night."

"I'm fine. Dray Eros gave me some kind of sobering concoction."

"Then what's wrong?"

I peel back the cover and peer up at him. To my

surprise, Fly is not looking hungover this morning either. In fact, he's looking his usual bright and dapper self.

"It's complicated," I tell him.

"One thing I'm learning, Cupcake, it always is with you." He examines my face. "Do I take it the rest of your evening was not a success?"

"Define success?"

"Did you get to fuck the Princes?"

"No," I shriek but I guess my eye must twitch or something.

"Hmmm," Fly says. "Something did happen though?"

I groan. "Something did happen."

"Are you going to tell me what?"

I shake my head.

"Spoil sport," he snips. "So why so unhappy about it?" Horror streaks across his face. "They didn't–"

"No!" I shriek again. "I just ..."

"Have some regret?" he says with sympathy. I nod. "Well, don't. Life's too short for that, Cupcake. And life is definitely too short to be lying about in bed. Especially on our one day off!"

"But there's nothing to do!" I whine.

"No problem," he says, tapping his fingers against his mouth, "luckily I have an idea. Get dressed and meet me outside in half an hour. I'm going to go see if Clare is still alive."

Thirty minutes later I'm hugging my jacket tight around me and waiting for Fly, the wind whipping loose strands of my hair around my face.

"What exactly did you have planned?" I call to him as he approaches with Clare by his side. "I hope it's indoors because it's a tad bit windy out here."

"I know," he says with a grin. "Perfect, isn't it?"

I glance at Clare who shrugs, then winces. "My head hurts so much!" she groans. "Why couldn't you leave me alone to die in peace?"

"Because a bit of fresh air to blow away the cobwebs is exactly what you need."

"It's a little bit more than fresh," I complain, yanking hair from my face.

"Come on you two, quit the complaining."

He hooks his arms through both of ours and drags us along the cobbled pathways and out to the edge of the campus. There he leads us right to where the manicured fields end and the moorland encroaches all the way up to the edge of the towers.

"Come on," he says, stepping onto the rough terrain.

"Where exactly are we going?" I say.

"That's the thing with surprises," he says, "if you tell the person what it is, you spoil it."

He marches us across the moorland and Clare groans, then makes a queasy face.

"I can't walk any further. I think I'm going to vomit." She peers at me. "How come you seem okay? Weren't you as drunk as I was?"

"Yes, but Dray Eros gave me something to sober me up – seems it cured any potential hangover too."

"See, being a thrall has its advantages," Fly points out. I think of the two awesome orgasms I was treated to last night – definitely another advantage. My cheeks pinken. Something Fly spots immediately.

"What?" he hisses.

"Huh?" I respond, pretending to straighten my jacket against the wind and not meeting his eyes.

"What was that?" he sweeps his forefinger in my direction. "That blush."

"I didn't blush."

"You're still blushing now, Cupcake." He turns to Clare. "She regrets something that happened last night – something that was obviously dirty enough to make her blush just thinking about it – but she won't give me the details."

"I imagine it's private," Clare says.

"Exactly," I respond.

"Yeah, but where's the fun in that!" Fly whines, walking us several hundred meters away from the tall buildings and then stopping.

"This should do it," he mumbles.

"Do what?" I say, spinning around. There is nothing here. Nothing to see and clearly nothing to do.

Fly unzips his jacket.

"Are we getting our own private strip show?" I ask. "Is this what this is? Couldn't we have done that indoors?"

"You wish, Cupcake," he says, pulling out a piece of material from inside his jacket. The cloth is multicolored and cut into the shape of a diamond and he holds it up to show us.

"A kite?" I say. This is not what I was expecting.

"Yep, a kite. It's the best I could do with the limited resources I had."

"You made it?" I say.

"I did. Had to sacrifice quite a good shirt for it too."

"Shhh, don't let the teachers hear. They'll have you carted off to Slate Quarter for manual craft work in no time."

"We can make things in Iron Quarter, you know."

"And in Granite," Clare pipes up.

"I used to make and fly these with my grandpa, before, you know, I became the disappointment." He smiles sadly.

Then hands me the kite. "Here, hold this out in front of you, at the bottom tip."

I do as he says, and he unwinds the string, stepping further and further away from me as he does. When he's content with the distance, he yells towards me.

"Okay, Briony, toss it up."

Bending my knees, I throw the kite up into the air. The wind catches it immediately and it swerves around like a crazed bird before crashing into the ground.

"Again," Fly commands me, untangling the string.

This time, I concentrate on making my throw straighter and higher and somehow Fly manages to time it with a tug on the string and before we know it, the kite is sailing up into the sky. Fly runs out the string and we watch it climb higher and higher into the gray clouds, bright and vibrant among them, a trail of bows bobbing after it.

"It's beautiful," I tell Fly as the three of us stand and watch it.

"It's not bad," he says.

"You and your grandpa used to make them?"

"Yeah, he showed me how. He was different too. We'd disappear together and for a moment I'd feel like maybe I did belong somewhere. After all, if the kite could escape all the way up there in the sky among the birds and the wind and the clouds, maybe I could belong somewhere just as crazy."

"Granite's not that crazy," Clare says matter-of-factly. "It's actually pretty boring."

"Maybe I won't fit in there either, then," Fly says, a little sadly.

I lean my head against his shoulder.

"Do you want a go, ladies?" he asks us both.

"I'm barely managing to remain upright," Clare tells him. "I cannot operate another vessel as well."

"How about you, Briony?"

"Are you sure? I wouldn't want to break it."

"Kites are meant to be broken. That's what my grandpa always said." He passes the string to me. "Hold it tight."

I'm thankful for the warning. The kite tugs against the string much more firmly than I expected, attempting to break free, and the whole line vibrates with tension.

We're so engrossed in watching the kite dance above our heads, we don't see the Smyte twins crossing the moorland from the woods, heading our way, until they're almost upon us, their wild long hair caught in the wind and the soles of their boots caked in mud.

Where the hell did they come from?

Their faces are almost identical but I'm beginning to be able to tell them apart. Henrietta's hair falls more to the left and she has the tiniest of scars above her right eyebrow. Lynette blinks a little more than her sister and talks less.

"Oh look," Henrietta says to her sister, loud enough to ensure we can hear. "How quaint. They're flying a kite."

Lynette giggles. "One they patched together themselves by the looks of it."

"Now don't be cruel, Linny. They don't have magic for these things, do they? Poor pathetic little souls."

She adopts an exaggerated expression of sympathy, curling down her bottom lip, but then her gaze lands on me. Her eyes narrow immediately.

"If it isn't that little bitch from Slate Quarter. The one who thinks she's worth more than she is."

Clare gasps. She was wholeheartedly convinced Thorne's speech the other day would end all the abuse directed at me. She's shocked to find the opposite.

I am not. I knew it would only make it worse. I know how people like the Smyte twins work.

It doesn't deter Clare though. My mild little friend – who possibly had all her sense pickled by alcohol last night – stares at Henrietta and says, "You can't talk to her like that."

Henrietta's face turns ugly. I doubt anyone has ever told her she can't do something – certainly not a commoner.

"What did you just say to me, scum?"

Clare immediately realizes her mistake and I step in front of her protectively.

"I-I-I-I just meant that Thor–"

"Are you still talking to me?!" Henrietta roars. "Who the hell do you think you are to dare to presume to tell me what I can and can't do? Do you know who I am?" We all look at her silently, sensing it would be better not to speak. "Well, do you?"

"We know," Fly says.

"Then you know what I can do!" Her eyes flicker with menace and she shoots her hand up into the sky, lightning racing from her fingertips and towards the clouds.

"Briony!" Fly shouts out.

But it's too late, Henrietta's lightning strikes the flimsy kite high above us and it bursts into flames, electricity shoots down the string and straight into my arm.

I don't even have time to scream. I'm tossed across the grass, and the lights flick out.

Chapter Forty-Six

B riony

I blink open my eyes and stare up into the concerned faces of Fly and Clare.

"Oh Briony, thank the stars," Clare says, rocking back onto her behind.

"Wh-wh-what happened?" I murmur. My ears are ringing and my tongue moves like a lead weight in my very dry mouth.

"You don't remember?" Fly says.

A bruise is forming on his right cheekbone and when I peer at Clare, I see she has blood trickling out of her nostrils.

"Last I remember we were flying a kite. But it looks like we were in a fight."

"Yeah," Fly says, helping me to roll up and sit. The motion makes me woozy but I'm more concerned about my friends. I can take a beating. Something tells me with two brothers, Fly has encountered more than his fair share too. But Clare? "Henrietta Smyte threw a bit of a hissy fit."

"What happened?" I say, pulling a tissue out of my pocket and passing it to Clare to dab at her nose. "Is it broken?" I ask her.

She shakes her head. "It looks more dramatic than it is. I always get a nosebleed in an emergency."

My brow wrinkles with confusion.

"We thought you were dead," Fly clarifies. "You got electrocuted by a kite and flew halfway across the moorland. That's how many times now, Cupcake?" The side of his mouth twitches.

"Near-death experiences? I lost count long ago." I reach out and touch the bruise on his cheek. "Did Henrietta do that too?"

"Yeah, I called her a bitch for zapping you with her magic."

"It was really badass," Clare adds.

"Yeah, until she struck me with her magic as well. I thought I was going to be fried toast."

"She did look like she wanted to kill us all," Clare says, shuddering which makes more blood run from her nose.

"If it hadn't been for that show of magic from the other side of the campus, she may have. I think the shadow weavers are out playing again. She obviously decided it looked more fun than torturing us."

"I think she may be insane," Clare whispers. "They say her mother is."

"I'm pretty certain all shadow weavers are," I growl.

"Are you going to tell Thorne about this?" Fly asks, pulling me up onto my feet.

"Nope," I say, peering down at my body. My clothes are

black and scorched with soot. Terrific. After all of my things were shredded, Clare donated some bits and pieces to me, but it's not like I have a lot of clothes to spare.

"I think you should tell Thorne," Clare says. "He'd put an end to stuff like this."

"And by stuff we mean, attempted murder," Fly says.

Clare adjusts her now wonky glasses and nods. "Or you could tell one of the teachers. Students – including shadow weavers – are not allowed to do stuff like this. You've read the rules."

"Clare, your friend is still in the clinic," I say. "They can do what they want."

Which is why I know my sister's death was no accident. Someone killed her. Of that I am certain.

Chapter Forty-Seven

B riony

My sister remains on my mind for the rest of the day and all through lessons over the next two. At lunch break on Wednesday, we find Clare already in the canteen, hunched over a book.

"What are you reading?" I ask Clare, attempting to twist my head around to read the text.

"Oh," she peers up at us, blinking behind her glasses, "I'm reading up on past trials."

"The first trial is ages away," Fly mutters, "and I don't want to have to think about it until I'm forced to."

"It's not ages away. It's three days," Clare says. "And I want to be prepared."

"How can we be?" I say.

Clare marks her page and closes the book. "I figure the academy trials have occurred every year for over five hundred, correct?" We both nod. "By this point, it must be pretty difficult to come up with anything original. I bet all the trials are just a variation on the very first few they devised."

"How's that helpful?" Fly says, grimacing as he chews a particularly tough bit of meat.

"If I can work out what the most common types of trials are, I can prepare for them," she explains.

"That's ... not a bad idea," I confess.

She nods. "Of course not."

I stare at Clare and then down at her book, an idea forming in my mind. I push back my chair and stand up.

"Woah," Fly cries. "What's the hurry? Lessons don't start for another twenty minutes."

"I'm not going to lessons."

"Right." He nods. "Did the alcohol from the other night fry your brain? You can't skip lessons."

"I can and I am."

"Well, sure you *can*, if you want to face the full force of Madame Bardin's wrath. I hear she reduced Marcus London – one of the biggest and most hardy of men from Iron Quarter by the way – to tears. And that's before she doled out his actual punishment for turning up to class ten minutes late."

"I'm not scared of Madame Bardin."

"It's Professor Tudor's lesson you'll be missing, though."

"I doubt he'll even notice I'm not there."

"But where are you going to go? What are you going to do? There's nothing to do around here – especially when everyone else is in lessons."

"I'm going to the library."

I leave Fly speechless and gaping into space and hurry out of the canteen.

I haven't visited the library yet. When I arrive at its twin metal doors, I suspect people rarely do. Inside the place is dark and gloomy, despite the long windows high up near the roof, and the air swirls with a thick mist of dust. It makes my eyes sting and has me coughing almost immediately. The large room itself – almost the same size as the Great Hall – is rammed with stacks of books, lined up like gravestones.

No librarian greets me, but there is a sign pinned to one of the first bookcases which indicates where different genres of books can be located. I run my eyes down the list past Fiction, Nonfiction and academic textbooks. There is nothing specifically about the academy, but I decide the history section may have something.

I weave in and out of the bookshelves, finding them jammed closer and closer together the further I walk, until soon I'm squeezing between them. It's like a maze – a maze I swear is moving around me – because every time I hit a dead end and turn around, I swear the bookcases are in different places than they were before. I start to panic, fearing I'm going to be lost in this library and will never find my way out, the gloom becoming more oppressive and the dust more suffocating.

The shelves have not been well kept. Some are almost empty, while others have been jammed with books at all sorts of angles. Books also lie abandoned across the floor, discarded like dead birds – dead birds that trip me up and have me stumbling. There's even a book caught up in the unused chandelier, thick cobwebs entombing the long-forgotten candles.

Finally, by some miracle and a lot of perseverance, I reach the history section of the library and find another sign, breaking the history genre into further sections – ancient, early and modern, and then under each of those more specific topics such as the Crystal Wars of the first century and the forming of the realm in the last millennia. Under modern history lies the history of the academy. The school has stood for the last five hundred years. As long as the realm itself – sorting the young people into their Quarters every year ever since.

I follow the sign's instructions and find a bookcase dedicated to the academy. There are biographies of famous headteachers, tomes on the architecture and design of the buildings, several books on the most famous – and infamous – trials that have been held at the academy, and then finally something more useful – a book that promises to list every important event that has ever occurred at the academy, from its opening to the present day. Surely my sister would be listed – even just as an endnote, an appendix to more interesting events. Although somehow, I doubt it.

With very little hope in my heart, I pull the thick book from the shelf, dust billowing into the air as I do, and flip over the hardcover, bound in a faded cloth. More dust has me choking and when I can see through the tears, I find the year she was here in the index, and flick to the pages.

Seeing the year gilded at the top of the page has my breath catching in my throat and I am back there, standing at the train station, waving her off, so sure the next time she returned would be with good news, that her talents would be discovered and she'd whisk us all away to better places.

Instead, five months later, my father and I had returned to that train station, two lone figures, waiting for the arrival of her coffin in the sleet, a coffin nailed shut. They said it would be too distressing to see her body, that there was nothing left of her face.

I can still feel the cold rain biting against my face, freezing the tears in my eyes, the stench of alcohol from my father distinct and undeniable. A stench that would accompany him thereafter forever more.

The coffin itself had been plain, the cheapest of wood, rough and awkward, hammered together with little care or consideration. On the lid her name scrawled in dark ink. Amelia Besheba Storm.

It was so ugly. So plain. Swallowing up the most beautiful, the most radiant, of creatures. My sister never stopped smiling, no matter how tough things got, no matter how hungry or frightened she was. Sunshine seemed to pour from every single one of her pores, residing in the strands of her hair. And they placed her in that ugly box as if she was no one special at all.

The truth had hit me. My sister would never again take my hand in hers, never braid my hair, never sing to me, never hug me close and whisper in my ear, 'it's okay, Briony, everything is going to be okay'.

Bile sloshes in my stomach.

Things were never the same again. Things were never okay.

I trace my fingers over the numbers that form that year. I wish I could go back there. I wish I could beg her to run away with me, or at the very least advise her to keep her secret quiet, to stay hidden. I wish I could have saved her.

But even shadow weavers can't roll back the hands of time. All I can do for her now is discover the truth – discover the truth and punish those responsible.

I run my finger down the page, scanning the information for my sister's name and I see how my hand is shaking, and the hair on my arm is standing on end. Am I frightened? I shiver.

"Miss Storm."

I yelp, the book flying out of my hands as I spin around

and find Professor Fox Tudor glaring right at me only a foot away.

I didn't hear him. How the hell did he creep up on me like that? Unless he was lurking about in the shadows already – or did he come straight from class? I've lost all track of time stumbling about in this library and have no idea whether class should be starting or finishing about now.

Slowly, like I'm not disturbed by the way he appeared out of nowhere and scared the living daylights out of me, I bend down and scoop up the book from the floor. I don't want to lose it – I haven't found the information I came here for yet.

"Can I ask why you are here in the library and not in my class?" the professor says, folding his arms over his wide chest and continuing to glare at me with those glowing eyes of his.

I'm tempted to ask him why he is here in the library and not in *his* class, but I have a feeling that wouldn't go down particularly well. And besides, maybe class is over? I have no idea what time it is.

"Looking for some information," I tell him, hugging the book close to my chest.

"And this was more urgent than attending class? So urgent you couldn't come to the library on your own time?"

"Yes."

His brows knit together. "Class isn't negotiable. I expect all my students to attend and to arrive on time." I don't speak, adopting that blank expression instead. He considers me. "What information were you looking for exactly? If you're searching for spells on how to turn three individuals into toads, I'm afraid it can't be done." I snort. "Not by you anyway."

"Could *you* turn them into toads?" I ask, curious.

The corner of his lip twitches ever so slightly – the movement so fleeting I almost miss it. "Yes, but it would get me into a hell of a lot of trouble. Of course, it might be worth it."

Do I want the Princes turned into toads? If you'd asked me before last Saturday I would most definitely have said yes. Now my feelings are all mixed up and I have no idea at all.

I shift my weight from one foot to the other, momentarily lost in my jumble of thoughts.

"Something tells me that wasn't what you were here for though."

I don't say anything. He remembers my sister. But I don't know if I can trust him. Really, I don't know if I can trust anyone, if I should.

"Tell me," he says, raising his chin, glowering at me. "I think I deserve to know what is more important than my class."

Is it me or is he taking a personal affront to me missing his class?

"There's no point in me attending your class, I'm no shadow weaver. I don't have any powers. None of us do – we all know it's a waste of time."

"Do we?" he snaps, dropping his arms and taking a decided step towards me. "Because you seem to keep forgetting that I was like you, Briony Storm. A boy from Slate Quarter and now I can do this."

He lifts his hand, shadows dancing forth and the books all rising from the shelves to join them, floating in the air like stars in the sky.

I flip my head back to watch them, transfixed by how pretty it looks, and then just as suddenly as they rose, they fall, clattering down onto the bookcases, the shelves and some onto my damn head. I shield my crown with my arm and mutter a curse under my breath.

"Your protectors aren't the only powerful ones in this school," he snarls, his shadows hissing in the air, "and just because you are their thrall does not mean you get to skip my lessons."

"I didn't say it did," I snap. "And I don't know how many times I have to tell you this, but I am not their thrall."

He takes another step towards me, and I can feel his shadows against my skin now. They don't crackle with electricity like Beaufort's do. They're cool and smooth, slipping over me like a caress or a touch.

"Then tell me, Briony Storm, why are you in the library and not in my lesson?"

I frown. Does that mean his lesson isn't over? Then why is he here, chasing me down?

I stare into those eyes of his and decide to take a gamble.

"To find out what happened to her. You couldn't tell me, so I decided to find out for myself."

"You already know what happened to her."

I snort. "I know what they told us happened."

"It was an accident, Briony. They happen, far more regularly than you'd suspect. We're dealing with dangerous and unpredictable forces at the academy. She was one of the unlucky ones; that's all."

I shake my head.

"No, she was special."

"Everyone is special to someone," he says, dismissively with that bitterness he seems to wear like a crown.

"You remember her – she was–"

"Barely. I barely remember her."

"She was special!"

"Special how?"

I open my mouth but no words will come out. How can I explain it? How can I even attempt to describe what she was? To capture all that she was in a couple of words – words that seem so feeble and hopelessly inadequate. It's not possible.

"I know something happened," I say, stubbornly.

"It did. Your sister was killed in crossfire while a group of shadow weavers were training."

"She wasn't stupid," I snap. "She was intelligent and she was careful. Why would she have been anywhere near a group of shadow weavers training? It doesn't make any sense."

"You want her death to have meaning," he says, "because she was special to you. But death never does. Like everything else in this goddamn life, it's random and callous and meaning*less*. Searching for a purpose or a reason in it will drive you to insanity." There's that bitterness again and I wonder what he can be so bitter about. He got out, didn't he? Escaped Slate Quarter and became a professor? His life seems pretty damn good to me, especially compared to all those lives being lived back home – to the life I was living back home.

"I don't believe that," I say with frustration.

"Believe it!" he barks, making me jump, "and realize that snooping about in libraries when you're meant to be in class is going to get you into trouble. Fuck, questioning what you've been told is going to get you into trouble."

"With who?"

"You said your sister was clever, I'm guessing that's a trait you didn't inherit."

"You're saying I can't ask questions?"

"Not when those questions sound very much like accusations."

"I'm not accusing–"

"Yes, you are. You're saying your sister died some other way – at least that's what you believe – which would have to mean someone lied about it."

"Yes," I say firmly.

"Sounds very much like an accusation to me."

I glare back at him. Maybe it is. And maybe I don't care if it gets me into trouble. Trouble seems to have followed me around from the day I arrived at this academy.

"Don't be stupid, Miss Storm. And make sure you're outside my classroom at 7 o'clock tonight."

"Why?"

"For your detention, of course. Did you really think you could miss my class and go unpunished? Now get to your next lesson."

I don't want to leave, but with him standing there glaring at me, I don't really have a choice. I could dig my heels in and refuse to go, but he's much bigger than me and I wouldn't put it past him to drag me there.

I set off, the bookshelves seeming to part and create a pathway for me this time.

"Miss Storm," he says, "leave the book here."

"But I–"

"Books cannot be removed from the library."

I want to argue that that makes it a pretty shitty library – even the public library back in Slate Quarter lets you borrow books – but I'm really done talking with him. I place the book down on the nearest shelf and storm out of the library, finding the door in a matter of minutes.

I don't care what he says. I know I'm right. Something happened to my sister. The story they told us was a lie.

Chapter Forty-Eight

Briony

I'm half tempted to wait around a corner and then creep back into the library and track down that book. The more I think about it, the stranger it seems that it took so long to find the right place in the library and was quick to find my way out. As if the library itself wanted to stop me in the first place and then throw me out in the second. That can't be right, though. My mind must be playing tricks on me. I was just frustrated and not concentrating properly on my way in.

However, though I want to go back, I have a funny feeling Professor Tudor will be waiting for me there again, ready to turf me out if I try. I'm going to have to be clever about sneaking back in – some time I know he'll be distracted – although who knows when that will be.

Do teachers have lives? It's not like the academy is situated near a town or any other form of entertainment. There's the moor, the forest and the distant train station – probably not so bad if you enjoy train spotting, which I doubt very much Fox Tudor does. No, he probably enjoys torturing students slowly and cruelly down in his dungeon to pass the time. Yep, I'm really looking forward to my detention.

Admitting temporary defeat, I set off towards my room to change into my tracksuit for the next lesson. Detention with Professor Tudor will be bad enough, I imagine it will be unbearable with the gruesome twosome. Halfway there my day gets even better when my period comes on and I'm forced to dash up the stairs as fast as I can.

Once I've cleaned myself up, taken some painkillers for the cramps I know will be incoming anytime soon, and changed, I hurry down to the field. I'm hungry and, with my period too, feeling pretty faint.

"Are you okay?" Fly asks, as I sidle up to him in the line along the field, Clare hovering at his other side.

"Yeah, why?"

"Professor Tudor, I thought he was going to blow the classroom to smithereens when he discovered you weren't in class today." He shivers and holds his hand to his chest. "I actually feared for my life. That man is terrifying."

"Was it you who told him where I was?" I say, glaring at him.

"No," he says, "cross my heart. And I'm telling you, I was shaking in my boots when he grilled me."

"How did he know then?"

He shrugs. "Sixth sense."

"He is a shadow weaver," Clare points out.

"Yeah," I say, bending down to tie my lace. "I had no idea he was."

"What do you mean?" Clare asks me. "All professors are."

"Oh," I say, jumping back up, "he came from Slate Quarter. You'd think one of our own turning out to have powers and making it as an academy professor would be big news back in our Quarter – the thing of legends. But I never heard anything about it."

"He came from Slate Quarter?" Fly says, staring at me in astonishment.

"You don't need to sound so surprised," I say, "we're not all feeble dunces. The occasional one of us makes it out of the shithole."

"But a shadow weaver. That's ... that's ..."

"Weren't you listening in his class? Some students from other Quarters do end up having powers."

"Yeah," Clare says, fiddling with her sweater, "but no one actually believes it. No one's ever heard of anyone who it's actually happened to."

"Well, it happened to him."

"Nah," Fly says, shaking his head adamantly. "You must be mistaking him for someone else. Someone who's like him."

"I very much doubt there are two men, both in their early thirties called Fox Tudor."

"Then, he must have had shadow weaver blood – his mom or dad must have been a shadow weaver."

"I don't think so," I say, thinking of Fox's parents – two of the most ordinary people you could meet.

"It doesn't happen otherwise," Clare insists.

"Maybe his dad isn't who they say he is," Fly says, waggling his eyebrows.

"Right," I say, "because shadow weavers are always

passing through our Quarter and having illicit affairs with very ordinary, very dull women who live there."

"Are they?" Clare says, surprised.

"No," I tell her. "I'd never seen a shadow weaver in the flesh until I came to the academy."

"Oh," Clare says.

"It has to be something like that," Fly insists. "People like us don't develop shadow weaving powers. It doesn't just arrive out of the blue."

"Then why tell us otherwise? Why put us through those lessons?" I point out.

Clare shrugs. "To give us hope or something."

"Hmmm," I say, not convinced, because I know Fox Tudor doesn't have a drop of shadow weaving blood in him – I'm sure of that – and yet he has the power.

Just like ...

"Anyway, what happened when Professor Doom and Gloom found you?" Fly says, interrupting my thoughts. "I thought the next time we saw you, you'd have no fingernails or something."

"I don't know yet. I have detention with him tonight." Fly and Clare both shiver. "It can't be any worse than hanging out with the Princes – or not hanging out with them more to the point."

Both Clare and Fly look at me.

"They keep leaving me and going off to parties, remember?" I say, neglecting to remind my friends about what happened when they returned.

Of course, I give myself away with a blush. Something Fly happily points out.

"I'm not blushing," I insist. "It must be a hot flush. I just got my period."

"Urgh," Clare says. "That's the worst."

"Can we change the subject?" Fly says, lowering his voice.

"So we can talk about sex and blowjobs but not periods?" I tease.

"It's just ... I don't ..."

I laugh. Stopping when the twin professors come marching towards us with amusement on their faces. This probably won't be good. Physical exercise is the last thing I feel like doing right now. The cramps have kicked in and all I want to do is curl up on my bed with a hot water bottle and my dog. None of those things are options though. My dog is hundreds of miles away, I don't have a hot water bottle and I've already cut class once today and will be suffering the consequences later. I also doubt a note from the nurse will cut it. I think you could lose a limb and be gushing blood from an open wound and they'd still have you undertaking drills.

The drills today are especially evil. If it was running around the grounds again, I'd probably be okay. Instead, it's circuits – sit-ups, press ups, burpees – the lot.

Of course, the shadow weavers and the Iron Quarter kids find the whole thing a breeze – even Fly seems to be coping all right. I, and most of the other kids from Slate and Granite Quarters, are not. My entire body screams with pain, my lungs burn and I want to die.

"Come on, you lazy fucks," one of the twins screams obnoxiously close to my ear, "move your butts. You're not even trying."

I yank myself up for another sit up, peering through my knees at the group of students that are finding this incredibly easy. Stanley is among them, of course, smiling and laughing as he does a series of press-ups one handed. I wish I had shadow weaver abilities because I'd use them to kick out the supporting arm and have him landing flat on his face. I smile to myself at the picture in my mind.

"If you're smiling, you're not working hard enough," the twin yells at me. "Come on, Madame Bardin is convinced there's Iron material among some of you weaklings – we've only got to get you trained."

Despite my ability to run fast, I know I don't have what it takes to be assigned Iron Quarter. I can't lift anything more than a couple of pounds. I can't jump over rocks. I definitely can't wrestle guys twice my size to the ground. This is a waste of time and is only going to result in more aches and pains.

Past Stanley and his new friends in Iron Quarter are the shadow weavers. Most of the girls aren't even trying – they haven't broken sweat and are gathered around gossiping. I note they aren't being shouted at. Among them are the Smyte twins – Henrietta and Lynette – both looking innocent, like butter wouldn't melt in their mouths – and not like they tried to kill me this weekend.

The boys, as well as one or two of the girls, however, are showing they are just as fit and just as strong as the kids from Iron Quarter. Probably because their diet has been considerably better than ours.

I spy Dray in among a group of shadow weavers, laughing as he works at sit-ups. I watch him snap up his body and peer over his knees, meeting my gaze immediately. He grins and winks at me and I roll back down to lie on the grass and stare up at the sky. When I drag my body up for another sit up, Dray isn't looking my way anymore and I spot Beaufort off to his side, concentrating as he lifts weights that look like boulders above his head.

Thorne isn't with them and it takes me a while until I

find him further out on the field, running sprints backwards and forwards, driving his body, his focus intense.

I roll back down again, my body tingling with that sensation from Saturday.

Desire?

I can't deny the three men are attractive. Especially when they're all hot and sweaty and looking impressive as hell.

But I don't want to feel desire for them. I don't want to feel anything but hate.

I grit my teeth and snap back up, three more times to complete the set and move on to a round of star jumps.

I doubt I look impressive. I suspect I look like a woman close to death. Flushed and messy and smelly. I glance at the shadow weaver girls with bitterness. Not a hair out of place, not a single bead of sweat broken.

Finally, when twin one blows his whistle and tells us we're done, I collapse down on the grass and attempt to catch my breath.

Clare hunches over her knees and peers down at me. She's bright red, and panting fast.

"You ... coming ... changing room," she huffs out. I shake my head. I won't be risking those changing rooms ever again. "Then ... see ... you ... canteen."

I peer up at the clock and groan. It's already six o'clock. Three hours that torture session lasted. Three hours! No wonder I feel like I'm dying.

"I have my detention at seven," I tell her. "By the time I've hobbled back to my room and cleaned up, I don't think I'll have time for dinner. I'll see you guys tomorrow."

Clare nods and limps away, moaning and groaning as she does.

I lie exactly where I am, staring up at the rapidly darkening sky, trying to find the energy to move.

"You want a hand up?"

I flip my head to one side and find Dray Eros, towering over me and holding out his hand.

He licks his lips, eyes traveling over me. "Or do you want me to join you down there?"

"I wouldn't if I were you," I say. "I stink."

"I thought we'd already established that you smell really damn good."

"Not right now I don't."

He squats down. "I'd like to lick the sweat off you." He glances over his shoulder. "I have a feeling it would piss off Beaufort though if I were that fucking public. Maybe later, huh?"

"Later?" I say.

"It's Wednesday, sweetheart. You know what that means." He winks again, stands and offers his hand out a second time. "Up we go."

"Not yet," I say, "it hurts too much."

"So you're just going to stay there?"

"Until I can move again, yes."

"What's wrong?" Beaufort says, appearing beside his friend and staring down at me with a frown. My hot skin seems to grow even hotter as he stares down at me – a mix of desire and anger sloshes around my tired body. He hasn't apologized about that argument. In fact, he hasn't spoken to me at all and I haven't spoken to him. I thought we were ignoring each other.

Obviously not, Beaufort Lincoln doesn't seem to hold a grudge.

"Nothing, I hurt everywhere so I'm just going to lie here until I can move again."

"You can't stay out here, it isn't safe," Beaufort says.

"She'll be fine," Dray says, lifting his chin out towards the field. "Thorne's here."

"Is Thorne even watching her?"

"I don't need babysitting," I point out. I'm ignored.

"Thorne's always watching her," Dray says, which is the most nonsense thing the crazy bastard has ever said. Apart from that weird little warning, the dude has hardly acknowledged my existence.

Beaufort lifts his gaze out to the field and I follow his example. Thorne's still out there, driving his body backward and forward across the field.

"What the hell is he even doing?" I ask.

"Making himself hurt probably," Dray says, like that explanation makes any sense. "It's his favorite pastime."

"Right," I mumble.

"You'll be safe with Thorne out here," Beaufort says, "but when he leaves, you leave, understood?" I stare at him, refusing to give my consent. "Understood?" he growls.

"Sure," I say, too tired to argue.

"We'll see you later."

What? No apology? No attempt to patch things up?

Nope, just back to treating me like they always do.

"Seriously?" I say, closing my eyes. When I open them again the other two shadow weavers have gone. In fact, everyone else has gone, leaving just me and pain-boy out here in the dusk.

I roll my head to the side. It's not just my muscles that hurt, the cramps are really painful now and I have a feeling moving is going to make them worse.

Through the darkness, I spy Thorne's large figure. He's no longer running. Instead, he stands with his arms outstretched, his shadow magic streaming across the field.

His shadows aren't silvery like Beaufort's, they're jet black – like the deepest part of the forest back home where the branches of the trees all tangle overhead, black like the darkest of winter nights. They streak across the space, and even from this distance, I feel their power, despite their darkness, a warmth brushing against my skin.

I can't read his face over the distance, but I can tell, by the stance of his legs, by the way he's bracing his body, that he's using all his strength to shoot those shadows across the field. Or maybe it's not that at all? Maybe he's using all his strength to wield those shadows, to control and bind them.

I shiver, thinking of my sister. Maybe Fox is right. Shadow weavers can unleash their powers out here with no restraint and no precautions. Maybe it would have been easy for her to take a wrong turning, to stumble somewhere she shouldn't have been, and end up caught in the crossfire.

No! Amelia was smart and careful. I just can't believe it.

With a dramatic groan, I roll up to sit and then heave myself up onto my feet.

My detention starts in twenty minutes and I have no desire to turn up a sweaty, broken mess.

Chapter Forty-Nine

F ox

Once upon a time, nights at the academy were the highlight of my entire short-lived existence. A chance for fun and frivolity that was seriously lacking in the mundane and misery of Slate Quarter.

That was a long time ago, though. It's been years since my nights could be considered anything close to fun or entertaining.

Perhaps tonight will be different.

Because tonight the girl is due here for her detention and, despite everything, despite the dangers, a sense of anticipation builds in the pit of my stomach. Another sensation I haven't experienced in a long, long time.

I wait at my desk, an unread book open on the surface, my gaze focused on the door, my ears alert for the sound of her tread on the steps, for the first hint of her scent. The anticipation in my stomach builds, and my hands ball into fists on my knees, my short nails pinching into my skin.

This is dangerous.

What was I thinking telling her to meet me down here alone? Where no one would find us. Where no one could stop me.

I screw shut my eyes.

I am being pessimistic. I am in control. I will maintain control.

For a moment, I believe it, and then I hear it. The first distant slap of her shoe on the stone.

With my eyes still closed, I inhale, deep and strong, sucking the air through my nose and into my mouth.

I groan as I catch the first taste of her and my tongue slides automatically along my lower lip.

The smell of her is even more potent today than before. More metallic, more raw. It has my aching stomach moaning in pleasure and in torture.

If only I could ...

The footsteps quicken as if she's trotting down those last few steps, and then there's the inevitable knock on the door.

My eyelids snap open.

"Come in," I boom.

The door creaks ajar, and she hesitates in the doorway, her eyes adjusting to the gloom.

"You know it's really bad for your eyes to be reading in the dark like this," she mumbles, spying the book on my desk.

"My eyes are perfectly fine, Miss Storm."

Perfectly fine because I can see the flush in her cheeks, the brightness of her eyes and the pulse dancing in her neck.

She steps inside the room and her scent follows in with her. It flies up my nostrils and smacks me right in the center of my brain; my stomach pangs more aggressively; my fists so taut now my nails cut into my flesh.

I hold my body in place and when I speak again, my voice sounds strangled in my throat.

"Take a seat."

She does as she's told, lowering herself carefully onto a bench, groaning under her breath as she does. The Edward professors had the students running circuits this afternoon. I imagine a wisp of a girl like her is feeling the effects.

She nibbles on her lip and waits for my next instruction. She's nervous. The majority of students are scared of me – not that they could tell you why. I've never warranted that fear. Unlike Madame Bardin, I don't mete out punishments left, right and center.

What does she expect I'll do to her? I very much doubt she suspects the one thing I want to do. The one thing I can't.

"What is this detention going to involve?" she asks with a little suspicion.

I rise to my feet slowly, and her head drops back and her gaze follows me upward. Casually, I stroll around my desk, trying my best not to betray the tension in my body. I pick a textbook off the top of the pile on the edge of my desk and toss it towards her. She reaches out and catches it between her hands.

"You can catch up on the lesson you missed."

"That's it?" she says with a relieved little giggle. "School work?"

"Miss Storm, I suspect you'd rather be elsewhere and not in a dungeon with me."

"Well," she says, smiling as she flips open the cover of the book, "it's not like I had anything better planned."

"Not partying with the Princes tonight," I hiss.

She ignores that comment, making a show of pretending to be very interested in the first page of the textbook.

"Don't you have something better to be doing yourself, Professor Tudor?"

I snort. "Anything would be better than this," I lie, because there isn't a single place I'd rather be than in her company, basking in her delicious scent, "so you'd better not skip my class again."

She runs her finger down the first page, pretending to read the text.

"We've covered that material already, Miss Storm. You need to turn to page twenty-two."

Blood rushes up to the surface of her cheeks, and my stomach moans silently.

She flips to the relevant page.

"Restrainments," she reads out.

"Yes, using shadow-weaving abilities to restrain another person."

"I don't have shadow-weaving abilities," she says, coldly.

"Doesn't mean you get to skip my lesson."

"It's a waste of my time and yours."

"I'll be the judge of that." I lean back against my desk. "Read the text aloud to me."

She fidgets on her seat and then begins. Her reading is a little stilted and I can't decide if that's because she's nervous or because the education system back in our Quarter is horseshit.

She describes the means by which a shadow weaver can use their powers to capture and restrain another person. The different ways it can be done and how it can be used.

When she finishes the section, she looks up at me.

I fold my arms over my chest. "Any questions, Miss Storm?" She shakes her head. "Then give it a try."

"There's no point."

"Do you really want to argue with me? This punishment is a light one. I can make it tougher if you'd prefer."

She glances towards the chains hanging from the walls and for the first time in forever I nearly burst into laughter. Is that what she thinks I would do? Chain her to the wall?

The idea has my stomach growling and I close my eyes and focus on breathing through my mouth.

When I open them again, she's staring at me with a mixture of trepidation and curiosity.

"Did you discover your abilities in one of these classes?" she asks me.

"No."

"So you already knew you had them?" I stare at her, unblinking. "I don't have the ability. I'd know if I did. I'm just an ordinary girl. There is nothing special about me."

The way she smells, the way that anticipation gurgles in my gut, tells me otherwise. She is special.

"Stand up, Miss Storm."

Reluctantly, and with some obvious discomfort, she rolls up onto her feet.

"Lift your hands and search for the shadows, beckon them forward like you've been told."

I watch her try. Nothing happens. I am not surprised. She's special but not like that. No one is. Not even me. All the crap they have me teach is bullshit. In the years I've been here, not one of my students from another Quarter has possessed the shadow-weaving ability.

It's just something they say. To give them hope.

I can't tell her any of this and my own frustration has me picking at the girl instead.

"You're not trying hard enough, Miss Storm," I taunt.

She drops her arms and glares at me. "I am."

"You're not. All you have to do is reach for the power and ..."

I raise my hand and the shadows slip from my fingers, racing across the space towards her. I couldn't stop them even if I wanted – and I don't. I want the excuse to touch her – even if it is only like this. My magic curls around her wrists, twines around her waist, slithers around her throat. The binds hold her in place and her emerald eyes widen in horror.

It would be so easy to close the distance between us, to close the distance and ...

But I'm not like her. I refuse to be.

"See," I whisper, my voice hoarse. Her skin against my magic is soft and smooth. I can feel her pulse. I can feel how very alive she is. "It's easy."

"For you," she says, holding as still as she can and refusing to struggle against my binds, that passive expression falling over her face.

She's so obviously a fighter, always champing at the bit to argue every opportunity she can. And then every so often she sees she is beat, that she is too weak to win, and that curtain falls over her face, all that fight hidden behind it.

It's the very opposite of provocative. It has shame creeping through me and my shadows retreating.

Where did she learn to do that? And more to the point, why?

I examine her face, noting her shoulders relaxing just a fraction as my shadows slide away. I walk closer to her, drawn by my unquenchable fascination.

My proximity makes that pulse in her throat dance even more beautifully for me, and it's so damn hard not to lean down, press my lips there, and …

"Do I scare you?" I whisper.

"A little," she confesses. "But I think maybe everyone in this place does. I don't think there is anyone I can truly trust."

I nod my head. That was the mistake I made. I was too trusting and look where the hell it led me. "You can't. You can't trust anyone."

"Not even you, Professor?"

I take another step forward and another and another until I am staring right down into her eyes. "Especially not me."

She's so beautiful. So eager. So hungry for everything. She reminds me in so many ways of myself – the way I once was. If I met her then, would it feel this way, or would it have been different? Would I even have noticed her? The quiet girl from Slate Quarter trying her best to hide how pretty she is, trying her best to survive.

I can't help myself. This close I see how fragile her skin is, how thin the tissue; I can see the veins knitted beneath the surface, can almost hear her heart beating frantically in her chest.

I inhale. The scent of her blood is so pungent, I swear. My eyes flash. I stumble away.

"Leave," I mumble, leaping back into the shadows where she can't see me, where I belong. "Leave now."

"Wh-wh-what?" she says.

"Detention is over. Get out."

She frowns. Then gathers up her belongings and, with a final peek over her shoulder, opens the door and steps outside.

I hold my breath until the door slams. Then I gasp, collapsing over my desk.

That was close. Far too close and far too dangerous.

And now I'm no longer hungry, I'm ravenous.

I fetch my dark cloak, fasten it around my neck and slip out into the night.

Chapter Fifty

Briony

Why does every one of my encounters with Fox Tudor leave me bewildered, confused and flustered? My heart is racing like a runaway train and all because the man stepped within a few centimeters of me. He didn't even touch me – not with his hands anyway. He did touch me with his magic. It was different again from Beaufort's and Thorne's. It was almost like it wasn't restraining me but holding me – holding me like he would if he were going to kiss me.

I knock my hand against my head. What the hell is wrong with me? One bit of fingering and all my thoughts have turned spicy and a little unhinged.

There is no plane of existence in which Fox Tudor would want to kiss me. Especially now he is a professor at the academy and would most definitely lose his job, his reputation and his livelihood.

Yet, no matter how many times I tell myself that, I can't shake that first instinct away and I can't stop imagining what it would be like to kiss a man like Professor Fox Tudor.

Intimidating probably.

Perhaps there's some god watching and judging my smutty thoughts, because I'm halfway back to the tower when the killer cramps start, forcing me to double over and groan. It's a really bad one – probably worsened by that torturous exercise session today. Muriel tried to convince me once that physical exercise helped lesson cramps but I've long suspected that was just another of her sadistic lies.

Clutching my stomach and bending double, I hobble across the remainder of the campus, up the stairs and collapse on my bed. It hurts too much to even attempt to remove my clothes and climb into my nightwear. Instead I pull the covers over me and pray for death. Fly isn't even across the hallway, to call for help and beg for painkillers. I've no more of my own.

After a few minutes, I hear the tower bell clang eight o'clock and I'm vaguely aware there's no way in hell I'm making it over to the Princes' tower tonight. I couldn't give less of a shit. There is nothing they could do to me that is worse than what my own body is currently doing.

I roll up into a ball, my teeth clattering and close my eyes. I do the thing I always did when the pain was too much. I take myself away. I close off my body from my mind and I disappear, somewhere my sister is, her arms around me, her soft voice whispering to me.

"Storm!"

The light kicks on, dazzling me back to the present. I groan as the pain batters my body once again and the light assaults my eyes.

"Where the hell have you been? You were due at our

place twenty minutes ago!" Beaufort's loud angry voice yells at me.

I wrap my arms over my head. "Leave me alone," I mutter.

Boots march across the floor and then a hand lands on my shoulder.

"What's wrong? What's wrong, little thrall?" That same hand comes to cup my face and turn it towards his. He's not alone. Dray hangs right by his shoulder. I blink up at them, tears I didn't even know I was crying blurring their features.

"Go away," I mumble.

"Did someone hurt you?" Dray growls, sounding remarkably like his wolf.

"No!"

"Are you sick?" Beaufort lays the back of his hand against my damp forehead.

"No, it's just my period. I got my period, that's all."

I hear Dray sniff. "Fuck, yeah. I can smell it – that's gross."

"Thanks a lot," I hiss. "Now please leave me alone. I'm not coming tonight. I don't care if you think you're going to drag me or whatever. It hurts too much." I clutch my stomach and moan.

Dray and Beaufort conspire in hushed tones, but I'm too out of it to work out the words. Then, in the next moment, I feel a pair of strong arms slide underneath me and scoop me up. Beaufort's arms. He holds me against his chest and marches me out of the room.

"I may be wrong, but I don't think there is any conceivable way that you could describe this as dragging, Beaufort Lincoln," I point out.

"I'm making an exception," he says with an expression that looks a lot more like a real smile than his usual smirk.

Dray trots along after us, bouncing up and down on his toes.

"I wanted to carry her," he whines.

"Tough shit," Beaufort says, taking the steps two at a time.

"But you get to have all the fun."

"She's sick," Beaufort says.

"And I smell bad, remember?"

"You still smell fucking amazing," he says grinning, "just not as a good as usual."

Beaufort's arms are strong and his embrace warm, and maybe I'm imagining it but I swear I feel his magic against my skin, soothing away the pain. I sink into his arms, resting my head against his chest and close my eyes.

I guess the pain and that exercise session plus all the tension with Professor Tudor has worn me out, because I jerk awake again a few minutes later as Beaufort carries me up the stairs in his own tower, Dray still behind us.

"Where are we going?" I murmur, sleepily. If he thinks he's going to get a repeat of last weekend's activities, he's going to be sorely disappointed. Even if I wanted to, which I don't – that was a one off, a stupid mistake – I don't think I could physically lower myself onto my knees tonight. My thighs will not do it.

"I've run you a hot bath."

"Are we joining her in it?" Dray says, eyes lighting up.

"No," Beaufort says firmly. "It's to make her feel better." He glances down at me. "That's correct, right?"

I nod my head, not that I was treated to many hot baths back home.

"We'll add some soothing salts in too," Dray pipes up.

"Are protectors meant to run their thralls baths?" It doesn't exactly sound like how things are meant to work.

"As your little slave, aren't I meant to be the one running baths?" I say, sarcastically.

Beaufort walks into the steamy bathroom and drops me down hard on my feet.

"I've told you before, the arrangement is reciprocal. You look after us and we look after you." He jerks his head towards the bath. "Get in."

"Erm, no."

Dray leans in the doorway, one foot crossed over the other ankle, gaze flicking eagerly between me and Beaufort.

"Don't argue with me, little thrall. You said it would make you feel better. We both saw how much pain you were in. Get in the damn bath."

"Not with the two of you standing there watching. Some privacy please."

"You shy?" Dray chuckles.

"It has nothing to do with being shy and a lot to do with privacy and respect," I say through gritted teeth as another cramp sears through my stomach. I really, really want to climb into that bath and sink into oblivion. I just don't want to do it with them watching.

"You're clearly exhausted," Beaufort says, "you fell asleep in my arms almost immediately. I'm not having you fall asleep in the bath and drowning."

"I won't."

"You're in obvious pain, little thrall, just get in the bath." Dray chuckles. I lift my chin stubbornly and shake my head, even though the cramps hurt like hell. "I'll tell you what, then. We'll turn around." He grabs Beaufort's arm and, after some tussling, forces him to turn his back on me, doing the same himself. "There you are. We promise not to peek."

I consider them. I don't really trust them not to peek. I

also really want to climb into that bath. It's been so long since I've had one, I can't even remember what it was like. But it smells divine and looks like heaven.

"Okay," I say, "but if you–"

"We won't," Dray promises.

Hunched over to protect my modesty as best I can, I slip off my clothes quickly and climb into the bath, sighing as I slip under the water. My eyes drift closed as the warmth of the water and salts soothe away the cramps and I tip back my head and lean it against the edge of the bath, my body completely submerged under the water.

"Wanna tell us about those scars, little thrall?" Dray growls from the other side of the bathroom.

My eyelids fly open. Both men are glaring at me, thunder clouding their expressions. It's pretty terrifying and I don't even know what I did wrong.

"You promised not to peek," I say, sinking deeper into the water.

"Was it the shithead from Slate Quarter?" Beaufort asks, his tone deadly. "The same one who gave you the black eye?"

"It's no one you know," I say, turning my head and peering down into the water; my body is obscured under the water, water that's slowly turning crimson with my blood.

It brings back flashes of memories, of running water turning red with my blood as I washed myself up as best I could in the freezing cold river.

Under the water, I can't see the disfigurements she left on my stomach, although I know the ones on my back are far far worse.

"How did it happen?" Beaufort asks.

I swim my hands through the water. I feel light-headed,

like I could float away, disassociate from the here and now and never have to answer these questions.

But then he's beside me, his fingers cupping my chin again, once more turning my face to meet his. "Tell me how they did it and who it was and I will kill them."

"You're not going to kill anyone," I snort.

"I am," he growls.

"It's in the past. It's over. I'm never going back there." Even if they send me back to Slate Quarter, I won't be going home. I'm not a child anymore. I'm free now and I have no intention of returning.

"No, you're not," Beaufort says, meeting my gaze with his silver one. "Because you're ours now."

I don't know why he says that because we all know, even if I relent and agree to be their thrall, this is only a temporary arrangement lasting as long as our time in the academy. Then I will most probably never see the three of them again.

I don't have long to mull it over though, because in the next moment they do something entirely unexpected. Dray comes to kneel on the other side of the bathtub and reverently, gently, with care and kindness they begin to wash me, soft sponges and fragrant soap gliding over my skin.

I'm too weak to argue about it. Too tired to push them away.

Instead, I close my eyes once more and dissolve into the feeling. If it's been a long time since anyone touched me with kindness, then I don't remember a time someone stroked and caressed me like this. Even Amelia was too busy to do anything but scrub the dirt from my body, hurriedly because the water was always too cold to make it pleasant.

When Dray reaches the scars on my stomach, he's even gentler, his brow furrowing as he does.

"I know it's really ugly," I mutter, wrapping my arms around my stomach in a bid to hide them from him. Maybe this will finally be the point when they realize they don't want me as a thrall.

"I didn't say they were ugly. Is that what you think? Is that why you were trying to keep them hidden?"

"They're not exactly beautiful, are they?"

He rocks back on his heels and drags his shirt over his head. His chest is sculpted and muscular, rows of tight abs running over his stomach. But he also has a scar of his own – a ragged one that runs in a circle over his shoulder and down his back.

"How did–" I gasp.

"Another shifter. He wasn't very friendly." He chuckles. "Don't worry he's dead now."

"Shit," I mumble, realizing it must have been a set of powerful jaws that made that scar, realizing it was probably Dray who killed the other shifter. "But I didn't notice it when you were–"

"Fur hides it."

"Did it hurt?"

He chuckles again. "Hurt like hell," he says, running his fingertips over the raised mangled flesh. "Do you think it's ugly?"

"No," I admit. I shrug. "It's kinda sexy." I peer down at my stomach. "My scars are not sexy."

"They're a testament of what you've been through – whatever that was," he adds, with a growl, "of what you survived. And that is beautiful."

I can't help smiling at the crazy bastard, an expression he studies with interest.

Beaufort taps my shoulder.

"Lean forward so I can do your back," he commands. I

pull a face. I don't want to. I only ever catch fleeting glances of my back in the mirror but I know it's as mangled and twisted as Dray's shoulder.

"Please," Dray adds with a set of puppy dog eyes that could melt the coldest of hearts.

With a little huff, I fold forwards, resting my cheek on my bent knees.

Beaufort mutters something under his breath and then he's gliding the sponge over my back. I barely feel it. I lost the sensation on the skin there long ago.

"Did it hurt?" Dray asks me, repeating my early question.

I consider whether to tell them the truth, and in the end – who knows what possesses me – I do.

"At first, yes. But I learned to disassociate from the pain. To take myself someplace else."

"It happened more than once," Beaufort says, his voice quiet but a current of rage quivering below the surface.

I close my eyes. "Many times."

I feel a slight tug at my scalp and then Beaufort is unwinding my hair and washing that too.

"She has the most beautiful hair," he murmurs to Dray, running his fingers through the strands and massaging my scalp. It's so good I let out a little sigh of pleasure. That man really does have exceedingly talented hands.

When they've finished washing me, Dray holds out the biggest, fluffiest of white towels I've ever seen and Beaufort holds out his hand to help me out. I hesitate again, but they've already seen me naked so I guess there is nothing left to be modest about.

"Don't you have a different towel?" I ask.

"This one not good enough for you, little thrall?" Dray

asks, one side of his mouth raised in a lopsided grin. "It's made from the finest cotton."

"I'll get blood all over it."

"Doesn't matter," Beaufort says, shaking his hand.

"Do you know how hard it is to get blood out of fabrics?!"

"Yes," they both answer together.

"Oh," I say, still thinking about their answer as I climb out of the bath and let Dray wrap me up in the towel.

"There're sanitary items just there," Beaufort says, pointing to a pile of items beside the sink, "and a set of my pajamas there."

"Pajamas?" I say, but they're already out of the bathroom.

I peer around looking for my own clothes to pull on instead and realizing they're gone. Sneaky. Seems I have no choice but to put on the plaid pants and baggy t-shirt unless I want to walk back to my room in the nude. Which I definitely do not.

I find a comb by the sink and brush out my hair, automatically going to tie it back up and then pausing. They've seen me naked. They've seen my scars. They've seen my hair. There's almost nothing left to hide. And so I leave it hanging loose and tiptoe out into the hallway.

"I'm in here," Beaufort says, standing by the chest of drawers he caught me at days ago. He's holding a glass of broth in his hands. "It has pain-easing qualities. It will help you sleep."

"Thank you," I say, taking it from him. "Do you have something I can put it in? I'm worried I'll have spilled it all by the time I get back to my room."

"You can sleep here tonight," he says casually. I raise an eyebrow at him. He shrugs and buries his hands deep into his pockets. "You'll be much more comfortable. That bed in your room is shit, whereas this one ..." He tilts his head towards his bed and I follow my gaze that way. "Plus there's a hot water bottle waiting for you."

The bed is huge with so many pillows and blankets I could roll myself up in. It's so tempting, especially as the soothing effects of the bath are fading.

I obviously have a serious lack of willpower today. These men are wearing me down.

That may have to be tomorrow-Briony's problem, though, because right now I want to curl up in that bed and sleep.

"If you're expecting ..." I nibble on my lip, because he's asking me to climb into his bed after all and I am not naïve, that has some definite connotations.

"I'm expecting you to get a good night's sleep. I doubt you've had one since you got here."

I don't tell him I've slept pretty well, that my bed in the tower may be shit but at least it's a bed and not the cold hard floor.

"Okay, then."

He raises his eyebrows. "What? No argument?"

"Your bed does look amazing." I sigh. I gulp down the draught and Beaufort walks me towards the bed and sweeps back the cover. There, as promised, is a fluffy-looking hot water bottle.

Feeling pretty self-conscious, I climb into bed, hugging the hot water bottle to my stomach and rolling onto my side.

Beaufort pulls the cover up around me and to my utter astonishment tucks me in.

"Good night, little thrall," he says, pressing his lips to my forehead, "sleep well."

Chapter Fifty-One

B eaufort

I close the door of my bedroom and pad down the staircase to the lower floor. Thorne's nowhere to be seen. For all I know, he's still out there on the field, tossing around his magic. The dude seems even more obsessive and insular than usual.

Dray, however, is waiting for me, big grin on his face, glass of whisky in his hand.

"That was fucking fun," he says.

"You think it's fun that someone abused and tortured our thrall?" I say quietly.

The grin falls from his face and something more sinister takes its place. Dray is one step away from being unhinged, hanging on to civility by the skin of his teeth. I've no doubt if the person responsible for those scars were here now, he'd

transform into his wolf and tear them limb from limb –
that's if I didn't get there first.

"Who do you think it was?" Dray asks, growling.

"Someone from home." I take up the glass of whisky
waiting for me on the mantelpiece and take a long drawn
out swig, enjoying the burn it causes right the way down my
gullet. "I'll have it looked into."

Dray rocks on his toes, swilling his drink around his
glass. "I could go ask a few questions of the shits from the
Slate Quarter."

I'm pretty sure by 'ask a few questions' he means 'torture until they tell me'.

"No," I say, "she won't want everyone knowing. You
saw how self conscious she was about it."

"She shouldn't be. That girl has a body made for sin,
and fuck I cannot wait to indulge in some filthy immorali-
ties." His eyes twinkle and he actually tips back his head
and howls towards the ceiling.

"Not tonight. She's resting."

He lowers his head. "I'm not a jackass."

I slump down into one of the armchairs, rest my drink
on my knee and stare off into the fire.

I wish I could access that vision again. I wish I had
control over the sight. I wish I could use it and bend it to my
will – rather than the hopeless way my gift presents in
flashes and glimpses.

Don't get me wrong, I like the girl. She's growing on me
and I like her a lot. Especially when she's down on her
knees sucking my cock with that pretty mouth of hers. Hell,
I even like it when she's arguing with me. But that doesn't
mean I understand. Why her?

A girl from Slate Quarter. A girl *abused* back in Slate Quarter. If I had any lingering hope she might be someone special after all, that maybe she'd have some unknown power soon to be revealed, well, the scars on her back have put heed to that.

She's no unrevealed shadow weaver. There is no way one of us could go through torture like that and not reveal our true nature.

"Where exactly is she resting?" Dray asks with suspicion.

"My bed."

"Not the room we have set up for our thrall on the fifth floor then?" he says with annoyance.

I take another sip of my drink, smiling into the liquid. "I thought she'd be more comfortable in *my* bed."

Dray slams his empty glass down on the mantelpiece.

"I'm going to go look for Thorne," he says sulkily.

Once he's gone, I fetch what's left of the bottle and climb back up the stairs, peering around the bedroom door to find the girl already fast asleep.

I stare at her enviously. I don't sleep much these days, too much raging around in my head, too much to consider, to think about, to prepare. That's if I want my future to pan out the way it should. Some days – every so often – I'm not sure I do.

Life in Slate Quarter may be grim, but I bet it's a hell of a lot simpler.

Quietly, I close the door again and retreat to my study, dumping the whisky bottle and the glass down on my desk and drawing up the chair. Across the surface of my desk lie open books, the recent accounts of events across the realm, letters from my family and my own notebooks, scribbled with my thoughts and memorandums.

Fresh accounts were delivered by raven to our tower this evening as usual, hand written and laid out across the scroll, tied with bine. I snip through the bind with my powers and unwind the tiny scroll. The writing that runs across its width is tinier still and I position it under the waiting magnifying glass and begin to read.

At some point I hear the door of the tower slam open and close, muffled voices and heavy footfall, then silence again. A sliver of moonlight moves across my desk from east to west as the hours pass and then slowly the first lights of dawn creep through the window.

I hear my bedroom door open.

I rest my pen down, sit back in my chair and peer out towards the landing through my open study doorway.

The girl steps out onto the landing, stretching her arms above her head and then spins her gaze around. She's dressed in her own clothes again but her golden hair remains loose and tangled around her shoulders and more color has returned to her cheeks.

"Contemplating some more snooping, little thrall?" I say.

The little thing jolts, her hand flying to her chest, before she spots me through the doorway. She pads my way, coming to a stop by my desk.

"I was wondering where you were. It's early, isn't it?"

I glance towards the clock on the wall.

"5:37am."

"Jeez," she mutters. She glances down at the paperwork spread across my desk. "Are you working? Shit, there isn't an assignment I don't know about, is there?"

"No, it's realm business."

"Realm business," she teases, "that sounds very important and mysterious." She strains her eyes towards my desk and I brush everything aside.

"Are you okay? Do you need anything?"

She shakes her head. "I feel much better. Still a little sore and uncomfortable. But the worst of it is over." She smiles at me. "I'm going to head back to my own room now. I need to be ready for class in a few hours."

I take her hand in mine, threading my fingers through hers.

"You could stay and have breakfast here with us."

She doesn't shake her head immediately and I take that as progress. She's tempted by the offer, tempted to spend more time with us.

"I'd happily eat you out for breakfast," I offer.

She rolls her eyes, but I don't miss the little shiver of desire. "You sound like Dray."

"Dray may be one crazy bastard but he does get some things right."

"I have my period, remember?" she says. I shrug. "I've got to go."

"In a moment," I tell her, pulling her towards me and reaching up with my free hand to cup the back of her head and draw her mouth right onto mine. I kiss her, deep and long and slow, exploring her mouth with my tongue, until she's sighing against my lips and her knees are buckling.

When I lean away, her eyes are closed and there's even more color in her cheeks. In the half-morning light, she looks so damn pretty. I'm not sure I've ever truly acknowledged it before, ever really understood. And when she opens her eyes, they are so green and vivid, I have to concede; she's probably the most beautiful woman I know.

Maybe it's not surprising that I want her so badly.

But that won't be today. She's already unhooking her hand from mine and pushing away.

"I'll see you on Friday." She frowns. "The trial," I clarify. The color drains from her face. "You're worried about it?"

"You aren't?" she scoffs.

"No, not really." And, stupidly, it hadn't occurred to me, or maybe I just hadn't given it any thought that she would be. The trials are difficult even for fairly accomplished shadow weavers. Of course, they'd be damn terrifying if you were a plain old commoner. "We could–"

"It's fine. We've been researching." She straightens her shoulders and lifts her chin – the way she does when she's being defiant. "You don't need to worry about me."

I nod, dragging her to me for one last kiss and then watching as she walks towards the staircase.

Of course, what she doesn't know – what she'll never understand – is that I will always worry about her. I will always want her safe.

Chapter Fifty-Two

B riony

I stroll through the campus in the half-light as the dawn crawls over the horizon. It's quiet, everyone still sleeping and the buildings still and peaceful. Even the ravens aren't flapping across the sky, screeching as usual.

Contentment hums in my belly and in my body. It isn't a feeling I think I've ever truly experienced before. It's strange, alien and pleasant. I could get used to it but I know that is a dangerous thing. This contentment won't last – it can't. One thing Slate Quarter teaches you is that hope is pointless. Sooner or later everything turns to shit. So no matter how nice the Princes seem, no matter how well they're treating me now, I can't – or won't – believe it will last.

I'm so engrossed in my thoughts, I don't realize where I am until I'm passing right outside the library.

I halt.

Everyone is sleeping. I imagine Professor Tudor will be sleeping as well.

This is my opportunity to go back inside and find that book. This is my opportunity to understand what really happened to my sister.

The only problem is, I don't have a light – it was dark enough in the library during the middle of the day, but in the half-light of dawn, I imagine it will be impassable.

I'm considering where best to steal a candle or even a lamp, when my eyes stray to the roof of the library and to the windows that run just beneath it, and I realize it's not dark in the library at all. The windows glow with an orange light. There's someone in there. In the early hours of the morning.

Before I can talk myself out of it, I'm creeping up the steps to the building and pulling at the heavy door. It's unlocked and I slip inside, hugging the shadows as I try to see who is in here this morning and what the hell they are doing.

Light flickers from somewhere deep in the stacks of the library and, faintly across the distance, I can hear voices – hushed voices despite the lateness of the hour. With my back tight to the wall, I strain my ears.

Two voices – one male, one female.

Maybe this is some illicit hook-up and I should get out of here before I'm accused of being a peeping tom. But then I recognize the first voice. Madame Bardin.

It makes no sense. Why would she be in here at this time of the morning?

I glide against the wall, edging closer.

"There are other ways. There is no need to resort to

such menial actions," she purrs, her voice seductive and dangerous.

Perhaps this is some rendezvous after all. Maybe with one of those twins. Maybe with both.

"Not ones I am willing to take," the other voice hisses back. A voice I know. A voice I know *well*.

Professor Tudor.

Madame Bardin and Fox Tudor.

Of course!

It would make sense – the woman is beautiful in a strangely intimidating way and Professor Tudor is the only young attractive teacher on campus – if you discount the gruesome twosome who may be young but are definitely not attractive. It was inevitable that they would end up together.

But why meet in the library? They must have their own private rooms. Unless this is their thing, some kind of kink.

I guess I shouldn't judge. I did let Beaufort Lincoln finger me on top of his chest of drawers. I did let two men bathe me.

Do I really want to overhear the two of them getting it on?

I should leave. This is a private moment and I don't want to be caught snooping yet again – especially when these two are likely to be a lot more angry about it than Beaufort. However, my feet don't move when I ask them to. Although the two of them together makes perfect sense, there's also something about it that is strange. Fox's tone isn't one of a lover and I can't help but hang about to hear more.

"There are other options open to you," Madame Bardin says, "you could find yourself a–"

"I said no!"

She laughs. "Always so noble, so full of ideals, so naïve. It's what I liked best about you."

Professor Tudor growls lowly which only makes Madame Bardin laugh harder.

"I'm not like you. I won't take another–"

"Ahhh," Madame says, cutting across the professor's words – her own suddenly shrill and full of tension. "Unless you've already found–"

"I haven't," he says abruptly.

There's a pause, one full of tension. I tiptoe forward, peering through the gaps in the bookcases until I see them.

They stand facing each other – Madame in a long black gown, cut low and clinging to her body. The professor dressed in his suit. Both wear long black cloaks pinned to their shoulders. Their hair is tussled, red lipstick smeared across their mouths and I was obviously wrong again. Maybe they are arguing now but before that they definitely were getting it on.

"You've found someone," Madame says, her voice quiet now and full of tension.

"No," Fox says, but the way his shoulders stiffen show me he's lying. Madame spots it too.

"You can't lie to me, Fox Tudor. You never could." She tilts her head to one side, wiping the lipstick from her mouth. "Who are they?" Professor Tudor stares back at her and says nothing.

"You don't want to share? And yet you used to be so eager to please me in every possible way." She smiles cruelly and steps towards him, snaking her hand down his torso.

"Not any more," he growls, snatching her hand away so violently, she stumbles, nearly losing her balance.

I gasp inadvertently at his violent behavior and immediately both their heads snap my way, eyes flashing in the dim light.

Shit!

"There's someone here," Madame says.

I smother another gasp, turn and race out of the library as quickly as I can, their footsteps discernible behind me.

"Stop!" the madame calls out.

But nothing in the world could compel me to stop. I don't think they saw me and I don't want them to know it was me spying on them.

I don't stop until I'm outside. Here, I spin my vision around, looking for somewhere to hide. Choosing one of the nearest towers, I duck inside, closing the door quietly behind me and sinking into the shadows of the stairwell.

I hear their footsteps again, out on the cobblestones and then their whispered voices.

"They're gone," Professor Tudor says.

"Did you see them? Did you see who it was?"

"No, I didn't."

"Hmmm," she says, not sounding convinced. "I don't like secrets, Fox."

"I am aware," he says, but then their voices fade as they move away.

I wait in the dark as long as I can bear it, just in case they are still lingering out on the pathway, and then I creep back out and hurry as quickly as I can back to my room. Inside, I beeline straight for my wardrobe, retrieving my bag from its hiding place and checking the contents. I shouldn't have left it unguarded for so long – the entire night. However, everything is as I left it and once I've hidden my bag again, I climb into bed, curl up under the covers and go over the events in the library.

The conversation was strange – their relationship even

stranger. Fox Tudor clearly hates Madame Bardin and yet if I'd been there a matter of minutes earlier, I'm sure I'd have seen the two of them all over each other. And the way she talked made it seem as if their relationship has been a long one. Maybe it's one of those love–hate things. Maybe they're exes. Maybe the sex is fueled by hate.

I imagine hate-fucking Beaufort Lincoln and decide it really is time to get out of bed because those thoughts are surprisingly hot.

I take a much needed cold shower – one advantage of living in this tower – and go in search of my friends.

Chapter Fifty-Three

B riony

The following day, Fly and I are going over likely trial scenarios yet again on our way to Professor Tudor's class, when we find our path blocked by Madame Bardin. One moment the path ahead is empty, the next she's standing right there – usual red lipstick painted on her lips, usual stern expression fixed to her face.

"Miss Storm," she says, attempting to wrestle her mouth into an unconvincing smile. "I would like a word."

"With me?" I say, utterly shocked. She's hardly said one word to me since I started at the academy – both in and out of class. She's far more interested in the shadow weaver students. She hardly gives us commoners a passing glance. Her sudden interest in me can mean only one thing. She knows it was me. My stomach plummets.

"Yes, you. Let's go to my office where we can talk in

private." She spins on her heels and starts pacing away and I take it I'm meant to follow her. I peer at Fly with alarm, an expression I find mirrored on his own face.

"What did you do?" he mouths at me.

"I don't know," I mouth back.

"Miss Storm?" Madame calls, and I jerk into action, hurrying along behind her.

Her office isn't anywhere near her classroom. It's housed in the same building as the Great Hall, up a grand staircase and along a plush-carpeted hallway. The door to her office stands directly alongside the one marked Head-teacher. I wonder if the elusive head is in there at this very moment. I wonder if anyone has actually checked he's still alive.

Madame Bardin unlocks her office door with a wave of her hand and we step through into an elegant room, the carpet a dark maroon, her desk carved from a polished ebony, and heavy velvet drapes hanging around the ancient windows.

"Please," she says, motioning towards a low maroon sofa that blends with the carpet, "sit."

I do as she says, finding myself sinking into the sofa and my knees nearly hitting my chin. I shuffle forward until I'm sitting on the edge and rest my hands in my lap.

What the hell is this about? Did she see me in the library yesterday?

Madame remains on her feet, leaning back against her desk and tossing her glossy hair over her shoulder.

"You don't mind if I smoke, do you?"

I do. Muriel smoked like a chimney and it's left me with an aversion to the smell, but I hardly think I can say no to the Madame.

I nod.

"Thank you." She opens one of the drawers, takes out a small silver case and a box of matches. She examines me as she opens the case and selects a slim cigarette.

"You're from Slate Quarter?"

I clear my throat. She makes me nervous. "Yes."

She clamps the cigarette between her lips, strikes the match and holds it to the end of the cigarette, all the time staring right at me. Then, she shakes away at the match until the flame extinguishes and takes a long drag, closing her eyes as she does. Her eyelids are painted a dark plum color and they're lined with black kohl that ends in a flick at the edge of her eyes. Her lids still closed, she plucks the cigarette from her mouth, and exhales a cloud of gray smoke; the smell doing nothing to lessen my unease.

"And did you know Professor Tudor back in Slate Quarter?" She opens her eyes and stares at me. Her irises are a violet that glow through the swirl of smoke from her cigarette.

"I knew of him, yes. But there isn't a person in Slate Quarter who didn't," I frown, "who doesn't."

"He's much older than you."

"Yes."

She takes another drag on the cigarette. "Ten years perhaps." I nod. "So you can't have been friends. Perhaps your families are acquainted."

"No."

"And yet you seem to have a friendship now?"

"What?" I say. Sure, Fox and I have had a couple of conversations – which, judging by his behavior and attitude, might be pretty rare – but we are most definitely not friends. Far from it. "He's my teacher."

"Yes, and any relationship between the two of you

would be highly irregular and, it goes without saying, inappropriate."

"There is no relationship," I say, confused. Why would anyone think there was? She's the one having a relationship with him.

She stubs out her half-smoked cigarette into a glass ashtray that rests on the top of her desk, and leans forward.

"If he's made a move on you," she adopts a concerned expression, "if he's said anything inappropriate to you–"

I shake my head. "I don't know where you'd get such an idea, but he hasn't."

She leans back, peers over her shoulder and then back at me.

"He is a very good looking man and charming. You won't be the first student at the academy to have developed a crush on the professor."

I frown. Hang on – is she accusing him of making a move or me?

"I don't have any feelings for the professor," I say with irritation.

"It's perfectly natural to feel that way about an older man with–"

"I don't. Professor Tudor and I have barely spoken since I started at the academy. I'm not interested in him – or anyone else for that matter."

Is that true? The way Beaufort kissed me this morning has me thinking I'd like him to do that again.

"Well, that is a relief, Miss Storm," she says, that forced smile returning once again to her mouth. "We could do without those kinds of ... complications." She beckons for me to stand and walks me to her office door. "Of course," she says, holding the door open, "if anything did happen. If the professor were to ... be sure to come and tell me imme-diately."

I mutter something indistinct and duck out of the room. If I did have any secret to tell, any concerns about the behavior of any of the faculty, Madame would be the last person in the realm I'd choose to confide in.

The very last.

Chapter Fifty-Four

F^{ox}

The students filter into the classroom one by one, and I scan my gaze among them. Anticipation races through my body, making my fingers tingle and my magic hiss.

But it's all for nothing. The girl is not among them.

Again.

For the second time, she has chosen to skip my lesson.

A storm of emotions erupts in my stomach. Disappointment. Rage. Irritation. Fear.

Is it because she knows the truth?

I close my eyes and battle the storm into submission.

I will not lose control. I will not betray the way I feel. I will not make the mistake of hunting her down again.

I wait until all the students are settled and then I ask calmly, hoping the strain in my voice does not give me away, "Miss Storm is not here."

"Thank goodness," one of the Smyte twins mutters under her breath. It's pathetically transparent how jealous so many of the other students are of her – just because she's caught the attention of the Princes. A bunch of spoiled, arrogant brats.

"Has she chosen to skip my class yet again?"

I direct my question towards her friend, who, despite my calm tone and calm demeanor, quakes on his seat.

"N-n-n-n-no," he stutters, swallowing hard. "I think she'll be along soon. She had to–"

"I'm not interested in hearing excuses!" I snap.

"But–" he protests feebly.

"Quiet!" I thunder. "You all have a duty to attend my class. But that duty does not just extend to yourselves. I expect all my students to be present and if they are not, that reflects on all of you." I glare at the students sitting in front of me, although I doubt they can see me hidden away in the shadows. "Therefore, you will all be punished for Miss Storm's tardiness."

"What the fuck?" some obnoxious shadow weaver shrieks from the front row.

"Silence!" I boom, my irritation getting the better of me. "Take out your pens and paper. I will not be teaching you until Miss Storm is good enough to join us. You will sit in silence, copying the following lines from the board." I brush my hands through the air and my shadows race towards the blackboard, scribbling nonsense sentences in white chalk.

"This isn't fair," Lynette Smyte moans.

"I'll be the judge of that."

"She's such a little bitch. Someone needs to put her in her place – once and for all," her sister whispers in her ear, so quietly I expect she thinks no one would hear.

"And I suppose, you think, you are the person who should do that, do you, Miss Smyte?" I ask her.

She peers through the shadows at me with a whole heap of disdain. "Yes."

"How?" I ask, the danger obvious in my voice.

"Fry her like a slice of bacon. It would be good practice." She smirks.

Anger crackles inside me. I'd like to fry Henrietta Smyte like a slice of bacon. Somehow, however, I manage to keep it together.

"It's not her fault," Briony's friend starts to protest, but any further words are interrupted by the opening of the door and the girl herself strolling through without a damn care in the world.

"You're late!" I roar.

"I am," she snaps back, meeting my angry glare with one of her own. For a moment, our eyes are locked together like that and her scent slithers towards me, softening everything inside me, making me hungry instead.

"We're copying lines from the board, Miss Storm. Take a seat. You can see me afterwards."

"Now she's here, can't we–" the first shadow weaver starts to argue.

"No," I say, then I lean back in my chair and spend the next ninety minutes watching her. Transfixed by her. Mesmerized by her.

●

"This is becoming a habit," I growl at her when we're once again alone. "Tell me what the hell makes you think you can miss my lessons? Because I'm pretty certain I made it clear last time that I won't tolerate it."

Perhaps being alone like this is dangerous and foolish. Perhaps I shouldn't fall for the temptation.

But we're here now. Once again alone.

She rolls her eyes at me like I'm being unreasonable. "It wasn't my choice." I snort. "Madame Bardin asked to see me."

An icy cold sweeps across my skin and into the pit of my stomach.

"Madame Bardin?" I say quietly.

"Yes, she asked to talk to me in her office. I couldn't exactly say no."

"Talk to you? Talk to you about what?"

The obnoxious expression falls away and the blood rushes to the surface of her cheeks. For the briefest of seconds it distracts me, my stomach moaning in agony.

"I'm not sure ..." she mutters. "It was private."

I stalk towards her and grab hold of her wrist. "What did she want to talk to you about, Briony?" It's the first time I've used her name, and the sound of it takes both of us by surprise. It sounds so personal, so intimate.

"You," she hisses. I nod. Me. I'm not surprised at all. But does that mean the Madame is aware about how I feel? I shouldn't be surprised. I'm only surprised the girl herself has not realized. It must be written all over my face. Clear in my every move. "She seems to be under this deluded impression that the two of us are ... I don't know what!"

My fingers are wrapped tightly around her wrist. Her pulse thunders beneath her skin – skin that is so delicate, so paper thin, so fragile.

I say nothing and my eyes stray to the pulse in her neck, thundering away too – the skin there just as vulnerable.

"Which is utterly ridiculous," she continues, "considering it's the two of you who are–"

"What?" I say, dropping her wrist.

Even more of that blood rushes to her cheeks. "I saw you together – this morning in the library. I know you're together."

"We are not together," I say firmly.

"Right," she says sarcastically, "not 'seeing each other' but still messing around. Whatever. I'm really not interested in becoming entwined in whatever sick games the two of you are playing."

"We're not playing any games," I say, although as soon as I say it I wonder if that's really true. "We're not together. We're not screwing around – if that is what you are insinuating. Whatever you thought you saw this morning, you didn't."

She glares at me and for the briefest flicker of a moment, I wonder why she cares, I wonder *if* she cares, I wonder if maybe she is jealous. But I bat those foolish ideas away.

Just because my thoughts about the girl are burgeoning on the obsessive, does not mean she feels the same way about me. And even if she did, so what? I will not go there. I refuse to go there.

"Madame Bardin is dangerous," I tell her.

"Is she an ex? Is that what this is about?"

I ignore her questions.

"Briony," I say earnestly, "do not meet with her alone. Even if she asks you to, do not. It isn't safe." She stares at me, disbelief written all over her face, waiting for me to say more, to explain myself. But how can I? "Trust me when I say, she is dangerous."

"Trust you?" she spits. "Why the hell would I trust you?"

Something pangs in my chest. Something I haven't felt in years and years. Is that hurt? Do I want her to trust me?

She'd be a fool to. And the girl is bright, I see that. She's no fool.

And yet, still I want her to trust me. Fuck, I want to protect her and devour her. I want it all.

"Fine," I concede. "You don't have to trust me. But for your own safety – for your own sake – heed this warning anyway."

Chapter Fifty-Five

B riony

With the next trial tomorrow, you can feel the tension growing among the students. The commoner students are quieter than usual – even those from Iron Quarter – and the shadow weavers are even more obnoxious. There're plenty of displays of their powers and I'm sure I'm not imagining that even more kids than usual are walking around with black eyes and busted noses.

I'm sort of thankful for the upcoming trial. It's going to be awful. I will probably end up with another broken nose and another sprained ankle, but at least it means everyone's attention is diverted onto that and not onto me and the Princes.

Even Fly and Clare show no interest in my complicated love life. Despite his earlier skepticism, Fly and I have joined Clare in researching everything we can about past trials – me keeping half an eye out for clues about my sister as I do.

Although we've spent every spare moment of the last few days going over possible trial scenarios and how we'd handle them, the evening before the trial – when we should probably be in bed resting – we're doing the same again.

There are several scenarios that have us beat – unless you're a shadow weaver with magical abilities there's no way you'd overcome the trial – but we have plans and ideas for the others. Of course, plans and ideas are one thing; putting them into execution is another.

"You know, I think it's going to be a maze," Clare says, looking up from her latest book as we lie out together on her bedroom floor.

"What makes you say that?" I ask, closing the old newspaper I was reading.

"I made a tally," she explains, holding up a piece of paper with a table drawn across it. "Mazes are the most frequent trial type to be set – especially for the early trials."

"Doesn't that make it less likely to be picked again this time?" Fly says, scratching his cheek and yawning.

"I don't think so. It's obviously a favorite with the trial setters and they haven't picked it for the last four years straight."

"Maybe," Fly says, sounding unconvinced.

"A maze doesn't sound so bad," I say.

Fly snorts. "Don't count on it."

"But aren't there ways to solve mazes?" I persist. "Even for those of us without shadow magic?"

"Yes," Clare says, slamming her book down in front of me. "There are!"

Clare spends the next hour going over the different

techniques. She'd probably spend longer still, but Fly cuts her off and insists we all go get some sleep.

"Techniques or not," he says, "we won't be able to solve any maze if we're so tired we can't sleep tonight."

"I don't know," I mull. "I think we should keep researching."

"Uh uh," he says, "trust me on this."

He drags me to my feet and we hug Clare good night. Then we make our way back to our tower. Despite the late hour, there are lights on all over the campus. I guess we weren't the only ones up studying tonight.

Outside our doors, Fly rests his hand on my shoulder.

"Okay?" he asks me.

"A little nervous," I say. "You?"

"Same." He kisses my forehead. "Try to get some sleep, Cupcake."

Once I'm in my room alone, I realize he never promised me tomorrow would go okay. Because he can't. He doesn't know. And there's a high probability it won't.

Without my friends close by, I feel suddenly more nervous, less sure of myself, less confident in all the plans we made.

I climb into the old pair of pajamas Clare has gifted me, flick off the light switch and snuggle into my bed.

The mattress doesn't feel nearly as comfortable as it usually does. It's scratchy, lumpy and hard. One night in a luxurious shadow weaver bed and I'm spoiled. But I don't think that's truly the problem. My mind buzzes with worries and I toss and turn unable to find sleep no matter how desperately I try.

I start to panic as the tower bell chimes two. Fly's right, without sleep I'll be even more hopeless at this trial – and while I'm not expecting to pick up any points, while I don't think I have any chance of making it into one of the other quarters, I want to make it out of the trial *alive*.

I flop over onto my back and stare up at the dark thatched roof, listening to the sounds of the creatures scurrying around inside. My heart beats loudly and my chest feels tight with worry. Speaking with Fly or Clare would make me feel better. It would probably calm me down. Lying here alone with only my spiraling thoughts for company isn't helping. But I can't wake them up in the middle of the night. They need their sleep as much as I do. It wouldn't be fair.

I close my eyes.

There is one person.

One person I could talk to. One person who is going to ace the trial, sleep or no sleep. One person who I shouldn't want to go and talk to – but I do.

I flip over onto my side, tucking my hands under my cheek.

I shouldn't be relying on other people for support or comfort. I shouldn't be trusting people.

Amelia was too trusting – so was I back then. I bet that was the true reason for her death.

I think of her now. Exactly my age. She seemed so old back then. Now I realize she wasn't. I am twenty-one and yet I feel like such a kid half the time. There is still so much to do, so much to learn. I don't want my story to end yet. I want to make it through this trial.

I fling back the thin blanket, slide on my boots, tug my coat over my pajamas and walk out of my room, locking the door behind me.

I creep down the staircase as quietly as I can, not wanting to wake anyone, also really not wanting anyone catching me on my way to where I'm going.

There is already so much gossip swirling around about me and to be caught creeping towards the Princes' tower in the middle of the night would churn that gossip up into a whirlwind.

The lights that were burning earlier are all extinguished now and the only other being I meet is an owl, swooping low over the towers on his way out towards the woods.

At the Princes' tower I hesitate. I'm not sure thumping on the door is going to wake them. This was probably a wasted night-time stroll. I try the door-handle anyway and to my surprise it clicks open.

I stand there dumbfounded as the door swings back and the dark hallway comes into view.

Do the Princes leave their tower unlocked? Or ... did the door open specifically for me?

I'm not sure how I feel about that. Flattered maybe? Another strange new sensation to add to my collection.

I step inside, closing the door quietly behind me as I slip off my boots and tiptoe up the staircase.

This is extremely, one hundred percent stupid and possibly deadly. If Beaufort, Dray or Thorne catch an intruder in their tower, they will probably shoot first, ask questions later. I was worried about dying or being injured in the trial, I am just as likely to be killed or hurt climbing their stairs. I keep climbing though. I'm committed now.

No turning back.

As I step out onto the landing, I find my suspicions were correct. Beaufort Lincoln is not sleeping in his bed. Beaufort Lincoln is once again sitting in his study. Beaufort Lincoln is staring right at me.

Chapter Fifty-Six

B eaufort

"I ... I couldn't sleep," she says.

I crook my finger and beckon her. Her hand rests on the banister. She doesn't move.

"You're worried about the trial."

She nods.

"Come here," I command and she stays where she is.

"Little thrall," I whisper, "you wanted to see me." She bites at her lip. She's always fighting this connection. But I'm no fool. I know now that she feels it. That she's finding it as hard as I am to resist. "So come here and see me." She creeps into my study like a shy little rabbit, stopping by my desk and leaning her hip against it. I can't help myself. I swivel my chair around to face her, taking a grip of her thighs and pulling her towards me.

This time, she comes willingly, a flush on her cheeks

and something in her eyes leading me to believe there's more than her fears about the trial on her mind. In fact, I believe she's come here seeking distraction from those fears.

"Do you always work this late?" she asks, as I draw my hands up her legs and squeeze her ass through the material of her sleep pants.

"I find it hard to sleep. I have a lot on my mind."

"You're a shadow weaver, what could you possibly have on your mind?"

"It's complicated."

"Have you ever had to worry if you'll have enough money to buy food for the next week? Have you ever worried there'll be no food left in the cupboard come tomorrow? Have you ever had to worry they'll take your home away?"

"No," I say, I dip my head to meet her gaze. "But I take it you have."

She nibbles at her lip and, shit, I want to do that. "Yes."

"Not anymore," I say.

She opens her mouth to say something, then changes her mind, meeting my gaze with her own instead.

"Tell me what you're worried about, little one."

She rolls her eyes. "Everything. I don't have powers like you. I may not make it out."

"You will," I say confidently.

"You don't know that for sure. Every year, students end up–"

"It won't happen to you," I say, that vision flickering in my mind.

I reach up and cup her cheek, stroking the pad of my thumb over her plump bottom lip.

Maybe she sees all the heat burning in my pupils, or maybe I'm thinking this is more than it is and all she wants is that distraction. Either way, a little whimper escapes her throat and the next thing I know, she's climbing up to straddle my lap.

"Shit," I mumble as she rubs her core against me.

"Maybe there's something that could help both of us to sleep."

"Don't you have your–" I start to say but I don't finish my words because she's kissing my mouth hungrily.

"It's over."

I smile against her lips. I should have known it would be like this. The girl does not act like she should. One moment she's hating on me, hissing and spitting into my face, the next she has her tongue inside my mouth.

I yank her closer still, so her sex is pressed right up against my erection and then I'm guiding her hips to rub against me.

She bites down hard on my bottom lip, making me groan.

"Not enough," she pants.

"Not enough?" I repeat. "You want more, little thrall?"

"Uh huh." She pants as I draw my hand up under her shirt and squeeze at her tit, finding her stiff nipple and brushing the pad of my thumb back and forth over it.

"What do you want?" I say, against her mouth. "Do you want to be fucked?"

She whimpers again and I think that's the closest I'm going to get to a yes.

"Because I really really want to fuck you, little thrall," I mutter, scrabbling to remove her pajama pants and then her panties; simple, plain things. I snap open the drawer of my desk, stuff the panties inside, and grasp around for a rubber. I break off our kiss to rip open the wrapper with my teeth.

Then I'm instructing her to lift up on her knees as I

unbuckle my belt and yank down my pants, freeing my stiff cock.

Her eyes are wide as I roll the rubber down my cock, and then my hands are back on her hips, firm, unyielding. I've waited long enough. I've been patient. Now I'm going to have the girl.

I brush my thumb over her stiff sensitive nub, and then I guide her down onto me.

We groan in unison as I push inside her and I know my cock inside her feels just as good as her pussy does wrapped tightly around my cock.

"Okay?" I say, my voice catching in my throat. She nods, resting her fingertips against my chest, tension on her face.

"Just ..." She shudders. "It's been a while ..." She swallows. "Go gently."

Go gentle?

I want to bite my own damn fist. All I want to do is slam her up and down my cock, to fuck her hard, to make her scream.

Maybe with any other girl I would. But I want this to be more than a one-time-only thing. I want her to enjoy it. I want to fuck her over and over again, willingly. I want her to want it.

"Then you take control, little thrall," I tell her. "You bounce up and down on my cock just how you want to."

A little strangled noise escapes her throat and then she's lifting up onto her knees, my cock slipping through her wet pussy, caressed by her velvety walls.

When she reaches the top, and only my cockhead lingers inside of her, she whimpers again and her fingernails dig into my shoulders.

"Does it feel good?" I murmur, looking up at her.

"Uh huh," she murmurs, gliding back down me.

It's slow and considered – a fucking tease of a fuck and maybe I like it this way. The girl has been teasing me right from day one and fuck I have loved it.

She circles her hips, moaning because that must feel good, before rising up again.

I lean forward and nip at her throat, threading open the buttons of her top and sliding it open. Her tits are a perfect handle of a size, her nipples pink and stiff and delicious. I lean in and capture them in my mouth, swirling my tongue around them, feeling them crinkle further still.

"Your pussy feels so damn good. So tight, so wet, so perfect."

I wonder why the fuck she ever fought this. All those weeks wasted when we could have been doing this and nothing else.

"Now I know how good you feel, I'm going to fuck you all the time. You're never going to leave my bed."

She sinks back down onto me, this time with a little more force and I grunt.

"Yeah, sweetheart, just like that."

"You're so ..." She screws up a brow.

"Big?" I suggest, smiling to myself. I've been told often enough that I am.

"Chauvinistic," she clarifies. "You say such sexist bullshit."

"I think you like what I say. I think you like my dirty mouth." I flick at her nipples, then lick up her neck and capture her mouth with mine, kissing her hard as her movements along my cock become faster, harder, more frantic.

I begin to meet her with a thrust from below every time she slams down on my cock and she lets out little cries of ecstasy, shaking her head from side to side as if she can't handle just how good this makes her feel, a blush blossoming across her flesh.

"I think you like my words. I think you like my fingers. And most of all I think you like my cock," I grunt.

And then I'm gathering her up into my arms and lifting her to lie on my desk. I push her down flat and paw at her tits, watching as she arches her back, pressing her breasts into my palms. I fuck her hard, the solid desk shaking beneath her and books crashing to the floor, my bottle of whisky tumbling that way too and smashing into a million pieces.

I want to see her come again. I want to make this good for her too. I press my thumb to her clit and soon it's quivering and she's writhing on my desk, ecstasy racing across her face. She cries out and with a grunt, I join her, collapsing over her, my brow damp with sweat.

I find her mouth again. I kiss her deep and slow as the aftermath of pleasure pulsates through my body, from my balls all the way to the top of my head and the tip of my toes. She kisses me back, sucking on my tongue and I find her hands and thread our fingers together. I have no desire to move. I'm still inside her and I want to remain there.

Because now I've had her, I'm never letting her go.

Chapter Fifty-Seven

B^{riony}

For a man who claims he doesn't sleep, Beaufort seems pretty passed out to me. He lies face down on the mattress, arms and legs slung wide, one arm draped over my waist.

I chew on my lip and stare up at the canopy of his four-poster bed.

I can't deny that that wasn't anything but good. So good I know I am doomed. Because it was like the sweetest of honeys, the most potent of opioids – one taste and I won't be able to help myself from coming back for more.

What the hell possessed me to come here tonight? What the hell compelled me to climb onto his lap like that? What the hell was I thinking?

I was thinking how good it would be for him to touch me again, to make me fall apart again. And it wasn't like I wanted it. I needed it. My body has been craving his touch all week. I am already an addict.

The orgasms Beaufort Lincoln sucks from my body are like thunder and lightning, summer and winter, life and death and everything in between. Like the molecules of my body, the make-up of my soul, are being rearranged completely.

I sigh and turn my head to peer at his face.

His eyelids are closed, a set of thick eyelashes resting against the curves of his cheekbones; his lips tremor as he breathes in and out, his chest rising and falling.

He looks almost harmless like this, almost vulnerable – as if his body doesn't possess the power and strength it does, as if his veins aren't brimming with the shadows he can wield. He may look gentle now – I may have seen a more gentle side to him – but he is dangerous and I have allowed myself to walk willingly into his lair.

As I watch him, his lids flicker open and his silver eyes focus in on my face. He lifts his hand to stroke my cheek.

"Okay, little thrall?"

I bite my lip and nod.

Am I?

I feel like a traitor. I feel like I've betrayed my sister and all for a good looking boy who makes me feel good. I am the worst of the worst.

"You're not worrying again?"

I shake my head and his finger meanders down my cheek, over my jaw and down my throat.

"You'll be safer with our collar on. And shit, our collar is going to look so good wrapped around your neck."

I pull away from his touch. "I'm not wearing a collar. Just because we slept together does not mean–"

He groans and flops back down on the mattress. "Not this bullshit again."

"It isn't bullshit," I say. I don't want to argue, not now when my skin is still tingling and my core buzzing and I feel ... content. Not when the trial is tomorrow and I have more important things to think about.

Then again, maybe this is my opportunity to make him understand my point of view.

He rolls over onto his back. "It is bullshit."

"Why do we have to label this thing between us as something? Why do we have to label it *that*? Can't we just enjoy each other's company?"

A wicked smile meanders over his lips. "I really fucking enjoy your company. But this isn't a negotiation. This doesn't work unless you are our thrall. All our thrall."

I tut. "Thorne doesn't even want me to be his thrall."

"Not true." He turns his head to look at me. "I don't understand. You like it when I touch you. You like it when I make you come. You came here tonight looking for it. And yet ... Why are you so against it?"

"I've told you."

He shakes his head. "Those aren't reasons. You know, I know, the entire damn academy knows, you are better off as our thrall. Even if you hated our very souls you'd be better off as ours. Even if we abused you and treated you badly you'd be better off with us."

"Because I'm so weak and pathetic I couldn't possibly look after myself?"

"Correct."

I scowl at him. "I'm stronger than I look and I'd rather take my chances on my own than belong to someone else."

"And end up dead."

Amelia. That plain wooden box.

I look away from him.

"Why are you so against it?" he repeats. "Why really?"

I snap my head back towards him. "Shadow weavers killed my sister!"

Shock spirals across his face, followed quickly by anger. "Who?"

"I ... I don't know. They never told us, but I intend to find out."

"How?"

"I'm not sure yet. I think there may be information in the lib–"

"No, how did they kill her?"

"I don't know–"

"You don't know? You must–"

"All they told us – all they *would* tell us – was that she was killed in crossfire between shadow weavers practicing at the academy."

"She died at the academy?" I nod. "Ahhhh," he says, the anger and tension leaving his face.

"What?" I say with irritation. "What do you mean by 'ahhh'?"

"It happens."

"What does?"

"Accidents. Especially here at the academy. You said it yourself, people die here. You can't hold all shadow weavers responsible for something–"

"Accident?" I snap, throwing back the covers and jumping up onto my knees. "It wasn't an accident. She was special. And so they killed her."

He rolls up to sit, the blankets coalescing around his waist.

"Why? Why would they kill her?"

I open my mouth. I don't have the answers to that. It's what I intend to find out.

"She wandered into crossfire," he says. "Unfortunate but—"

"That's what they told us. It's all just a lie. I know it isn't true."

"Why wouldn't it be?"

My heart pounds in my ears and in my throat. I could tell him the whole truth. The reason I know this could never have been an accident. But then I remember Professor Tudor's warning. Throwing around accusations could land me in trouble. I've already said too much.

"Training often leads to collateral damage," he says. "People get hurt. People die. It's the way of the fucking world."

I leap out of the bed. "My sister was not collateral damage. And maybe I don't like this world! It's corrupted and unfair and molded to benefit people like you!"

"Me? To *benefit* me?" He laughs bitterly.

"Yes, you and all the other shadow weavers too. It's down to plain old luck where we're born and yet you live in luxury and splendor while the rest of us shiver in the cold, scrabbling about to find enough food to eat. Have you ever actually been to Slate Quarter? Because that picture down there on your wall is so embellished it's laughable!"

"It's only fair that those taking the highest risks should reap the highest rewards."

"You don't think working in a mine has its risks, working the land all through the winter?"

He scoffs. "You can't possibly conceive how dangerous the threat to our realm really is. Because you've never faced the demons and the monsters that are out there. You don't understand how hard my kind are working every minute of every day to protect this realm. How much we are risking. Why? Three alone were killed last month! You're naïve," he says patronizingly and I have a deep desire to slap my hand across his face. Instead, I rummage around the room, looking for clothes I can pull on my body.

"And you're a dick."

"I'm sorry about your sister but you can't–"

"I don't want to talk about it anymore."

I find my pajamas discarded in a pile in the corner.

"What the fuck are you doing now?" he says with irritation of his own.

"Leaving," I tell him, pulling on my pants and my shirt.

"It's the middle of the night!"

"So what?"

"It's not safe out there."

"Because other shadow weavers might come for me? Like they did my sister, you mean? You know what, I think you're the monsters!" He glares at me. "I made it here on my own tonight, didn't I? I've survived the last twenty-one years just fine. I can look after myself."

"Really because all the black eyes, broken noses and sprained ankles suggest otherwise. And as I understand it, they weren't from shadow weavers."

I'm half tempted to tell him about the way Henrietta struck me with lightning, but I am done with this conversation.

I storm towards the door.

"This is over," I tell him, with my hand on the door knob.

"No, it's not. This won't ever be over."

I open my mouth to argue with him, but it's pointless. He's as stubborn as I am. I'm not going to waste my time arguing over the point. This was a mistake. A huge one.

I've been keeping my sister's death a secret for a reason. I don't know what happened to her and I don't know why she was killed. There's a possibility I could be in danger too.

I trusted him. What a fool I am! Because, he just dismissed my sister's death as meaningless as if it was no more important than breaking a vase or stepping on a snail. He is as conceited and cruel as I first suspected.

From now on I'm going to have nothing to do with him or his brothers – no matter the cost.

Chapter Fifty-Eight

B^{riony}

I storm back to my tower so angry I could trash my own room tonight, shaking so hard I can barely unlock my own door.

I want to scream. I want to tear everything down.

This world is so unfair, so twisted, so corrupt. It took my mother and my sister. It broke my father and gave me a woman that abused me. And now it wants to torture me some more.

I throw myself on the bed and pummel my fists and my legs against the hard mattress, hitting as hard as I can, until I'm choking on my own strangled breaths and the tears hurtle down my cheeks.

I'm such a fool. What did I think would happen? That he'd believe me? That he'd help me? That he'd understand?

He is a shadow weaver. He'll never understand what it's

like to have your only hope ripped away, to have the most precious person in your life torn from you. I shouldn't have trusted him.

I lie there sobbing until there are no more tears to cry and the tower bell strikes five in the morning.

And then I stop.

This is pathetic and hopeless and ridiculous.

There is nothing to be gained from feeling sorry for myself. Might as well use all this anger, channel it somewhere useful.

I settle on the floor with my notebook and pencil.

The library may be out of bounds for now but I can still attempt to make progress on the mystery of my sister's death. I'm going to start by writing down everything I know – the indisputable facts and the ones I don't believe, as well as everything I've learned about the academy since coming here.

Before I begin, I lift my bag from its hiding place in my wardrobe and, as I do every morning and every evening, check the contents.

Then I lick the tip of my pencil, press it to my page and begin.

After an hour, I've scribbled notes across pages and pages of my notebook. It hasn't led me to any new insights or brainwaves but at least I feel like I'm taking action.

Fly and Clare knock on my door at seven as planned and, after gathering up all my notes, I invite them in. Both of them are still dressed in their pajamas. We planned one last cramming session before getting ready for the trial.

"Hey Cupcake, how did you ..." Fly trails off, spotting my tear-stained face. "What's wrong?"

I've been dreading this moment. I hoped I could pretend like nothing had happened. But Fly is far too observant for that. What exactly am I going to tell them and what am I going to keep to myself? I've already made the mistake of divulging my secret tonight. Can I truly trust my friends?

"Hmmm," I say, contemplating this dilemma.

"Cupcake, you're scaring me. Did something happen?"

I sigh, finding it hard to meet his eyes. "I couldn't sleep last night–"

"Me neither," Clare says.

"–so I went to see Beaufort Lincoln."

"Ooooh!" Fly says.

Clare adjusts her glasses and examines my face. "There's more isn't there?"

I fidget on the floor. "Well, yes ... Beaufort and I slept together."

"Slept together as in the same bed or slept together slept together?" Fly asks.

"We had sex on his desk."

Clare's mouth falls open and relief floods over Fly's face before he rocks backwards and kicks his feet against the floor.

"Oh my gosh!" he squeals.

"Was it good?" Clare asks.

"Don't be stupid. It was Beaufort Lincoln. Of course it was good. She's just full of the usual good-girl guilts," Fly dismisses, then sees the expression on my face and adds: "It was good, right?"

"Yeeeeessss," I say, "but then we had this massive fight right after, where he revealed just what an asshole he is."

"Isn't that how your budding relationship goes? You fight, you make up, you fight again."

"This was a big one. It's over between us. I don't care what they say or do, I don't want anything more to do with any of them."

"Oh," Fly says, all the joy on his face quickly evaporating.

"What was it about?" Clare asks.

"Huh?"

"The fight. What was it about?"

"My sister," I say.

They both gape at me blankly. "You had a massive blow up about your sister?" Fly says.

"Did I know you had a sister?" Clare asks, straightening her glasses again.

I stare at my two friends and weigh up the decision in my mind. I've known them for only three weeks and what do I really know? Yet, I trust them. I trust them to have my back.

"I don't anymore. She died. Here at the academy."

"Oh my gosh," Fly repeats, this time with sympathy. "Bri– I had no idea." He shakes his head. "You never said anything."

I drop my gaze to my lap, my notebook resting on my thighs; I straighten the loose pages escaping the cover.

"It's not exactly the bright, cheery topic you bring up when trying to make new friends," I say, managing a half smile.

"But we're old friends now," Fly protests, resting his hand on my shoulder. "We've known each other for three long weeks."

"They have been long, haven't they?" I say, peering up into his face, which is a mistake because his eyes are brimming with empathy – such a strong contrast to Beaufort's – and it has my eyes stinging with tears again.

"How did she die?" Clare asks softly.

"They say she was killed in an accident. That she strolled into the crossfire of shadow weavers practicing their magic. But I don't believe it. She wasn't stupid," I say with steel, waiting for them to challenge me. They don't, they both nod.

"You think something else happened to her?" Clare asks.

I nod. "And I'm going to find out what."

"How exactly?" Clare says.

I drum my fingers against the cover of my notebook and bite my cheek. "I haven't worked that out yet. I tried searching for information in the library but Professor Tudor stopped me before I got anywhere." I don't divulge what happened on my most recent trip to the library. I may be feeling more trusting, but I'm not quite ready to reveal all my secrets just yet. Especially as those secrets could get my friends into trouble.

"It all makes sense now," Fly says.

"What does?"

"The reason you hate shadow weavers so much."

"Can you blame me?"

"Well, I don't exactly get on with my brothers," Fly says, "they are a bunch of shitheads who have made my life unbearable for the last twenty-one years. As bad as it sounds, I wouldn't hate the person who removed them from my life. But I'm guessing you and your sister ..."

"She was older than me. She was like a mom to me. She took care of me. And she was beautiful and clever and so so special."

Fly smiles at me. "Then I can totally understand why you hate those shadow weavers."

"But the Princes weren't the ones that killed your sister, were they?" Clare says with confusion. "If she was older than you, they would have been kids when she was at the academy."

"It doesn't matter," Fly says. "It's made her distrustful of them all."

"Not just distrustful," I clarify. "I hate them. They don't care about us. They've bent and corrupted this world for their own gain. And Beaufort confirmed all my worst suspicions about them tonight."

Clare lunges forward and wraps her arms around me. "I'm sorry, Briony."

I pat her back. "It's okay. I'm fine. And it's better this way. I don't need any distractions like those three. I need to find the truth."

Chapter Fifty-Nine

D^{ray}

I wake up to the sound of angry footsteps on the stairway and the front door slamming shut.

I roll to the edge of the bed, stumble to my feet and, rubbing sleepy crust from my eyes, stagger to the window. I am not a fucking morning person and whoever the hell has woken me at this freaking early hour is going to pay for it.

Only it turns out the person responsible is our little thrall.

I lean against the frame and watch her scuttle away, thunder all over her face.

Now ain't that curious. I didn't even know our little thrall was visiting. That certainly wasn't planned.

I'm suddenly more awake than if I'd downed ten straight shots of coffee.

I gaze up towards the ceiling. I bet Beaufort is responsible.

I find him pacing in his study wearing nothing but a pair of boxers. To be fair, I'm wearing even less.

I lean against the doorway, spinning a toothpick between my lips and consider him. As I do, my nose twitches. It smells strongly of our little thrall in this room. Fucking strongly of her. My intuition was correct.

"You want to tell me what happened with our little brat of a thrall?" I ask, crossing my right foot over my left and chewing on the toothpick.

"Nothing happened," he says, halting at his desk, picking up a note that lies on its surface and turning it over in his hands, refusing to look my way.

"Do you know how many more olfactory receptor neurons a wolf has compared to a human?" I say.

Beaufort sighs, lowers the note, and, collapsing into the chair, looks up at me. "No," he says with irritation. "I don't."

"Fifty-six times. Which means," I say, pushing off the doorframe and striding into the room, "I can smell a hell of a lot better than you can, my friend. I know you fucked her in here." I sniff at the air and a grin stretches across my face. "Fuck, was it on your desk?"

He frowns at me and I take that for all the confirmation I need.

"So you fucked her." I nod to myself, twisting the toothpick in my fingers. "Why does that mean she is now storming away looking like she might kill someone?"

"She's always angry. She doesn't want to be our thrall. She's made that clear. Nothing's changed."

"Dude," I snort, "are you really that bad a fuck?"

He pushes back his chair, hands tight on the armrests and glowers at me. "Trust me, she had a good time."

"So why isn't she wearing our collar and perched on your lap, purring like a good little kitten?"

"If you'd ever met a fucking kitten, you'd know the last thing they do is sit nicely in your lap. They're more likely to scratch at your face and claw your eyes out."

Yeah, that does sound more like our little thrall. Kitten – seems the perfect way to describe her.

"And yet they'd still be back for more of that affection." I chuckle. "So tell me, Beaufort, what the fuck happened?"

He sighs again, and leans back in his chair, resigned to tell me the truth.

"We argued."

"So what. You argue. She argues. It's what you both love to do."

"It was more than that this time." He scrubs his hand over his face. "The girl hates us, Dray," he says, with an emotion I haven't seen since we were kids. Beaufort, unlike Thorne, does have them, he just keeps them very well hidden. "She really fucking hates us."

"She's always put on this act–"

"It isn't an act. She ... has her reasons."

I consider him some more, snapping the toothpick between my fingers. "But you said–"

"I know what I saw," he snaps.

"Maybe you were wrong. Maybe you misinterpreted–"

"I didn't," he says coolly. "There was no mistaking it. I saw it in the vision. She is meant to be ours. Whether she hates us or not."

Whether she hates us or not.

No one hates me. Not really. And any that have hated me – any enemies, for example – are now dead. I don't think our little kitten would hate me if she got to know me better.

I'm not Beaufort and I sure as hell ain't Thorne. Look how much she liked me in my wolf-form.

Which gives me an idea.

I wait until just before breakfast time, slip outside and jog out to the trees. Transforming's easiest out where nature rules, where all my wolfish instincts take over. Sure, if I need to I can transform whenever and wherever I please – it's what makes me one of the most powerful shifters in the realm. But I've always preferred to do it in private, underneath the trees, where the ground is soft and organic beneath my feet.

I shrug off the pants and shirt I'm wearing, tip back my head and let the shadows overtake my body, let them twist bone, shape muscle, stretch skin, until I'm forced down onto four paws and the world has shifted on its axis.

I'm still me, hidden beneath this fleece of fur. Only fucking wilder, fucking stronger, and definitely more fucking impulsive.

I fucking love it.

I lean back on my paws, stretching out my back, swiveling my ears, and then nipping at my tail.

Like this, the world loses its colors; everything is muted, less bright, less vibrant. But the smells. Fuck, the smells! Millions of them all competing for my attention, all screaming out some story, promising some freaking amazing adventure. Sharp, sour, sweet, pungent, putrid.

And the sounds too. I can hear the path of a small rodent as he scurries through the distant undergrowth; can hear the ruffle of an owl's feathers in the branches high above me, and hear the faintest whisper of voices from the academy far away.

I indulge in my wolfish side for just a moment, following the scent of a squirrel through the trees. I soon catch up with him and then it's a chase. Me crashing through the undergrowth and leaping over discarded branches and broken brambles, hot on his tail. I nearly catch him, but then he's scrambling up a tree and out of reach.

I stand panting, the adrenaline soaring through my veins. I let it fade and yank myself back. There was a reason for transforming. Another scent I intend to hunt out. One that stinks of sex – of wet pussy and soft limbs.

I drag my tongue over my snout and then I sprint off in the direction of the academy.

I can smell the humans before they see me, and so I hug the shadows. I don't want anyone to see me but her. Not in this moment anyway. I track through the campus until I reach the tower that houses her room, then still hidden from view, I drop down onto my stomach, rest my head on my front paws and wait.

Time passes, my perception of it distorted in my wolf form. He's more patient than me – even if he is wilder. But eventually I catch a hint of her scent. I lift my head and peer through the gloom. My wolf eyes may not be able to detect the colors my human ones can, but my vision in the half-light is far sharper. Soon I see her turn the corner, alone, her coat pulled tightly around her to ward off the cold and her head bowed down. I jump up onto my paws and trot towards her.

I'm guessing the little kitten is lost in her thoughts, because she doesn't register my presence until I nudge my snout against her side and whine.

She jolts, jumping away, her hands raised like she's either about to surrender or about to fight.

I sit, dragging my paw through the air and whining a second time.

"Oh, it's you," she says flatly, which was not the reception I was hoping for. The last time we met in my wolf form, she was all fucking over me. "Go away. I don't need this today. The trial starts in less than an hour."

If I could laugh, I would. Because, yeah, I'm not leaving.

I stare at her with what I'm guessing are a pair of adorable puppy eyes and whine some more.

"Don't look at me like that. I know who you are under all that fur and you can't fool me with this cutesy thing."

Me, cute? I'm not sure it's how the last person I ripped apart would have described me. But if the little kitten wants to call me cute, then I won't be complaining.

I stand and pad towards her. She doesn't try to turn away or run. She's smart and she knows I'm faster than she is. Does she also know how much I like to fucking chase? In fact, this would be so much more fun if she were to run. Then I could hunt her down and ...

"What do you want?" she says, scowling at me.

I nudge my nose against her hand and then lick at her fingers. Her skin tastes divine. But it's her pussy I really want to eat.

She snatches her hand away from my mouth and crosses her arms over her chest, staring off into space and not at me.

I rub my head and body against her legs hoping she'll relent and pet me, but she only huffs in annoyance.

I huff myself through my nostrils and sink to the ground, looking up at her again with hurt eyes.

She glances at me but refuses to relent.

This isn't working.

Time for a new plan.

I close my eyes and the shadows creep from my veins, wrestling the wolf back into submission. My body trans-forms again. This time skin retracts, bones shorten, muscles turn. It hurts. Of course it fucking does. But it's a part of who I am.

I roll up to stand on my bare feet, towering above the little kitten.

"Jeez," she says, jumping away from me and bringing her hand to cover her face. "You're ..."

"Yes sweetheart I am," I say, letting the pecs on my chest dance for her.

"You need to put some clothes on."

"Nah," I say.

"You'll freeze to frigging death."

I shrug my shoulders. "I don't feel the cold. Blood runs hot." I stare at her with heat in my eyes. The kitten's green eyes dart down towards my cock and away again. I chuckle. "Like what you see?" I run my fingers through my hair. "I hear you have a thing for riding cock. Wanna go back to my room and ride mine?"

She glowers at me – just like Beaufort did earlier. The two of them are more alike than they realize. I'd say that's half the reason for whatever the hell argument they had.

"Do you get a kick out of swinging your cock about and flashing girls – who by the way really don't want to see your cock!"

I ruffle my hair, then hold up my forefinger between us.

"One – I'm not swinging my cock – but if that's something you want to see ..." She shakes her head adamantly and I hold up another finger. "Two, actually, kitten, most girls want to see my cock." I shrug. "What can I say, most girls want to suck it too."

"Leave me alone."

"Just because Beaufort pissed you off in some way–"

"You all piss me off. I already told you multiple times, I don't want to be your thrall, I want nothing to do with you."

I take a step towards her. "For someone who wants nothing to do with us, it sounds like you had rather a lot to do with Beaufort."

My gaze flicks across her face as her cheeks pinken.

"That ... that was a mistake."

"Mistakes can be fun." I lick my lips. "Wanna make a mistake with me, little kitten? Wanna make one all over my face as I lick out your pussy?"

And to my utter fucking delight, she draws back her hand and slaps me hard across the face. This is starting to become a habit. Our very own brand of foreplay. I love it.

Stars spin across my vision and my senses tingle, my magic electric, all the blood rushing down towards my cock.

I go to grab her, but the little thing is quick, and she's slipping out of reach and scurrying away, up into her tower – just like that squirrel in the tree.

Fuck, that was fun.

The more I play with the little thing, the more I like her.

Chapter Sixty

B riony

I knock on Fly's door. He skipped breakfast this morning, saying he was too nervous to eat. I wish I'd done the same, that way I could have missed that awkward encounter with Dray.

Fly steps out onto the landing and shuts his door behind him.

"Looking dapper today," I tell him, taking in the way he's styled his tracksuit and combed his hair this morning.

"Cupcake, if I'm going to die today, then I'm going to at least die looking good."

"You're not going to die, Fly," I say, although I'm sure the nerves are apparent in my voice. "Trials aren't meant to be deadly, remember? They're meant to fish us out before we are actually killed," I say, parroting something we've read and heard thousands of times, even if I don't believe it, even if it was those fears that led me straight into Beaufort's arms last night. "They try their best to keep casualties to a minimum."

He takes my hand and squeezes it. "You're right. Both of us are going to ace this trial. I was a little skeptical when you dragged that scrawny little thing to our lunch table–"

"Do you mean Clare?" I ask.

He nods. "But it was genius. All the studying up on different trials actually makes me feel like we stand a chance – not just of surviving unhurt, but of actually coming out of it with some points."

"And Clare is also, you know, fun to be around and a good friend."

"That too," he says, winking at me. "I have a feeling we're all going to end up old friends together in Granite Quarter."

I smile back, although I know his cheer this morning is an act. I can feel his hand shaking in mine.

We meet Clare outside her tower. She's looking as nervous as I feel, a tissue pressed to her nostrils because she has another nose bleed.

"Remember," Clare says as we walk along together, "if you meet a pool of water do not wade into it, and if you find anything that looks like nightshade, pocket it."

"We know," Fly says, "we went over this already."

She nods, then sniffs and presses the tissue more firmly to her nose. "And if your path is blocked by green fire, it may look and feel hot but you can cross unharmed. It won't burn you."

"Yep, we went over that too," I say, squeezing her arm. "Are you okay, Clare?"

She sighs. "Not really. No offense, Briony, but I really don't want to end up in Slate."

"None taken," I tell her. "And you won't. You know more than anyone. You're going to be fine." I hand her some clean tissue from my own pocket. "Come on. Let's hurry up. We might be able to see something and, I don't know, that could be helpful."

The others nod and we pick up the pace, jogging across the campus to the far field where we've been instructed to gather for the trial this morning. It's funny – I'm about to face something incredibly dangerous. And yet – despite my nerves, that argument with Beaufort and all those tears this morning – I don't feel half as downbeat, half as miserable, as I did that day I arrived at the academy. Three weeks have passed and, despite the attempts on my life, the breaking of my nose and the situation with the Princes, I realize things are not all bad. In fact, I feel pretty damn good. I have a feeling that's down to the two friends I have walking with me. I'd forgotten how good it is to have a friend, to have someone on your side, and all of a sudden a wave of panic hits me.

I stop dead in my tracks.

"What's wrong?" Clare asks, fiddling with the material she's tied around the back of her head to keep her glasses fixed firmly to her face.

I reach out and take her hand in my right and Fly's in my left.

"You will be careful, won't you? Don't do anything stupid or ... I couldn't bear to lose either of you."

"You're not going to get rid of me that easily, Cupcake. I don't know, you may be weird as hell with very bad fashion sense, but I kinda like you."

Clare chuckles, causing more blood to trickle from her nose, but my face remains deadly serious.

"Promise me," I whisper.

Fly squeezes my hand again.

"I promise."

"Me too," Clare says, inhaling and then nodding.

It seems we aren't the only ones that had the bright idea of arriving at the trial site early. Half the students, excluding the shadow weavers, are already here milling about and talking to one another quietly. They aren't the only ones. All the faculty staff are here including the gruesome twosome, Madame Bardin, and Professor Tudor – plus a collection of other adults, all dressed in their finery. I assume they must be representatives from the different Quarters because among them, is our very own director dragged all the way from Slate Quarter, looking a lot less confident than he usually does and dressed in a suit that is worn and drab. To think, he always used to look so well dressed to me before.

However, what we can't see is the trial site itself. A large fence has been erected, blocking our view of the fields, the moorland and the forest beyond. To one side, a stand has also been built with rows of seating. The chairs at the front are padded and large, the ones further up the stand plain old benches. Some of the adults are already seated.

"What are all those people from the Quarters doing here?" I ask the other two.

"It's part of the rules," Clare whispers to me. "There has to be representatives from all the Quarters here to oversee the trials – to ensure they're fair and to help decide how points are awarded."

I snort. "I don't see why they'd bother."

"Because sometimes – very rarely mind you," Clare says with sarcasm, "there are kids who are good academically and physically and could reasonably be placed in Iron or

Granite. Sometimes both Quarters want them. There needs to be a way of deciding."

"And sometimes," Fly says, staring off towards the stands, "kids do well in these trials but the Quarters don't want them anyway because they don't meet the ideal, they don't fit in. There has to be a way to make it fair."

"Fair," I snort, "nothing about this is fair."

Clare shushes me and even Fly looks a little uncomfortable with that remark, especially when the Empress herself appears in a swirl of mist in the next moment, accompanied by her troop of guards and a flurry of trumpets. Madame Bardin hurries off to meet her and I peer up at the clock tower. Fifteen minutes until this ordeal begins.

More and more of the students trickle in from the campus but it's not until the Empress and Madame Bardin are standing waiting on a stage that's been erected right in front of the giant fence, and the large clock is about to strike ten, that the shadow weaver students come strolling out onto the field. They aren't wearing their black tracksuits and I realize no one actually instructed us to wear our uniforms today. Instead, they're dressed in the clothes many were wearing the day we arrived: bright colorful outfits that make them look more like gods than young adults who have only just passed through puberty.

Instinctively, I search for Beaufort, Dray and Thorne among the group, finding them leading the pack. Beaufort has purpose engrained across his brow, his gaze focused right ahead. Dray bounces along on his toes, lazy grin on his face as he chews his gum, gaze flicking everywhere. And Thorne has the usual blank expression he always wears as if this day is like any other.

Dray's eyes find me among the crowd but today I'm not rewarded with my usual wink or the usual smile that makes me think he'd like to devour me for dinner. No, his gaze doesn't linger on me at all, simply passes over me as if I'm of no interest at all. I should be pleased with that. It suggests that perhaps those three men have finally gotten the message. But to my surprise, disappointment sparks in my belly instead. Really? Do I actually care?

I don't have time to analyze this strange response, though, because Madame is clapping her hands, the sound magically amplified, and drawing everyone's attention away from the shadow weavers and to the stage.

"Welcome, Empress." The Empress inclines her head ever so slightly. She's dressed in another beautiful gown – this one the color of the sky on a cloudless day, the crown once again woven into her hair and decorated with small blue flowers. "Welcome distinguished guests from across the realm." She points out towards the people who have now taken their seats in the stands. "And welcome students to the first real Firestone Academy trial of the year. Before we begin, I will remind you of the rules."

"Where's the Head teacher?" I whisper to Fly and Clare. "You'd think he'd at least show up for this."

Fly shrugs and Clare places her finger to her lips.

"Students will complete the trial set for them alone and without assistance. You may not collaborate or help other students. Doing so will see you severely punished.

"You will enter the trial site one at a time and you will have sixty minutes to complete the trial. You may take no objects or devices into the trial site. The judges," she points out to the observers sitting in the front row of the stands – two spaces remaining – one I assume for the Empress and one for Madame, "will award points for your performance under the categories of magic, physical abilities, and mental aptitude. At the end of your time at the academy, when all the trials have been completed, your points will be totaled and will determine to which Quarter of the realm you will be sent."

There's some murmuring among the students. This isn't new news – we all know that is how things supposedly work – and yet to hear it spoken by Madame Bardin right before this trial makes it all real. The first night had been something minor – the points up for grabs minimal. This is it. The real deal. Our destinies start here.

"The order by which students will enter the trial site has been set." She waves her hand and a large list of names appears pinned to the fence in front of us. At the very top: Thorne Cadieux.

"I think you're right at the bottom," Fly whispers to me, squinting towards the list.

"Figures," I say, "of course, they'd have us Slate kids going out last."

"No, I mean right at the bottom. I think you're last."

"Seriously?" I say. "Do they think I am that awful?"

"The order might not have anything to do with ability. It may be determined by some other factor," Clare says.

I look at her cynically. "Then why are the Princes top of the list?"

I peer through the crowd towards them, trying to determine if the order has rattled them. It seems strange to me that Beaufort isn't going first. Then again, maybe I understand less about the three shadow weavers than I thought.

"When your name is called, you will step forward. I wish every student the best of luck. *Through trials to truth.*" She smiles that strange smile. "And now, Her Majesty the Empress will address you."

There is loud applause from the crowd in the stands.

The Empress takes Madame Bardin's place. Her eyes

scan over us students just like they did the day we arrived at the academy.

"Young and loyal subjects of the realm. We come here today to observe your talents and your skills. This is your opportunity to show the realm the very best of yourself. Go forth and do me proud. *By trial and truth, your Quarter calls!*"

More loud applause erupts once she finishes speaking and for a second time her gaze sweeps across the students. This time her gaze lingers for just a fraction of time on the Princes and then, to my utter astonishment, me. Her eyes are a dark gray, like stormy skies, and I swear, even from this distance, I feel her magic tingle against my skin. I don't break the eye contact, but soon her penetrating gaze is moving on, across the students, leaving me just as bewildered as I did that day out there on the platform when Beaufort captivated me with a similar stare.

Fly knocks me out of it, though, nudging me hard in the ribs.

"Come on," he says, "we have to wait over there."

I follow him over to a roped-off section of grass where we've been told we must wait. There are separate areas for the kids from Iron, Granite and Slate. I hug both Fly and Clare goodbye and go stand with the kids from my own Quarter.

It isn't exactly comfortable – forty of us crammed onto a tiny section of grass. There's not enough space to sit and even if there were, the ground is too hard and too cold. Which makes it even more infuriating that the shadow weavers have been given a large section with comfortable-looking chairs. Not that many of them are choosing to use them. They're all pacing, or jumping up and down on the spot, some stretching out. It's a sharp contrast to our group where most people are either praying to the stars or rocking backward and forward in semi-comatose states.

"Thorne Cadieux," a loud voice booms across the grounds.

I rise up on my tiptoes in an attempt to see over the heads in front of me.

I can just make out the quietest of the Princes, strolling across to the tall fence. He looks neither scared nor relaxed. Not even buzzed. He walks calmly, ignoring all the eyes on him.

One of the gruesome twins steps out to meet him and leads him to a door in the fence. He says a few words to him but none of it is discernible over the distance. Then the whistle sounds, the door swings open and Thorne steps through.

Immediately the door slams behind him, offering no glimpse of what lies beyond and the voice calls out the name of the next student to face the trial.

Beaufort Lincoln.

Several people actually slap Beaufort on the back as he strides past, or wish him luck. There's even a trickle of applause from the stand.

He reaches the fence and a moment later he disappears through the door, the voice calling up Dray next.

The last of the Princes milks his moment of limelight for all its worth, waving to the crowd and receiving some whoops of encouragement and even a cry of, "Go for it, Dray!"

But it doesn't last long, then he's gone and the next shadow weaver is called forward. It seems they'll be going before us, not hanging around in the cold to stew in their own thoughts. I can't help feeling that this must be an advantage.

As more and more students disappear behind the fence, sounds begin to travel towards us. Screams and screeches, thuds and cracks. Once or twice we even see the flash of magic up in the sky. I study the faces of the spectators seated in the stands. From their angle they can see behind the fence and observe what is happening. There are some definite winces; once or twice some of the spectators even cover their eyes with their hands. But there are other spectators whooping with delight, bouncing up and down in their seats with excitement, even laughing.

I watch as the first of the Iron Quarter kids set off, Fly among them. I cross my fingers and say a silent prayer for him. Next it's the Granite kids. Clare looks petrified when her name is called and I send her all the good luck vibes I can muster. And then it's just us Slate kids left waiting.

Of course, Stanley is billed to go first, and he turns to us all, hands on hips, giant smirk on his face. There's still a blue tinge to his left eye and a scab under his right, but that beating obviously didn't knock the obnoxiousness out of him.

"Good luck, losers. You're going to need it." His eyes find me and he mouths, "Especially you."

I flick my gaze away from him and don't give him the benefit of a reaction. I don't even watch as he jogs towards the fence when his name is called.

Soon enough, I'm the last one left out there in the holding pen and I can feel eyes from the spectators flicking from the action to me. There's some murmuring in the crowd. I have really failed at this disappearing act. Last girl standing. I bet, just like me, they're all wondering why. Or maybe they think I'm going to be utterly awful and therefore a good source of entertainment.

I glare back at them and several actually jolt and turn to look away. All but one.

Professor Fox Tudor.

Those rust-colored eyes of his glow over the distance and I swear I can almost feel the cool lick of his shadow magic against my skin. Then he nods. The tiniest of gestures. Something private that I think is meant just for me. A gesture of encouragement.

Does it work? I'm not sure. I still feel pretty petrified as my name is called and I walk towards that door.

One half of the gruesome twins barks orders at me, but I can't hear what he's saying over the sound of my heart thumping in my ears. And then the whistle pierces through my skull, the door opens and I step through.

Chapter Sixty-One

T horne

I step through the doorway and into a maze, tall rambling hedgerows blocking my view and my path.

Immediately, I sense danger. It is nothing I can see. Nothing I can hear. But I do feel it right in the core of my body.

Beneath my feet the earth is hard and solid and above me the sky has changed – full of angry clouds, thunder and lightning crashing between them. It means little light filters down towards me. I look up and behind me, searching for the stand full of spectators but the hedges are too tall – formed from a tangle of brambles and vines.

I look down at my hands and carefully remove the leather gloves. Then I close my eyes and let my shadow magic race from my fingertips, it skids and swerves ahead of me through the maze, round corners and bends, through and past the dead-ends, searching for whatever this maze hides, seeking out the danger. There are several obstacles, both organic and inorganic, that block the path. My magic scorches easily through them all, driving deeper into the heart of the maze, halting when it reaches the center. My magic doesn't recognize what lies there, but it is neither threat nor reward. I think it is simply the end.

I sigh in annoyance. This was easy. Too damn easy. Not a challenge at all.

I set off at a steady pace. The shadows have cleared a path for me and now all I need to do is follow it.

As I walk, I think of the girl. How hard will she find this? How dangerous?

The traps laid out were nothing for my magic. But for a girl without any? Without even brute strength to aid her?

I don't like the idea of leaving her to her fate.

It is forbidden to help her. It is against the rules to provide aid to any other student. Do I care?

If I'm caught, I'd be expelled from the trial and stripped of my points.

I stare down at my bare hands and ask myself again, do I care?

I walk around corners, passing over and through the remains of the traps laid out. Most of the students out there won't make it this far. They definitely won't make it to the center.

Three more minutes and I'm there. The heart of the maze – a square bordered by low-manicured hedgerows, a fountain spurting water in the center, a dark crystal spinning in the current. My intuition tells me that if I reach out and take it, the trial will be complete.

I call the shadows back to me, feeling them drive back inside me like a thousand knives – sharp, lethal, deadly.

I unhook my gloves from my belt and tug them back onto my hands, the leather feeling stiff and even more confining than it did before. Thunder booms above my head, shaking the fountain and the bushes. I reach forward, through the cold water, and take hold of the crystal in my hand.

"Trial completed," a voice whispers.

Immediately the ground spins away, and I'm gone.

Gone all but for a sliver of shadow I leave behind.

Something to protect her.

Chapter Sixty-Two

B riony

Lightning streaks across the sky above me and thunder roars. The air is icy cold and I hug my arms around me and consider my surroundings. Immediately, I recognize this trial for what it is.

A maze. It's a maze. I laugh out loud. I can't believe it; Clare was right.

I mean, I'm sure it won't be as easy as a straightforward maze. I'm sure they'll have thrown in a bunch of other challenges along the way, but if I follow Clare's rule, then maybe – just maybe – there's a chance I might actually complete this trial. Or at least complete it enough to earn some points.

Straight in front of me, a tall wall of sharp brambles blocks my path, leaving me with the option of turning left or right. I go with the left, keeping my hand hovering along the surface of the thorns as I run along paths, swerve around corners and meet dead-ends. I know this method through the maze is time consuming so I need to be quick about it, especially as I'm forced to double back on myself several times, but I'm sure I'm drawing closer to the center of the maze – I'm sure I can feel it.

Of course, I should know better. Life doesn't work that way for a girl from Slate Quarter. Whenever you think you're on to a good thing, it's snatched away. As soon as you rise, you fall. As soon as you feel just a teensy bit confident, the realm shows you exactly why you shouldn't be.

Because blocking my path is the biggest dog I've ever seen. It's as big as a bear and covered in mangy fur, scabs on its legs and its back. Spit drools from its open jaws and its eyes wild and frantic.

It spots me, draws back its cracked lips and growls, showcasing rows and rows of sharp teeth.

I don't think this is going to be a situation like Dray's wolf. I don't think I'll be charming this dog-like creature and making a new friend. For the briefest of moments, I stare at the creature, and terror and panic overtake me, making my body shake and bile rise up in my throat. Then I pull myself together and run.

I have two legs. The dog has four. But it doesn't look healthy and I am fast. It's possibly the only thing I have going for me. And so I run as fast as I can, driving my legs and my arms forward with all my might, swerving and diving round corners, trying to make my path random in the hope I'll lose the creature.

Behind me I hear the thunder of its paws on the hard ground and its panted breath. It's right behind me, chasing me as I take a hard right, and then two lefts.

It's going to catch me. I know it's inevitable and I try to form a plan as I run.

Do I wrap myself up into a ball, protect my head and my face and wait for the trial masters to save me – hoping I still have a throat left by the time they fish me out of this maze? Or do I attempt to fight the beast off, hold it at bay with my hands and my feet as best I can?

Neither option seems great. Both will involve me losing large chunks of flesh.

I keep running, searching the ground for some kind of weapon as I do, the paws still thundering, the beast still coming, and then, suddenly, a shriek of pain, followed by a whimper. The thumping paws stop.

I don't hang about to find out what the hell just happened. Perhaps the beast stumbled, perhaps it tripped. If it did, this is my chance to get away.

I sprint haphazardly through the maze, left and right, right and left, running and running, until I hear nothing but my own feet and my own breath.

I've lost it. I'm sure I've lost it.

I hunch over my knees, bile sloshing in my stomach and my throat, my lungs burning and my heart hammering. I close my eyes and try to catch my breath.

I'm okay.

I. Am. Okay.

All right, I may have lost my bearings, I may be lost completely, but I'm alive; I'm uninjured. There was no real chance I was going to complete this maze anyway. Maybe I'm better off concentrating on staying safe, running down the clock and coming away unscathed. I'm sure I'll earn a few points from the progress I made. It's better than dying.

Only, the maze has other ideas. It obviously doesn't want me waiting in one place. It wants me moving. I only notice when something sharp scrapes against my arm. I cry out and find the brambles from the walls of the maze curling onto the pathway, curling towards me.

I squeal, jumping out of the way, as a limb covered in long sharp thorns swings dangerously close to my face. I back away from the brambles, only to find the path behind me also blocked.

Shit! Why the hell did I think not moving would be a good idea?

Hardly entertaining for the spectators watching us as we make our way through this trial.

I peer through the brambles in front of me, searching for a way through, and then turn and do the same in the other direction. The brambles are moving too quickly, already blocking both directions; soon they'll envelop me completely. I have a choice to make. Start moving or be strangled to death by these murderous plants. I grit my teeth and, with my arms over my head in a bid to protect my face, I plow straight ahead.

I try to duck and dive through the moving brambles. But it's hopeless, they are too dense, and I scream as my flesh is torn to pieces. The pain is awful, but I'm used to that. It isn't new. I search for that place I can go to for escape, I try to disassociate from my mind. I keep moving.

A bramble catches me by the ankle, coiling around my leg, and then another catches my arm, another tightening around my middle.

I struggle as best I can, trying to pull the brambles away with my hands even as the thorns sink into the sensitive flesh of my palms. But then one catches me by the throat and I know this is the end.

I close my eyes and wait for the trial masters to save me, hoping with every bone in my body that they do.

Chapter Sixty-Three

B riony

"Please," I whisper.

The bramble around my throat loosens.

I flick open my eyes, expecting to find myself back in the academy.

I'm not. I'm still in the maze, surrounded by the vines, only they're no longer moving. I scrabble at the vine wrapped around my throat and pull it away.

Unlike before, it doesn't struggle back, it simply tumbles to the ground, its limbs slowly turning black as it does.

What the hell?

The rot continues, racing along the brambles as they fall to the ground, crack and snap. I brush them away from my body, and they fall away like dead leaves from a tree.

I don't understand it. Did the trial masters cut off the

attack before it could become deadly? Does that mean I failed? Then why leave me in the maze?

I peer down at my tracksuit. It's shredded along both arms, down my legs and over my stomach. Gripping the material in my hands, I rip off a section and use it to dab at the cuts that litter my body, holding it against the deepest of slices to stem the blood. Then I pick through the shriveling, dying brambles and continue on my way.

The trial may be over and I may already have failed, but I'm not going to risk it by remaining in one place. I'm going to keep moving. I'm going to continue on my way. Who knows what might come for me next time if I remain in one place.

I peer up at the sky. My time must nearly be up, surely, but with the heavy storm clouds it's impossible to tell how many minutes have passed.

I walk along one pathway, take a left, another left and then three rights in a row, and then, to my utter astonishment, I walk out into the center of the maze. The hedgerows here are boxed and neatly trimmed and a water fountain gurgles away.

Alongside the clear water stands Madame Bardin, wrapped in the thick black cloak I saw her wearing that morning in the library.

"Madame Bardin!" I say, surprised – although it would make sense she'd be waiting at the end of the maze – at the end of the trial. "Am I done?"

"You are indeed, congratulations."

Once again, I'm taken aback, as she holds out her manicured hand for me to shake.

With a pride I haven't experienced in years – which may be I've never experienced – I step forward and take her hand in mine.

Only she doesn't shake it like I expect, she squeezes it hard in her own and yanks me towards her.

"And how exactly is that possible? Only a handful of students have made it to the center of this maze, Miss Storm. Only a handful – powerful shadow weavers with abilities you couldn't even dream of." She glares at me. "I think you're hiding something from us, Miss Storm. I think you are trying to deceive us."

"Wh-wh-what?" I say.

"An ordinary girl like you could not complete a maze like this. There must be something special about you," she spits, like she can hardly believe it's true. "What is it?" She squeezes my hand so hard my eyes water and her magic crackles against my skin. "Either tell me, or I'll be forced to drag it from you."

"I don't know what you're talking about. There is nothing special about me. I don't have any powers, if that's what you mean. I just got lucky."

"Lucky?" she hisses. "You expect me to believe that?!"

She pushes me away. I stumble backward but manage to remain on my feet. Only for a moment though, because then something hard and heavy hurtles into my stomach and knocks me to the ground, holding me in place against the earth.

Her shadow magic.

It's cold like Professor Fox's, only far more so. Like ice against my skin; like needles piercing my flesh.

"Tell me," she growls.

"There's nothing to tell," I growl right back up at her. Anyone could see that. Anyone who had been watching my progress through the maze would know that.

She raises her right hand above her head, then brings it crashing down. Lightning shrieks from her fingertips and streaks across the space between her. I try to twist away, but the shadows pin me down and the electricity smacks into me. It courses through my body, making every muscle fry with a cold heat. I scream in agony, writhing on the floor. Tears swim from my eyes down my cheeks and I smell burning in the air.

"You ungrateful, deceptive little bitch." She drops her hand and the lightning stops. "Tell me!" she screeches, her eyes wild.

"There's nothing to tell," I croak, my voice raw and scratchy from screaming. Her hand rises into the air. "No!" I scream but it's too late, more lightning comes snaking towards me. It's even worse the second time and I start to disassociate once more.

I'm far away. Her words float towards me garbled and muddled but I catch elements of them as my vision swims in and out of focus.

"Why you? ... I've seen the way he looks at you ... he wants you ... there must be a reason for it ... you're hiding something ..."

Beaufort? Is that what this is about?

Or does she know what I'm really hiding? The object I'm hiding in my closet. The truth about Amelia.

Darkness swoops towards me, then retreats. I try to stay conscious. I need to get away. I don't want her to kill me.

I attempt to crawl, to heave my body away. But it doesn't respond to my command. It hurts too much and the weight of the shadows pinning me down are too great.

I'm like a cat, I think to myself. How many times have I blundered seriously close to death and yet survived? Well just like any other cat, it seems my luck has run out.

The darkness becomes more oppressive, her words ever more distant, until I don't hear them at all.

And then everything stops.

Chapter Sixty-Four

B riony

Is this death?

Am I floating somewhere in the abyss of time and space?

But no, I feel the ground beneath my body. Hard and cold.

My body!

I still feel my body. Sore and raw but no longer ... no longer screaming with agony.

I flick open my eyes. At first the dim light is overwhelming, and my eyes swim with tears, but then gradually the world comes back into focus.

Madame Bardin stands just where she was. Her attention is no longer focused on me. The lightning no longer streams from her fingertips and her words are no longer directed my way.

Instead, she's grappling with a dark wisp of shadow coiling around her body. She attempts to shake it off with her own magic, to wrestle it away. Yet, despite the faintness of the shadow, it is strong, stronger than her own magic.

She begins to panic, scrabbling, twisting her body round and round just like I'd done when those brambles had encased me.

Then her eyes land on me.

"Are you doing this?" she yells with venom. "Is this you?"

"N-n-no," I mutter.

"Then help me, you stupid wretch. Don't just lie there, help me!"

Is she kidding me? One minute she's frying me to death, the next she wants my help? What – so that she can fry me some more?

I stare up at her. Even if I did want to help her – which to be clear, I do not – I can't. My body is too weak. My muscles are not functioning as they should, my heart still skittish in my chest.

"We'll pretend this never happened. I will promise never to bother you again," she says with a lot less venom and a lot more desperation this time, grappling with a shadow that weaves its way around her throat. "Just let me go! Let me go!"

I don't know what possesses me. I'm not in control of those shadows. I don't know who the hell is – or how and why they've intervened. But I take my opportunity anyway.

"You swear?" I say, lifting my head from the ground to stare right at her. "You swear to leave me alone?"

"I do," she snarls.

"Then make the promise," I tell her. "Make me the promise."

She scowls at me, then rests her hand over her heart, her magic pulsating around her fingers. "I promise," she says.

To my utter astonishment, the strange shadow drifts away from her.

Despite the pain it causes me, I jerk up into a crouching position. I don't trust Madame Bardin to keep her promises – even if she sealed that one with her magic. Fox was right. She is dangerous and crazy as hell.

However, she doesn't come for me again; she is swishing her dark cloak around her body and melting away into the air.

I let out a noise – halfway between a sigh of relief and a self-pitying sob.

Unfortunately, I'm not out of danger yet. Seems that mystery shadow wasn't on my side after all, because now it is drifting towards me. I scrabble backwards, desperately searching for another plan. I won't be able to outrun this or keep it at bay. If Madame Bardin couldn't overcome it, what chance do I have?

I collapse back down onto the grass instead and an uncontrollable laughter takes over me as the shadow inches towards my toes.

Just when I thought I was safe, just when I thought this was over, fate has to come along and spit in my eye and teach me I'm wrong? Yet again!

At least I'll die laughing. I think Amelia would be proud of that. Fly would probably get a kick out of it too.

Except, the shadow makes no move to harm me. Instead, it dances around my body, floating close towards my skin and then darting away, as if it wants to touch me, but daren't. I watch it. Up close I see how it glitters, swirls and shimmers. It's almost beautiful in a deadly kind of way.

I reach out my hand to touch it myself. The shadow backs away almost immediately, like a scared little rabbit.

"It's okay," I whisper. "I won't hurt you."

The shadow hesitates, then creeps closer, right to my fingertip. A mere millimeter separating my flesh from the wisp of magic. I can feel its heat. I stare up into its depths utterly captivated.

"You're really quite something, aren't you?" I say. "Thank you. For helping me."

I don't know who I'm thanking or why they helped me. However, there's no doubt in my mind that someone did help me.

The shadow floats in place for a minute longer, then glides away towards the fountain at the center of this maze. It swirls around and around the stone monument. It's trying to tell me something.

With a lot of effort and even more pain, I stumble up onto my feet and hobble that way.

The aroma of burned hair and flesh lingers in my nostrils. What the hell must I look like? If it's half as bad as I feel, then hideous, most definitely hideous.

The shadow floats by the trickling water of the fountain and as I inspect closer I spot a crystal spinning under the water. I understand what I have to do.

"Thank you," I whisper a second time and then I reach out and take the cool crystal in my hand.

Immediately, the ground beneath my feet jerks away and the world around me spins and then I land with a thud on solid ground.

"Finally."

I blink and find the second half of the gruesome twosome standing right in front of me, a pen and clipboard in his hands. We're somewhere out in the academy grounds and the sky above us is already black with night.

"What the hell happened?" he grunts with annoyance. "Didn't you hear my whistle? You've been in the maze for over two hours."

"I-I-I have?" I say. "Shouldn't I have been whisked out after one?"

"Exactly," he snaps, with even more annoyance, scribbling something on his board. "Your completion of the maze won't count. You were out of time." He glares at me as if I might dare to challenge him. I'm not going to bother. After all, someone helped me in there. Helping others is against the rules – yet, if anyone found that out, I'm sure I'd be the one to be punished. Then again, I'm sure Madame Bardin is going to find a way to punish me anyway. I don't trust that promise of hers one bit and I doubt she is the type of person to take kindly to being beaten like that.

"Can I go?" I say.

"Huh?" he says, still scribbling. "Yeah," he waves his hand in my direction without looking down at me again, "if you're injured at all, take yourself along to the clinic."

I wrap my arms around my body and set off back to my room. The air is frigid, making my already injured muscles ache and my teeth chatter together. Every step is painful. Tears snake down my face and drip off my chin.

Yet, there's this peculiar warmth in my stomach, one that's urging me back to my room. I pick up my pace and hurry along.

The main campus is busy with people tonight. The ball to celebrate the completion of the first trial won't happen for a few days yet – everybody needs time to recover. But that hasn't stopped people from partying already. Several are out on the paths, drinking, talking, going over the trial. Some are wrapped in bandages. I can hear music wafting from the towers, more chatter and laughter too.

I have a strong desire to find Fly and Clare, swap stories and take a swig or two of Fly's liquor. This strange sensation has other plans though and soon I'm rounding the corner to my own tower.

Rounding the corner and halting.

There are three figures lingering at the entrance.

Beaufort, Dray and Thorne.

Chapter Sixty-Five

B eaufort

"You're sure she's safe?" Dray says, kicking at a loose pebble on the pathway as he leans against the walls of her tower.

"I told you what I saw. She has to be."

Only problem is, by our calculations, the girl should have been back from the trial over an hour ago – sooner if, like most of the commoners, she was in danger and had to be fished out. Rumor has it, less than a fifth of the students completed the maze – most of the shadow weavers.

So where the hell is she?

We've already searched for her in the commoners' clinic, their canteen and the rooms of both her friends. Hell, Dray even went back and looked for her in our tower on the off-chance she headed that way – probably in the hope we'd heal whatever injuries she most probably has picked up.

I wince at the thought. I may be fuming at her. Her

words may have cut deeper than I'd ever care to admit. But the girl has gotten under my skin and into my blood, as ingrained there as my magic itself, and I cannot shake her. I don't like the idea of her being hurt. I want her safe. I want her safe by my side – even if she's hissing and spitting at me the whole time.

This rift between us is unsustainable. Time to heal it.

"Here she comes," Dray says, catching her scent and nudging me rather too aggressively with his elbow.

I glare at him, then peer through the darkness and see her hobbling towards us. My breath catches in my throat. She is hurt.

"Briony," I call out, already striding towards her, the other two right by my side. "What the hell happened? Are you hurt?"

"Happened?" she says. "Nothing happened." She wipes her hands over her face.

She's lying. Her clothes are torn to shreds, cuts litter her skin, burns mark her face, and some of her hair has been scorched away. Okay, lots of the students are walking around looking like shit tonight – nobody looks like this.

But it's the something in her eyes that confirms to me she's lying.

"Nothing happened?!" Dray says. "You think we're stupid or something?" She stares at him silently and he frowns. "Where have you been, kitten?"

"None of your business." She stares right ahead, not meeting my eyes.

"It is our business," I snap. I came to make up with her, to tell her I'm sorry, to take care of her, but already this damn conversation has twisted in some other direction. Why does she have to be so obstinate? Why does it make my hackles rise?

"Just leave me alone," she says, tears trickling from her eyes. She swipes at them. "I want nothing to do with–"

"Where are you hurt?" Thorne cuts right across her, glaring at her with such ferocity I'm surprised the girl isn't shaking in her shredded boots.

"I'm not ..." It's clear she was going to argue that she wasn't hurt, but something about the way Thorne is glaring at her, has her changing tact. "It's not that bad."

"Then why do you smell like you've been fried in a pan?" Dray says, nostrils quivering. "No one else smells like this." He turns towards Thorne, tilting his head. "Was there something in that maze that could do this?"

Thorne shakes his head.

"What happened?" I growl.

"It doesn't concern you," she says, dragging her eyes away from Thorne and attempting to push her way past us. Thorne steps backward as she steps towards him but I block her path.

"You need healing," I say, trying to make my voice gentler. She's hurt. I don't like seeing her like this. I want to make her better. I want to lay my hands on her again. I want to mend the argument between us.

"I don't need your help. I don't need anything from you."

"Let us heal you!"

"No," she cries, desperately shaking her head. "I don't want anything from you. I want nothing to do with you."

"Don't be a fool. Tell us what happened and we'll sort it out."

"No!"

"For star's sake, Briony! Why not?"

"Because I don't trust you!" I stare at her dumbfounded. She doesn't trust us. After everything we've done for her. "How could I? How can I trust anyone in this place?"

"Damn it, Beaufort, just tell her," Thorne mutters.

Immediately her eyes snap from me to him.

"Tell me what?"

I stare back at her. There are tiny puncture marks on her throat, a burn mark across her left cheek, bruising on her forehead and her right eye is slightly swollen. The remnants of old tear tracks are visible on her face.

"There's something special about you, Briony Storm."

She flinches and then she shakes her head again. "There isn't."

"Stop toying with her, and tell her," Thorne growls.

"Tell me what?"

I stare into her emerald eyes. They swim with pain and anger and curiosity. All the things I've come to associate with her.

"I'll tell you," I whisper to her, "if you tell me what happened to you out there in the maze."

Something did happen – I'm sure of it. Two hours she was gone. We searched for her everywhere. The only place she could have been was in that maze. And she comes back looking like this.

"Let's go somewhere private to talk," I say softly, reaching for her elbow.

She stares back at me, her gaze flicking ever so gently from side to side as if she's attempting to peer deeper, see further, inside my soul, as if she's weighing up whether she can trust me or not.

"No," she says finally and something inside me cracks. And then before any of us knows it, she's darting away and scurrying towards her tower.

"Should we go after her?" Dray asks.

I watch her wince as she leans against the heavy door and disappears inside. My chest feels tight and painful as if she took a knife and plunged it straight between my ribs.

She doesn't trust me. She doesn't trust any of us.

I almost laugh. Something hurt her in that maze – maybe even someone. It wasn't us and yet she seems to think that we are the ones to fear.

Then, suddenly, I understand. The pain in my chest intensifies. She thinks we were responsible for whatever happened today.

But why? Why would she think that?

I screw up my face trying to make sense of it, trying to recall the argument last night, to go over what she told me, what she said. Her sister. Her sister's death. All this mistrust, all this suspicion, this inability to be with us, stems back to that.

Why? Why the hell does she think her sister was murdered? It makes no sense at all.

"It's time she knew," Thorne says steely. He's said more in the last two minutes than he has the last seven days.

I scrub my hand through my hair. My body and my magic still buzzes with the adrenaline of that trial. Sure, it wasn't as challenging as I'd have liked. But it was still a lot of fun. That adrenaline was fading fast; the girl has reignited it.

How does she do this to me?

"I agree," I say, "it's time she knew." I turn my back on the tower and stride away. "But not tonight."

Tonight, I find out who the hell hurt her in that maze.

Then I'll show her who was truly responsible.

And then I am going to make them pay for it.

Chapter Sixty-Six

B^{riony}

I storm up the tower steps as fast as my legs carry me, my mind crashing around with a million thoughts.

I've always suspected there must be a reason the Princes chose me to be their thrall. It's certainly not down to my ravishing good looks, dazzling personality or realm-beating abilities. There had to be another reason.

It seems I was right.

I knew it and yet, is it crazy that that hurts? Had I begun to believe that they truly saw something in me no one else did?

Stupid girl; stupid, stupid girl. Of course there had to be an ulterior motive.

These are shadow weavers. They only care about themselves. They're only out for themselves. The rest of us —

we're just dispensable. Collateral damage – that's what Beaufort called us.

Do I want to know what that ulterior motive is? Hell yeah! But I won't play Beaufort Lincoln's games.

I don't know what the hell went on in that maze – why I was in there far longer than I should have been, why I wasn't whisked out when my life was in danger, why Madame Bardin chose to attack me like that – Madame Bardin! A teacher!

Turns out the Princes aren't the only thing I was correct about. This place has secrets to hide. This place is not all it pretends to be. I was right to be distrustful.

I was right to hide the truth about my sister.

I don't trust those in charge of the realm. I don't trust those running this academy. I don't trust shadow weavers. I certainly don't trust the Princes. They've been keeping secrets of their own. For all I know, they were responsible for what happened in that maze. For all I know, my sister is the reason they want me close.

No, from now on, I'm keeping all my secrets to myself. I won't be sharing anything at all. And that includes my biggest secret of all.

I unlock my room and rush inside, skidding across the floor and halting in front of the wardrobe. I fling back the doors and pull out the blankets and covers, finding my bag buried at the bottom.

The pull is even stronger than before, even more incessant. Just like it was the very first day – that day we buried my sister and the grief had drowned me in its darkness, the day I'd fled away from my home, from my dad and into the forest, and there I'd first felt it. This strange sensation – forcing my footsteps right towards it. Pulling me its way. Calling to me.

I kneel down on the hard floor and drag my bag carefully onto my lap. My hands are shaking as I draw the zipper down and pull open the bag, then I reach inside.

As always the stone is warm against my palms as I heave it out of its hiding place with both my hands and into my lap. My heartbeat slows and the warmth in my stomach reverberates throughout my body as I do.

The stone is oval shaped, the size of a loaf of bread, only heavier, much heavier. It's a deep black but its surface is smooth – like polished coal. I sweep my palms over it, turning it in my hands and then I understand why it's called me, why it's beckoned me here.

How long have I owned this stone? How long have I kept it hidden? Nine long years I've guarded it. Since that day we buried my sister.

But tonight something is different. Something has changed.

Along the surface of the stone run two fine fissures.

The stone is cracking – cracking open.

Yeah, perhaps I've been lying all along ... perhaps I'm not the girl they think I am ... perhaps I'm not so ordinary after all.

*** End of book 1 ***

Briony's story will continue in book 2 of the Firestone Academy series, **Spark of Sorcery**.

If you can't wait that long, you can find a bonus scene on my website — it's where you'll find all my bonus content.

. . .

Want somewhere to discuss this story and chat with other readers? Come join my exclusive reader Facebook group.

If you enjoyed this story, please consider leaving a rating or review — it's a huge help to indie authors like me!

Also by Hannah Haze

All available on Amazon and Kindle Unlimited.

Paranormal RH romance
The Firestone Academy
Storm of Shadows
Spark of Sorcery
Taste of Thorns
Lure of Lightning

The Arrow Hart Academy
Fractured Fates
Twisted Ties
Shattered Stars
Burdened Bonds
Destined Dawn

Contemporary RH omegaverse
The Rockview Omegaverse
Pack Rivals Part I

Pack Rivals Part II
Pack Choice
Pack Gamble Part I
Pack Gamble Part II
Pack Education Part I
Pack Education Part II

In With The Pack
In Deep - Rosie's story
In Trouble - Connie's story
In Knots - Alexa's story
In Doubt - Giorgie's story
In Control - Sophia's story
In Stockings (Christmas Novella)

Contemporary MF omegaverse series
The Alpha Rock Stars
The Rockstar's Omega
Rocked by the Alpha
Fourth Base with the Alpha

Contemporary MF omegaverse standalones
Oxford Heat
The Alpha Escort Agency
Omega's Forbidden Heat

Contemporary MF omegaverse novellas
The Omega Chase
Online Heat
Christmas Heat

Alien omegaverse MF romance series

Also by Hannah Haze

The Alpha Prince of Astia
<u>Alien Desire</u>
<u>Alien Passion</u>

About the Author

A recovering cynic, Hannah grew up swearing she would never marry. Then in 2001, she met her husband and has been a card-carrying romantic ever since. Despite being an avid writer and reader, Hannah decided to do the sensible thing and study science at university, putting authoring ideas to one side.This all changed when she discovered the joys of a good romance book and came to the realisation that love stories are always the best ones.

She now uses her knowledge of chemical bonds and reactions to ensure her books are full of sparks. In fact the electricity between her characters is sure to set your pulse racing and your heart fluttering.

Hannah loves reading to her three children, including doing all the silly voices, and going for long walks in the countryside (the muddier the better). Her head is always full of new story ideas and you are most likely to find her avoiding the demands of her very naughty cat as she attempts to write them all down.

Sign up to my newsletter:
www.hannahhaze.com/about

Join my reader groups:

https://www.facebook.com/groups/hannahhazehotro
mancereads

https://www.facebook.com/groups/softandsteamy
omegaverse

Visit my website:
www.hannahhaze.com

Catch me on TikTok:
www.tiktok.com/@hannahhaze_author

Acknowledgments

As always I have lots of people to thank who have helped me along the way...

Firstly, a massive thank you to my readers for their continued support and encouragement. It means the world to me that the stories I write bring enjoyment to others.

Another massive thank you to my amazing beta reader team who help me to make my stories so much better. Thank you Kiki, Courtney, Sara, Aimee, Donna, Jenna, Jessie, Brandy, Leandri and Melissa.

Thank you to Christian for a simply stunning cover, to James for wading through all my terrible spelling mistakes and my PA team at Dragonfire for all their support.

And finally, thank you to Mr. D, Stephy, my children and the rest of my family. Love you all x

www.ingramcontent.com/pod-product-compliance
Lightning Source LLC
Chambersburg PA
CBHW070734120726
47910CB00001B/100